WHISKEY BEACH

BY NORA ROBERTS

Hot Ice	True Betrayals	Northern Lights
Sacred Sins	Montana Sky	Blue Smoke
Brazen Virtue	Sanctuary	Angels Fall
Sweet Revenge	Homeport	High Noon
Public Secrets	The Reef	Tribute
Genuine Lies	River's End	Black Hills
Carnal Innocence	Carolina Moon	The Search
Divine Evil	The Villa	Chasing Fire
Honest Illusions	Midnight Bayou	The Witness
Private Scandals	Three Fates	Whiskey Beach
Hidden Riches	Birthright	

SERIES

IRISH BORN TRILOGY
Born in Fire
Born in Ice
Born in Shame

DREAM TRILOGY
Daring to Dream
Holding the Dream
Finding the Dream

CHESAPEAKE BAY SAGA
Sea Swept
Rising Tides
Inner Harbor
Chesapeake Blue

GALLAGHERS OF ARDMORE TRILOGY
Jewels of the Sun
Tears of the Moon
Heart of the Sea

THREE SISTERS ISLAND TRILOGY
Dance Upon the Air
Heaven and Earth
Face the Fire

KEY TRILOGY
Key of Light
Key of Knowledge
Key of Valor

IN THE GARDEN TRILOGY
Blue Dahlia
Black Rose
Red Lily

CIRCLE TRILOGY
Morrigan's Cross
Dance of the Gods
Valley of Silence

SIGN OF SEVEN TRILOGY
Blood Brothers
The Hollow
The Pagan Stone

BRIDE QUARTET
Vision in White
Bed of Roses
Savor the Moment
Happy Ever After

THE INN BOONSBORO TRILOGY
The Next Always
The Last Boyfriend
The Perfect Hope

E-BOOKS BY NORA ROBERTS

BY NORA ROBERTS AND J. D. ROBB

Remember When

J. D. ROBB

Naked in Death
Glory in Death
Immortal in Death
Rapture in Death
Ceremony in Death
Vengeance in Death
Holiday in Death
Conspiracy in Death
Loyalty in Death
Witness in Death
Judgment in Death
Betrayal in Death

Seduction in Death
Reunion in Death
Purity in Death
Portrait in Death
Imitation in Death
Divided in Death
Visions in Death
Survivor in Death
Origin in Death
Memory in Death
Born in Death
Innocent in Death
Creation in Death
Strangers in Death

Salvation in Death
Promises in Death
Kindred in Death
Fantasy in Death
Indulgence in Death
Treachery in Death
New York to Dallas
Celebrity in Death
Delusion in Death
Calculated in Death

ANTHOLOGIES

From the Heart
A Little Magic
A Little Fate

Moon Shadows
(with Jill Gregory, Ruth Ryan Langan, and Marianne Willman)

THE ONCE UPON SERIES
(with Jill Gregory, Ruth Ryan Langan, and Marianne Willman)
Once Upon a Castle
Once Upon a Star
Once Upon a Dream

Once Upon a Rose
Once Upon a Kiss
Once Upon a Midnight

Silent Night
(with Susan Plunkett, Dee Holmes, and Claire Cross)

Out of This World
(with Laurell K. Hamilton, Susan Krinard, and Maggie Shayne)

Bump in the Night
(with Mary Blayney, Ruth Ryan Langan,
and Mary Kay McComas)

Dead of Night
(with Mary Blayney, Ruth Ryan Langan,
and Mary Kay McComas)

Three in Death
Suite 606
(with Mary Blayney, Ruth Ryan Langan,
and Mary Kay McComas)

In Death
The Lost
(with Patricia Gaffney, Mary Blayney, and Ruth Ryan Langan)

The Other Side
(with Mary Blayney, Patricia Gaffney, Ruth Ryan Langan,
and Mary Kay McComas)

Time of Death
The Unquiet
(with Mary Blayney, Patricia Gaffney, Ruth Ryan Langan,
and Mary Kay McComas)

ALSO AVAILABLE . . .

The Official Nora Roberts Companion
(edited by Denise Little and Laura Hayden)

WHISKEY BEACH

NORA ROBERTS

DOUBLEDAY LARGE PRINT HOME LIBRARY EDITION

G. P. PUTNAM'S SONS, NEW YORK

Large print ed.

This Large Print Edition, prepared especially for
Doubleday Large Print Home Library, contains
the complete, unabridged text of the original
Publisher's Edition.

PUTNAM

G. P. PUTNAM'S SONS
Publishers Since 1838
Published by the Penguin Group
Penguin Group (USA) Inc.,
375 Hudson Street, New York, New York 10014, USA

Penguin Books Ltd, Registered Offices:
80 Strand, London WC2R 0RL, England

ISBN 978-1-62490-204-8

Printed in the United States of America

Gift 10/13

This is a work of fiction. Names, characters, places, and incidents either are the product of the author's imagination or are used fictitiously, and any resemblance to actual persons, living or dead, businesses, companies, events, or locales is entirely coincidental.

To my sons and
the daughters they gave me.
And all that comes from that.

The dragon-green, the luminous, the dark,
the serpent-haunted sea.

—James Elroy Flecker

Dark

The mass of men lead lives of quiet desperation. What is called resignation is confirmed desperation.
—HENRY DAVID THOREAU

One

Through the chilly curtain of sleet, in the intermittent wash of the great light on the jutting cliff to the south, the massive silhouette of Bluff House loomed over Whiskey Beach. It faced the cold, turbulent Atlantic like a challenge.

I will last as long as you.

Standing three sturdy and indulgent stories above the rough and rugged coast, it watched the roll and slap of waves through the dark eyes of windows, as it had—in one incarnation or another—for more than three centuries.

The little stone cottage now housing tools and garden supplies spoke to its humble beginnings, to those who'd braved the fierce and fickle Atlantic to forge a life on the stony ground of a new world. Dwarfing those beginnings, the spread and rise of golden sand walls and curving gables, the generous terraces of weathered local stone sang to its heyday.

It survived storm, neglect, careless indulgence, dubious taste, the booms and the busts, scandal and righteousness.

Within its walls, generations of Landons had lived and died, celebrated and mourned, schemed, thrived, triumphed and languished.

It had shone as bright as the great light that swept the water off Massachusetts' rocky and glorious north shore. And it had huddled, shuttered in the dark.

It had stood long, so long now it simply was Bluff House, reigning above the sea, the sand, the village of Whiskey Beach.

For Eli Landon it was the only place left to go. Not a refuge as much as an escape from everything his life had become over the past eleven horrible months.

He barely recognized himself.

The two-and-a-half-hour drive up from Boston over slick roads left him exhausted. But then, he admitted, fatigue cozied up to him like a lover most days. So he sat outside the house, in the dark, sleet splatting off his windshield, his roof, while he debated the choices of gathering enough energy to go inside or just staying put, maybe sliding into sleep in the car.

Stupid, he thought. Of course he wouldn't just sit there and sleep in the car when the house, with perfectly good beds to choose from, stood only a few feet away.

But neither could he drum up the enthusiasm for hauling his suitcases out of the trunk. Instead he grabbed the two small bags on the seat beside him, ones holding his laptop and a few essentials.

Sleet slapped at him when he climbed out of the car, but the cold, that whistling Atlantic wind, cut through the outer layers of lethargy. Waves boomed against the rock, slapped against the sand, combining into a constant hissing roar. Eli dragged the house keys out of his jacket pocket, stepped onto the shelter of the wide stone portico to the massive double entrance doors hewn more than a century before from teak imported from Burma.

Two years, he thought—closer to three—since he'd been here. Too busy with his life, with work, with the disaster of his marriage to drive up for a weekend, a short vacation, a holiday visit with his grandmother.

He'd spent time with her, of course, the indomitable Hester Hawkin Landon, whenever she'd come to Boston. He'd called her regularly, e-mailed, Face-booked and Skyped. Hester might have been cruising toward eighty but she'd always embraced technology and innovation with curiosity and enthusiasm.

He'd taken her to dinner, to drinks, remembered flowers and cards, gifts, gathered with her and his family for Christmas, important birthdays.

And that, he thought as he unlocked the door, was all just rationalization for not taking the time, making the time, to come to Whiskey Beach, to the place she loved most, and giving her real time, real attention.

He found the right key, unlocked the door. Stepping inside, he flicked on the lights.

She'd changed some things, he noted, but Gran embraced change even as she managed to embrace traditions—that suited her.

Some new art—seascapes, garden-scapes—splashing soft color against rich brown walls. He dumped his bags just inside the door, took a moment to just look around the glossy spill of the entrance hall.

He scanned the stairs—the grinning gargoyle newel posts some whimsical Landon had commissioned—and up where they curved gracefully right and left for the north and south wings.

Plenty of bedrooms, he thought. He just had to climb the stairs and pick one.

But not yet.

Instead he walked through to what they called the main parlor with its high, arch-ing windows facing the front garden—or what would be once winter opened its claws.

His grandmother hadn't been home for over two months, but he didn't see a speck of dust. Logs lay in the hearth framed by the gleam of lapis and ready to light. Fresh flowers stood on the Hepplewhite table she prized. Pillows sat fluffed and welcoming on the three sofas ranged around the room, and the wide planked chestnut floor gleamed like a mirror.

She'd had someone come in, he decided, then rubbed his forehead where a headache threatened to bloom.

She'd told him, hadn't she? Told him she had someone looking out for the place. A neighbor, someone who did the heavy cleaning for her. He hadn't forgotten she'd told him, he'd just lost the information for a moment in the fog that too often crawled in to blur his mind.

Now looking out for Bluff House was his job. To tend to it, to, as his grandmother had asked, keep life in it. And maybe, she'd said, it would pump some life back into him.

He picked up his bags, looked at the stairs. Then just stood.

She'd been found there, there at the base of the steps. By a neighbor—the same neighbor? Wasn't it the same neighbor who cleaned for her? Someone, thank God, had come by to check on her, and found her lying there unconscious, bruised, bleeding, with a shattered elbow, a broken hip, cracked ribs, a concussion.

She might've died, he thought. The doctors expressed amazement that she'd stubbornly refused to. None of the family routinely checked on her daily, no one thought to call, and no one, including himself, would have worried if she hadn't answered for a day or two.

Hester Landon, independent, invincible, indestructible.

Who might have died after a terrible fall, if not for a neighbor—and her own indefatigable will.

Now she reigned in a suite of rooms in his parents' home while she recovered from her injuries. There she'd stay until deemed strong enough to come back to Bluff House—or if his parents had their way, there she would stay, period.

He wanted to think of her back here, in the house she loved, sitting out on the terrace with her evening martini, looking out at the ocean. Or puttering in her garden, maybe setting up her easel to paint.

He wanted to think of her vital and tough, not helpless and broken on the floor while he'd been pouring a second cup of morning coffee.

So he'd do his best until she came home. He'd keep life in her house, such as his was.

Eli picked up his bags, started upstairs. He'd take the room he'd always used on visits—or had before those visits stretched out fewer and farther between. Lindsay had hated Whiskey Beach, Bluff House, and had made trips there into a cold war with his grandmother rigidly polite on one side, his wife deliberately snide on the other. And he'd been squeezed in the middle.

So he'd taken the easy way, he thought now. He could be sorry about that, sorry he'd stopped coming, sorry he'd made excuses and had limited his time with his grandmother to her trips to Boston. But he couldn't turn back the clock.

He stepped into the bedroom. Flowers here, too, he noted, and the same soft green walls, two of his grandmother's watercolors he'd always particularly liked.

He put his bags on the bench at the foot of the sleigh bed, stripped off his coat.

Here, things had stayed the same. The little desk under the window, the wide atrium doors leading to the terrace, the wingback chair and the little footstool with the cover his grandmother's mother had needlepointed long ago.

It occurred to him that for the first time in a very long time he felt—almost—at home. Opening his bag, he dug out his toiletry kit, then found fresh towels, fancy seashell soaps. The scent of lemons in the bath.

He stripped down without glancing at the mirror. He'd lost weight, too much weight, over the last year. He didn't need to remind himself of it. He turned on the shower, stepped in, hoping to burn some of the fatigue away. He knew from experience if he went to bed exhausted and stressed, he'd sleep fitfully, wake with that dragging hangover.

When he stepped out he grabbed one of the towels from the stack, again caught the whiff of lemon as he scrubbed it over his hair. Damp, it curled past the nape of his neck, a mop of dark blond longer than it had been since his early twenties. But then he hadn't seen his usual barber, Enrique, for nearly a year. He hardly had the need for a hundred-fifty-dollar haircut, or the collection of Italian suits and shoes packed in storage.

He was no longer a sharply dressed criminal attorney with a corner office and the fast track to full partner. That man had died along with Lindsay. He just hadn't known it.

He tossed back the duvet, as fluffy and white as the towel, slid in, switched off the light.

In the dark he could hear the sea, a steady growl, and the sizzle of sleet against the windows. He closed his eyes, wished as he did every night for a few hours of oblivion.

A few was all he got.

God damn, he was pissed. Nobody, absolutely nobody, he thought as he drove through the hard, freezing rain, could trip his switch like Lindsay.

The bitch.

Her mind, and apparently her morals, worked like no one else's he knew. She'd managed to convince herself, and he was sure any number of her friends, her mother, her sister, and Christ knew, that it was *his* fault their marriage had deteriorated, *his* they'd gone from couples counseling to a trial separation to a legal battle in preparation for divorce.

And *his* fucking fault she'd been cheating on him for well over eight months— five more than the "trial" separation she'd campaigned for. And somehow it was on him that he'd found out about her lying, cheating, conniving ass before signing on the dotted line so she could walk away with a fat settlement.

So they were both pissed, he decided— he that he'd been an idiot, and she that he'd finally clued in.

No doubt it would be his fault they'd had a bitter, vicious and public fight about her adultery that afternoon in the art gallery where she worked part-time. Bad timing, bad form on his part, he admitted, but right now? He didn't give a shit.

She wanted to blame him because

she'd gotten sloppy, so sloppy his own sister had seen his estranged wife and another man all over each other in a hotel lobby in Cambridge—before they'd gotten on the elevator together.

Maybe Tricia had waited a couple days to tell him, but he couldn't blame her. It was a lot to tell. And he'd taken another couple to absorb it before he'd manned up, hired an investigator.

Eight months, he thought again. She'd been sleeping with someone else in hotel beds, in B &Bs, God knew where else—though she'd been too smart to use the house. What would the neighbors think?

Maybe he shouldn't have gone, armed with the investigator's report and his own fury, to the gallery to confront her. Maybe the two of them should've had more sense than to start a shouting match that carried through the place and out to the street.

But they'd both have to weather the embarrassment.

One thing he knew: the settlement wouldn't be so sweet for her now. All concept of clean and fair, and no need to stick hard to the prenup? Done. She'd find that out when she got home from her charity auction and found he'd taken the painting he bought in Florence, the Deco diamond that had been his great-grandmother's and had come to him, and the silver coffee set he had no interest in but was another family heirloom he'd be *damned* if she'd throw into the community property pot.

She was going to find herself batting in a new ball game.

Maybe it was petty, maybe it was stupid—or maybe it was right and just. He couldn't see through the anger and betrayal, and simply didn't care. Riding on that anger, he pulled up in the driveway of the house in Boston's Back Bay. A house he'd believed would serve as a solid foundation for a marriage that had begun to show some cracks. One he'd hoped would one day house children, and one that, for a short time, had plastered over those cracks as he and Lindsay had outfitted it, chosen furnishings, debated, argued, agreed—all of which he considered normal—over little details.

Now they'd have to sell it, and both likely walk away with half of little to nothing. And instead of renting a condo for what he'd hoped would be the short term, he'd end up buying one.

For himself, he thought as he climbed out of the car and into the rain. No debates, arguments or agreements necessary.

And, he realized as he jogged to the front door, that came as a kind of relief. No more holding time, no more maybes, no more pretense his marriage could or should be saved.

Maybe in her lying, deceitful, cheating way, she'd done him a favor.

He could walk away now without guilt or regret.

But he'd damn well walk away with what was his.

He unlocked the door, stepped into the wide, gracious foyer. Turning to the alarm pad, he keyed in the code. If she'd changed it, he had his ID, listing his name and this address. He'd already worked out how to handle any police or security questions.

He'd simply say his wife had changed

the code—true enough—and he'd forgotten it.

But she hadn't. The fact that she hadn't
was both relief and insult. She thought
she knew him so well, was so sure he'd
never enter the house that was half his
without her permission. He'd agreed to
move out, to give them both some space,
so he'd never intrude, never push too
hard.

She assumed he'd be fucking civilized.

She was soon to discover she didn't
know him at all.

He stood a moment, absorbing the
quiet of the house, the *feel* of it. All those
neutral tones serving as a backdrop of
splashes and flashes of color, the mix of
old, new, cleverly quirky adding style.

She was good at it, he could admit
that. She knew how to present herself,
her home, knew how to arrange success-
ful parties. There had been some good
times here, spikes of happiness, stretches
of contentment, moments of easy com-
patibility, some good sex, some lazy Sunday mornings.

How did it all go so wrong?

"Screw it," he muttered.

Get in, get out, he told himself. Being in the house just depressed him. He went upstairs, directly to the sitting room off the master bedroom—noted she had an overnight bag on the luggage rack, half packed.

She could go wherever the hell she wanted to go, he thought, with or without her lover.

Eli focused in on what he'd come for. Inside the closet, he keyed in the combination for the safe. He ignored the stack of cash, the documents, the jewelry cases holding pieces he'd given her over the years, or she'd bought for herself.

Just the ring, he told himself. The Landon ring. He checked the box, watched it wink and flash in the light, then shoved it into the pocket of his jacket. Once the safe was secured again and he started back down, it occurred to him he should've brought bubble wrap or some protection for the painting.

He'd grab some towels, he decided, something to shield it from the rain. He took a couple of bath sheets from the linen closet, kept going.

In and out, he told himself again. He

hadn't known how much he wanted out of that house, away from the memories—good and bad.

In the living room he took the painting off the wall. He'd bought it on their honeymoon because Lindsay had been so taken with it, with the sun-washed colors, the charm and simplicity of a field of sunflowers backed by olive groves.

They'd bought other art since, he thought as he wrapped the towels around it. Paintings, sculptures, pottery certainly of greater value. They could all go in the communal pile, all be part of the mechanism of negotiation. But not this.

He laid the padded painting on the sofa, moved through the living area with the storm slashing overhead. He wondered if she was driving in it, on her way home to finish packing for the overnight trip with her lover.

"Enjoy it while it lasts," he murmured. Because first thing in the morning, he was calling his divorce attorney and letting him off the leash.

From now on, he intended to go for the throat.

He turned into the room they'd fashioned into a library and, as he started to hit the light switch, saw her in a shuddering burst of icy lightning.

From that moment to the answering bellow of thunder, his mind went blank.

"Lindsay?"

He slapped at the switch as he lurched forward. Inside him waged a war between what he saw and what he could accept.

She lay on her side in front of the hearth. Blood, so much blood on the white marble, the dark floor.

Her eyes, that rich chocolate that had so captivated him once, were filmed glass.

"Lindsay."

He dropped down beside her, took the hand stretched out on the floor as if reaching. And found her cold.

In Bluff House, Eli woke, dragging himself out of the blood and shock of the recurring dream and into sunlight.

For a moment he just sat as he'd reared up, disoriented, hazy. He stared around the room, remembering as his thumping heart leveled again.

Bluff House. He'd come to Bluff House.

Lindsay had been dead nearly a year. The house in the Back Bay was finally on the market. The nightmare was behind him. Even if he still felt its breath on the back of his neck.

He shoved at his hair, wished he could delude himself so he could just go back to sleep, but he knew if he closed his eyes again, he'd be right back in the little library, right back beside the body of his murdered wife.

And yet he couldn't think of a single good reason to get out of bed.

He thought he heard music—dim, distant. What the hell was that music?

He'd gotten so used to noises—voices, music, TV mumbling—during the last few months in his parents' house he hadn't registered there shouldn't be music, or anything but the sound of the sea or the wind.

Had he turned on a radio, a television, something, and forgotten? It wouldn't be the first time since his long downward spiral.

So, a reason to get up, he decided.

As he hadn't brought in the rest of his

bags, he yanked on the jeans he'd worn the day before, grabbed the shirt and shrugged into it as he started out of the bedroom.

It didn't sound like a radio, he realized as he approached the stairs. Or not just a radio. He recognized Adele easily enough as he moved through the main floor, but clearly heard a second female voice forming a kind of passionate—and loud—duet.

He followed the sound, winding through the house toward the kitchen.

Adele's singing partner reached into one of the three cloth market bags on the counter, drew out a small bunch of bananas and added them to a bamboo bowl of apples and pears.

He couldn't quite get his mind around it, any of it.

She sang full out, and well—not with Adele's magic, but well. And looked like a fairy, of the long and willowy variety.

A mass of long curls the color of walnut tumbled around her shoulders, spilled down the back of a dark blue sweater. Her face was . . . *unusual*, was all he could think. Long, almond-shaped eyes, the sharp nose and cheekbones, the top-heavy mouth down to the mole at its left corner struck him as just a little other-worldly.

Or maybe it was just his fogged brain and the circumstances.

Rings glinted on her fingers. Dangles swung from her ears. A crescent moon hung around her neck, and a watch with a face as round and white as a baseball rode her left wrist.

Still belting it out, she lifted a quart of milk, a pound of butter from the bag, started to turn toward the refrigerator. And saw him.

She didn't scream, but did take a stumbling step back, and nearly bobbled the milk.

"Eli?" She set down the milk, laid a beringed hand on her heart. "God! You scared me." With a throaty, breathless laugh, she shook back all that curling hair. "You aren't due until this afternoon. I didn't see your car. But I came in the back," she continued, gesturing toward the door leading out to the main terrace.

"I guess you came in the front. Why wouldn't you? Did you drive up last night? Less traffic, I guess, but crappy roads with the sleet.

"Anyway, here you are. Would you like some coffee?"

She looked like a long-legged fairy, he thought again, and had a laugh like a sea goddess.

And she'd brought bananas.

He just stared at her. "Who are you?"

"Oh, sorry. I thought Hester told you. I'm Abra. Abra Walsh. Hester asked me to get the house ready for you. I'm just stocking the kitchen. How's Hester? I haven't spoken to her for a couple of days—just quick e-mails and texts."

"Abra Walsh," he repeated. "You found her."

"Yes." She dug a bag of coffee beans out of a sack and began to fill a machine much like one he'd used daily at his law offices. "Horrible day. She didn't come to yoga class—she never misses. I called, but she didn't answer, so I came over to check. I have a key. I clean for her."

While the machine hummed, she put

an oversize mug under the spout, then continued putting away the groceries. "I came in the back—habit. I called for her, but . . . Then I started to worry maybe she wasn't feeling well, so I walked through to go upstairs. And she was lying there. I thought . . . but she had a pulse, and she came around for a minute when I said her name. I called for an ambulance, and I got the throw off the sofa because I was afraid to move her. They were quick, but at the time, it seemed like hours."

She got a carton of cream out of the refrigerator, added it to the mug. "Counter or breakfast nook?"

"What?"

"Counter." She set the coffee down on the island. "That way you can sit and talk to me." When he just stared at the coffee, she smiled. "That's right, isn't it? Hester said a dollop of cream, no sugar."

"Yeah. Yes, thanks." Like a man sleepwalking, he moved to the island, sat on the stool.

"She's so strong, so smart, so herself. She's my hero, your grandmother. When I moved here a couple of years ago, she was the first person I really connected with."

She just kept talking. It didn't matter if he listened, she thought. Sometimes the sound of someone's voice could be comfort, and he looked as if he needed comfort.

She thought of the photos Hester had shown her of him, from a few years back. The easy smile, the light in his Landon blue eyes—crystal blue with a dark, dark rim around the iris. Now he looked tired, sad and too thin.

She'd do what she could to fix that.

So thinking, she took eggs, cheese, ham out of the refrigerator.

"She's grateful you agreed to stay here. I know it upset her thinking of Bluff House empty. She said you're writing a novel?"

"I . . . mmmm."

"I've read a couple of your short stories. I liked them." She put an omelet pan on the stove to heat. While it did, she poured a glass of orange juice, put some berries in a little colander to wash, bread in the toaster. "I wrote bad romantic poetry when I was a teenager. It was even worse when I tried to set it to music. I love to read. I admire anyone who can put words together to tell a story. She's so proud of you. Hester."

He looked up then, met her eyes. Green, he realized, like a sea in thin fog, and as otherworldly as the rest of her.

Maybe she wasn't here at all.

Then her hand lay over his, just for a moment, warm and real. "Your coffee's going to get cold."

"Right." He lifted the mug, drank. And felt marginally better.

"You haven't been here for a while," she continued, and poured the egg mixture into the omelet pan. "There's a nice little restaurant down in the village—and the pizza parlor's still there. I think you're pretty well stocked now, but the market's still there, too. If you need anything and don't want to go into the village, just let me know. I'm in Laughing Gull Cottage if you're out and want to stop in. Do you know it?"

"I . . . yes. You . . . work for my grand-mother?"

"I've cleaned for her once or twice a

week, as she's needed it. I clean for a few people—as they need it. I teach yoga five times a week, in the church basement, and an evening a week in my cottage. Once I convinced Hester to try yoga, she was hooked. I do massages"— she gave him a quick grin over her shoulder—"therapeutic. I'm certified. I do a lot of things, because a lot of things interest me."

She plated the omelet with the fresh berries and toast. Set the plate in front of him, added a red linen napkin and flatware. "I have to go, I'm running a little late."

She folded the market bags into an enormous red tote, slipped on a dark purple coat, wound a scarf of striped jewel tones around her neck, yanked on a purple wool cap.

"I'll see you the day after tomorrow, about nine."

"The day after tomorrow?"

"To clean. If you need anything in the meantime, my numbers—cell and home— are on the board right there. Or if you're out for a walk and I'm home, stop by. So . . . welcome back, Eli."

She walked to the patio door, turned, smiled. "Eat your breakfast," she ordered, and was gone.

He sat, staring at the door, then looked down at his plate. Because he couldn't think of anything else to do, he picked up his fork and ate.

Two

Eli wandered the house, hoping it might help him orient. He hated this feeling of free-floating, just drifting from place to place, thought to thought, without any sense of anchor or root. Once he'd had structure in his life, and purpose. Even after Lindsay's death, when the structure broke to pieces, he'd had purpose.

Fighting against spending the rest of his life in prison equaled a strong, defined purpose.

And now with the threat less immediate, less viable, what purpose did he have? His writing, he reminded himself.

He often thought the process and the escape of writing had saved his sanity.

But where was his anchor now? Where was the root? Was it Bluff House? As simple as that?

He'd spent time in this house as a boy, as a young man, so many summers with the beach always tantalizingly close, so many winter holidays or weekends, watching snow heap itself on the sand, on the rocks jutting through it.

Simple times—innocent? Had they been? Sand castles and clambakes with family, with friends, sailing with his grandfather in the pretty sloop he knew his grandmother still kept moored in Whiskey Beach marina, and noisy, crowded, colorful Christmas dinners, with all the fireplaces snapping and sizzling.

He'd never imagined himself wandering through these rooms like a ghost straining for the echoes of those voices or the faded images of better times.

When he stood in his grandmother's bedroom, it struck him that while she'd made changes here—the paint, the bedding—much remained just as always.

The big fabulous four-poster where his

own father—due to a blizzard and a rapid labor—had been born. The photograph of his grandparents, so young and vibrant and beautiful on their wedding day more than a half century before still stood, as it always had, in its gleaming silver frame on the bureau. And the view from the windows of the sea, the sand, the jagged curve of the rocky coastline remained constant.

Suddenly he had a vivid, movie-stream memory of a summer night, a wild summer storm. Thunder crashing, lightning whipping. And he and his sister, who'd been spending the week at Bluff House, running in terror to his grandparents' bed.

What had he been—five, or maybe six? But he could see it all, as if through a clear, crystal lens. The flashes of light outside the windows, the wonderful big bed he had to climb up to. He heard his grandfather—and wasn't it odd to just that moment realize how much his father had come to resemble his grandfather at a similar age?—laughing as he'd hauled the terrified Tricia into the bed.

They're having a wild party up there tonight! It's heaven's rock concert.

Even as the image faded, Eli felt steadier.

He walked to the terrace doors, flipped the lock and stepped out into the wind and cold.

The waves kicked, riled up by the strong, steady wind that tasted of snow. On the tip of the headland, the far end of that curve, the bride-white tower of the lighthouse rose above a tumble of rocks. Far out in the Atlantic, he saw a speck that was a ship plying those restless waters.

Where was it going? What did it carry?

They'd played a game long ago, a variation on A is for Apple. It's going to Armenia, Eli thought, and it's carrying artichokes.

For the first time in too long, as he hunched his shoulders against that ice-pick cold, he smiled.

To Bimini with baboons. To Cairo with coconuts. To Denmark with dental floss, he thought as the speck vanished.

He stood a moment longer before stepping back inside, back into the warm.

He needed to do something. He should go out, get his stuff. Unpack, settle in.

Maybe later.

He walked out again, wandered again, all the way to the third floor that had once served—before his time—as the servants' domain.

Storage now, ghost-draped furniture, chests, boxes, most in the wide space while the warren of rooms where maids and cooks had slept stood empty. Still, with no purpose in mind, he walked through them to the sea side, and the gable room with its wide, curved windows facing the sea.

The head housekeeper's room, he thought. Or had it been the head butler's? He couldn't remember which, but whoever had slept there claimed prime territory, down to the private entrance and terrace.

No need for all that staff now, or to keep the third floor furnished, maintained, even heated. His practical Gran had closed that off years ago.

Maybe one day whoever was in charge would repurpose it, bring it back, shake off all those ghost cloths and strike up the warmth and light.

But right now it felt as empty and cold as he did.

He went down again, continued to wander.

And found more changes.

In what had been one of the second-floor bedrooms, his grandmother had re-imagined, redesigned it into an office/sitting room. A study, he supposed. Complete with a computer station on a gorgeous old desk, a reading chair and what he thought of as an afternoon nap sofa. More of her art—petal pink peonies spilling out of a cobalt vase, mists rising over windswept dunes.

And the view, of course, spread out like a banquet for a hungry soul.

He moved into the room, to the desk, and pulled the sticky note off the monitor.

Hester says:
    Write here, and why aren't you
already?
    Relayed by Abra.

He frowned at the note a moment, not sure he appreciated his grandmother's using her neighbor to relay her orders. Then, the note still in his hand, he looked around the room, the windows, even into the little bathroom, the closet that now held office supplies as well as linens, blankets and pillows. Which meant, he concluded, the sofa was a pullout.

Practical again. The house held a dozen bedrooms or more—he couldn't remember—but why waste space when you could multipurpose?

He shook his head at the glass-fronted mini-fridge stocked with bottled water and his own guilty favorite since college, Mountain Dew.

Write here.

It was a good space, he thought, and the idea of writing held a lot more appeal than unpacking.

"Okay," he said. "All right."

He went to his room, retrieved his laptop case. He slid the keyboard and monitor to the far left, gave himself room for his own tool. And since it was there, what the hell, got a cold bottle of the Dew. He booted up, plugged in his thumb drive.

"Okay," he said again. "Where were we?"

He opened the bottle, chugged as he brought up his work, did a quick review. And with one last glance at the view, dived in.

He escaped.

Since college, he'd written as a hobby—an interest he'd enjoyed indulging. And it had given him some pride when he'd sold a handful of short stories.

In the past year and a half—when his life began to shake into the dumpster—he'd found writing offered him better therapy, a calmer mind than a fifty-minute hour with a shrink.

He could go away into a world he created, he—to some extent, anyway—controlled. And oddly felt more himself than he did outside that world.

He wrote—again, to some extent—what he knew. Crafting legal thrillers—first in short stories, and now this terrifying and seductive attempt at a novel—gave him an opportunity to play with the law, to use it, misuse it, depending on the character. He could create dilemmas, solutions, tightrope along the thin and slippery line, always shifting between the law and justice.

He'd become a lawyer because the law, with all of its flaws, all of its intricacies and interpretations, fascinated him. And because the family business, the industry of Landon Whiskey, just wasn't a fit for him as it was for his father, his sister, even his brother-in-law.

He'd wanted criminal law, and had pursued that goal single-mindedly through law school, while clerking for Judge Reingold, a man he admired and respected, and into Brown, Kinsale, Schubert and Associates.

Now that the law had failed him in a very real sense, he wrote to feel alive, to remind himself there were times truth held out against lies, and justice found a way.

By the time he surfaced, the light had changed, gone gloomy, softening the tones in the water. With some surprise he noted it was after three; he'd written solidly for nearly four hours.

"Hester scores again," he murmured.

He backed up the work, switched to e-mail. Plenty of spam, he noted—and deleted. Not much else, and nothing he felt obliged, right then, to read.

Instead he composed a post to his parents, and another to his sister with nearly the same text. No problems on the drive, house looks great, good to be back, settling in. Nothing about recurring dreams, sneaking depression or talkative neighbors who fixed omelets.

Then he composed another to his grandmother.

I'm writing here, as ordered. Thank you. The water's gone to rippling steel with fast white horses. It's going to snow; you can taste it. The house looks good, and feels even better. I'd forgotten how it always made me feel. I'm sorry—don't tell me not to apologize again—I'm sorry, Gran, I stopped coming. But I'm sorry now almost as much for me as for you.

Maybe if I'd come to you, to Bluff House, I'd have seen things more clearly, accepted things, changed things. If I had, would it have all gone so horribly wrong?

I'll never know, and there's no point in the what-ifs.

What I'm sure of is it's good to be

here, and I'll take care of the house until you come home. I'm going to take a walk on the beach, come back and start a fire so I can enjoy it once the snow starts to fall.

I love you,
Eli

Oh, P.S. I met Abra Walsh. She's interesting. I can't remember if I thanked her for saving the love of my life. I'll make sure I do when she comes back.

After he sent the e-mail, it occurred to him that while he couldn't remember if he'd thanked her, he did remember he hadn't paid her for the groceries.

He wrote himself a note on the pack of Post-its he found in the desk drawer, stuck it to the computer monitor. He forgot too easily these days.

No point in putting off unpacking, he told himself. If nothing else, he needed to change the clothes he'd worn two days straight. He couldn't let himself go down that road again.

He used the lift writing had given him,

dragged on his coat, remembered he'd yet to put on shoes, then went out for his bags.

In the unpacking he discovered he hadn't packed sensibly. He hardly needed a suit, much less three of them, or four pairs of dress shoes, fifteen (Jesus Christ!) ties. Just habit, he told himself. Just packing on autopilot.

He hung, folded in drawers, stacked up books, found his phone charger, his iPod. Once some of his things worked their way into the room, he found it did make him feel more settled in.

So he unpacked his laptop case, tucked his checkbook—had to pay the neighbor when she cleaned—in the desk drawer along with his obsessive supply of pens.

He'd go for a walk now. Stretch his legs, get some exercise, some fresh air. Those were healthy, productive things to do. Because he didn't want to make the effort, he forced himself as he'd promised himself he would. Get out every day, even if it's just a walk on the beach. Don't wallow, don't brood.

He pulled on his parka, shoved the keys in his pocket and went out the terrace doors before he changed his mind.

He forced himself to cross the pavers against the maniacal bluster of wind. Fifteen minutes, he decided as he headed for the beach steps with his head down and his shoulders hunched. That qualified as getting out of the house. He'd walk down, head in one direction for seven and a half minutes, then walk back.

Then he'd build a fire, and sit and brood in front of it with a glass of whiskey if he wanted to.

Sand swirled up from the dunes to dance while the wind sweeping in from the sea kicked at the sea grass like a bully. The white horses he'd told his grandmother about reared and galloped over water of hard, icy gray. The air scored his throat on each breath like crushed glass.

Winter clung to Whiskey Beach like frozen burrs, reminding him he'd forgotten gloves, a hat.

He could walk thirty minutes tomorrow, he bargained with himself. Or pick one day of the week for an hour. Who said it had to be every day? Who made the rules? It was freaking cold out there, and even an idiot could look at that bloated sky and know those smug, swirling clouds were just waiting to dump a boatload of snow.

And only an idiot walked on the beach during a snowstorm.

He reached the bottom of the sand-strewn steps with his own thoughts all but drowned out in the roar of water and wind. No point in this, he convinced himself, and on the edge of turning around and climbing up again, lifted his head.

Waves rolled out of that steel-gray world to hurl themselves at the shore like battering rams, full of force and fury. Battle cry after battle cry echoed in their unrelenting advance and retreat. Against the shifting sand rose the juts and jumble of rock it attacked, regrouped, attacked again in a war neither side would ever win.

Above the battle that bulging sky waited, watched, as if calculating when to unleash its own weapons.

So Eli stood, struck by the terrible power and beauty. The sheer magnificence of *energy*.

Then, while the war raged, he began to walk.

He saw not another soul along the long beach, heard only the sound of the bitter wind and angry surf. Above the dunes the homes and cottages stood with windows shut tight against the cold. No one moved up or down the beach steps or stood on bluff or cliff as far as he could see. No one looked out to sea from the pier where the turbulent surf hammered mercilessly at the pilings.

For now, for this moment, he was alone as Crusoe. But not lonely.

Impossible to be lonely here, he realized, surrounded by all this power and energy. He'd remember this, he promised himself, remember this feeling the next time he tried to make excuses, the next time he tried to justify just closing himself in.

He loved the beach, and this stretch remained a sentimental favorite. He loved the feel of it before a storm—winter, summer, spring, it didn't matter. And the *life* of it during the season when people dived into the waves or stretched out on towels, or settled onto beach chairs under umbrellas. The way it looked at sunrise, or felt in the soft kiss of summer twilight.

Why had he robbed himself of this for so long? He couldn't blame circumstances, couldn't blame Lindsay. He could, and should, have come—for his grandmother, for himself. But he'd chosen what had seemed the easier way than explaining why his wife hadn't come, making excuses for her, for himself. Or arguing with Lindsay when she'd pushed for Cape Cod or Martha's Vineyard—or an extended vacation on the Côte d'Azur.

But the easier way hadn't made it easier, and he'd lost something important to him.

If he didn't take it back now, he'd have no one to blame but himself. So he walked, all the way to the pier, and remembered the girl he'd had a serious, sizzling summer flirtation with just before he'd started college. Fishing with his father—something neither of them had even a remote skill for. And further back to childhood and digging in the sand at low tide for pirate treasure with fleeting summer friends.

Esmeralda's Dowry, he thought. The old and still vital legend of the treasure stolen by pirates in a fierce battle at sea, then lost again when the pirate ship, the infamous *Calypso*, wrecked on the rocks of Whiskey Beach, all but at the feet of Bluff House.

He'd heard every variation of that legend over the years, and as a child had hunted with his friends. They'd be the ones to dig up the treasure, become modern-day pirates with its pieces of eight and jewels and silver.

And like everyone else, they'd found nothing but clams, sand crabs and shells. But they'd enjoyed the adventures during those long-ago, sun-washed summers.

Whiskey Beach had been good to him, good for him. Standing here with those wicked combers spewing their foam and spray, he believed it would be good for him again.

He'd walked farther than he'd intended, and stayed longer, but now as he started back he thought of the whiskey by the fire as a pleasure, a kind of reward rather than an escape or an excuse for a brood.

He should probably make something to eat as he hadn't given a thought to lunch. He hadn't, he realized, eaten anything since breakfast. Which meant he'd reneged on another promise to himself to regain the weight he'd lost, to start working on a healthier lifestyle.

So he'd make a decent meal for dinner, and get started on that healthier lifestyle. There had to be something he could put together. The neighbor had stocked the kitchen, so . . .

As he thought of her, he glanced up and saw Laughing Gull nestled with its neighbors beyond the dunes. The bold summer-sky blue of its clapboard stood out among the pastels and creamy whites. He remembered it as a soft gray at one time. But the quirky shape of the place with its single peaked roof gable, its wide roof deck and the glass hump of a solarium made it unmistakable.

He saw lights twinkling behind that glass to stave off the gloom.

He'd go up and pay her now, he decided, with cash. Then he could stop thinking about it. He'd walk home from there, renewing his memory of the other houses, who lived there—or who had.

Part of his brain calculated that now he'd have something cheerful—and true—to report home. Went for a walk on the beach (describe), stopped by to see Abra Walsh on the way home. Blah, blah, new paint on Laughing Gull looks good.

See, not isolating myself, concerned family. Getting out, making contacts. Situation normal.

Amused at himself, he composed the e-mail as he climbed. He turned down a smooth cobble path between a short yard laid out with shrubs and statuary—a fanciful mermaid curled on her tail, a frog strumming a banjo, and a little stone bench on legs of winged fairies. He was so struck by the new—to him—landscaping and how perfectly it suited the individuality of the cottage, he didn't notice the movement behind the solarium until he had a foot on the door stoop.

Several women on yoga mats rose up—with varying degrees of fluidity and

skill, to the inverted V position he identified as the Downward-Facing Dog.

Most of them wore the yoga gear—colorful tops, slim pants—he'd often seen in
the gym. When he'd belonged to a gym.
Some opted for sweats, others for shorts.

All of them, with some wobbles,
brought one foot forward into a lunge,
then rose up—with a couple of teeters—
front leg bent, back leg straight, arms
spread front and back.

Mildly embarrassed, he started to step
back, to back away, when he realized the
group was following Abra's lead.

She held her position, her mass of hair
pulled back in a tail. The deep purple top
showed off long, sculpted arms; the
stone-gray pants clung to narrow hips,
slid down long legs to long, narrow feet
with toenails painted the same purple as
the top.

It fascinated him, tugged at him as
she—then the others—bowed back, front
arm curved over her head, torso turning,
head lifting.

Then she straightened her front leg,
cocked forward, leaning down, down

until her hand rested on the floor by her front foot, and her other arm reached for the ceiling. Again her torso turned. Before he could step back, her head turned as well. As her gaze swept up, her eyes met his.

She smiled. As if he'd been expected, as if he hadn't been—inadvertently—playing Peeping Tom.

He stepped back now, making a gesture he hoped communicated apology, but she was already straightening up. He saw her motion to one of the women as she wove through the mats and bodies.

What should he do now?

The front door opened, and she smiled at him again. "Eli, hi."

"I'm sorry. I didn't realize . . . until I did."

"God, it's freezing! Come on inside."

"No, you're busy. I was just walking, then I—"

"Well, walk in here before I freeze to death." She stepped out on those long bare feet, took his hand.

"Your hand's like ice." She gave it a tug, insistent. "I don't want the cold air to chill the class."

Left without a choice, he stepped in so

she could close the door. New Agey
music murmured like water in a stream
from the solarium. He could see the
woman at the rear of the class come back
up to that lunging position.

"I'm sorry," he said again. "I'm inter-
rupting."

"It's all right. Maureen can guide them
through. We're nearly finished. Why don't
you go on back to the kitchen? Have a
glass of wine while I finish up?"

"No. No, thanks." He wished, almost
desperately, he hadn't taken the impulsive detour. "I just— I was out for a walk,
and I just stopped by on the way back
because I realized I didn't pay you for the
groceries."

"Hester took care of it."

"Oh. I should've figured that. I'll talk to
her."

The framed pencil sketch in the entry
distracted him for a moment. He recognized his grandmother's work even without the *H. H. Landon* in the bottom corner.

He recognized Abra as well, standing
slim and straight as a lance in Tree position, her arms overhead, and her face
caught on a laugh.

"Hester gave it to me last year," Abra said.

"What?"

"The sketch. I talked her into coming to class to sketch—a gateway to persuading her to practice. So she gave this to me as a thank-you after she fell in love with yoga."

"It's great."

He didn't realize Abra still had his hand until she took a step back, and he was forced to step forward. "Shoulders down and back, Leah. That's it. Relax your jaw, Heather. Good. That's good. Sorry," she said to Eli.

"No, I'm sorry. I'm in the way. I'll let you get back to it."

"Are you sure you don't want that glass of wine? Or maybe, considering . . ." She closed her other hand around his, rubbed at the cold. "Some hot chocolate?"

"No. No, but thanks. I need to get back." The friction of her hands brought on a quick, almost painful warmth that emphasized he'd let himself get chilled down to the bone. "It's . . . going to snow."

"A good night to be in with a fire and a

good book. Well." She let go of his hand to open the door again. "I'll see you in a couple of days. Call or come by if you need anything."

"Thanks." He walked away quickly so she could close the door and keep the heat in.

Instead she stood in the open door, looking after him.

Her heart—one some often told her was too soft, too open—just flooded with sympathy.

How long had it been, she wondered, since anyone but family had welcomed him out of the cold?

She shut the door, moved back to the solarium and, with a nod for her friend Maureen, took over again.

As she completed final relaxation, she saw the snow Eli had predicted falling thick and soft outside the glass so her cozy space felt just like the inside of a fanciful snow globe.

She thought it perfect.

"Remember to hydrate." She lifted her own water bottle as the women rolled up their mats. "And we still have room in tomorrow morning's East Meets West class in the Unitarian Church basement at nine-fifteen."

"I *love* that class." Heather Lockaby fluffed her short cap of blond hair. "Winnie, I can pick you up on the way if you want."

"Give me a call first. I'd love to try it."

"And now"—Heather rubbed her hands together—"was that who I thought it was?"

"Sorry?" Abra responded.

"The man who came in during class. Wasn't that Eli Landon?"

The name brought on an immediate murmur. Abra felt the benefits of her hour's yoga practice dissolve as her shoulders tightened. "Yes, that was Eli."

"I *told* you." Heather elbowed Winnie. "I told you I'd heard he was moving into Bluff House. Are you seriously doing the cleaning there while he's in the house?"

"There's not a lot to clean if nobody's living there."

"But Abra, aren't you nervous? I mean, he's accused of murder. Of killing his own wife. And—"

"He was cleared, Heather. Remember?"

"Just because they didn't have enough evidence to arrest him doesn't mean he isn't guilty. You shouldn't be alone in that house with him."

"Just because the press likes a good scandal, especially where sex, money and bedrock New England families are involved, doesn't mean he isn't innocent." Maureen arched fiery red eyebrows. "You know that old rule of law, Heather. Innocent until proven guilty?"

"I know he got fired—and he was a criminal defense lawyer. Seems fishy, if you ask me, that they'd fire him if he wasn't guilty. And they said he was the prime suspect. Witnesses heard him threaten his wife the same *day* she was killed. She'd have gotten a pile of money in a divorce. And he had no business being in that house, did he?"

"It was his house," Abra pointed out.

"But he'd moved out. I'm just saying where there's smoke . . ."

"Where there's smoke sometimes means someone else started the fire."

"You're so trusting." Heather gave Abra

a one-armed hug—as sincere as it was patronizing. "I'm just going to worry about you."

"I think Abra has a fine feel for people and can take care of herself." Greta Parrish, the senior of the group at seventy-two, pulled on her warm and practical wool coat. "And Hester Landon wouldn't have opened Bluff House for Eli—always a well-mannered young man—if she had the smallest doubt of his innocence."

"Oh, now I've nothing but affection and respect for Ms. Landon," Heather began. "Every one of us hope and pray she'll be well enough to come home soon. But—"

"No buts." Greta yanked a cloche cap over her steel-gray hair. "That boy's part of this community. He may have lived in Boston, but he's a Landon, and he's one of us. God knows he's been through the wringer. I'd hate to think anyone here would add to his troubles."

"I—I didn't mean that." Flustered, Heather looked from face to face. "Honestly, I didn't. I'm just worried about Abra. I can't help it."

"I believe you are." Greta gave Heather

a brisk nod. "I believe you've no reason to. This was a very nice practice, Abra."

"Thank you. Why don't I drive you home? It's snowing pretty hard."

"I believe I can manage a three-minute walk."

Women bundled up, filed out. Maureen lingered.

"Heather's an ass," Maureen stated.

"A lot of people are. And a lot of people will think the way she does. If he was suspected, he must be guilty. It's wrong."

"Of course it is." Maureen O'Malley, her short, spiky hair as fiery as her eyebrows, took another pull from her water bottle. "The problem is, I don't know if I'd think the same, at least in some little cynical pocket, if I didn't know Eli."

"I didn't realize you did."

"He was my first serious make-out."

"Hold that." Abra pointed with both index fingers. "Just hold that. That's a glass-of-wine story."

"You don't have to twist my arm. Just let me text Mike that I'm going to be about another half hour."

"You do that. I'll pour the wine."

In the kitchen Abra chose a bottle of Shiraz while Maureen plopped down on the sofa in the cozy living area.

"He says that's fine. The kids haven't killed each other yet, and are currently in the happy throes of snowstorm." She looked up from her phone, smiled when Abra handed her the wine, took a seat. "Thanks. I'll consider this girding my loins before I walk next door into the battle and feed the troops."

"Make out?"

"I was fifteen, and while I had been kissed, that was the first *kiss*. Tongues and hands and heavy breathing. Let me say first, the boy had most excellent lips, and very nice hands. The first, I'll also admit, to touch these amazing ta-tas." She patted her breasts then sipped her wine. "But not the last."

"Details, details."

"July Fourth, after the fireworks. We had a bonfire on the beach. A bunch of us. I had permission, which was hard-won, let me tell you, and which my kids will likely have a harder time winning due to my experience. He was so cute. Oh my God, Eli Landon up from Boston for a month—and I set my sights on him. I was not alone."

"How cute?"

"Mmm. That curling hair that would get more sun-streaked every day, those fabulous crystal blue eyes. And he had a smile that would just knock you senseless. An athletic build—he played basketball, as I remember. If he wasn't at the beach—shirtless—he was at the community center playing ball—shirtless. Let me repeat: Mmm."

"He's lost weight," Abra mentioned. "He's too thin."

"I saw some pictures, and the news clips. Yeah, he's too thin. But then, that summer? He was so beautiful, so young and happy and *fun*. I flirted my butt off and that July Fourth bonfire paid the dividends. The first time he kissed me we were sitting around the fire. Music banging out, some of us dancing, some of us in the water. One thing led to another, and we walked down to the pier."

She sighed with the memory. "Just a couple of hormonal teen-agers on a warm summer night. It didn't go any farther than it should have—though I'm sure my father would have disagreed—but it was the headiest moment of my life to that date. Seems so sweet and innocent now, but still ridiculously romantic. Surf and sea and moonlight, music from down the beach, a couple of warm, half-naked bodies just beginning to understand, really, what they were for. So . . .”

“So? So?” Leaning forward, Abra circled both hands in a hurry-up gesture. “What happened then?”

“We went back to the bonfire. I think it might have gone farther than it should have if he hadn’t taken me back to the group. I was so unprepared for what happens inside your body when someone really flips that switch. You know?”

“Oh boy, do I.”

“But he stopped, and after, he walked me home. I saw him a few more times before he went back to Boston, and we had a few more lip-locks—but nothing hit me like the first. The next time he came down, we were both dating someone. We never reconnected, not that way. He probably doesn’t even remember that July Fourth with the redhead under the Whiskey Beach pier.”

"I bet you're selling yourself short."

"Maybe. If we ran into each other when he'd come up to visit, we'd have a nice little chat—the way you do. Once I ran into him in the market when I was enormously pregnant with Liam. Eli carried my bags out to the car. He's a good man. I believe that."

"You met his wife?"

"No. I saw her once or twice but never met her. She was gorgeous, I'll give her that. But I wouldn't say she was the type who enjoyed those nice little chats outside the market. Word was there was no love lost between her and Hester Landon. Eli came up alone or with the rest of his family a few times after they were married. Then he just didn't come. At least not that I know of."

She looked at her watch. "I've got to get home. Feed the rampaging horde."

"Maybe you should go by and see him."

"I think it might feel like an intrusion at this point—or like I was morbidly curious."

"He needs friends, but you may be right. It may be too soon."

Maureen carried her empty wineglass to the kitchen, set it down. "I know you, Abracadabra. You won't let him wallow, not for long." She pulled on her coat. "It's your nature to fix things, heal things, kiss it where it hurts. Hester knew just what she was doing when she asked you to look after him and the house."

"Then I better not let her down." She gave Maureen a hug before she opened the back door. "Thanks for telling me. Not only a sexy story of teenage lust, but it gives me yet another perspective on him."

"You could use a lip-lock or two."

Abra held up her hands. "Fasting."

"Yeah, yeah. I'm just saying should the opportunity arise—he's got great lips. See you tomorrow."

Abra watched from the door while her friend hustled through the thick snow, and until she saw the back door light on the house next door shut off.

She'd build a fire, she decided, have a little soup, and give Eli Landon some serious thought.

Three

Maybe he'd lost some progress over-all, Eli admitted, but he'd stuck with the book for the best part of the day, and he'd produced there.

If he could keep his brain fired up, he'd write from the time he woke until the time he crashed. And okay, maybe that wasn't healthy, but it would be productive.

Besides, the snow hadn't relented until mid-afternoon. His vow to get out of the house at least once every day had to bow to two feet of snow and counting.

At one point when he simply couldn't think clearly enough to put coherent words on the page, he continued his exploration of the house.

Tidy guest rooms, pristine baths—and to his surprise and puzzlement, the former upstairs parlor, north wing, now held a cross trainer, free weights, a massive flat-screen. He wandered the room, frowning at the yoga mats neatly rolled on a shelf, the towels tidily stacked, the large case of DVDs.

He opened that, flipped through the pages. Power yoga? His *grandmother*? Seriously? Tai chi, Pilates . . . *Getting Ripped*?

Gran?

He tried to imagine it. He had to believe he owned a damn good imagination or he'd never make a decent living writing novels. But when he tried to picture his watercoloring, pencil-sketching, garden-clubbing grandmother pumping iron, it failed him.

Yet Hester Landon never did anything without a reason. He couldn't deny the setup and layout of the room showed careful thought and good research.

Maybe she'd decided she needed a convenient place to exercise when, like today, the weather prohibited her famous three-mile daily walks. She could have hired someone to outfit the room.

No, she never did anything without a reason—and she never did anything half-way.

And still he couldn't imagine her sliding in a DVD with the goal of getting ripped.

Idly, he flipped through a couple more DVDs in the case, and found the sticky note.

Eli, regular exercise benefits body, mind and spirit. Now, less brooding and more sweating.
   I love you,
   Gran via Abra Walsh

"Jesus." He couldn't decide whether to be amused or embarrassed. Just how much had his grandmother told Abra anyway? How about a little privacy?

He shoved his hands in his pockets and walked to the window facing the beach.

While the sea had calmed, it remained gray under a sky the color of a faded bruise. Waves flopped up against the snow-covered beach, slowly, gradually nibbling away at that rippled blanket of white. The white mounds of dunes rose, sea grasses poked out like needles in a pincushion. They trembled in the wind, bent to the force of its hands.

Snow buried the beach steps, lay thick and heavy on the rails.

He saw not a single footprint, yet the world outside wasn't empty. Far out in that gray forever he saw something leap—just a blur of shape and movement, here then gone. And he watched gulls wing over the snow, over the sea. In the snow-muffled quiet, he heard them laughing.

And thought of Abra.

He glanced back, gave the cross trainer an unenthusiastic study. He'd never liked putting in miles on a machine. If he wanted to work up a sweat, he'd play some round ball.

"Don't have a ball, a hoop," he said to the empty house. "And I do have a couple feet of snow. I should shovel the walk maybe. Why? I'm not going anywhere."

And that last statement, he thought,

had been part of the problem for nearly a year.

"Okay, fine. But I'm not doing any freaking power yoga. God, who thinks of that stuff? Maybe ten or fifteen on that damn machine. A couple of miles."

He'd put in some miles on the jogging path along the Charles, usually working it in a couple times a week in decent weather. He'd considered a treadmill at his gym a last resort, but he'd put in plenty of time there, too.

He could certainly handle his grand-mother's little cross trainer.

Then he could e-mail her, tell her he'd found the note, done the deed. And if she wanted to communicate with him on something, just *communicate*. No need to bring her yoga buddy into every damn thing.

He approached the cross trainer with inherent dislike, glanced at the flat-screen. No, no TV, he decided. He'd stopped watching when he'd seen his own face on the screen too often, heard the commentary, the debates on his guilt or innocence, the truly horrible rundowns of his personal life, factual and not.

Next time, if there was one, he thought as he stepped on, he'd dig out his iPod, but for now he'd just get it done and stay inside his own head.

To get a feel for it, he gripped the handles, pushed with his feet. And his grandmother's name flashed on the display screen.

"Huh." Curious, he studied the pad, called up her stats.

"Whoa. Go, Gran."

According to her last entry, which he realized was the day she'd taken the fall, she'd logged three miles in forty-eight minutes, thirty-two seconds.

"Not bad. But I can whip ya."

Intrigued now, he programmed for a second user, keyed in his name. He started slowly, giving himself a chance to warm up. Then pushed it.

Fourteen minutes and one-point-two miles later, drenched with sweat, his lungs burning, he surrendered. Gasping for breath, he staggered to the minifridge, grabbed a bottle of water. After guzzling, he dropped to the floor, lay flat on his back.

"Jesus Christ. Jesus, I can't even keep up with an old lady. Pitiful. Pathetic."

He stared up at the ceiling, struggling to get his breath back, disgusted to feel the muscles in his legs actually quivering with shock and fatigue.

He'd played basketball for goddamn Harvard. At six-three, he'd made up for his relative disadvantage in height with speed and agility—and endurance.

He'd been a fucking athlete once, and now he was weak and soft, underweight and slow.

He wanted his life back. No, no, that wasn't accurate. Even before the nightmare of Lindsay's murder, his life had been impossibly flawed, deeply unsatisfying.

He wanted *himself* back. And damned if he knew how to do it.

Where had he gone? He couldn't remember what it felt like to be happy. But he knew he had been. He'd had friends, interests, ambitions. He'd had fucking *passion*.

He couldn't even find his anger, he thought. He couldn't even dig down and find his anger over what had been taken from him, over what he'd somehow surrendered.

He'd taken the antidepressants, he'd talked to the shrink. He didn't want to go back there. He couldn't.

And he couldn't just lie there on the floor in a sweaty heap. He had to do *something*, however incidental, however ordinary. Just do the next thing, he told himself.

He pushed to his feet, limped his way to the shower.

Ignoring the voice in his head that urged him to just lie down, sleep off the rest of the day, he dressed for the cold, layering sweatshirt over insulated shirt, getting a ski cap, gloves.

Maybe he wasn't going anywhere, but that didn't mean the walkways, the driveway, even the terraces shouldn't be cleared.

He'd promised to tend to Bluff House, so he'd tend to Bluff House.

It took hours, with snowblower, snow shovel. He lost count of the times he had to stop, to rest when his pulse beat pounded alarm bells in his head, or his arms shook like palsy. But he cleared the driveway, the front walk, then a decent path across the main terrace to the beach steps.

And thanked God when the light faded to dusk and made continuing with the other terraces impractical. Inside, he dumped his outdoor gear in the mud-room, walked like a zombie into the kitchen where he slapped some lunch meat and Swiss cheese between two slices of bread and called it dinner.

He washed it down with a beer, simply because it was there, eating and drinking while he stood over the sink and looked out the window.

He'd done something, he told himself. He'd gotten out of bed, always the first hurdle. He'd written. He'd humiliated himself on the cross trainer. And he'd tended to Bluff House.

All in all, a pretty decent day.

He popped four Motrin, then dragged his aching body upstairs. He stripped, crawled into bed, and slept until dawn. Dreamlessly.

It surprised and pleased Abra to find the driveway cleared at Bluff House. She'd fully expected to slog through two feet of untrampled snow.

Normally, she'd have walked from her cottage, but opted against navigating deep snow or thin ice on foot. She pulled her Chevy Volt behind Eli's BMW, grabbed her bag.

She unlocked the front door, cocked her head to listen. When silence greeted her, she decided Eli was either still in bed or closed up somewhere in the house.

She hung her coat in the closet, changed her boots for work shoes.

She started a fire in the living room first, to cheer the room, then headed to the kitchen to make coffee.

No dishes in the sink, she noted, and opened the dishwasher.

She could track his meals since he'd arrived. The breakfast she'd made him, a couple of soup bowls, two small plates, two glasses, two coffee mugs.

She shook her head.

This wouldn't do.

To corroborate, she checked cupboards, the refrigerator.

No, this wouldn't do at all.

She turned the kitchen iPod on low, then gathered ingredients. Once she'd made up a bowl of pancake batter, she went upstairs to find him.

If he was still in bed, it was time he got up.

But she heard the clicking of a keyboard from Hester's home office, smiled. That was something anyway. Moving quietly, she peeked through the open doorway to see him sitting at the wonderful old desk, an open bottle of Mountain Dew (mental note to pick up more for him) beside the keyboard.

She'd give him a little more time there, she decided, and went straight into his bedroom. She made the bed, pulled the laundry bag out of the hamper, added bath towels.

She checked other baths on the way back in case he'd used hand towels or washcloths, checked the gym.

Back downstairs, she carted the bag into the laundry room, sorted, separated and started a load. And shook out, hung up his outdoor gear.

Not a lot to tidy, she realized, and she'd

given the house a thorough cleaning the day before he'd arrived. While she could always find something to do, she calculated the time. She'd make him a kind of brunch before she rolled up her sleeves and really got to work.

The next time she went upstairs, she deliberately made noise. When she reached the office, he was up and moving to the door. Probably with the intention of closing it, she thought, so she stepped in before he could.

"Good morning. It's a gorgeous day."

"Ah—"

"Fabulous blue skies." With her trash bag in hand, she walked over to empty the basket under the desk. "Blue sea, sun sparkling off the snow. The gulls are fishing. I saw a whale this morning."

"A whale."

"Just luck. I happened to be looking out the window just as it sounded. Way out, and still spectacular. So." She turned. "Your brunch is ready."

"My what?"

"Brunch. It's too late for breakfast, which you didn't eat."

"I had . . . coffee."

"Now you can have food."

"Actually, I'm . . ." He gestured to his laptop.

"And it's annoying to be interrupted, to be hauled off to eat. But you'll probably work better after some food. How long have you been writing today?"

"I don't know." It *was* annoying, he thought. The interruption, the questions, the food he didn't want to take time for. "Since about six, I guess."

"Well, God! It's eleven, so definitely time for a break. I set you up in the morning room this time. The view's so nice from there, especially today. Do you want me to do any cleaning in here while you eat—or ever?"

"No. I . . . No." After another slight pause. "No."

"I got that. Go ahead and eat, and I'll do what I have to do on this level. That way if you want to go back to work, I'll be downstairs where I won't bother you."

She stood between him and his laptop, smiling genially in a faded purple sweatshirt with a peace sign dead center, even more faded jeans and bright orange Crocs.

As arguing seemed time-consuming and futile, he simply walked out of the room.

He'd meant to stop and have something—maybe a bagel, whatever. He'd lost track of time. He *liked* losing track of time because it meant he was inside the book.

She was supposed to clean the house, not take on the position as his damn keeper.

He hadn't forgotten she was coming. But his plan to stop writing when she arrived, to grab that bagel and take it with him on a walk, to call home while he was out, well, the book sucked that away.

He turned left, into the glass-walled curve of the morning room.

Abra was right. The view was worth it. He'd take that walk later if he could find a reasonable route with the snow. At least he could get to the beach steps, take some pictures with his phone, send them home.

He sat at the table with its covered plate, its short pot of coffee, crystal glass of juice. She'd even taken one of the flowers from the living room arrangement and tucked it in a bud vase.

It reminded him of the way his mother had put a flower or some game or book or toy on the tray when she brought food to his sickbed when he was a boy.

He wasn't sick. He didn't need to be mothered. All he needed was someone to come in and clean so he could write, live, shovel damn snow if it needed shoveling.

He sat, wincing a little at the stiffness in his neck, his shoulders. Okay, the Shovel Snow for Pride Marathon had cost him, he admitted.

He lifted the dome.

A puff of fragrant steam rose from a stack of blueberry pancakes. A rasher of crisp bacon lined the edge of the plate and a little clear bowl of melon garnished with sprigs of mint sat beside it.

"Wow."

He simply stared a moment, struggling between more annoyance and acceptance.

He decided both worked. He'd eat because it was here, and now he was damn near starving, and he could be annoyed about it.

He spread some of the butter she'd scooped into a little dish over the stack, watched it melt as he added syrup.

It felt a little Lord of the Manor—but really tasty.

He knew very well he'd been raised in privilege, but pretty brunches with the morning paper folded on the table hadn't been everyday events.

The Landons were privileged because they worked, and worked because they were privileged.

As he ate he started to open the paper, then just set it aside. Like television, newspapers held too many bad memories. The view contented him, and letting his mind just drift, he watched the water, and the drip of melting snow as the sun bore down.

He felt . . . almost peaceful.

He looked over when she came in. "Second floor's clear," she told him, and started to lift the tray.

"I'll get it. No," he insisted. "I'll get it. Look, you don't have to cook for me. It was great, thanks, but you don't have to cook."

"I like to cook, and it's not all that satisfying to cook just for myself." She followed him into the kitchen, then continued on to the laundry room. "And you're not eating properly."

"I'm eating." He mumbled it.

"A can of soup, a sandwich, a bowl of cold cereal?" She carried in a laundry basket, sat in the breakfast nook to fold. "You don't have secrets from the housekeeper," she said easily. "Not about eating, showering and sex. You need to put on about fifteen pounds, I'd say. Twenty wouldn't hurt you."

No, he hadn't been able to find his anger for months, but she was drawing him a map. "Listen—"

"You can tell me it's none of my business," she said, "but that won't stop me. So I'll cook when I have time. I'm here anyway."

He couldn't think of a reasonable way to argue with a woman who was currently folding his boxers.

"Can you cook?" she asked him.

"Yeah. Enough."

"Let's see." She cocked her head, swept that green-eyed gaze over him. "Grilled cheese sandwiches, scrambled eggs, steak on the grill—burgers, too—and . . . something with lobster or clams."

He called it Clams à la Eli—and really wished she'd get out of his head. "Do you mind read as well as make pancakes?"

"I read palms and tarot, but mostly for fun."

It didn't surprise him, he realized, not in the least.

"Anyway, I'll make up a casserole or two, something you can just heat and eat. I'll be going to the market before I come back. I marked my days on the calendar there so you'll have a schedule. Do you want me to pick up anything for you, besides more Mountain Dew?"

Her brisk, matter-of-fact details clogged up his brain. "I can't think of anything."

"If you do, just write it down. What's your book about? Or is that a secret?"

"It's . . . A disbarred lawyer looking for answers, and redemption. Is he going to lose his life, literally, or get it back? That kind of thing."

"Do you like him?"

He stared at her a moment because it was exactly the right question. And the kind he wanted to answer rather than brush off or avoid. "I understand him, and I'm invested in him. He's evolving into someone I like."

"Understanding him is more important than liking him, I'd think." She frowned as Eli rubbed at his shoulder, the back of his neck. "You hunch."

"I'm sorry?"

"Over the keyboard. You hunch. Most people do." She set the laundry aside, and before he realized what she meant to do, she'd stepped up to dig her fingers into his shoulder.

Pain, sudden and sweet, radiated straight down to the soles of his feet. "Look, ow."

"Good God, Eli, you've got rocks in there."

Annoyance edged to a kind of baffled frustration. Why wouldn't the woman leave him alone? "I just overdid it yesterday. Clearing the snow."

She lowered her hands as he stepped back, opened the cupboard for the Motrin.

Partly overdoing, she thought, partly keyboard hunch. But under all that? Deep, complex and system-wide stress.

"I'm going to get out for a while, make some phone calls."

"Good. It's cold, but it's beautiful."

"I don't know what to pay you. I never asked."

When she named a price, he reached for his wallet. Found his pocket empty. "I don't know where I left my wallet."

"In your jeans. Now it's on your dresser."

"Okay, thanks. I'll be right back."

Poor, sad, stressed Eli, she thought. She had to help him. She thought of Hester, shaking her head as she loaded the dishwasher. "You knew I would," she murmured.

Eli came back, set the money on the counter. "And thanks if I don't get back before you leave."

"You're welcome."

"I'm just going to . . . see what the beach is like, and call my parents, my grandmother." And get the hell away from you.

"Good. Give them all my best."

He stopped at the door to the laundry room. "You know my parents?"

"Sure. I've met them several times when they've come here. And I saw them when I came to Boston to visit Hester."

"I didn't realize you came into Boston to see her."

"Of course I did. We just missed each other, you and I." She started the machine and turned. "She's your grandmother, Eli, but she's been one to me, too. I love her. You should take a picture of the house from down at the beach and send it to her. She'd like that."

"Yeah, she would."

"Oh, Eli?" she said as he turned to the laundry room and she walked over to pick up the laundry basket. "I'll be back about five-thirty. My schedule's clear tonight."

"Back?"

"Yeah, with my table. You need a massage."

"I don't want—"

"Need," she repeated. "You may not

think you want one, but trust me, you will after I get started. This one's on the house—a welcome back gift. Therapeutic massage, Eli," she added. "I'm licensed. No happy endings."

"Well, Jesus."

She only laughed as she sailed out. "Just so we understand each other. Five-thirty!"

He started to go after her, make it clear he didn't want the service. And at the jerk away from the door, dull pain shot across the back of his shoulders.

"Shit. Just shit."

He had to ease his arms into his coat. He just needed the Motrin to kick in, he told himself. And to get back inside his own head without her in it, so he could think about the book.

He'd walk—somewhere—call, breathe, and when this nagging stiffness, this endless aching played out, he'd just text her—better to text—and tell her not to come.

But first he'd take her advice, go down to the beach, take a picture of Bluff House. And maybe he'd wheedle some information out of his grandmother about Abra Walsh.

He was still a lawyer. He ought to be able to finesse some answers out of a witness already biased in his favor.

As he followed the path he'd cut down through the patio, he glanced back and saw Abra in his bedroom window. She waved.

He lifted his hand, turned away again.

She had the kind of fascinating face that made a man want to look twice.

So he very deliberately kept his gaze straight ahead.

Four

He enjoyed the walk on the snowy beach more than he'd anticipated. The winter-white sun blasted down, bounced off the sea, the snow, sent them both sparkling. Others had walked before him, so he followed the paths they'd cut down to the wet and chilly strip of sand the sweep of waves had uncovered.

Shore birds landed on the verge to strut or scurry, leaving their shallow stamps imprinted before water foamed over and erased them. They called, cried, chattered, made him remember the advance of spring despite the winterscape around him.

He followed a trio of what he thought might be some sort of tern, stopped, took a couple more pictures and sent them home. Walking on, he checked the time, calculated the schedule back in Boston before he tried his parents' house line.

"And what are you up to?"

"Gran." He hadn't expected her to answer. "I'm taking a walk on Whiskey Beach. We've got a couple feet of snow. It looks a lot like it did that Christmas back when I was, I don't know, about twelve?"

"You and your cousins and the Grady boys built a snow castle on the beach. And you took my good red cashmere scarf and used it as a flag."

"I forgot that part. The flag part."

"I didn't."

"How are you?"

"Coming along. Annoyed with people who won't let me take two steps without that damn walker. I'll do *fine* with a cane."

As he'd had an e-mail from his mother detailing the battle of the walker, he'd come prepared. "It's smarter to be careful, and not risk another fall. You've always been smart."

"That roundabout won't work with me, Eli Andrew Landon."

"You haven't always been smart?"

He made her laugh, considered it a small victory. "I have, and intend to continue. My brain's working just fine, thank you, even if it can't pull out how I fell in the first place. I don't even remember getting out of bed. But no matter. I'm healing, and I *will* be done with this old-lady-invalid walker. What about you?"

"I'm doing okay. Writing every day, and making what seems like real progress on the book. I feel good about that. And it's good to be here. Gran, I want to thank you again for—"

"Don't." Her voice held the hard edge of New England granite. "Bluff House is as much yours as mine. It's family. You know there's firewood in the shed, but if you need more you talk to Digby Pierce. His number's in my book, in the desk in the little office, and in the far right drawer in the kitchen. Abra has it if you can't find it."

"Okay. No problem."

"Are you eating properly, Eli? I don't want to see skin and bones the next time I lay eyes on you."

"I just had pancakes."

"Ah! Did you go into Cafe Beach in the village?"

"No . . . actually, Abra made them. Listen, about that—"

"She's a good girl." Hester rolled right over him. "A fine cook, too. If you have any questions or run into any problems, you just ask her. If she doesn't have the answer, she'll find it. She's a smart girl, and a very pretty one, as I hope you noticed unless you've gone blind as well as skinny."

He felt a warning tingle at the back of his neck. "Gran, you're not trying to fix me up with her, are you?"

"Why would I have to do something like that? Can't you think for yourself? When have I ever interfered in your love life, Eli?"

"Okay, you're right. I apologize. It's just . . . You know her a lot better than I do. I don't want her to feel obliged to cook for me, and I don't seem to be able to get that across to her."

"Did you eat the pancakes?"

"Yes, but—"

"Because you felt obliged to?"

"Point taken."

"Over and above that, Abra does what she likes, I can promise you. That's something I admire about her. She enjoys life and lives it. You could use a bit of that."

That warning tingle resounded. "But you're not trying to fix me up?"

"I trust you to know your own mind, heart and physical needs."

"Okay, let's move on from there. Or move laterally from there. I don't want to offend your friend, especially when she's doing my laundry. So, as I said, you know her best. How do I, diplomatically, convince her I don't want or need a massage?"

"She offered you a massage?"

"Yes, ma'am. Or she informed me she'd be back at five-thirty with her table. My 'No, thanks' didn't make a dent."

"You're in for a treat. That girl has magic hands. Before she started giving me weekly massages, and talking me into doing yoga, I lived with lower back pain, and an ache right between my shoulder blades. Old age, I decided, and accepted. Until Abra."

He realized he'd walked farther than he intended when he spotted the steps leading up to the village. The few seconds it took him to shift direction, decide to go up, gave Hester an opening.

"You're a bundle of stress, boy. Do you think I can't hear it in your voice? Your life went to hell in a handbasket, and that's not right. It's not fair. Life too often isn't either. So it's what we do about it. What you've got to do now is the same as everybody's telling me I have to do. Get healthy, get strong, get back on your feet. I don't like hearing it either, but that doesn't mean it's not the simple truth."

"And a massage from your pancake-making neighbor's the answer?"

"It's one of them. Listen to you, huffing and puffing like an old man."

Insulted—mortified—he pivoted to the defensive. "I walked all the way to the village—and some of that through this damn snow. And I'm climbing steps."

"And these excuses from a former Harvard basketball star."

"I wasn't a star," he muttered.

"You were to me. You are to me."

He paused at the top of the steps—yeah, to catch his breath, and to wait for the heart she'd managed to stir to settle.

"Did you see my new gym?" she asked him.

"I did. Very nice. How much can you bench-press, Hester?"

She laughed. "You think you're smart and sassy. I'm not going out scrawny and used up, I'll tell you that. You make use of that gym, Eli."

"I did—once already. I got your memo. I'm standing across from The Lobster Shack."

"The best lobster rolls on the North Shore."

"Things haven't changed much."

"Here and there, but the foundation's what counts. I expect you to remember yours. You're a Landon, and you've got the grit of Hawkin blood that comes down through me. Nobody holds us down, not for long. You take care of Bluff House for me."

"I will."

"And remember. Sometimes a pancake is just a pancake."

She made him laugh. The sound might've been rusty, but it was there. "Okay, Gran. Use the walker."

"I'll use the damn walker—for now—if you get that massage."

"All right. Check your e-mail for some pictures. I'll call you in a couple days."

He passed places he remembered— Cones 'N Scoops, Maria's Pizza—and new enterprises like Surf's Up with its beach-pink clapboard. The white spire of the Methodist church, the simple box of the Unitarian, the dignified edifice of the North Shore Hotel, and the charm of the scattering of B&Bs that would welcome tourists through the season.

Light traffic chugged by, then petered out almost completely as he made his way home.

Maybe he'd go back to the village on the next clear afternoon, pick up some postcards, write quick notes to make his parents—and the couple of friends he could still claim—smile.

It couldn't hurt.

And it couldn't hurt to check out some of the shops, old and new, get a feel for the place again.

Remembering his foundation, so to speak.

But right now he was tired, and cold, and wanted home.

His car sat alone in the driveway, and that was a relief. He'd stalled long enough for Abra to finish. He wouldn't have to make conversation, or avoid it. Considering the state of his boots, he circled around, let himself in through the laundry room/mudroom.

His shoulder felt fine now, he decided as he took off his gear. Or close enough. He could text Abra, tell her the walk had worked out the kinks.

Except for that deal he'd made with his grandmother. So he'd keep the deal—but he could put it off for a few days. He had a couple hours to work that out, he thought. He was a lawyer, for Christ's sake—practicing or not—and a writer. He could compose a clear and reasonable communication.

He stepped out into the kitchen, spotted the sticky note on the counter.

Chicken and potato casserole in the freezer.

Fireboxes restocked.

Eat an apple, and don't forget to hydrate after your walk. See you at 5:30ish.

Abra

"What are you, my mother? Maybe I don't want an apple."

And the only reason he got water out of the fridge was that he was thirsty. He didn't want or need somebody telling him when to eat, when to drink. The next thing, she'd tell him to remember to floss or wash behind his ears.

He'd go up, dig into some research, then compose that text.

He started out, cursed, circled back and grabbed an apple out of the bamboo bowl because, damn it, now he wanted one.

He knew his irritation was irrational. She was being kind, considerate. But at the base of it he just wanted to be left alone. He wanted space and time to find his footing again, not a helping hand.

There'd been plenty of those hands at

the outset, then fewer and fewer as friends, colleagues, neighbors had started to distance themselves from a man suspected of killing his wife. Of smashing in her skull because she'd cheated on him, or because a divorce would cost him a great deal of money.

Or a combination thereof.

He didn't intend to reach out for those hands again.

In his stocking feet, still a bit chilled from the long walk, he detoured to the bedroom for shoes.

He stopped, the apple halfway to his mouth, and frowned at the bed. Moving closer, he peered down and choked out his second laugh of the day—a definite record.

She'd folded, twisted, curved a hand towel into what looked like some strange bird squatting on the duvet. It wore sunglasses with a little flower tucked between the cloth and the earpiece.

Silly, he thought—and sweet.

He sat on the edge of the bed, nodded at the bird. "I guess I'm getting a massage."

He left the bird where it was, went into the office.

He'd do some research, maybe fiddle around with the next scene, just get that springboard.

But out of habit he checked his e-mail first. Among the spam, a post from his father, another from his grandmother in response to the photos he'd sent her, he found one from his lawyer.

Rather not, he thought. Rather not click on it. But then it would just be there, waiting, waiting.

With the muscles in his shoulders twisting into fists, he opened the e-mail.

He cut through the legalese, set aside the assurances, even the questions of approach, and focused on the ugly center.

Lindsay's parents were, once again, making noises about filing a wrongful death suit against him.

It was never going to end, he thought. Never going to be over. Unless and until the police caught whoever was responsible for Lindsay's death, he was the default.

Lindsay's parents despised him, abso-

lutely and without a sliver of doubt believed he murdered their only child. If they
went forward with this—and the longer
he remained the default, the more likely
they'd do just that—everything would be
dredged up again, swirled into the media
hot box to cook and bloat. And spill over
not only him but his family.

Again.

Assurances the case was unlikely to
go forward now, or to gain much traction
if and when, didn't help. They would beat
that drum, for sure, righteous in their certainty that they sought the only justice
available to them.

He thought of the publicity, all those
talking heads discussing, analyzing,
speculating. The private investigators the
Piedmonts would hire—likely already
had—who would come here to Whiskey
Beach and bring that speculation, that
doubt, those questions with them to the
only place he had left.

He wondered if Boston PD's Detective
Wolfe had any part in their decision. On
bad days, Eli considered Wolfe his personal Javert—doggedly, obsessively pur-

suing him for a crime he didn't commit. On better ones, he thought of Wolfe as stubborn and wrongheaded, a cop who refused to consider that the lack of evidence might equal innocence.

Wolfe hadn't been able to put a case together that convinced the prosecutor to file. But that hadn't stopped the man from trying, from edging over the line of harassment until his superiors had warned him off.

At least officially.

No, he wouldn't put it past Wolfe to encourage and abet the Piedmonts in their quest.

Braced on his elbows, Eli rubbed his hands over his face. He'd known this was coming, he'd known this other shoe would drop. So maybe, in a horrible way, it was better to get it done.

Agreeing with the last line of Neal's e-mail, *We need to talk,* Eli picked up the phone.

The headache was a tantrum inside his skull, kicking, punching, screaming. Reassurances from his lawyer did little to alleviate it. The Piedmonts made noises about a suit to increase pressure, to keep the media interested, to float the idea of a settlement.

None of those opinions, even though he agreed with them, reassured.

The suggestions to keep a low profile, not to discuss the investigation, to reengage his own private investigator hardly helped. He already intended to keep a low profile. Any lower, he'd be interred. Who the hell would he discuss *anything* with? And the idea of pumping money and hope into private investigation, which hadn't turned up anything genuinely helpful the first time around, just added a layer of depression.

He knew, as his lawyer knew, as the police knew, that the more time that passed, the less likely they'd find solid evidence.

The most likely endgame? He'd remain in limbo, not charged, not cleared, and shadowed by suspicion for the rest of his life.

So he had to learn to live with it.

He had to learn to live.

He heard the knock at the door, but didn't fully register the sound, the reason, until the door opened. He watched Abra muscling in a huge padded case, a bulging tote.

"Hi. Don't mind me. You just stand there while I drag all this in by myself. No, no problem at all."

She'd nearly managed it by the time he crossed over. "I'm sorry. I meant to get in touch, to tell you this just isn't a good time."

She leaned back against the door to close it, let out an audible *whew*. "Too late," she began, then her easy smile faded when she focused on his face. "What's wrong? What happened?"

"Nothing." Not much more than usual, he thought. "This just isn't a good time."

"Do you have another appointment? Are you going out dancing? Do you have a naked woman upstairs waiting for hot sex? No?" she answered before he could. "Then it's as good a time as any."

Depression spun into annoyance on a finger snap. "How about this? No means no."

Now she blew out a breath. "That's an excellent argument, and I know I'm being pushy, even obnoxious. Chalk it up to keeping my promise to Hester to help, and the fact that I can't stand seeing anyone— anything—in pain. Let's make a deal."

And damn it, that reminded him of his earlier one with his grandmother. "What are the terms?"

"Give me fifteen minutes. If after fifteen minutes on the table you don't feel better, I'll pack it up, get out and never bring up the subject again."

"Ten minutes."

"Ten," she agreed. "Where do you want me to set up? There's plenty of room up in your bedroom."

"Here's fine." Stuck, he gestured toward the main parlor. He could push her out of the house faster from there.

"All right. Why don't you start a fire while I set up? I'd like the room warm."

He'd intended to light a fire. He'd gotten distracted, lost track of time. He could start a fire, give her ten minutes—in exchange for her leaving him the hell alone.

But it still pissed him off.

He hunkered down by the hearth to stack kindling. "Aren't you worried about being here?" he demanded. "Alone with me?"

Abra unzipped the cover on her portable table. "Why would I be?"

"A lot of people think I killed my wife."

"A lot of people think global warming is a hoax. I don't happen to agree."

"You don't know me. You don't know what I might do under any given set of circumstances."

She set up her table, folded away the cover, movements precise and practiced—and unhurried. "I don't know what you'd do under any given set of circumstances, but I know you didn't kill your wife."

The calm, conversational tone of her voice infuriated him. "Why? Because my grandmother doesn't think I'm a murderer?"

"That would be one reason." She smoothed a fleece cover on the table, covered it with a sheet. "Hester's a smart, self-aware woman—and one who cares about me. If she had even the smallest doubt, she would have told me to stay away from you. But that's just one reason. I have several others."

As she spoke she set a few candles around the room, lit them. "I work for your grandmother, and have a personal friendship with her. I live in Whiskey Beach, which is Landon territory. So I followed the story."

The lurking black cloud of depression rolled back in. "I'm sure everybody did around here."

"That's natural, and human. Just as disliking, and resenting, the fact that people are talking about you, reaching conclusions about you, is natural and human. I reached my own conclusion. I saw you, on TV, in the paper, on the Internet. And what I saw was shock, sadness. Not guilt. What I see now? Stress, anger, frustration. Not guilt."

As she spoke she took a band from around her wrist and, with a few flicks, secured her hair in a tail. "I don't think the guilty lose much sleep. One other— though as I said I have several—you're not stupid. Why would you kill her the same day you argued with her in public? The same day you learned you had a lever to dump some dirt on her in the divorce?"

"First degree wasn't on the table. I was pissed. Crime of passion."

"Well, that's bullshit," she said as she retrieved her massage oil. "You were so passionate you went into your own house and prepared to take three items—arguably your property? The case against you didn't stand, Eli, because it was, and is, weak. They proved the time you entered because you switched off the house alarm, and have the time of your nine-one-one call, and because people know the time you left your office that evening. So you were in the house for less than twenty minutes. But in that small window of time you went upstairs, into the safe—taking only your great-grandmother's ring—came down, took the painting you'd bought off the wall, wrapped it in bathroom towels, killed your wife in a fit of passion, then called the police. All in under twenty minutes?"

"The police reconstruction proved it was possible."

"But not probable," she countered. "Now we can stand here debating the case against you, or you can just take my word that I'm not worried you're going to kill me because you don't like hospital corners on your bed or the way I fold your socks."

"Things aren't as simple as you make them."

"Things are rarely as simple or as complicated as anyone makes them. I'm going to use the powder room to wash up. Go ahead and undress, get on the table. I'll start you faceup."

In the powder room Abra shut her eyes, did a full minute of yoga breathing. She understood perfectly well he'd lashed out at her to push her out, scare her off. But all he'd done was annoy her.

In order to expel stress, dark thoughts, frustrations with massage, she couldn't hold on to any of her own. She continued to clear her mind as she washed her hands.

When she stepped back in, she saw him on the table, under the top sheet— and board stiff. Didn't he understand that even that weighed on his innocence for her? He'd made a bargain, and though he was angry, he'd keep it.

Saying nothing, she dimmed the lights, walked over to turn on her iPod to sooth-

ing music. "Close your eyes," she murmured, "and take a deep breath. In . . .
out. Another," she said as she poured the
oil into her hands. "One more."

As he obeyed, she pressed her hands
on his shoulders. They didn't even touch
the table, she noted. So stiff, so knotted.

She stroked, pressed, kneaded, then
slid her hands up along the column of his
throat before she began a light facial
massage.

She knew a headache when she saw
one. Maybe if she could bring him some
relief there, he'd relax a little before she
began the heavy work.

It was hardly his first massage. Before
his life had shattered he'd used a mas-
seuse named Katrina, a solidly built, mus-
cular blonde whose strong, wide hands
had worked out tensions built up from
work, strains generated from sports.

With his eyes closed, he could almost
imagine he was back in the quiet treatment room of his club, having his muscles soothed after a day in court, or a
couple hours' competing on one.

Besides, in a few minutes, the deal

would be met, and the woman who wasn't the sturdy Katrina would be gone.

Her fingers stroked along his jaw and pressed under his eyes.

And the screaming violence of the headache quieted.

"Try another breath. Long in, long out." Her voice melted into the music, just as fluid and soft.

"That's good. Just in, then out."

She turned his head, worked those fingers up one side of his neck, then the other, before she lifted his head.

Here, the firm, deep press of her thumbs brought a quick, stunning pain. Before he could tense against it, it released, like a cork from a bottle.

Like breaking up concrete, Abra thought, an inch at a time. So she closed her eyes as she worked, visualized that concrete softening, crumbling under her hands. When she moved to his shoulders, she increased the pressure, degree by degree.

She felt him relax—a little. Not enough, but even that slight yield equaled a victory.

Down his arm, kneading the tired muscles all the way down to his fingertips. Part of her mind might have smiled smugly when that ten-minute deadline went by unnoticed, but she focused the rest on doing the job.

By the time she lifted the face rest, she knew he wouldn't argue.

"I want you to turn over, scoot up and lower your face into the rest. Let me know if you need me to adjust it. Take your time."

Zoned, half asleep, he simply did as he was told.

When the heels of her hands pressed into his shoulder blades, he nearly moaned from the glorious mix of pain and release.

Strong hands, he thought. She didn't look strong. But as they pushed, rubbed, pressed, as her fists dug into his back, aches he'd grown used to carrying rose to the surface, and lifted out.

She used her forearms, slick with oil, her body weight, knuckles, thumbs, fists. Every time the pressure hovered on the edge of too much, something broke free.

Then she stroked, stroked, stroked, firm, rhythmic, constant.

And he drifted away.

When he surfaced, floating back to consciousness like a leaf on a river, it took him a moment to realize he wasn't in bed. He remained stretched out on the padded table, modestly covered by a sheet. The fire simmered; candles glowed. Music continued to murmur in the air.

He nearly closed his eyes and went under again.

Then he remembered.

Eli pushed himself up on his elbows to look around the room. He saw her coat, her boots, her bag. He could smell her, he realized, that subtle, earthy fragrance that mixed with the candle wax, the oil. Cautious, he pulled the sheet around him as he sat up.

He needed his pants. First things first.

Holding the sheet, he eased off the table. When he reached for his jeans, he saw the damn sticky note.

Drink the water. I'm in the kitchen.

He kept a wary eye out as he pulled on his pants, then picked up the water bottle she'd left beside them. As he shrugged on his shirt he realized nothing hurt. No headache, no toothy clamps on the back of his neck, none of those twinges that dogged him after his attempts to get some exercise.

He stood, drinking the water in the room soft with candlelight and firelight and music, and realized he felt something he barely recognized.

He felt good.

And foolish. He'd given her grief, deliberately. Her answer had been to help him—*despite* him.

Chastised, he made his way through the house to the kitchen.

She stood at the stove in a room redolent with scent. He didn't know what she stirred on the stove, but it awakened another rare sensation.

Genuine hunger.

She'd chosen grinding rock for her kitchen music, turned it down low. Now he felt a twinge—of guilt. No one should be forced to play good, hard rock at a whisper.

"Abra."

She jolted a little this time, which reassured him. She was human after all.

When she turned, she narrowed her eyes, held up a finger before he could speak. Stepping closer, she gave him a long study. Then she smiled.

"Good. You look better. Rested and more relaxed."

"I feel good. First, I want to apologize. I was rude and argumentative."

"We can agree there. Stubborn?"

"Maybe. All right, I can concede stubborn."

"Then, clean slate." She picked up a glass of wine, lifted it. "I hope you don't mind, I helped myself."

"No, I don't mind. Second, thank you. When I said I felt good . . . I don't remember the last time I did."

Her eyes softened. Pity might have made him tense again, but sympathy was a different matter.

"Oh, Eli. Life sure can suck, can't it? You need the rest of that water. To hydrate, and for flushing out the toxins. You may feel some soreness tomorrow. I really had to dig down. Do you want a glass of wine?"

"Yeah, actually. I'll get it."

"Just sit," she told him. "You should stay relaxed, absorb that for a while. You should consider booking a massage twice a week until we really conquer that stress. Then weekly would do, or even every other week if that doesn't work for you."

"It's hard to argue when I'm half buzzed."

"Good. I'll write the appointments down on your calendar. I'll come to you for now. We'll see how that goes."

He sat, took his first sip of wine. It tasted like heaven on his tongue. "Who are you?"

"Oh, such a long story. I'll tell you one day, if we get to be friends."

"You've washed my underwear and had me naked on your table. That's pretty friendly."

"That's business."

"You keep cooking for me." He angled his chin toward the stove. "What is that?"

"Which?"

"The thing, on the stove."

"The thing on the stove is a good hearty soup—vegetables, beans, ham. I gave it a mild kick as I wasn't sure how spicy you can handle. And this?" She turned, opened the oven. More scent poured out and stirred that burgeoning appetite. "Is meat loaf."

"You made a meat loaf?"

"With potatoes and carrots and green beans. Very manly." She set it on the stove. "You were out over two hours. I had to do something."

"Two . . . two *hours*."

She gestured absently at the clock as she got down plates. "Are you going to ask me to dinner?"

"Sure." He stared at the clock, then back at Abra. "You made meat loaf."

"Hester gave me a list. Meat loaf was in the top three. Plus I think you could use some red meat." She began to plate the meal. "Oh, by the way. If you ask for ketchup to put on this, I'll hurt you."

"So noted, and accepted."

"One more stipulation." She held the plate just out of reach.

"If it's legal, I can almost guarantee agreement in exchange for meat loaf."

"We can talk about books, movies, art, fashion, hobbies and anything in that general area. Nothing personal, not to-night."

"That works."

"Then let's eat."

Five

In the church basement, Abra brought her class out of final relaxation slowly. She'd had a class of twelve that morning, a solid number for the time of year, the time of day.

The number kept her personal satisfaction high, and her budget steady.

Conversation broke out as her ladies—and two men—got to their feet, began rolling up their mats, or the extras she always carted in for those who didn't bring their own.

"You had a really good practice today, Henry."

The sixty-six-year-old retired vet gave

her his cocky grin. "One of these days I'm going to hold that Half Moon longer than three seconds."

"Just keep breathing." Abra remembered when his wife had first dragged him—mentally kicking and screaming—to her class, Henry hadn't been able to touch his toes.

"Remember," she called out, "East Meets West on Thursday."

Maureen walked over as Abra rolled up her own mat. "I'm going to need it, and some serious cardio. I made cupcakes for Liam's class party today. And ate two of them."

"What kind of cupcakes?"

"Double chocolate, buttercream frosting. With sprinkles and gumdrops."

"Where's mine?"

Maureen laughed, patted her stomach. "I ate it. I have to go home, grab a shower, put on Mom clothes and take the cupcakes in. Otherwise, I'd beg and bribe you to take a run with me so I could burn that double chocolate off. The kids have an after-school playdate, I'm caught up on paperwork, and filing, so I have no excuse."

"Try me later, after three. I've got to work until then."

"Eli?"

"No, he's on tomorrow's schedule."

"Still going good there?"

"It's only been a couple weeks, but yeah, I'd say it is. He doesn't look at me like 'What the hell is she doing here?' every time he sees me. It's more like every other time now. When I'm there during the day, he's usually closed up in his office writing—and he avoids me by slipping outside for a walk when I head up to do the upstairs. But he's eating what I leave for him, and doesn't look as hollow."

Abra zipped her personal mat into its bag. "Still, every time I give him a massage—I've managed four now—it's like starting from scratch. He carries so much tension, plus he's at that keyboard for hours a day."

"You'll crack him, Abracadabra. I have every faith."

"That's my current mission." Abra pulled on her hoodie, zipped it. "But right now I've got some new jewelry to take into Buried Treasures—so fingers crossed there—then I'm running some errands for Marcia Frost. Her boy's still got that virus and she can't get out. I've got a massage booked at two, but I'm up for a run after that."

"If I can juggle it in, I'll text you."

"See you later."

While her class headed out, Abra secured her mats, tucked her iPod into her bag. As she pulled a jacket over her hoodie, a man came down the stairs.

She didn't recognize him, but he had a pleasant enough face. Baggy eyes that made him look tired, a thick crop of brown hair, a slight paunch, which would have improved if he didn't slouch.

"Can I help you?"

"I hope so. Are you Abra Walsh?"

"That's right."

"I'm Kirby Duncan." He held out his hand to shake, then offered her a business card.

"Private investigator." Instinctively, her barriers went up.

"I'm doing some work for a client, out of Boston. I'm hoping I can ask you a few questions. I'd love to buy you a cup of coffee if you can spare me a few minutes."

"I've already had my quota for the day."

"I wish I could stick with a quota. God knows I drink too much coffee. I'm sure that coffee shop just down the street serves tea, or whatever you like."

"I have an appointment, Mr. Duncan," Abra said as she pulled on boots. "What's this about?"

"Our information indicates you're working for Eli Landon."

"Your information?"

His face remained pleasant, even affable. "It's no secret, is it?"

"No, it's not, and it's also none of your business."

"Gathering information is my business. You must be aware Eli Landon is a suspect in the murder of his wife."

"Is that accurate?" Abra wondered as she pulled on her cap. "I think it's more accurate to say after a year of investigating, the police haven't been able to gather the evidence to show Eli Landon had anything to do with his wife's death."

"The fact is, a lot of prosecutors won't

take on a case that's not a slam dunk. That doesn't mean there isn't evidence, there isn't a case. It's my job to gather more information—let me get that for you."

"No, thanks, I'm used to carrying my own. Who do you work for?" Abra asked him.

"Like I said, I have a client."

"Who must have a name."

"I can't divulge that information."

"Understood." She smiled pleasantly, walked to the stairs. "I don't have any information to divulge either."

"If Landon is innocent, he has nothing to hide."

She paused, looked Duncan in the eye. "Seriously? I doubt you're that naive, Mr. Duncan. I know I'm not."

"I'm authorized to compensate for information," he began as they went up the steps into the little church proper.

"You're authorized to pay for gossip? No, thanks. When I gossip, I do it for free." She walked out and turned toward the parking lot and her car.

"Are you personally involved with Landon?" Duncan called out.

She felt her jaw tighten, cursed the fact he'd ruined her post-yoga mood. She tossed her mats, her bag in the car, opened the door. And in a wordless reply to his question, shot up her middle finger before she got in, turned the key and drove off.

The encounter kept her in a state of irritation as she segued from job to job, task to task. She considered canceling her massage booking but couldn't justify it. She couldn't penalize a client because some nosy detective from Boston was poking around in her life. Because he'd dug under her skin so quickly she'd been rude.

Not her life, she reminded herself, not really. Eli's.

Regardless, it struck her as monumentally unfair and intrusive.

She knew all about unfair and intrusive.

When Maureen texted her about taking a run, she nearly made an excuse. Instead, she decided the exercise and company might be just what she needed.

She changed, zipped on her hoodie, pulled on her cap, tugged on fingerless gloves and met her friend at the beach steps.

"I need this." Maureen jogged in place. "Eighteen kindergartners on a sugar high. Every teacher in America should have their salaries doubled and get a bouquet of roses every freaking week. And a bottle of Landon Whiskey's gold label."

"I take it the cupcakes were a success."

"They were like locusts," Maureen said as they started down to the beach. "I'm not sure there was a stray sprinkle left. Everything okay?"

"Why?"

"You've got that little deal here." Maureen tapped herself between her eyebrows.

"Damn." Instinctively, Abra rubbed at the spot. "I'm going to get lines there. I'm going to get culverts there."

"No, you won't. You only get that crease when you're really upset or pissed off. Which is it?"

"Maybe both."

They started off at a light jog, the ocean frothing on one side, the sand with its clumps and pockets of snow on the other.

Knowing her friend, Maureen said nothing.

"Did you see that guy when you were leaving class this morning? About average height, brown hair, nice face, little paunch?"

"I don't know . . . maybe, yeah. He held the door for me. Why? What happened?"

"He came downstairs."

"What happened?" Maureen stopped dead, then had to kick up her pace as Abra kept going. "Honey, did he try something? Did he—?"

"No. No, nothing like that. This is Whiskey Beach, Maureen, not Southie."

"Still. Damn it. I shouldn't have left you alone down there. I was thinking cupcakes, for God's sake."

"It wasn't anything like that. And who taught that course on self-defense for women?"

"You did, but that doesn't mean your best friend just strolls off and leaves you alone that way."

"He's a private detective from Boston. Come on," Abra said when Maureen stopped again. "Keep up. I have to run this mood off."

"What did he want? That bastard's still in prison, isn't he?"

"Yes, and it wasn't about me. It was about Eli."

"Eli? You said private detective, not the police. What did he want?"

"He called it information. What he wanted was for me to gossip about Eli. He wanted dish and dirt, and he offered to *pay* me. Looking for an inside man," she spewed. "Somebody who'd spy on Eli and pass on what he's doing, what he's saying. I don't even know because Eli's not doing or saying *anything*. And when I told him, basically, to get lost, he asked if Eli and I were involved. Which sounded a hell of a lot like asking if Eli and I were screwing like bunnies. I didn't like it. I didn't like him. And now I'm going to get culverts on my face."

Temper and exercise pinkened Maureen's face. Her voice, breathless with both, lifted over the surge and crash of waves. "It's none of his damn business if you *are* screwing like bunnies. Eli's wife's been dead a year, and they were already in the middle of a divorce. And they don't have anything but the most circumstantial of evidence against him. The cops can't prove anything, so now they're reaching, digging in the dirt."

"I don't think cops hire PI's."

"I guess not. Who does?"

"I don't know." As her muscles warmed, as the chilly air washed over her face, Abra found her mood leveling. "Insurance company? Maybe his wife had insurance, and they don't want to pay. Except he said he was hired by a client. And he wouldn't tell me who. Maybe insurance company lawyers, or, I don't know, the dead wife's family, who's always trashing him in the press. I don't know."

"I don't know either. Let me ask Mike."

"Mike? Why?"

"He deals with lawyers and clients all the time."

"Real estate lawyers and clients," Abra pointed out.

"A lawyer's a lawyer, a client's a client.

He might have an idea. He'll keep it confidential."

"I'm not sure that part matters. If this guy hunted me down, who knows who else he's talking to? It's all getting stirred up again."

"Poor Eli."

"You've never believed he did it either."

"No."

"Why do you believe him, Maureen?"

"Well, as you know, I got my detective's license from TV. That said, why would a man who never exhibited violent behavior suddenly bash his wife in the head with a fireplace poker? She cheated on him, and that pissed him off. It also made her look bad as they moved forward with the divorce. Sometimes I want to bash Mike's head in with a poker."

"You do not."

"Not literally, but my point is I really love Mike. I think you have to really love or really hate somebody to want to bash their brains in. Unless it's about something else. Money, fear, revenge. I don't know."

"So who did it?"

"If I knew that and could prove it, I'd be promoted from detective to lieutenant. Or captain. I'd like to be captain."

"You already are. Captain of the good ship O'Malley."

"That's true. You can be captain of the made-for-TV police department in charge of clearing Eli Landon once and for all."

At her friend's silence, Maureen slapped out a hand to hit Abra's arm. "That was a joke. Don't even think about getting involved in any of it. It'll blow over, Abra. Eli will get through it."

"What could I do?" And the question, Abra decided, didn't promise *not* to do something.

When they turned at the halfway point to jog back, she realized she was glad she'd come out. A good way to think, to shove away a bad mood, to get some perspective. She'd missed running during the cold grip of winter, missed the sound of her own feet slapping against the sand while she gulped in the sea air.

She wasn't one to wish time away, not even a minute, but she could, deeply, long for spring and the summer that followed.

Would Eli still be at Bluff House, she wondered, when the air began to warm and the trees to green? Would spring's balmy breezes blow away the shadows that dogged him?

Maybe those shadows needed a little help on their way out the door. She'd think about it.

Then she saw him, standing at the water's edge, hands in his pockets, gaze on the far horizon.

"There's Eli now."

"What? Where? Oh, shit!"

"What's the problem?"

"I didn't imagine running into him the first time when I'm sweaty and red-faced and huffing. A woman likes to hold a certain standard for chance meetings with her first serious make-out partner. Why did I wear my oldest jogging pants? These make my legs look like tree stumps."

"They do not. I'd never let you wear pants that made your legs look like tree stumps. You're insulting my code of friendship."

"You're right. That was small and selfish of me. I apologize."

"Accepted, but watch it. Eli!"

"Shit," Maureen grumbled again when he turned. Why hadn't she at least stuck some lip gloss in her pocket?

Abra lifted a hand. She couldn't see his eyes, not when he wore sunglasses. But he didn't just wave and walk away. He waited, and she took that as a positive sign.

"Hi." She stopped, braced her hands on her thighs as she stepped one leg back to stretch. "If I'd seen you earlier, we'd have talked you into a run."

"Walking's more my speed these days." His head turned a fraction before he took off his sunglasses.

For the first time Abra saw him smile, all the way through, when his gaze held, and warmed on Maureen's face.

"Maureen Bannion. Look at you."

"Yeah, look at me." With a half laugh she lifted a hand to push at her hair, before remembering she wore a ski cap. "Hello, Eli."

"Maureen Bannion," he repeated. "No, sorry, it's— What is it?"

"O'Malley."

"Right. The last time I saw you, you were . . ."

"Hugely pregnant."

"You look great."

"I look sweaty and windblown, but thanks. It's good to see you, Eli."

When Maureen just moved in, wrapped her arms around Eli for a good, hard hug, Abra thought that, just that, was why she'd fallen in love with Maureen so fast, so completely. That simple, straightforward compassion, that naturally inclusive heart.

She saw Eli close his eyes, and wondered if he thought of a night under the Whiskey Beach pier when everything had been simple, had been innocent.

"I've been giving you time to settle in," Maureen said as she eased back. "Looks like time's up. You need to come to dinner, meet Mike, the kids."

"Oh, well . . ."

"We live in Sea Breeze, right next door to Abra. We'll set it up, and we'll catch up. How's Hester?"

"Better. A lot better."

"You tell her we miss her in yoga class. I've got to run—ha ha—and pick my kids up from a playdate. Welcome back, Eli. I'm glad to know you're back at Bluff House."

"Thanks."

"Talk to you later, Abra. Hey, Mike and I plan on having a date night at the Village Pub on Friday. Talk Eli into coming."

With a quick wave, she ran off.

"I didn't realize the two of you knew each other," Eli began.

"BFFs."

"Uh-huh."

"It's not just for teenagers. And BFFs of any age tell each other *everything*."

He started to nod, then she saw it hit him. "Oh. Well." He slid his sunglasses back into place. "Hmmm."

With a laugh, she gave him a poke in the belly. "Sweet and sexy teenage secrets."

"Maybe I should avoid her husband."

"Mike? Absolutely not. Besides hitting very high on my personal scale of adorable, he's a good man. A good daddy. You'll like him. You should drop into the pub Friday night."

"I don't know it."

"It used to be something else. Katydids."

"Right. Sure."

"It went downhill, I'm told. Before my

time. New name, new owners the last three years. It's nice. Fun. Good drinks, good crowd and live music Friday and Saturday nights."

"I'm not really looking to socialize."

"You should. It'll help with that stress level. You smiled."

"What?"

"When you recognized Maureen, you smiled. A real one. You were happy to see her, and it showed. Why don't you walk with me?" She gestured up the beach in the direction of her cottage. Rather than give him a chance to decline, she just took his hand, began to walk.

"How are you feeling?" she asked. "Since the last massage."

"Good. You were right, I usually feel it some the next day, but that eases off."

"You'll get more benefits when we finally break up those knots, get you used to being loose. I'm going to show you some yoga stretches."

No, she couldn't see his eyes, but she could see the wariness of his body language. "I don't think so."

"It's not just for girls, you know." She let out a long sigh.

"Is something wrong?"

"I'm having a mental debate with myself. Whether or not I should tell you something. And I think you have a right to know, even though it's probably going to upset you. I'm sorry to be the one to upset you."

"What's going to upset me?"

"A man came in to talk to me after my morning class. A private detective—investigator. His name's Kirby Duncan, from Boston. He said he has a client there. He wanted to ask me questions about you."

"Okay."

"Okay? It's *not* okay. He was pushy, and he said he'd *compensate* me for information, which I find personally insulting, so that's not okay. It's harassment, which is also not okay. You're being harassed. You should—"

"Tell the cops? I think that ship's sailed. Hire a lawyer? I've got one."

"It's not right. The police hounded you for a year. Now they or somebody's hiding behind lawyers and detectives to keep on hounding you? There should be a way to make them stop."

"There's no law against asking questions. And they're not hiding. They want
me to know who's paying for the questions, the answers."

"Who? And don't say it's none of my
business," she snapped out in case he
tried to. "That jerk approached *me*. And
he implied I refused to cooperate because we had a personal relationship,
which easily translated to sleeping with
you."

"I'm sorry."

"No." As he'd pulled his hand free, she
just grabbed it again. "You *won't* be sorry.
And if we did have a personal relationship, the kind he meant? It's none of his
damn business. We're adults, we're single. And there's nothing wrong, nothing
immoral, nothing period about you moving on with your life. Your marriage was
over before your wife died. Why shouldn't
you have a life that includes a relationship with me, or anyone?"

Her eyes, he noted, turned a particularly glowing green when she was angry.
Really angry.

"It sounds like this upsets you more
than me."

"Why aren't you angry?" she demanded. "Why aren't you seriously pissed?"

"I spent plenty of time being pissed. It didn't help a hell of a lot."

"It's intrusive, and it's—it's vindictive. What's the point in being vindictive when . . ." It hit her, clear and strong. "It is her family, isn't it? Lindsay's family. They can't let go."

"Could you?"

"Oh, stop being so damn reasonable." She stalked away, toward the verge of foaming water. "I think, if she'd been my sister, my mother, my daughter, I'd want the truth." She turned around, faced him where he stood, just watching her.

"How is hiring someone to come here, ask questions here, a way to find the truth?"

"So, it's not especially logical." He shrugged at that. "And it's not going to be productive, but they believe I killed her. To them there's no one else who could have or would have."

"That's close-minded and short-sighted. You weren't the only person in her life, and not, even at the time she died, the most important. She had a lover, she had a part-time job, she had friends, worked on committees, she had family."

She stopped, noting the way he frowned at her. "I told you I followed the case, and I listened to Hester. She felt able to talk to me when it was harder to talk to you or your family. I was someone who cared about her but was not really connected. So she could unload on me."

He didn't speak for a moment, then nodded. "It must've helped her to have you to unload on."

"It did. And I know Hester didn't like her, not one bit. She would've tried to, and would have made her welcome."

"I know that."

"What I'm saying is Hester didn't like her, and it's very unlikely Hester was the only person in the world who didn't. So like most people, Lindsay had enemies, or at least people who didn't like her, had grudges or hard feelings."

"None of them were married to her, had a public fight with her the day she died or discovered her body."

"With that line of thinking I hope to hell you didn't ever consider representing yourself."

He smiled a little. "That would give me a fool for a client, so no, but those are all valid points. Add all that to her family's list of grievances. I put my needs and ambitions above hers and didn't make her happy, so she sought happiness else-where. She told them I neglected her then complained about the time she spent on her own interests, that she thought I was having affairs, that I was cold and ver-bally abusive."

"Even though there was never one shred of evidence—even after a thorough police investigation—that you were hav-ing affairs—and she was? Or that you were in any way abusive?"

"I was pretty verbal the last time I spoke to her, publicly."

"You both were, from what I read. And all right, I understand the need for family to support, to rationalize, to do whatever comforts. But siccing a private detective on you, here? There's nothing here. You haven't been here in years, so what could he find?"

Yeah, he could see having her to un-load on had helped his grandmother. De-spite his own reluctance to cover old ground, he knew it helped him. "It's not that so much as letting me know they're not going to let me walk away quietly. Her parents are dangling the threat of a wrongful death suit."

"Oh, Eli."

"I'd say this is just a way to let me know they're using all their options."

"Why don't their options include hounding her lover, or someone else she might've been involved with?"

"He had a solid alibi. I didn't."

"What's so solid about it?"

"He was home with his wife."

"Well, I read all that, heard all that, but his wife could be lying."

"Sure, but why? His wife, mortified and angry when she learned from the police he'd had this affair, with someone they both knew, reluctantly swore he'd been home since before six that evening. Their stories about the timeline, what they did, during the key time, meshed. Justin Suskind didn't kill Lindsay."

"Neither did you."

"Neither did I, but when you factor opportunity, I had it, he didn't."

"Whose side are you on?"

He smiled a little. "Oh, I'm on my side. I know I didn't kill her, just like I know, with what they have, I look guilty."

"Then they need more. How do you get more?"

"We've pretty much tapped that out."

"They've hired a PI. You hire a PI."

"Did that, got nothing that helped."

"So just give up? Stop that." She gave him a light shove. "Hire another one and try again."

"Now you sound like my lawyer."

"Good. Listen to your lawyer. You don't just lie back and take it. That's from experience," she added. "It's that long story I'll tell you one day. For now, I'm saying taking it makes you feel sad and weak and cowardly. It makes you feel like a victim. You're not a victim if you don't allow it."

"Did someone hurt you?"

"Yes. And for too long I did what you're doing. I just accepted it. Fight back, Eli." She laid her hands on his shoulders. "Whether or not they ever believe you're innocent, they'll know you're not their whipping boy. And you'll know it, too."

On impulse she rose to her toes,

brushed her lips lightly over his. "Go call your lawyer," she ordered, then walked away toward the beach steps.

From above, on the long headland, Kirby Duncan snapped photos through his long lens.

He'd figured something was going on between Landon and the long-stemmed brunette. Didn't mean squat, of course, but his job was to document, to ask questions, to keep Landon off balance.

People made more mistakes when they were off balance.

Six

When Abra came into Bluff House to clean, the scent of coffee greeted her. She scanned the kitchen—he kept it clean and tidy—then, since he hadn't done so, began to make a shopping list.

When he came in, she stood on a step stool polishing the kitchen cabinets.

"Morning." She sent him a casual smile over her shoulder. "Been up awhile?"

"Yeah. I wanted to get some work in." Particularly since the damn dream had wakened him just before dawn. "I need to go into Boston today."

"Oh?"

"I'm meeting with my lawyer."

"Good. Have you eaten?"

"Yes, Mom."

Unoffended, she kept polishing. "Will you have time to see your family?"

"That's the plan. Look, I don't know when I'll be back. I may end up staying overnight. I'll probably stay over."

"No problem here. We can reschedule your massage."

"I'll leave your money. The same as the last time?"

"Yes. If there's a difference either way, we'll adjust it next week. Since you won't be working, I'll give your office a quick pass, and I promise not to touch anything on your desk."

"Okay." He stood where he was, watching her. She wore a plain black T-shirt today—conservative for her—with snug black pants and red high-top Chucks.

Chains of little red balls swung at her ears, and he noted a little bowl with several silver rings on the kitchen island. He supposed she'd taken them off to avoid getting polish on them.

"You were right the other day," he said at length.

"I love when that happens." She stepped down from the stool, turned. "What was I right about this time?"

"About fighting back. I let that slide. I had reasons, but they're not working. At least I need to be armed, so to speak."

"That's good. No one should have to tolerate being harassed and hounded, and that's what Lindsay's family is doing. They're not going to go through with this suit."

"They're not?"

"There's nothing there, legally, for them to go through with. Not that I can see, and I've watched a lot of lawyer shows."

He let out a half laugh. "That would qualify you."

Pleased with his reaction, she nodded. "I could make a living. They're just ha-beasing their corpus and whereforing the heretofore to screw with you."

"That's . . . a unique argument."

"And rational. They probably think if they can string this out, keep chipping away at you, maybe they'll uncover new evidence against you. Or at the very least, they'll beat you up, bury you in documents and writs and whatever so you'll offer a financial settlement. Which would prove, to their mind, your guilt. They're grieving, so they lash out."

"Maybe you could make a living."

"I like *The Good Wife*."

"Who?"

"It's a lawyer show. Well, it's really a character study, and sexy. Anyway, what I'm saying is, it's good you're going to meet with your lawyer, that you're taking steps. You look better today."

"Than what?"

"Than you did." Resting her polishing hand on her hip, she angled her head. "You should wear a tie."

"A tie?"

"Normally I don't see the point in a man putting a noose around his neck, which ties are, essentially. But you should wear a tie. It'll make you feel stronger, more in control. More yourself. Plus you have a whole collection upstairs."

"Anything else?"

"Don't get a haircut."

Once more, she simply baffled him. "No haircut because?"

"I like your hair. It's not lawyerly, but it's writerly. A little shaping if you absolutely feel it's necessary, and which I could actually do for you myself but—"

"No, you absolutely couldn't."

"I could on the element of skill. Just don't whack it into the suit-and-tie lawyer look."

"Wear a tie, but keep the hair."

"Exactly. And pick up some flowers for Hester. You should be able to find tulips by now, and they'd make her think of spring."

"Should I start writing this down?"

She smiled as she came around the island. "Not only looking better, but feeling better. You're getting some sass back that's not just knee-jerk temper-based." She brushed at the lapels of his sport coat. "Go pick out a tie. And drive safe." She boosted up, kissed his cheek.

"Who are you? Really?"

"We'll get to that. Say hi to your family for me."

"All right. I'll see you . . . when I do."

"I'll reschedule the massage, note it on your calendar."

She walked around the island, climbed back on the stool and went back to her polishing.

He picked out a tie. He couldn't say putting it on made him feel stronger or more in control, but it did—oddly enough—make him feel more complete. With that in mind, he got out his brief-case, put in files, a fresh legal pad, sharp-ened pencils, a spare pen and, after a moment's thought, his mini recorder.

He put on a good topcoat, caught a glimpse of himself in the mirror.

"Who are *you*?" he wondered.

He didn't look the way he used to, but neither did he look quite the way he'd grown accustomed to. No longer a law-yer, he thought, but not yet proven as a writer. Not guilty, but not yet proven in-nocent.

Still in limbo, but maybe, maybe fi-nally ready to begin climbing out.

He left Abra's money on his desk on his way downstairs, then headed straight out with her cleaning music—vintage Springsteen today—rolling after him.

He got into the car, realizing it was the

first time he'd been behind the wheel since he'd parked it on arrival three weeks before.

It did feel good, he decided. Taking control, taking steps. He turned on his own radio, let out a surprised laugh when The Boss jammed out at him.

And thinking it was almost like having Abra for company, he drove away from Whiskey Beach.

He didn't notice the car slide in behind him.

Since the day was relatively mild, Abra opened doors and windows to let the air wash through. She stripped Eli's bed, spread on fresh sheets, fluffed the duvet. And after a few minutes' thought, fashioned a fish from a hand towel. After digging through what she thought of as her emergency bag of silliness she came up with a little green plastic pipe for its mouth.

Once the bedroom met her standards, the first load of laundry chugged in the washer, she turned her attention to the office.

She'd have loved to fuss around the desk—in case he'd left any notes or clues about his work in progress. But a deal was a deal. Instead she dusted, vacuumed, restocked his bottled water and Mountain Dew. Wrote the next message Hester had dictated on a Post-it, stuck it to a bottle. After wiping down the leather desk chair, she stood awhile studying his view.

A good one, she thought. Wind and sun had all but vanished the snow. Today the sea spread in a good, strong blue, and the sea grass swayed in the breeze. She watched a fishing boat—dull red against deep blue—lumber over the water.

Did he think of it as home now? she wondered. That view, that air, the sounds and scents? How long had it taken her to feel at home?

She couldn't recall, not specifically. Maybe the first time Maureen knocked on her door holding a plate of brownies and a bottle of wine. Or maybe the first time she walked that beach and felt truly quiet in her mind.

Like Eli, she'd escaped here. But she'd

had a choice, and Whiskey Beach had been a deliberate one.

The right one, she thought now.

Absently, she traced a finger along her left ribs, and the thin scar that rode them. She rarely thought of it now, rarely thought of what she'd escaped from.

But Eli reminded her, and perhaps that was just one of the reasons she felt compelled to help him.

She had plenty of others. And, she thought, she could add a new one to the mix. The smile she'd watched bloom over his face when he recognized Maureen.

New goal, she determined. Giving Eli Landon reasons to smile more often.

But right now, she needed to put his underwear in the dryer.

Eli had barely settled in Neal Simpson's waiting area, declined the offer of coffee, water or anything else made by one of the three receptionists, when Neal himself strode out to greet him.

"Eli." Neal, fit in his excellent suit, shot out a hand, took Eli's in a firm grip. "It's good to see you. Let's go on back to my office."

He moved athletically through the slickly decorated maze of the Gardner, Kopek, Wright and Simpson offices. A confident man, an exceptional attorney who at thirty-nine had grabbed full partner and put his name on the letterhead of one of the top firms in the city.

Eli trusted him, had to. Though they'd worked in different firms, often competing for the same clients, they'd moved in similar circles, had mutual friends.

Or had, Eli thought, as most of his had slipped away under the constant media battering.

In his office with its wide, wintry view of the Commons, Neal ignored his impressive desk and gestured Eli to a set of leather chairs.

"Let's take a minute first," Neal began as his attractive assistant brought in a tray with two oversize mugs filled with frothy cappuccino. "Thanks, Rosalie."

"No problem. Can I get you anything else?"

"I'll let you know."

Neal sat back, studying Eli as his assistant stepped out, shut the door. "You look better."

"So I'm told."

"How's the book going?"

"Some days better than others. Altogether not bad."

"And your grandmother? She's recovering from her accident?"

"She is. I'm going by to see her later. You don't have to do this, Neal."

Brown eyes shrewd, Neal picked up his mug, settled back with it. "Do what?"

"The small talk, the relax-the-client routine."

Neal sampled the coffee. "We were friendly before you hired me, but you didn't hire me because we were friendly. Or that wasn't at the top of the list. When I asked you why you'd come to me, specifically, you had several good reasons. Among them was you believed the two of us approached the law and our work along similar lines. We represent the whole client. I want to know your state of mind, Eli. It helps me decide what actions or non-actions to recommend to you. And how much I'll have to persuade you to take a recommendation you might not feel ready for."

"My state of mind changes like the goddamn tide. Right now it's . . . not optimistic but more aggressive. I'm tired, Neal, of dragging this chain behind me. I'm tired of regretting I can't have what I had, even not knowing if I want it anymore. I'm tired of being stuck in neutral. It may be better than sliding off a cliff in reverse, the way it felt a few months ago, but it sure as hell isn't moving forward."

"Okay."

"There's nothing I can do to change how Lindsay's parents—or anyone else—thinks or feels about me. Not until Lindsay's killer is found, arrested, tried, convicted. And even then, some will think I somehow slipped through the fingers of justice. So screw that."

Neal sipped again, nodded. "All right."

Eli pushed to his feet. "I need to know for me," he said, pacing the office. "She was my wife. It doesn't matter that we'd stopped loving each other, if we ever did. It doesn't matter that she cheated on me. It doesn't matter that I wanted the marriage over, and her out of my life. She was my wife, and I need to know who came in our home and killed her."

"We can put Carlson back on."

Eli shook his head. "No, he played it out. I want someone fresh, someone who comes into this fresh, starts at the beginning. That's not a dig at Carlson. His job was to find evidence to support reasonable doubt. I want new blood, not looking for evidence to prove I didn't do it, but to find who did."

On his legal pad, Neal made a lazy, looping note. "To go into it without automatically eliminating you?"

"Exactly. Whoever we hire should look at me, and hard. I want a woman."

Neal smiled. "Who doesn't?"

With a half laugh Eli sat again. "That would be me for the past eighteen months."

"No wonder you look like shit."

"I thought I looked better."

"You do, which only shows how bad it got. You specifically want a female investigator."

"I want a smart, experienced, thorough female investigator. One Lindsay's friends would be more apt to talk to, to open up with than they were with Carlson. We agreed with the police determination that Lindsay either let her killer into the house, or the killer had a key. No forced entry, and after she got home at four-thirty, coded in, the next coding in was my own at about six-thirty. She was attacked from behind, meaning she turned her back on her killer. She wasn't afraid of him. There wasn't a fight, a struggle, a botched burglary. She knew and didn't fear her killer. Suskind's alibied, but what if he wasn't her only lover? Just the latest?"

"We went down that avenue," Neal reminded him.

"So we go down it again, slower, taking a detour if it looks promising. The cops can keep the case open, can keep scraping away at me. It doesn't matter, Neal. I didn't kill her, and they've exhausted every angle trying to prove I did. It's not about making that stop, not anymore. It's about knowing, and being able to put it away."

"Okay. I'll make some calls."

"Thanks. And while we're on PI's— Kirby Duncan."

"I already made calls there." He rose,

went to his desk and brought back a file. "Your copy. Basically? He runs his own bare-bones firm. He does have a reputation for slipping around the edges, but he hasn't been formally cited. He was a cop for eight years, BPD, and still has plenty of contacts there."

As Neal spoke, Eli opened the file, read the report.

"I figured Lindsay's family hired him, but he seems too low-key, too basic for them." Frowning over the details, he searched for another angle, other possibilities. "I'd think they'd go for the flash, the fancier firm, higher tech and profile."

"I agree, but people can make decisions like this based on a lot of factors. They might've gotten a recommendation from a friend, an associate, another family member."

"Well, if they didn't hire him, I can't think who would."

"Their attorney neither confirms nor denies," Neal told him. "At this point, she's under no obligation to disclose the information. Duncan was a cop. It's possible he and Wolfe know each other, and Wolfe decided to make an investment.

He's not going to tell me, if that's the case."

"Doesn't seem like his method either, but . . . There's nothing we can do about Duncan asking questions around Whiskey Beach, whoever his client is. No law against it."

"Just as you're under no obligation to speak with him. That doesn't mean our own investigator can't ask questions about him, gather information about him. And it doesn't mean we can't let it leak that we've hired someone to do just that."

"Yeah," Eli agreed. "It's time to stir the pot."

"The Piedmonts are, at this point, just making noise, trying to gin up doubt about your innocence, keep their daughter's case in the media storm, which has ebbed, and in the public eye. The side benefit of that is making your life as uncomfortable as possible. So this latest push with a PI might've come from them."

"They're screwing with me."

"Bluntly, yeah."

"Let them. It can't be any worse than it was when this was a twenty-four/seven circus. I got through that, I'll get through this." He believed that now. He wouldn't simply exist through it, but *get* through it. "I'm not going to just stand there while they take shots at me, not this time. They lost their daughter, and I'm sorry, but trying to fuck me over isn't going to work."

"Then when their lawyer floats the idea of a settlement, which I expect she will at some point, that's a firm no."

"That's a firm fuck you."

"You are better."

"I spent most of the last year in a fog—shock, guilt, fear. Every time the wind changed, blew in a little clear, all I could see in it was another trap. I'm not out of the fog yet, and Jesus, I'm afraid it may roll back in and choke me, but right now, today, I'm willing to risk one of those traps to get the hell out and breathe fresh air again."

"Okay." Neal balanced a silver Montblanc pen over his legal pad. "Let's talk strategy."

When he finally left Neal's office, Eli walked across to the Commons. He asked himself how he felt being back in

Boston, even for a day. He couldn't quite find the answer. Everything here remained familiar, and there was comfort in that. There was hope and appreciation for the first green spears pushing up out of winter ground toward spring sun.

People braved the wind—not too much bluster in it today—to eat their lunch on benches, to take a walk as he did or just to cut through on their way to somewhere else.

He'd loved living there, he remembered that. That sense of familiarity again, the sense of place and purpose. He could walk from there if he wanted a good, strong hike, to the offices where he'd once entertained and strategized with clients as Neal had done with him.

He knew where to get his favorite coffee, where to grab a quick lunch or to have a long, lingering one. He had his favorite bars, his tailor, the jeweler where he'd most often bought Lindsay's gifts.

None of those were his anymore. And as he stood there, studying the hearty green of daffodils waiting to erupt, he realized he didn't regret it. Or not as keenly as he once had.

So he'd find a new place to get not really a haircut, and buy tulips for his grand-mother. And before he went back to Whiskey Beach, he'd pack up the rest of his clothes, his workout gear. He'd get serious about reclaiming the parts of his life that were still there to be taken, and start really letting go of the rest.

By the time he parked in front of the beautiful old redbrick home on Beacon Hill clouds had rolled in over the sun. He thought the oversize bouquet of purple tulips might offset that. He balanced them in one arm while he maneuvered the big bowl of forced hyacinths—one of his mother's favorites—out of the car.

He could admit the drive, the meeting, the walking, had left him more tired phys-ically than he liked. But he wasn't going to let his family see it. Maybe the day had gone gloomy, but he clung to that hope he'd pulled to him in the Commons.

Even as he crossed to the door, it opened.

"Mr. Eli! Welcome home, Mr. Eli."

"Carmel." He would have hugged their longtime housekeeper if his arms had been free. Instead he bent down to her five feet of sturdy joy to kiss her cheek.

"You're too skinny."

"I know."

"I'm going to have Alice fix you a sandwich. You're going to eat it."

"Yes, ma'am."

"Look at those pretty flowers!"

Eli managed to pull a tulip from the bunch. "For you."

"You're my sweetheart. Come in, come in. Your mother will be home very soon, and your father promised to be home by five-thirty so he wouldn't miss you if you don't stay. But you're going to stay, have dinner. Alice is making Yankee pot roast, and vanilla bean crème brûlée for dessert."

"I'd better save her a tulip."

Carmel's wide face warmed with a smile, an instant before her eyes filled.

"Don't." Here was the pain, the distress he'd seen on the faces of people he loved every day since Lindsay's murder. "Everything's going to be fine."

"It will. Of course it will. Here, let me take that bowl."

"They're for Mom."

"You're a good boy. You've always been a good boy, even when you weren't. Your sister's coming to dinner, too."

"I should've bought more flowers."

"Hah." She'd blinked away the tears and now gave the air a brush with her hand to send him on his way. "You take those to your grandmother. She's up in her sitting room, probably on that computer. You can't keep her off it, all hours of the day and night. I'll bring you the sandwich, and a vase for those tulips."

"Thanks." He started toward the wide and graceful staircase. "How is she?"

"Better every day. Upset still she can't remember what happened, but better. She'll be happy to see you."

Eli walked up, turned at the top of the steps to the east wing.

As Carmel predicted, his grandmother sat at the desk, tapping away at her laptop.

Back and shoulders ruler-straight, he noted, under her tidy green cardigan. Her silver-streaked dark hair stylishly coiffed.

No walker, he noted with a shake of his

head, but her cane with its silver tip in the shape of a lion leaned against the desk.

"Rabble-rousing again?"

He came up behind her, pressed his lips to the top of her head. She just reached up, took his hand. "I've been rousing the rabble all my life. Why stop now? Let me look at you."

She nudged him back while she swiveled in the chair. Those nut-brown eyes studied him without mercy. Then her lips curved, just a little.

"Whiskey Beach is good for you. Still too thin, but not so pale, not so sad. You brought me some springtime."

"Abra gets the credit. She told me to get them."

"You were smart enough to listen to her."

"She's the type who rarely if ever takes no for an answer. I figure that's why you like her."

"Among other reasons." Her hand reached out, gripped his for a moment. "You are better."

"Today."

"Today's what we've got. Sit down.

You're so damn tall you're giving me a crick in my neck. Sit, and tell me what you've been up to."

"Working, brooding, feeling sorry for myself, and decided the only thing in that mix that makes me feel like me is working. So I'm going to try to do something to eliminate the need for brooding and self-pity."

Hester gave him a satisfied smile. "There now. That's my grandson."

"Where's your walker?"

Her face reset into haughty lines. "I retired it. The doctors put enough hardware in me to hold a battleship together. The physical therapist works me like a drill sergeant. If I can tolerate that, I can damn well get around without an old-lady walker."

"Are you still hurting?"

"Here and there, from time to time, and less than I was. I'd say, about the same as you. They won't beat us, Eli."

She, too, had lost weight, and the accident as well as the difficult recovery had dug more lines into her face. But her eyes were as fierce as ever, and he took comfort in that.

"I'm starting to believe that."

While Eli talked with his grandmother, Duncan pulled his car to the curb, studied the house through the long lens of his camera. Then, lowering it, he took out his recorder to add to his notes for the day.

He settled in to wait.

Seven

Part of the job was boredom. Kirby Duncan slouched in his nondescript sedan, nibbling on carrot sticks. He had a new lady friend, and the potential for sex convinced him to drop ten pounds.

He'd managed two.

He'd moved the car once in the past two hours, and considered moving it again. Instinct told him Landon was probably settled in for a while—family dinner most likely as Duncan had snapped shots of the mother, the father and most recently the sister with husband and toddler in tow.

But his job was to sit on Landon, so sit he would.

He followed the job into Boston—an easy tail even with traffic—to the building that housed Landon's lawyer. That had given him an opportunity to do a casual walk-around of Landon's car. Nothing to see there.

Some ninety minutes later he'd followed Landon around the Commons, then tailed him to a high-priced salon, waiting while Landon got a trim. Not that Duncan saw much difference for the fifty-plus the snip cost.

But it took all kinds, Christ knew.

Landon made another stop at a florist, came out loaded.

Just a guy running a few errands in the city before he paid a visit to family. Ordinary crap.

In fact, as far as Duncan could see, all Landon did was ordinary crap, and not a hell of a lot of that. If the guy killed his wife and got away with it, Landon sure wasn't out celebrating.

His report, to date, ran pretty thin. A few walks on the beach, the encounter with the sexy housekeeper and the

woman who'd given Landon a solid
squeeze—and turned out to be the married mother of three.

He figured there was some heat between Landon and the housekeeper, but
he couldn't connect them prior to Landon's return to the house at the beach.

Still, his background check showed
him Abra Walsh had a history of hooking
up with violent types, which would make
Landon the perfect match—if he bashed
the wife's head in, which Duncan had
come to doubt. Maybe Landon was her
current choice, he thought, but current
was key as he couldn't find one crumb to
start a trail cozying the two of them up
before the murder.

Even the thin report he had didn't hold
with the client's insistence Landon was
guilty, or with the certainty of Duncan's
old friend Wolfe, one of Boston's finest,
that Landon had snapped and bashed
his cheating wife's brains in.

The longer he watched, the less guilty
the poor bastard looked.

To draw out information, he'd tried the
direct approach, as with sexy housekeeper, and the more circular style with

the clerk at the B&B and a couple others. Just commenting on the big house on the bluff, asking, as any tourist might, about its history, its owners.

He'd gotten an earful there about a fortune built initially on booze, from pirate plunder to distilleries to running whiskey during the bad old days of Prohibition. Legends of stolen jewels hidden for generations, family scandals, the expected ghosts, heroes, villains right up to Eli Landon's scandal.

His most entertaining source had been the pretty clerk in a gift shop who'd been happy to spend a half hour on a gloomy, preseason afternoon gossiping with a paying customer. Gossips often stood as a PI's best friend, and Heather Lockaby had been plenty friendly.

She felt *terrible* for Eli, Duncan recalled. Deemed the dead wife a cold, unfriendly snob who couldn't even take the time to pay visits to Eli's elderly grandmother. She'd gone off track with Hester Landon's fall, but he'd reeled her back easily enough.

According to the loose-tongued Heather, Landon hadn't lacked for female companionship during his summers and breaks at Whiskey Beach, or during his teens and twenties in any case. He'd liked to party, to suck down beers at the local watering holes and ride around in his convertible.

Nobody, according to Heather, expected him to settle down and get married before he hit thirty. And there'd been *plenty* of speculation about *that*, which had died off when no baby came along.

It was *obvious* there was trouble in paradise when Eli stopped bringing her to Bluff House, then when he stopped coming. Nobody blinked an eye when word circulated about a divorce.

And she, personally, *knew* before it came out that the cold fish of a wife was having an affair. It just stood to reason. She didn't blame Eli one bit for being upset and lighting into her. No, she didn't. And *if* he killed her, and naturally she didn't think that for a minute, she was sure it had been an accident.

He didn't ask how smacking a woman on the back of the head with a poker a few times equaled accident, as he'd already dropped two hundred and fifty bucks on whatnots to keep her talking, and outside of the entertainment value, she'd given him nothing.

Still, he found it interesting that at least some of the locals suspected the favored son of murder. And suspicion opened doors. He'd be knocking on them in the days to come and earn his fee.

For now, he considered moving on, calling it a day. Or at least taking a quick bathroom break.

He shifted his numb ass side to side as his cell phone rang.

"Duncan." He shifted again at his client's voice. "As it happens I'm sitting outside his parents' house on Beacon Hill. He drove into Boston this morning. I'll have a report for you by—"

He shifted butt cheeks again as the client interrupted with a spate of questions.

"Yeah, that's right. He's been in Boston all day, met with his lawyer, got a haircut, bought some flowers."

The client paid the bills, he reminded himself as he logged the call in his book. "His sister and her family went in about a half hour ago. Looks like full family visit. Given the timing, I'd say he's here for dinner at least. I don't think there's going to be any more activity here so . . . If that's what you want. I can do that."

It's your money, Duncan thought, and resigned himself to a long evening. "I'll contact you when he comes out."

When the phone clicked in his ear, Duncan shook his head. Clients paid the bills, he thought again, and ate another carrot stick.

Maybe he'd been gone only a few weeks, but it felt like a homecoming. Logs snapped and flamed in the big stone fireplace, the old dog Sadie curled in front of it. Everyone sat around what they called the family parlor, with its familiar mix of antiques and family photos, red lilies in a slim vase on the piano, as they might have sat, talked, sipped wine on any evening before the world collapsed.

Even his grandmother, who rather than object had enjoyed having him carry her down the steps and depositing her in her favored wingback chair, chatted away as if nothing had changed.

The baby helped, he supposed. Pretty

as a gumdrop, fast as lightning, the not-quite-three-year-old Selina just filled the room with energy and fun.

She demanded he play, so Eli sat on the floor and helped build a castle out of blocks for her princess doll.

A simple thing, an ordinary thing, and something that reminded him he'd once imagined having kids of his own.

He thought his parents looked less strained than they did when he left for Whiskey Beach a few weeks before. The ordeal they'd been through had deepened the creases in his father's face, brought a near-translucent pallor to his mother's.

But they'd never wavered, he thought.

"I'm going to feed this very busy girl." Eli's sister laid a hand over her husband's for a squeeze as she rose. "Uncle Eli, why don't you give me a hand getting her set up?"

"Ah . . . sure."

Since Selina, her doll dangling from her fingers, lifted her arms, beamed that irresistible smile, he scooped her up to carry her into the kitchen.

The broad-shouldered Alice ruled over

the expansive six-burner stove. "Hungry, is she?"

Selina immediately deserted Eli, stretching her arms out for the cook. "There's my princess. I've got her," she told Tricia, expertly securing Selina to the shelf of her hip. "She can eat and keep me company—and Carmel, too, once I tell her we've got our girl to ourselves. We'll have dinner on the table for the rest of you commoners in about forty minutes."

"Thanks. If she gives you any trouble—"

"Trouble?" Eyes popping comically wide, Alice spoke with exaggerated shock. "Look at that face."

Laughing, Selina wrapped her arms around the cook's neck and gave her version of a whisper. "I have cookies?"

"After your dinner," Alice whispered back. "We're fine." She made a shooing gesture. "Go relax."

"Be good," Tricia warned her daughter, then took her brother's hand. At nearly six feet, with a toughly toned body and a determined will, she easily pulled him out of the kitchen, then away from the parlor toward the library. "I want a minute with you."

"I figured. I'm fine. Everything's fine, so—"

"Just stop."

Unlike their more soft-spoken, diplomatic mother, Tricia took her personality clues from her straight-ahead, flinty and opinionated paternal grandfather.

Which could be why she now served as COO of Landon Whiskey.

"We're all being very careful to talk about anything but what happened, what's happening and how you're dealing with it. And that's fine, but now it's you and me. Face-to-face, no e-mail, which you can carefully compose and edit. What's going on with you, Eli?"

"I'm writing pretty steadily. I'm taking walks on the beach. I'm eating regular meals because Gran's housekeeper keeps making them."

"Abra? She's gorgeous, isn't she?"

"No. She's interesting."

Amused, Tricia sat on the arm of a wide leather chair. "Among other things. I'm glad to hear all that, Eli, because it sounds like just what you should be doing right now. But if it's all going so well, why are you back in Boston?"

"I can't come in, see my family? What am I, banished?"

And even then the way her finger shot up, pointed, reminded him of their grandfather.

"Don't evade. You didn't have any plans to come back until Easter, but here you are. Spill it."

"It's no big deal. I wanted to talk, face-to-face, with Neal." He glanced toward the doorway. "Look, I don't want to upset Mom and Dad, there's no point. And I can see they look less stressed. The Piedmonts are making noises about a wrongful-death suit."

"That's bullshit, just bullshit. It's straight-out harassment at this point, Eli. You should . . . talk to Neal," she ended, and blew out a breath. "As you did. What does he think?"

"He thinks it's noise, at least for now. I told him to hire a new investigator, to find a woman this time."

"You're coming back," Tricia stated, and her eyes filled.

"Don't. Jesus, Tricia."

"It's not just that—you—or not altogether. It's hormones. I'm pregnant. I cried this morning singing 'Wheels on the Bus' with Sellie."

"Oh. Wow." He felt a grin start up from his feet, straight up through his heart. "That's good, right?"

"It's great. Max and I are thrilled. We're not telling anybody yet, though I think Mom suspects. I'm only about seven weeks. What the hell." She sniffed back the tears. "I'll clear it with Max. We'll tell everybody at dinner. Why not make it a celebration?"

"And keep the topic off me."

"Yes, don't say I never did anything for you." She rose, wrapped her arms around him. "I'll shift everyone's focus *if* you promise no more careful e-mails, not to me. You tell me when you're having a bad day. And if you are, and you want company, I can work it so Sellie and I come up for a couple days. Max if he can manage it. You don't have to be alone."

She would, he thought. Tricia would shuffle, realign, reschedule—she was an expert at it—and she'd do it for him.

"I'm doing okay alone, no offense. I'm figuring things out I let go of for too long."

"The offer stands. And we won't wait for one if you're still there this summer. We'll just come. I'll float like the whale I'll be by then and let everybody wait on me."

"Typical."

"Say that when you haul around an extra twenty pounds and obsess about stretch marks. Go ahead back. I'm just going to peek in and make sure Selina hasn't sweet-talked Alice into those pre-dinner cookies."

At nine o'clock that evening, Abra finished her at-home yoga class, grabbed a bottle of water as her students rolled up mats.

"Sorry I was a little late," Heather said—again. "Things just got away from me today."

"It's no problem."

"I hate missing the warm-up breathing. It always helps me." Heather let out a sigh, pushed air down with her hands and made Abra smile.

Nothing brought Heather down. She

imagined the woman talked in her sleep, just as she did through a sixty-minute massage.

"I ran out of the house like a maniac," Heather continued. "Oh, I did notice Eli's car wasn't at Bluff House. Don't tell me he's already gone back to Boston."

"No."

Unwilling to leave it at that, Heather zipped up her coat. "I just wondered. It's such a big house. With Hester, well, she's a fixture, if you know what I mean. But I imagine, especially with everything he must have on his mind, Eli just rattles around in that place."

"Not that I've noticed."

"I know you see him when you go over to take care of the house, so that's *some* company. But I'd just think, with all that time on his hands, well, he wouldn't know what to do with himself. That can't be healthy."

"He's writing a novel, Heather."

"Well, I know that's what he *says*. Or that's what people say he says, but he was a lawyer. What does a lawyer know about writing novels?"

"Oh, I don't know. Ask John Grisham."

Heather opened her mouth, closed it again. "Oh, I guess that's true. But still—"

"Heather, I think it's starting to rain." Greta Parrish stepped up. "Would you mind giving me a ride home? I think I may have a little cold coming on."

"Oh, well, sure I will. Just let me grab my mat."

"You owe me," Greta murmured as Heather dashed off.

"Big time." She gave the older woman a grateful squeeze of the hand, then hurried off to look busy stacking mats.

The minute her house was empty, she let out a sigh.

She loved her at-home classes, the intimacy, the casual conversations before and after. But there were times . . .

After she'd straightened the sunroom, she went upstairs, put on her favorite pajamas—fluffy white sheep frolicking over a pink background—then walked back down.

She intended to pour herself some wine, build up the fire and snuggle in with a book. The sound of rain plopping on her deck made her smile. A rainy night, a fire, a glass of wine—

Rain. Damn it, had she closed all the windows in Bluff House?

Of course she did. She wouldn't have forgotten to . . .

Did she? Absolutely every one? Like the one in Hester's home gym?

Squeezing her eyes tight, she tried to visualize, tried to see herself walking through, securing the windows.

But she just couldn't remember, just couldn't be sure.

"Hell, hell, hell!"

She wouldn't relax until she'd checked, and it would take only a few minutes. In any case, she'd made that turkey stew earlier. She'd take the container she'd culled out for Eli down with her.

She pulled it out of the refrigerator, then took off her cozy socks to stick her feet in her ancient Uggs. She pulled her coat over her pj's, grabbed a hat and, dragging it over her head, jogged out to her car.

"Five minutes, ten tops, then I'm back home with that glass of wine."

She zipped down to Bluff House, un-surprised by a rumble of thunder. Late March equaled crazy in the weather department. Thunder tonight, snow or sixty and sunny tomorrow. Who knew?

She made the dash through the rain, heading straight for the front entrance, keys in one hand, turkey stew in the other.

She booted the door closed with her hip, reached out to flip the light switch so she could key in the alarm code.

"Great. Perfect," she muttered when the foyer remained dark. She knew all too well the iffy power in Bluff House during a storm, or in Whiskey Beach altogether. She flicked on the little penlight on her key ring and followed the tiny beam to the kitchen.

She'd check the windows, then she'd report the power outage—and the fact that the backup generator had failed. Again. She wished Hester would update that old monster. She worried how Hester would get by in a serious power outage, no matter how the woman pointed out she'd been through plenty of them and knew how to hunker down.

In the kitchen, she retrieved a full-size flashlight out of the drawer. Maybe she should go down into the basement, check the generator. Of course she didn't know what to check, but maybe.

She started for the door, stopped. Dark, cold, potentially damp. Spiders.

Maybe not.

She'd just leave a note for Eli. If he came home in the middle of the night to no power, no heat, no light, he could bunk on her sofa. But first she'd check the windows.

She hurried upstairs. Naturally, the window she'd worried about was secured, and naturally *now* she could clearly remember pulling it shut, flipping the latch.

She went back down, turned toward the kitchen. She wasn't easily spooked, but she wanted to get home, wanted out of the big, dark, empty house and into her own cozy cottage.

Thunder rolled again, made her jump this time, made her laugh at herself.

The flashlight flew out of her hand when he grabbed her from behind. For an instant, just an instant, full, mindless panic struck. She struggled helplessly, clawing at the arm hooked tight around her neck.

She thought of a knife held to her throat, of the blade skipping down her ribs, slicing flesh on the way. Terror shoved the scream from her guts to her throat where the arm chained it down to a choked wheeze.

It cut off her air, had her fighting to draw a breath until the room started to spin.

Then survival kicked in.

Solar plexus—hard elbow jab. Instep. Full-force stomp. Nose—a hard turn as the grip loosened, then a slam with the heel of her hand where instinct told her the face would be. Groin, fast, furious upward jerk of the knee.

Then she ran. Instinct again driving her blindly toward the door. Her hands struck it with enough force to shoot pain up her arms, but she didn't stop. She dragged the door open, ran to her car, dragging her keys out of her pocket with a shaking hand.

"Just go, just go, just go."

She hurled herself into the car, jabbed the key in the ignition. Her tires squealed as she threw the car in reverse. Then she whipped the wheel, shot it into drive, floored it.

Without conscious thought she drove past her own house, slammed the brakes in front of Maureen's.

Light. People. Safety.

She ran to the door, shoved it open, stopping only when she saw her friends snuggled up in front of the TV.

Both of them lunged to their feet.

"Abra!"

"Police." The room spun again. "Call the police."

"You're hurt! You're bleeding!" Even as Maureen rushed to her, Mike grabbed his phone.

"I am? No." Swaying, she looked down at herself as Maureen grabbed her. She saw the blood on her hoodie, on the pajama top beneath.

Not from the knife, no. Not this time. Not her blood.

"No, it's not mine. It's his."

"God. Was there an accident? Come sit down."

"No. No!" Not her blood, she thought again. She'd gotten away. She was safe.

And the room stopped spinning. "Someone was in Bluff House. Tell the police someone was in Bluff House. He grabbed me." Her hand went to her throat. "He was choking me."

"He hurt you. I can see it. You sit. You sit down. Mike."

"Cops are coming. Here." He tucked a throw around Abra when Maureen led her to a chair. "You're okay now. You're safe now."

"I'm going to get you some water. Mike's right here," Maureen told her.

He knelt down in front of her. Such a good face, Abra thought as her breathing labored. A caring face with dark puppy-dog eyes.

"The power's out," she said, almost absently.

"No, it's not."

"At Bluff House. The power's out. It was dark. He was in the dark. I didn't see him."

"It's all right. The police are coming, and you're all right."

She nodded, staring into those puppy-dog eyes. "I'm all right."

"Did he hurt you?"

"He . . . He had his arm tight, tight around my throat, and my waist, I think. I couldn't breathe, and I got dizzy."

"Honey, there's blood on you. Will you let me take a look?"

"It's his. I hit him in the face. I did SING."

"You what?"

"SING," Maureen said as she came in with a glass of water in one hand, a glass of whiskey in the other. "Self-defense. Solar plexus, instep, nose, groin. Abra, you're a miracle."

"I didn't think. I just did it. I must've given him a nosebleed. I don't know. I got loose, and I ran. I ran out and came here. I feel . . . a little sick."

"Sip some water. Slowly."

"Okay. All right. I need to call Eli. He needs to know."

"I'll take care of it," Mike told her. "Just give me the number, and I'll take care of it."

Abra sipped, breathed, sipped again. "It's on my phone. I didn't take my phone. It's at home."

"I'll get it. I'll take care of it."

"I didn't let him hurt me. Not this time." Abra clamped a hand on her mouth as the tears came. "Not this time."

Maureen sat beside her, drew Abra into her arms and rocked.

"Sorry. Sorry."

"Shh. You're okay."

"I am okay." But Abra held tight. "I should be dancing. I didn't fall apart—until now. I did everything right. He didn't hurt me. I didn't let him hurt me. It just . . . it brings it back."

"I know."

"But that's done." She eased back, rubbed tears away. "I handled it. But for God's sake, Maureen, somebody broke into Bluff House. I don't know where they were or what they were doing. I didn't notice anything out of place, but I only went up to the gym, into the kitchen. I nearly went into the basement to check the generator, but . . . He could've been down there. He must've cut the power to get in. The power was down. I—"

"Drink this now." Maureen pushed the whiskey into her hand. "And just take it slow."

"I'm all right." She took a slow sip of whiskey, breathed out when it ran warm down her sore throat. "It started to storm, and I couldn't remember if I'd closed all the windows. It nagged me, so I drove down. I just thought the power had gone out. I didn't see him, Maureen, or hear him. Not with the rain and the wind."

"You made him bleed."

Calmer now, Abra looked down. "I made him bleed. Good for me. I hope I broke his goddamn nose."

"I hope so, too. You're my hero."

"You're mine. Why do you think I came straight here?"

Mike came back in. "He's on his way," he told them. "And the police are headed down to Bluff House. They'll be here to talk to you after they do whatever they do." He walked over, handed Abra a sweatshirt. "I thought you might want this."

"Thanks. God, Mike. Thanks. You're the best."

"That's why I keep him." After a bolstering pat of her hand on Abra's thigh, Maureen rose. "I'm going to make coffee."

As she walked out, Mike crossed over to turn off the TV. He sat, took a sip of Abra's whiskey. Smiled at her.

"So, how was your day?" he asked, and made her laugh.

Eight

Eli made it from Boston to Whiskey Beach in under two hours. He'd driven in then out of the teeth of the storm as it blew south. The twenty-minute hell he'd navigated in its center helped keep his mind focused.

Just drive, he'd told himself. And don't think outside of the car and the road.

Little fingers of fog swirled up from the road as he barreled through the village. Streetlights threw out wavery beams to glisten on puddles, on streams snaking into gutters, then he was out of the lights, away from the storefronts and restaurants and taking the curve on the beach road.

He yanked the wheel, swung to the shoulder in front of Laughing Gull. Even as he strode toward the narrow front porch, the door in the neighboring cottage opened.

"Eli?"

He didn't know the man who stepped out, dragging on a light jacket as he crossed the short patch of lawn.

"Mike O'Malley," he said as he held out a hand. "I've been keeping an eye out for you.

The voice on the phone, of course. "Abra."

"She's with us." He gestured toward his house. "She's okay—mostly it just shook her up. There are a couple cops down at Bluff House. You'll want to talk to them. I—"

"Later. I want to see Abra."

"Back in the kitchen." Mike led the way.

"Did he hurt her?"

"Shook her up," Mike repeated, "scared her. He had her in a chokehold so she's a little raw. But it looks like she hurt him a lot more than he did her. He gave her some bruises, but she made him bleed."

Eli registered the pride in Mike's voice, assumed it was meant to be reassuring. But he wanted to see for himself. Needed to see.

He heard her voice as they turned out of a cozy living room and into a wide-open kitchen/great room. She sat at a table in a baggy blue hooded sweatshirt, thick pink socks on her feet. She looked up, a combination of sympathy and apology on her face. Surprise replaced it when he knelt at her feet, took her hands.

"Where's the ring?"

"Shut up." He scanned her face, then lifted his fingers, gently, to the raw marks on her neck. "Where else are you hurt?"

"I'm not." Her hands squeezed his, in gratitude, in reassurance. "I'm not. He scared me."

Eli looked to Maureen for corroboration.

"She's okay. If I didn't think that, she'd be in the ER, whether she liked it or not." Maureen pushed up, gestured toward the coffeepot and whiskey bottle that stood side by side. "Which do you want, or a combination thereof?"

"Coffee. Thanks."

"I'm sorry we had to call you, sorry we had to upset your family," Abra began.

"They're not upset. I told them the power was out, and I wanted to come back and check on things. I'd decided to come back tonight anyway."

"Good. There's no point in them worrying. I don't know if anything was taken," Abra continued. "The police said nothing looked out of place, but what do they know? These two wouldn't let me go down and walk through. Maureen's pretty scary when she's in protective mode."

"If there was a burglary and something *was* taken, what would you do about it?" Maureen stopped, held up her hands to Eli. "Sorry. We've been in that loop for the last half hour." She handed Eli coffee. Before she could offer milk or sugar, he downed half of it black.

"I'll go down, talk to the cops, take a look."

"I'll go with you. First," Abra said when Maureen started to protest, "I defended myself, didn't I? Second, I'll have police and Eli. Third, I know more about what's in the house and where it goes than anybody but Hester. Who isn't here. And last?"

She rose, hugged Maureen fiercely. "Thanks, not only for the socks, but for looking out for me. Thanks." She turned to hug Mike in turn.

"Come back here and sleep in the guest room," Maureen insisted.

"Sweetie, the only reason that asshole was interested in me was because I came into the house when he thought he had it to himself. He's not going to come sneaking into mine. I'll see you tomorrow."

"I'll make sure she's all right," Eli said. "Thanks for the coffee . . . and everything else."

"She's got Mom worry genes," Abra told him when she stepped outside with Eli. "We all know this wasn't about me."

"You were the one attacked, so it's very much about you. I'm driving."

"I'll follow you in my car, otherwise you'll just have to drive me back."

"That's right." He took her arm, steered her to his car.

"Fine. Everyone's got Mom worry genes tonight."

"Tell me what happened. Mike didn't give me the details."

"When the storm rolled in, I couldn't remember if I'd closed all your windows. I aired out the house today, and couldn't remember if I closed the window in Hester's gym. It nagged at me, so I went down to check. Oh, I took a container of turkey stew—with dumplings—down while I was at it."

"Speaking of Mom genes."

"I prefer 'helpful-neighbor genes.' The power was out. I feel stupid now as I didn't think twice about it, or the fact that it hadn't been out in the area, at least not five seconds earlier. I was just annoyed. I used my little flashlight to go back to the kitchen, got a bigger one."

She let out a huff of breath. "I didn't hear anything, didn't *feel* anything, which pisses me off as I like to think I've got this little sixth sense thing going on. Major fail on that tonight. So, I went upstairs, and of course I had closed the window. Then I came down again, nixed the idea of going into the basement to see if I could get that old generator running, which even eliminating spiders, dark, spooky, I don't know the first thing about generators. Then he had me."

"From behind."

"Yes. There was thunder, and the rain and wind, but still I hate knowing I didn't hear or feel anything until he grabbed me. After my initial panic, kicking, clawing at his arm—"

"Skin or cloth?"

"Cloth." Little details, she acknowledged. The former criminal attorney would think of them, just as the police had. "Wool, I think. Soft wool. A sweater or coat. My mind wasn't that sharp as my air supply was cut off. Lucky for me, without consciously thinking I went into defense mode. I taught some classes on it. SING. That's—"

"I know what it is. You remembered how to use it?"

"Some part of me did. I told the police this already," she said when he pulled up at Bluff House. "I jammed back with my elbow, and it took him by surprise. And hurt him, at least a little, enough his grip loosened some because I could breathe.

I stomped on his foot, which probably didn't hurt as much as throw him off since I was wearing Uggs. Then I swung around and aimed toward his face. I couldn't see it in the dark, but had the sense of it. Heel of the hand. Then the coup de grâce."

"Knee to the balls."

"And I know that hurt him. I didn't really register it at the time as I was running like a maniac for the door, for my car, but I'm pretty sure I heard him go down. And the nose shot worked, too, because he bled on me."

"You're pretty calm about it."

"Now. You didn't see me curled up in Maureen's arms crying like a baby."

But the idea of it tightened every muscle in his body. "I'm sorry about this, Abra."

"Me, too. But it's not your fault, and it's not mine." She got out of the car, smiled at the deputy who approached. "Hi, Vinnie. Eli, this is Deputy Hanson."

"Eli. You probably don't remember me."

"Yeah, I do." The hair was shorter, and brown rather than bleached blond, the face fuller. But Eli remembered. "Surfer dude."

Vinnie laughed. "Still am when I can grab a board and a wave. Sorry for the trouble here."

"So am I. How did he get in?"

"He cut the power. Shorted it out, and jimmied the side door—the one going into the laundry room. So he knew or suspected there was an alarm. Abra said you left late this morning, went into Boston."

"That's right."

"So your car wasn't here all day, into the evening. You can take a look around, see if there's anything missing. We called the power company, but they're probably not going to get on this until tomorrow."

"Soon enough."

"We didn't find any vandalism," Vinnie continued as he led the way. "We got some blood on the floor right in the foyer, and on Abra's pajama top and hoodie. It's enough for DNA if he's in the system, or if we get him. But that's not going to be quick."

He opened the front door, shone his light, then picked up the flashlight Abra had dropped and he'd already set on a table in the foyer.

"We get a break-in now and then, on rental cottages empty during the off season. But that's mostly kids looking for a place to hang out, have sex, smoke dope or, at worst, vandalize or steal some electronics. This doesn't look like kids. None of the local boys would risk Bluff House, for one thing."

"Kirby Duncan. Boston PI. He's been poking around, asking questions about me."

"It wasn't him," Abra said, but Vinnie took out his book, noted down the name.

"It was dark. You didn't see his face."

"No, but I had an up-close-and-personal with his build. Duncan's soft in the middle, paunchy, and this man wasn't. And Duncan's shorter, more beefy."

"Still." Vinnie tucked his book away again. "We'll talk to him."

"He's at Surfside B-and-B. I poked around," Abra explained.

"We'll check it out. There's some easily portable valuables in the house, and electronics. You've got a nice laptop upstairs, there's flat-screen TVs. I imagine Ms.

Hester's got jewelry in a safe. Maybe you had some cash sitting around?"

"Yeah, some." Eli took the kitchen flashlight, started upstairs. He checked the office first, booted up his laptop.

If Duncan had been after anything, he suspected it would be a look at his personal e-mail, files, Web history. So he ran a quick diagnostic.

"Nothing since I shut it down this morning. That shows." He opened drawers, shook his head. "It doesn't look like anything's been gone through. And nothing's missing in here."

Eli walked out and into his bedroom. He opened a drawer, saw the couple hundred in cash he kept for easy access. "If he was up here," Eli said as he shone the light, turned a circle, "he left everything just the way I did."

"It could be Abra interrupted him before he got started. Look, you should take your time, take a good look around. You may want to wait until you've got some light. We'll be doing drive-bys, but he'd be pretty damn stupid to come back at this point. It's late," Vinnie added, "but I don't have a problem rousting a private investigator out of bed. I'll follow up with you tomorrow, Eli. Do you want a lift home, Abra?"

"No thanks. You go ahead."

With a nod, he took out a card. "Abra's got one, but keep this around. You call me if you find anything missing, or have any more trouble. And if you pick up a board, we could see if you remember any of those lessons I gave you back in the day."

"In March? The water's freaking freezing."

"That's why real men wear wet suits. I'll keep in touch."

"He hasn't changed much," Eli commented when Vinnie's footsteps receded. "Well, the hair. I guess bleached-out shoulder-length isn't police issue."

"But I bet it was cute on him."

"You know each other? Before tonight, I mean."

"Yeah. He lost a bet with his wife last year and had to take one of my yoga classes. Now he's a semi-regular."

"Vinnie's married?"

"With one and a half kids. They live

down in South Point and throw exceptional barbecues."

Maybe Vinnie had changed, Eli thought
as he continued to scan the room. He remembered a rail-thin guy, perpetually
high, who'd lived for the next wave and
dreamed of moving to Hawaii.

The beam passed over the bed, then
came back to shine on the hand towel,
the pipe-smoking fish. "Really?"

"I'm going to see if I can manage a
guard dog next. Maybe a rottweiler or a
Doberman. Maybe it'll work."

"You're going to need a bigger towel."
He scanned her face in the dim light.
"You've got to be tired. I'll take you
home."

"More wired than tired. I should've
skipped the coffee. Look, you shouldn't
stay here without any power. It's going to
get colder, and no lights, no pump, so no
water. I've got a more-or-less guest room
and a really comfortable sofa. You can
take either."

"No, that's okay. I don't want to leave
the house empty after this. I'm going to
go down and bang on the generator."

"All right. I'll go down, too, make girl

noises and hand you inappropriate tools. You're gawky yet, but you should be able to stomp on any spiders. It's wrong, I know, considering the good work they do, but I have a thing about spiders."

"I can make manly noises and get my own inappropriate tools. You should get some sleep."

"I'm not ready." She gave a kind of shaking shrug. "Unless you have strong objections to my company down there, I'd rather stick around. Especially if I can have a glass of wine."

"Sure." He suspected, whatever she'd said to Maureen, she had nerves about being alone in her own house.

"We'll both get drunk and bang on the generator."

"That's a plan. I did a kind of half-assed cleaning down there before you came, at least in the main area, the wine cellar, seasonal storage. I don't really go beyond there, and I don't think Hester has in years. The rest of the place is huge and dark, dank and just pretty scary," she told him as they started downstairs. "It's not my favorite place."

"Spooky?" he said, and turned the

flashlight under his chin for a horror-movie effect.

"Yes, and stop that. The furnaces make grunting and grinding noises, things clang and creak. And there's too many strange little rooms and spaces. It's *The Shining* of basements. So . . ."

She stopped in the kitchen, got out the wine herself. "Courage from the grape, which may also counteract the very late-night coffee and adventure. How was everything at home? In Boston?"

"It was good. Really." If she needed to talk about something else, he could talk about something else. "Gran looks stronger, my parents look less stressed. And my sister's expecting her second child. So there was something to celebrate."

"That's wonderful."

"It switched the gears, if you know what I mean," he said as she poured wine for both of them. "Instead of being careful not to talk about why I moved here, we stopped thinking about it."

"To fresh starts, new babies and electricity." She tapped her glass against his.

After one sip she decided to take the bottle down to the basement. Maybe she *would* get a little drunk. It might help her sleep.

The basement door creaked. Naturally, she thought, and hooked a finger in one of Eli's belt loops as he started down. "So we don't get separated," she said when he glanced back.

"It's not the Amazon."

"In basement terms it is. Most houses around here don't even *have* basements, much less Amazon basements."

"Most aren't built on a cliff. And part of it's above ground level."

"A basement's a basement. And this one's too quiet."

"I thought it made too many noises."

"It can't make them without the furnaces, the pumps and God knows what other intestines are down here. So it's too quiet. It's waiting."

"Okay, you're starting to freak me out."

"I don't want to be freaked out alone."

At the base of the steps, Eli took a flashlight from its wall charger in a well-stocked and meticulously organized wine cellar.

There'd been a day, he imagined, when every niche would have held a bottle—

the hundreds of them systematically turned by the butler. But even now he calculated a solid hundred bottles of what would be exceptional wines.

"Here. Now if we get separated you can send me a signal. I'll get the search party."

She released his belt loop, turned on the flashlight he gave her.

Like caves, that's how she thought of Bluff House's basement. A series of caves. Some of the walls were the old stone where the builders had simply carved through. There were passages and low archways, section to section. Normally, she could have flipped switches and flooded it with welcome light, but now her beam shimmered and crossed with Eli's.

"Like Scully and Mulder," she commented.

"The truth is out there."

Appreciating him, she smiled and stayed close behind him as he ducked an archway, turned left and stopped, with Abra bumping into him.

"Sorry."

"Hmm." Eli shone the light on the

chipped red paint of the mammoth machine.

"It looks like something from another world."

"Another time, anyway. Why haven't we updated this? Why haven't we hard-wired a new generator into the house?"

"Hester didn't mind power outages. She said they helped remind her to be self-sufficient. And she liked the quiet. She's well-stocked with batteries, candles, wood, canned goods and so on."

"She's going to be self-sufficient with a new, reliable generator after this. Maybe this bitch is just out of gas." He gave it a light kick. He took a glug of wine, set the glass down on another utility shelf and, crouching down, opened a five-gallon gas can. "Okay, we've got gas here. Let's check the creature from another world."

Abra watched him circle behind it. "Do you know how it works?"

"Yeah. We've gone up against each other a few times. It's been a while, but you don't forget." He looked back at her. His eyes widened as he aimed the light on her left shoulder. "Ah . . ."

She jumped, spun around in circles,

glass in one hand, bottle in the other. "Is it on me? Is it on me? Get it off!"

She stopped when he laughed—full, deep, helpless laughter that struck a wonderful and warm chord inside her even as it infuriated.

"Damn it, Eli! What *is* it with men? You're all such children."

"You took out an intruder, in the dark, alone. Then you squeal like a girl over an imaginary spider."

"I am a girl, so I naturally squeal like one." She topped off her glass, drank. "That was mean."

"But funny." He gripped the gas cap on the generator, twisted. Got nothing. He rolled his shoulders, tried again. "Suck it."

"Want me to loosen it for you, big boy?" She fluttered her lashes.

"Go ahead, yoga girl."

She flexed her biceps, came around with him so they stood hip to hip. After two mighty attempts, she stepped back. "Apologies. It's obviously welded on."

"No, it's rusted and old and whoever put it on last time was showing off. I need a wrench."

"Where are you going?"

He stopped, turned back. "Tool department's back here, or it used to be."

"I don't want to go back there."

"I can get the wrench all by myself."

She didn't much want to stay where she was alone, either, but couldn't bring herself to admit it. "Well, keep talking. And don't make any stupid gagging or choking or screaming sounds. I won't be impressed."

"If the basement monster attacks, I'll fight him off in silence."

"Just keep talking," she insisted as he walked deeper into the dark. "When did you lose your virginity?"

"What?"

"It's the first thing that came to my mind. I don't know why. I'll go first. The night of my senior prom. It's a cliché for a reason. I thought it was forever, Trevor Bennington and I. It was two and a half months, six if you count pre-sex. . . . Eli?"

"Right here. Who dumped whom?"

"We just drifted apart, which is unsatisfying. We should've had some drama, some deception and fury."

"Not all it's cracked up to be." His voice echoed eerily, making Abra turn to *ujjayi* breathing as she skimmed her flashlight around the area.

She heard a kind of thump, a curse. "Eli?"

"Damn it, what's that doing here?"

"Don't be funny."

"I just rapped my damn shin on a damn wheelbarrow because it's sitting in the middle of the damn floor. And . . ."

"Are you hurt? Eli . . ."

"Come back here, Abra."

"I don't wanna."

"There's no spiders. I need you to see this."

"Oh God." She inched her way along. "Is it alive?"

"No, nothing like that."

"If this is a stupid boy trick, I'm going to be *very* unamused." She breathed easier when her light hit him. "What is it?"

"It's that." He pointed with his light.

The floor, a combination of packed earth and stone, gaped open. The trench ran nearly wall to wall, as wide as six feet, as deep as three.

"What . . . was something buried there?"

"Somebody obviously thinks so."

"Like . . . a body?"

"I'd say a body's more likely to be buried than disinterred in a basement."

"Why would anyone dig down here?
Hester never said anything about excavation." She ran her light over a pickax,
shovels, buckets, a sledgehammer. "It
would take forever to dig in this ground
with hand tools."

"Power tools make noise."

"Yes, but . . . Oh my God. That's what
this was about tonight? Coming down
here to dig for . . . whatever. The legend?
Esmeralda's Dowry? That's ridiculous—
and that has to be it."

"Then he's wasting time and effort. For
Christ's sake, if there was treasure, don't
you think we'd know, or have found it by
now?"

"I'm not saying—"

"Sorry—sorry." He paced away. "All
this wasn't done just tonight. This is
weeks of work, a few hours at a time."

"Then he's been down here before. But
he cut the power, jimmied the door. Hester changed the alarm code," Abra remembered. "She asked me to change

the code when she got out of the hospital. She was upset, and it didn't make any sense at the time, but she insisted. A new code, and to rekey the locks. I just did it, about a week before you moved in."

"She didn't just fall." The sudden certainty of it punched like a fist. "The son of a bitch. Did he push her, trip her, just scare her so she lost her footing? Then he left her there. He left her on the floor."

"We need to call Vinnie."

"It can wait till morning. This isn't going anywhere. I turned the wrong way. To get the wrench. I got mixed up. It's been years since I've been down here, and I went the wrong way. We used to scare ourselves spitless in here when we were kids. It's the oldest part of the house. Listen."

When he fell silent, she heard it clearly. The grumble of wave over rock, the moan of wind.

"Sounds like people—dead people, we'd think. Pirate ghosts, and dead witches from Salem, whatever. I can't remember the last time I was back this far. Gran wouldn't come back here. She didn't keep anything back here. I just turned the wrong way, otherwise I might never have found this."

"Let's get out of here, Eli."

"Yeah." He led her out, stopped before the first turn to pluck an old adjustable wrench from a shelf.

"It's the jewels, Eli," she insisted as they picked their way back to the generator. "It's the only thing that makes sense. You don't have to believe they exist. He does. Legend deems them priceless. Diamonds, rubies, emeralds— flawless, magical, exquisite. And gold. A queen's ransom."

"A rich duke's daughter's ransom, if you want to be accurate." He fought off the gas cap with the wrench. "They existed, and would probably be worth a few million, a lot of millions at this point. They're also somewhere at the bottom of the ocean with the ship, the crew and the rest of the booty." He peered in, shining the light. "Dry as an old virgin's . . . as dust," he corrected. "Sorry."

"You were about to be very vulgar."

She held the light while he filled the tank. Picked up her glass and held the light while he fiddled with switches, some kind of gauge.

He punched the power button. The machine belched, farted, coughed. Eli went through the routine again, then a third time—and it caught.

"Let there be light," she announced.

"In a few well-selected locations." He took the glass she offered him, and his hand brushed hers. "Jesus, Abra, you're freezing."

"Imagine that, in a damp, unheated basement."

"Let's get upstairs. I'll get a fire started." Instinctively he wrapped an arm around her shoulders.

And instinctively, she leaned into him as they walked.

"Eli? I don't want to believe it, but could whoever did this be local? They had to know you weren't at home. They couldn't have risked cutting the power and breaking in if you were here. It was early, really. Not long after nine-thirty."

"I don't know the locals the way I used to. But I know there's a PI at one of the local B-and-Bs. It'd be his job to know I wasn't here."

"It wasn't him. I'm sure of it."

"Maybe not. But he's working for someone, isn't he?"

"Yes. Yes, he is. Or with someone. Do you really think he—or they—hurt Hester?"

"She started downstairs in the middle of the night. None of us could ever figure out why. I'm going to start looking at this, all this, from a different angle. In the morning," he added as they reached the kitchen.

He set down the flashlight, the glass, then rubbed her arms. "It's colder in the Amazon than I thought."

She laughed, shook her hair back, lifted her face.

They stood, bodies close, his hands slowing to a stroke instead of a rub.

She felt the flutter in her belly, one she'd ignored since she began her sexual fast, and the lovely rise of heat behind it.

She watched his eyes change, deepen, flick down and linger on her lips before coming back to hers. And, drawn, she leaned toward him.

He stepped back, dropped his hands.

"Bad timing," he said.

"Is it?"

"Bad timing. Trauma, upset, wine. Let me get a fire started. You can warm the chill off before I take you home."

"All right, but tell me it cost you a little."

"A lot." For another moment, his eyes stayed steady on hers. "A hell of a lot."

That was something, she supposed, as he walked away. She took another sip of wine even as she wished they'd chosen another way to warm the chill off.

Nine

When Kirby Duncan closed the door after the county deputy left, he walked straight to the bottle of Stoli on the windowsill, poured two fingers.

Son of a bitch, he thought as he downed it.

It was a damn good thing he'd had receipts—one for a fancy coffee a few blocks from the Landon house, and another for gas and a ham and cheese at a pit stop a few miles south of Whiskey Beach.

Once he'd determined Landon had

been driving home, he pulled off to fuel up the car and himself. Damn good thing. The receipts proved he hadn't been anywhere near Bluff House at the time of the break-in. Otherwise, he was damn near sure he'd have been explaining himself to the local cops, in-house.

Son of a bitch.

Could be coincidence, he thought. Somebody just happens to pick the exact night he reports to his client Landon is in Boston for the evening for a break-in?

And pigs fly south for the winter.

He didn't like being played. He'd stand behind or in front of a client, as need be, but not when the client screwed with him.

Not when a client used him—without his knowledge or consent—to break into a house. And sure as hell not when the client roughs up a woman.

He'd have taken a tour inside Bluff House himself if the client had directed him, and he'd have taken his lumps if he'd been caught at it.

But he wouldn't have laid hands on a woman.

Time to put cards on the table, he decided, or for the client to find a new dog, because this dog didn't hunt for clients who knocked women around.

Duncan snatched his cell phone off the charger, made the call. He was just pissed enough not to give a good damn about the hour.

"Yeah, it's Duncan, and yeah, I got something. What I've got is a county deputy questioning me over a break-in and an attack on a woman at Bluff House tonight."

He poured himself another shot of vodka, listened a moment. "You don't want to bullshit me. I don't work for people who bullshit me. I've got no problem doing a dance for the locals, but not when I don't know the tune. Yeah, they asked who I was working for, and no, I didn't tell them. This time. But when I've got a client who uses me to clear a path to break into the house of the guy I'm paid to investigate, and that client goes after a woman in the house, I've got my own questions. What I do from here on depends on the answers. I'm not risking my license. Right now I've got information about a crime that includes assaulting a

woman, and that makes me an accessory. So you better have some damn
good answers or we're done, and if the
cops come back on me, I give them your
name. That's right. Fine."

Duncan checked the time. What the
hell, he thought, he was too pissed to
sleep anyway. "I'll be there."

He sat at his computer first, typed up
detailed notes. He intended to cover
every square inch of his ass. And if necessary, he'd take those detailed notes
straight to the county sheriff.

The break-in was one thing, and bad
enough. But the assault on the woman?
That tipped the scales.

But he'd give the client a chance to explain. Sometimes the dumb shits just
watched too much TV, got in over their
heads, and God knew he'd had dumb
shits for clients before this.

So they'd clear the air, and he'd make
his position just as clear. No more bullshit.
Leave the investigating to the profes-
sionals.

Calmer now, Duncan dressed. He gar-
gled away the vodka. Never a good idea
to meet a client with alcohol on the breath.

He strapped on his 9mm out of habit, then dragged on a warm sweater, topped it with a windbreaker.

He pocketed his keys, his recorder, his wallet, then slipped out of his room by his private entrance.

That little perk had cost him an extra fifteen a day, but it kept his cheerful hostess from knowing his comings and goings.

He considered his car, then opted to walk. The drive to and from Boston, the hours outside the Landon house, he could use the walk.

While he considered himself an avowed urbanite, he liked the quiet of the village, the middle-of-the-night Brigadoon feel to it with everything shut down, closed up, and the sound of waves rumbling nearby.

A few fingers of ground fog crawled in, adding to the otherworldly atmosphere. The storm had passed, but it left the air thick with wet, and the sky too heavy to show the moon.

The flick and flash of the lighthouse on the point added to the out-of-time feel. He headed toward it, using the time to decide just how to handle the situation.

All in all, now that he'd calmed down, it was probably best to call it a day. If you couldn't trust the client, the work suffered. Added to it, Landon didn't do a goddamn thing. After several days of surveillance, of interviewing the locals, the most damaging information was wholesale gossip from a chatty gift shop clerk.

Maybe Landon killed his wife— doubtful, but maybe. But Duncan didn't foresee any major revelations bursting out of the beach town or the house on the bluff.

Maybe he'd be persuaded to stay on the job—if it meant going back to Boston, doing some digging there, taking a look at the reports, the evidence from another angle. Talking the case over with Wolfe.

But question-and-answer time first.

He wanted to know why his client broke into the house. And he wanted to know if it was the first time.

Not that Duncan objected to a little *professional* B&E. But it was just stupid to think there was something inside that house to tie Landon to the murder of his wife, back in Boston, a year earlier.

And now the local cops would keep closer tabs on the house, on Landon and on the PI hired to snoop.

Amateurs, Duncan thought, puffing a little as he climbed the steep path to the rocky point where the Whiskey Beach lighthouse speared up into the gloom.

Fog swirled, clawing up a little higher here, muffling his footsteps, turning the lashing of water against rock into an echoing drumbeat.

Spoiled the view, too, he realized when he'd reached the lighthouse. Maybe he'd make a hike back if the next day came clear, on his way back to Boston.

Decision made, he realized. A job could bore you. A client could piss you off. An investigation could hit a dead end. But when you combined all three in one? It was time to cut your losses.

He shouldn't have popped off at the client the way he did, he admitted. But Jesus, what a bone-headed move.

He turned at the sound of footsteps, saw the client step through the fog.

"You put me in a hell of a spot," Duncan began. "We need to get this sorted out."

"Yes, I know. I'm sorry."

"Well, we can call bygones on that if you—"

He didn't see the gun. As with the footsteps, the fog muffled the shots so they sounded low, thick, odd. They puzzled him in that instant of shocking pain.

He never reached for his own gun; it never occurred to him.

He fell, eyes wide, mouth working. But the words were only gurgles. He heard, as if from a great distance, his killer's voice.

"I'm sorry. It wasn't supposed to be like this."

He didn't feel hands searching, taking his phone, his recorder, his keys, his weapon.

But he felt cold—biting, numbing cold. And unspeakable pain through it as his body was dragged to the edge over rocky ground.

For an instant he thought he was flying, wind rushing cool over his face. Then the thundering water swallowed him as he hit the rocks below.

Not supposed to be like this. Too late, much too late to turn back. Moving forward was the only choice. No more mistakes. No more hiring detectives—*anyone*—who couldn't be trusted, who couldn't be loyal.

Do what needed to be done until it was done.

Maybe they'd suspect Landon had killed the detective, as they had with Lindsay.

But Landon *had* killed Lindsay.

Who else could have? Would have?

Maybe Landon would pay for Lindsay through Duncan. Sometimes justice was serpentine.

For now, the most important thing was to clear out the detective's room, take everything that could possibly connect them. And the same needed to be done in Duncan's office, at his home.

A lot of work.

Best get started.

When Eli came downstairs in the morning he checked the living room. The throw he'd tucked around Abra when she conked out on the sofa lay artfully spread over the back. And, he noted, her boots weren't by the front door.

Better, he thought. Much less awkward after that unexpected and uncomfortable moment between them the night before. Better that he had the house to himself again.

More or less, he thought when he smelled coffee—saw the fresh pot—and the Post-it.

Did the woman have stock in the company? A never-ending supply?

Omelet in warming drawer. Don't
forget to turn it off. Fresh fruit in fridge.
 Thanks for letting me stay on the
couch.
 I'll check in later. CALL Vinnie!

"All right, all right. Jesus, do you mind if I have coffee first, see if I have a few brain cells to fire up?"

He poured coffee, added his dollop of cream and rubbed the insistent knots at the back of his neck. He'd call Vinnie; he didn't need to be reminded. He just wanted a minute before dealing with cops and questions. Again.

And maybe he didn't want a damn omelet. Who asked her to make a damn omelet? he thought as he yanked the warming drawer open.

Maybe he just wanted . . . Damn, it looked really good.

He scowled at it, then took it out, grabbed a fork. And ate it while wandering to the window. Somehow, however stupid, it felt less like caving if he ate standing up.

Balancing the plate, he went outside, onto the terrace.

Brisk but not brutal today, he noted. And that brisk breeze blew the world clear again. Sun, surf, sand, sparkle—it eased some of the knots.

He watched a couple walking on the beach, hand in hand. Some people, he thought, were made for companionship, for coupling. He could envy them. He'd made such a mess of his only serious attempt he'd only escaped divorce through murder.

What did that say about him?

He took another bite of omelet as the strolling couple stopped to embrace.

Yes, he could envy them.

He thought of Abra. He wasn't attracted to her.

And how incredibly stupid was it to lie to himself? Of course he was attracted. She had that face, that body, that *way*.

He'd rather not be attracted to her, that was accurate. He didn't want to think about sex. He didn't want to think about sex with her.

He just wanted to write, to escape into a world he created and to find his way back into the world he lived in.

He wanted to find out who killed Lindsay and why, because until he did, no amount of ocean breezes would blow that world clear again.

But wants didn't deal with what was. And what was? A hole in the basement floor dug by a person or persons unknown.

Time to call the cops.

He went inside, set the plate in the sink and saw Abra had set Vinnie's card against the kitchen phone.

He wanted to roll his eyes, but it saved him a trip upstairs to dig through his pants pocket where he'd stuck the card Vinnie'd given him.

He dialed the number.

"Deputy Hanson."

"Hey, Vinnie, it's Eli Landon."

"Eli."

"I've got a problem," he began.

Within the hour, Eli stood with the county deputy studying the trench in the old basement.

"Well." Vinnie scratched the back of his head. "That's an interesting problem. So . . . you haven't been digging holes down here?"

"No."

"Are you sure Miss Hester didn't hire somebody to . . . I don't know. New plumbing lines or something?"

"I can be pretty sure of that. I can be pretty sure if she did, Abra would know about it. And since it's obviously in prog-ress, I can be pretty sure if it's legitimate work, the person responsible would have contacted me."

"Yeah. That's not a hundred percent, but it's close. And one more added on. If this was hired work, I'd've probably heard about it by now. Still, do you mind asking your grandmother?"

"I don't want to do that." Eli had juggled the pros and cons of that half the night. "I don't want to upset her. I can look through her files, her bills. If she hired somebody, she had to pay. I'm no expert, Vinnie, but I'd say this is too deep for water pipes or what have you. Plus, what the hell would she be doing having something like that installed back here?"

"Just trying to eliminate the simple. Something like this? It's going to take some time with these hand tools. Time and determination. And it meant getting in and out of the house."

"Abra told me my grandmother had her change the alarm code and get the doors rekeyed. After she fell."

"Huh." Vinnie's gaze shifted from the trench to Eli's. "Is that right?"

"Gran didn't have a reason, not one she could articulate, but she was adamant about it. She doesn't clearly remember the fall, but I wonder if there's an instinct, some buried memory, something that had her insisting on changing the security."

"You find a hole in the basement and now you think Miss Hester's fall wasn't an accident."

"Yeah, nutshell. Abra was assaulted last night. He had to cut the power to get in. He wasn't expecting her. He knew I wasn't here. Maybe he's working with Duncan. Duncan knew I was in Boston. You said he showed you receipts, gave you timelines. He could've given the person who broke in the all-clear. I'm in Boston, get in, get digging."

"For what?"

"Vinnie, you and I might shake our heads at the whole Esmeralda's Dowry nonsense, but plenty don't."

"So somebody gets Ms. Landon's key and passcode, copies them. I can go with that. It's not that hard. He uses them to gain access to the basement, starts digging his ass off. One night he attacks her, knocks her down the stairs."

"She can't remember. Yet."

As the image came, as it always did, of her lying broken, bleeding, Eli paced off the fury. "Maybe she heard something and came down. Maybe she just came down then heard something. She tried to get back up. Her bedroom door's thick as a plank, and locks from the inside. Get in, call the cops. Or maybe he just scared her and she tripped. Either way, he left her there. Unconscious, bleeding, broken. He left her."

"If it happened that way." Vinnie put a hand on Eli's shoulder. "If."

"If. A lot of activity here for a couple weeks after she fell. The police, Abra in and out getting things for Gran. But then it settles down a little, and he can come back, keep digging. Until word gets out I'm coming to stay. Until Abra changes the security. Vinnie, he had to know the house would be empty for several hours yesterday. It had to come from Duncan."

"We'll talk to Duncan again. Meanwhile, I'm going to get somebody in here to take pictures, measurements. We'll take the tools in. We'll get them processed, but that's going to take a little time. We're small fries around here, Eli."

"Understood."

"Get that security fixed. We'll add a

couple more drive-bys. You ought to think about getting a dog."

"A dog? Seriously?"

"They bark. They have teeth." Vinnie's shoulders lifted in a rolling shrug. "We're not exactly a hotbed of crime over at South Point, but I like knowing there's a dog in my house when I'm not. Anyway, I'll get some people out here. Why dig way back here?" Vinnie wondered as they started back.

"It's the oldest part of the house. This section was here when the *Calypso* went down off the coast."

"So what's his name, the survivor?"

"Giovanni Morenni, according to some. José Corez, according to others."

"Yeah, them. And I've heard other stories that say it was Captain Broome himself. Arrgh!"

"And a hearty yo-ho," Eli added.

"Either way, he drags the dowry box—which conveniently came ashore with him—up here, buries it? I always like the one where he stole a boat, went out and buried it on one of the offshore islands."

"There's the one where my ancestor

came down, found him, brought him and the treasure to the house and nursed him back to health."

"My wife likes that one. It's romantic. Except for the part where your ancestor's brother kills him and throws his body off the bluff."

"And the dowry's never seen again. The fact is, whatever the theory, the man who did this is a believer."

"Looks that way. I'll stop by the B-and-B, take another pass at Duncan."

It wasn't the way Eli would've chosen to spend the day, dealing with cops, the power company, insurance company, alarm security techs. The house felt too crowded, too busy, and brought home to him how much he'd grown accustomed to space, quiet, solitude. He'd discovered an aptitude for quiet and solitude at odds with the life he once led. Gone were the days filled with appointments, meetings, people, the evenings filled with parties and events.

He wasn't sorry about it. If a day spent

answering questions, making decisions, filling out forms struck as an anomaly, he decided he could live with it.

And when at last the house and grounds were empty again, he let out one sigh of relief.

Before he heard the mudroom door open.

"Jesus, what now?" He crossed over, opened the interior door.

Abra took one of the market bags weighing down her shoulders, set it on the washer. "You needed a few things."

"I did?"

"You did." She pulled out a bottle of laundry detergent, put it inside a white cabinet. "It looks like you're hooked back up."

"Yeah. We've got a new security code." He dug in his pocket for the note, handed it to her. "You'll need it, I guess."

"Unless you want to run downstairs on my mornings." She glanced at it, tucked it in her purse. "I ran into Vinnie," she continued, moving past Eli and into the kitchen. "So I told him I'd pass along that Kirby Duncan appears to have checked out. He didn't formally, as in telling Kathy at the B-and-B he'd be leaving early, but his things are gone. Vinnie said to call if you had any questions."

"He just left?"

"So it seems," she said as she emptied the bags. "Vinnie's going to reach out, don't you love that? Such a cop term. He'll reach out to the Boston PD, as if they'll follow up with Duncan due to the excavation in your basement. But since he's gone he can't snoop around and invade your privacy. That's good news."

"Did the client pull him back? I wonder. Fire him? Did Duncan just cut his losses?"

"Can't say." She tucked a box of wheat crackers into a cupboard. "But I do know he was paid up through Sunday, and had made some noises about possibly extending his stay. Then poof, packed up and gone. I'm not sorry. I didn't like him."

With the groceries put away, she folded her bags, slid them into her purse. "So, I think this calls for a celebration."

"What does?"

"No snooping private investigations, the power's back on and your security is once more secure. That's a productive day after a really crappy night. You should come into the pub for a drink later. Good music tonight, and you can hang out with Maureen and Mike."

"I lost most of the day on all this. I need to catch up."

"Excuses." She tapped a finger to his chest. "Everybody can use a little lift on a Friday night. A cold beer, some music and conversation. Plus your waitress, who would be me, wears a really short skirt. I'm going to grab a water for the ride," she said, turning to open the fridge.

He slapped a hand on the door, making her eyebrows arch as she turned back. "No water for me?"

"Why do you keep pushing?"

"I don't think of it that way." He crowded her in, she realized. Interesting. And whether he realized it or not, sexy. "I'm sorry that you do. I'd like to see you there in a casual, social setting. Because it would be good for you, and because I'd like to see you. And maybe you need to see me in a short skirt so you can decide if you're interested in me or not."

He crowded her in a bit more, but instead of stirring caution or wariness— probably his intent—it stirred lust.

"You're pushing buttons you shouldn't."

"Who can resist pushing a button when it's right there?" she countered. "I don't understand that kind of person or that kind of self-denial. Why shouldn't I want to know if you're attracted to me before I let myself be any more attracted to you? It seems fair."

So much going on in there, she thought. Like a storm circling.

Hoping to calm it, she laid a hand on his arm. "I'm not afraid of you, Eli."

"You don't know me."

"Which would be part of my point. I'd like to know you before I get in any deeper. Anyway, I don't have to know you, the way you mean, to have a sense of you or to be attracted. I don't think you're a nice harmless teddy bear any more than I think you're a cold-blooded killer. There's a lot of anger under the sad, and I don't blame you for it. In fact, I understand it. Exactly."

He shifted back, and his hands found his pockets. Self-denial, she thought, because she knew when a man wanted to touch her. And he did.

"I'm not looking to be attracted to you or involved with you. Or anyone."

"Believe me, I get that. I felt exactly the same way before I met you. It's why I've been on a sexual fast."

His eyebrows drew in. "A what?"

"I've been fasting from sex. Which could be another reason I'm attracted. Fasts have to come to an end sometime, and here you are. New, good-looking, intriguing and clever when you forget to brood. And you need me."

"I don't need you."

"Oh, bullshit. Just bullshit." The quick flash of temper caught him off guard, as did the light shove. "There's food in this house because I put it there, and you're eating it because I fix it for you. You've already put on a few pounds, and you're losing that gaunt look in your face. You have clean socks because I wash them, and you have someone who listens when you talk, which you occasionally do without me using verbal crowbars to open you up. You have someone who believes in you, and everyone needs that."

She stalked over, grabbed her purse, then slammed it down again. "Do you think you're the only one who's ever gone through something horrible, something out of their control? The only one who's been damaged and had to learn to heal, to rebuild a life? You can't rebuild a life by building barriers. They don't keep you safe, Eli. They just keep you alone."

"Alone works for me," he snapped back.

"Just more bullshit. Some alone, some space, sure. Most of us need it. But we *need* human contact, connections, relationships. We need all of it because we're human. I saw the way you looked when you recognized Maureen on the beach that day. Happy. She's a connection. So am I. You need that as much as you need to eat and drink and work and have sex and sleep. So I make sure you have food and I stock water and juice and Mountain Dew because you like it, and I make sure you have clean sheets to sleep on. Don't tell me you don't need me."

"You left out the sex."

"That's negotiable."

She believed in instinct, so went with it. She simply stepped forward, grabbed his face in both hands and planted her lips on his. Not sexual, she thought, as much as elemental. Just human contact.

Whatever it stirred in her, she was fine with it. She *liked* feeling.

She stepped back, leaving her hands where they were for another moment. "There, that didn't kill you. You're human, you're reasonably healthy, you're—"

It wasn't instinct, but reaction. She'd flipped the switch so he grabbed on and plunged into the blast of light.

And her.

He yanked her around, trapping her between his body and the kitchen island. And gripping her hair—that mass of wild curls—wrapped it around his hand.

He felt her hands once again press to his face, felt her lips part under his, felt her heart slam against his.

He felt.

The pulsing in the blood, the ache of awakening need, the sheer grinding glory of having a woman caught against him.

Warm, soft, curves and angles.

The smell of her, the sound of surprised pleasure in her throat, the slide of lips and tongues slammed into him like a tsunami. And for now, for this one moment, he wanted to just be swept away.

She slid her hands into his hair, and her

own need spiked when he lifted her off
her feet. She found herself on the counter, legs spread as he pressed between
them, and a white-hot, *glorious* lust bursting in her center.

She wanted to wrap her legs around
his waist so they could both just ride, just
ride—hot and hard. But once again instinct took over.

No, not without thought, she warned
herself. Not without heart. They'd both
be sorry for that in the end.

So she laid her hands on his face, yet
again, stroked his cheeks as she drew
back.

His eyes, fierce blue heat, stared into
hers. In them she saw some of that anger
she'd recognized under lust.

"Well. You're alive, and more than reasonably healthy from where I'm sitting."

"I'm not sorry for that."

"Who asked for an apology? I pushed
the buttons, didn't I? I'm not sorry either.
Except for the fact I have to go."

"Go?"

"I have to change into that short skirt
and get to work, and I'm already running
a little behind. The good news is that

gives us both time to consider if we want to take the next natural step. That's also the bad news."

She slid off the counter onto her feet, heaved out a breath. "You're the first man who's tempted me to break my fast in a long time. The first one I think would make the fast and the breaking of it worthwhile. I just need to know we wouldn't be mad at each other if I did. Something to consider."

She picked up her purse, started out. "Come out tonight, Eli. Come into the pub, listen to some music, see some people, have a couple beers. First round's on me."

She walked out, made it all the way to her car before she pressed a hand to her fluttering belly, let out a long, unsteady breath.

If he'd touched her again, if he'd asked her not to go . . . she'd have been very late for work.

Ten

Eli argued with himself, weighed the pros, the cons, his own temperament. In the end he justified going to the damn bar because he hadn't gotten out of the house for his self-imposed hour that day. This would serve as his hour.

He'd check out what the newish owners had done, have a beer, listen to a little music, then go home.

And maybe Abra would get off his back.

And if under it he proved to himself as much as to her he could walk into the village bar, have a beer, with no problem, so much the better.

He liked bars, he reminded himself. He liked the atmosphere, the characters, the conversations, the companionship of having a cold one in company.

Or he had.

Added to it, he could consider it a kind of research. Writing might be a solitary profession—which he'd discovered suited him down to the ground—but it did require seeing, feeling, observing and the rare interaction. Otherwise he'd end up writing in a vacuum.

So, keeping to his vow of an hour out of the house, and getting some local color that might end up painted into his story somewhere made sense.

He decided to walk. For one, it left his car in the drive and that might, in addition to the lights he'd left on, convince any potential B&E candidate the house was occupied.

And it gave him a good solid walk for the exercise portion of his day.

Situation normal, he told himself.

Then he stepped into the Village Pub, and disorientation.

Gone was the watering hole where he'd bought his first legal drink—a bottled Coors—on his twenty-first birthday. No more dark and slightly dingy walls, no more frayed fishing nets, plaster seagulls, tattered pirate flags and gritty seashells that had made up the incessantly seafaring decor.

Dark bronze ceiling fixtures with amber shades replaced the ship's wheels and added moody lighting. Paintings, wall sculptures and a trio of his grandmother's pencil sketches depicted local scenes.

Somewhere along the way someone had sanded and scraped off years of grime, spilled beer and very likely old puke stains so the wide-planked wood floor gleamed.

People sat at tables, in booths, on leather love seats or on the iron stools lining the long paneled bar. Others took to a postage-stamp dance floor, just a scattering of them yet, to boogie and shake to the five-piece band currently doing a very decent job covering the Black Keys' "Lonely Boy."

Instead of the campy pirate costumes,

the staff wore black skirts or pants and white shirts.

It threw him off. And though the former Katydids had been on the crumbling edge of a shit hole, he kind of missed it.

Didn't matter, he reminded himself. He'd get a beer like any normal guy might on a Friday night. Then he'd go home.

He started toward the bar when he spotted Abra.

She was serving a table of three men—young twenties by Eli's gauge— balancing a tray with one hand while she set pilsner glasses on the table.

The skirt—short as advertised— showed a lot of long, toned legs that appeared to start somewhere around her armpits and ended in high black heels. The snug white shirt emphasized a lean torso and the impressive cut of biceps.

He couldn't hear the conversation over the music. He didn't need to, not to recognize the easy and overt flirting on all sides.

She gave one of the men a pat on the shoulder that had him grinning like a moron as she turned.

And her eyes met Eli's.

She smiled, warm and friendly, as if that mouth with the accent of the ridiculously sexy mole hadn't been plastered to his just a couple hours earlier.

She turned the tray under her arm and walked toward him through the moody light and music, hips swaying, sea goddess eyes glowing, mermaid hair tumbled and wild.

"Hi. Glad you could make it."

He thought he could devour her in one, greedy gulp. "I'm just going to get a beer."

"This is the place for it. We've got eighteen on tap. What's your pleasure?"

"Ah . . ." Getting her naked didn't seem like the appropriate response.

"You should try a local." The quick laugh in her eyes made him wonder if she'd read his mind again. "Beached Whale gets high marks."

"Sure, fine."

"Go on over and sit with Mike and Maureen." She gestured. "I'll bring the Whale."

"I was just going to go to the bar and—"

"Don't be silly." She took his arm, pulled him—weaving when necessary. "Look who I found."

With an easy welcome, Maureen patted the empty chair beside her. "Hi, Eli. Have a seat. Sit back here with us old farts so we can actually have a conversation without screaming."

"I'll get your beer. And the nachos should be up," Abra told Mike.

"Great nachos here," Mike said as Abra scooted off, and Eli—with little choice—took a seat.

"They used to serve bags of stale potato chips and bowls of peanuts of dubious origin."

Maureen grinned at Eli. "Those were the days. Mike and I try to get in here once a month anyway. A little adult time, and on weekends or in season it's a great place to people-watch."

"There's a lot of them."

"The band's popular. That's why we got here early enough to grab a table. Did you get your power back on and everything?"

"Yeah."

Maureen gave his hand a reassuring pat. "I didn't have much time to talk to Abra today, but she said somebody'd been digging down in the basement."

"Yeah, what's that about?" Mike leaned forward. "Unless you want it to all go away for a couple hours."

"No, it's okay." In any case Bluff House was a key part of the community. Everyone would want to know. He gave them the basic rundown, then shrugged. "My best guess is treasure hunter."

"Told you!" Maureen slapped her husband on the arm. "That's what *I* said, and Mike's all poo-poo. He has no fantasy gene."

"I do when you put on that little red number with the cutouts on your—"

"Michael!" His name came out on a choked laugh.

"You walked into it, honey. Ah." Mike rubbed his hands together. "Nachos. You're in for a treat," he told Eli.

"Nachos, loaded, three plates, extra napkins." Abra set them down smoothly. "And a Beached Whale. Enjoy. First one's on me, remember," she said when Eli reached for his wallet.

"When's your break?" Maureen asked her.

"Not yet." So saying, she answered a signal from another table.

"How many jobs does she have?" Eli wondered.

"I can't keep up. She likes variety." Maureen scooped nachos onto her plate. "Acupuncture's next."

"She's going to stick needles in people?"

"She's studying how to. She likes taking care of people. Even the jewelry she makes is to help you feel better, happier."

He had questions. A lot of them. And considered how to ask without moving it toward cross-examination mode. "She's managed that variety in a short amount of time. She hasn't lived here that long."

"Going on three years, from Springfield. You should ask her about that sometime."

"About what?"

"About Springfield." Eyebrow cocked, Maureen nipped into a nacho. "And what you'd like to know."

"So, what do you think about the Red Sox's chances this year?"

Maureen gave her husband a gimlet eye as she picked up her glass of red. "More subtle than just telling me to shut up."

"I thought so. Nobody I like talking

baseball with better than your grandmother."

"She's a fan," Eli said.

"She can reel off stats like nobody else.
You know I get into Boston every couple
weeks. Do you think she'd be up for a
visit?"

"I think she'd like it."

"Mike coaches Little League," Maureen explained. "Hester's a non-official
assistant coach."

"She loves watching the kids play." As
the band took a break, Mike caught
Abra's attention, circled his finger in the
air for another round. "I hope she gets
back for at least part of the season."

"We weren't sure she was going to
make it."

"Oh, Eli." Maureen closed her hand
over his.

He'd never said that out loud, he realized. Not to anyone. He wasn't sure
why it had come out now, except he
had all these new images of his grandmother in his mind, images he'd missed.
Yoga and Little League and pencil
sketches in a bar.

"The first few days . . . She's had two surgeries on her arm. Her elbow just . . . shattered. Then her hip, and the ribs and head trauma. Every day, touch and go. Then when I saw her yesterday—" Had it only been yesterday? "She's up and using a cane because walkers are for old ladies."

"That sounds like her," Maureen concurred.

"She lost so much weight in the hospital, and now she's filling out again. She looks stronger. She'd like to see you," he said to Mike. "She'd like you to see her when she's doing so much better."

"I'll make a point of it. Are you telling her about the break-in?"

"Not yet anyway. There's not a lot to tell. And I'm wondering how many times whoever was in there last night has been in there before. If he was there the night she fell."

As Eli lifted his beer to drain it, he caught the look Mike and Maureen exchanged.

"What?"

"That's exactly what I said when we

heard about the digging." Maureen gave Mike an elbow poke. "Didn't I?"

"She did."

"And he said I read too many mystery novels, which is impossible. You can never read too many books, any kind."

"I'll really drink to that." Still Eli just turned his glass in circles as he studied Maureen. "But why did you think it?"

"Hester's . . . I hate using 'spry,' because people use that for old people, and it's almost insulting. But she is. Plus, I bet you've never seen her in a yoga class."

"No, I haven't." And wasn't sure his mind could take it.

"She's got great balance. She can hold a tree pose, and Warrior Three, and . . . What I'm saying is she's not wobbly or shaky. Not that she couldn't have fallen. Kids fall downstairs. But it just didn't seem like Hester."

"She doesn't remember," Eli commented. "Not the fall or even getting out of bed."

"That's not unexpected, right, not after hitting her head that way. But now we know you've had somebody sneaking into the house who's crazy enough to dig in the basement, I wondered about it. And whoever it was who broke in put some bruises on Abra. If she hadn't fought back, known what to do, he could've hurt her more. If he'd do that, he might've scared Hester or he might've even pushed her."

"Round two!" Abra carried the tray to the table. "Uh-oh, solemn faces."

"We were just talking about Hester, and the break-in last night. I wish you'd stay with us for a couple nights," Maureen fretted.

"He broke into Bluff House, not Laughing Gull."

"But if he thought you could identify him—"

"Don't make me agree with Mike."

"I do not read too many mysteries. I read your short stories," she told Eli. "They were great."

"Now you leave me no choice but to get this round."

Abra laughed, gave him the tab. She ran a hand casually over his hair, left it on his shoulder.

Maureen gave Mike a light kick under the table.

"Maybe Eli could come talk to our book club, Abra."

"No." He felt panic lodge in his throat, gulped some beer to loosen it. "I'm still writing the book."

"You're a writer. We've never had a real writer at book club."

"We had Natalie Gerson," Abra reminded her.

"Oh, come on. Self-published poetry. Free verse. Terrible self-published free-verse poetry. I wanted to stab myself in the eye before that night was over."

"I wanted to stab Natalie in the eye. I'm taking five," Abra decided, and leaned a hip on the table.

"Here, sit down." Eli started to rise, but she just nudged him down again. "No, I'm good. Eli never talks about his book. If I were writing a book I'd talk about it all the time, to everyone. People would start to avoid me, so I'd seek out complete strangers and talk about it until they, too, avoided me."

"Is that all it takes?"

She gave him a punch on the arm. "I thought about writing songs once. If it hadn't been for the fact I can't read music, and didn't have any song ideas, I'd've been great."

"So you turn to acupuncture."

She grinned at Eli. "It's an interest and, since you brought it up, something I was going to talk to you about. I need to practice, and you'd be perfect."

"That's a terrible idea."

"I could work on a release of tension, and an opening of creativity and concentration."

"Could you? In that case, let me think about it. No."

She leaned toward him. "You're entirely too close-minded."

"And needle-puncture free."

She smelled heady, he realized, and she'd done something dark and dramatic to her eyes. When her lips curved, all he could think of was the way they'd felt against his.

Yeah, one big, greedy bite should do it.

"We'll talk." Abra stood, took her tray and walked over to a neighboring table to take an order.

"Don't be surprised to find yourself lying on a table with needles sticking out of your bare flesh," Mike warned him.

The hell of it was, he wouldn't be surprised. At all.

He stayed more than an hour, enjoyed the company. It occurred to him he wouldn't have to argue with himself the next time he considered dropping into the bar.

Progress, he decided, as he said good night to Maureen and Mike, and headed out.

"Hey!" Abra bolted out after him. "You don't say good night to your friendly waitress?"

"You were busy. Jesus, get inside. It's cold out here."

"I've got heat to spare after running around in there for the last three hours. You looked like you enjoyed yourself."

"It was a nice break. I like your friends."

"Maureen was your friend before she was mine, but yeah, they're the best. I'll see you on Sunday."

"On Sunday?"

"Your massage. It remains therapeutic," she said when she caught the look on his face. "Even if you stop stalling and kiss me good night."

"I already left you a tip."

She had an irresistible laugh, a sense of happy his system wanted to absorb like water. To prove he could, he moved in, taking his time, this time. He laid his hands on her shoulders, then slid them down her, feeling the warmth she still held from all the body heat pulsing inside the bar.

Then he leaned down, took her mouth.

Slow and smooth this time, she thought, soft and dreamy. A lovely contrast to the earlier shock and urgency. She slid her arms around his waist, let herself drift.

He had more to give than he believed, more wounds than he could admit. Both sides of him pulled at her.

When he eased back, she sighed. "Well, well, Eli, Maureen's absolutely right. You have skills."

"A little rusty."

"Me, too. Won't this be interesting?"

"Why are you rusty?"

"That's a story that calls for a bottle of wine and a warm room. I have to get back in there."

"I want to know the story. Your story."

The words pleased her as much as a bouquet of roses. "Then I'll tell you. Good night, Eli."

She slipped back inside, to the music, the voices. And left him stirred, and wanting. Wanting her, he realized, more than he'd wanted anything but peace for much too long.

Eli worked through a rain-drenched Saturday. He let the story absorb him until, before he realized the connection, he'd written an entire scene with wind-driven rain splatting against the windows where the protagonist found the key, metaphorically and literally, to his dilemma while wandering his dead brother's empty house.

Pleased with his progress, he ordered himself away from the keyboard and into his grandmother's gym. He thought of the hours spent in his Boston fitness center, with its sleek machines, all those hard bodies, the pumping music.

Those days were done, he reminded himself.

It didn't have to mean he was.

Maybe the jelly bean colors of his grandmother's free weights struck him as mildly embarrassing. But ten pounds remained ten pounds. He was tired of feeling weak and thin and soft, tired of allowing himself to coast, or worse, just tread water.

If he could write—and he was proving that every day—he could pump and sweat and find the man he used to be. Maybe better, he mused as he picked up a set of purple dumbbells, he'd find the man he was meant to be.

He wasn't ready to face the mirror, so he started his first set of biceps curls standing at the window, studying the storm-churned waves battering the shore. Watched water spume up against the rocks below the circling light of the white tower. Wondered what direction his hero might take now that he'd turned an important corner. Then wondered if he'd written his hero around that corner because he felt he'd turned, or at least approached a turn of his own.

Christ, he hoped so.

He switched from weights to cardio,

managed twenty minutes before his lungs burned and his legs trembled. He stretched, guzzled water, then went back to another round of weights before he flopped, panting, onto the floor.

Better, he told himself. Maybe he hadn't made it a full hour and felt as if he'd just completed a triathlon, but he'd done better this time.

And this time he made it to the shower without limping.

Very much.

He congratulated himself again on the way downstairs on a hunt for food. He actually wanted food. In fact, he was damn near starving, and that had to be a good sign.

Maybe he should start writing these small progressions down. Like daily invocations.

And that struck him as even more embarrassing than lifting purple weights.

When he stepped into the kitchen, the smell hit him seconds before he spotted the plate of cookies on the island. Any idea of slapping together a sandwich went out the rain-washed window.

He lifted the ubiquitous sticky note on

the film of plastic wrap, read as he pulled the wrap up and snagged the first cookie.

Rainy day baking. I heard your keyboard clacking, so didn't want to interrupt. Enjoy. See you tomorrow about five.

Abra

Should he reciprocate for all this food she kept making? Buy her flowers or something? One bite told him flowers wouldn't make the grade. He grabbed another cookie, hit the coffeemaker. He decided he'd build a fire, pick a book at random out of the library and indulge himself.

He built the fire to roaring. Something about the light, the snap, the heat meshed perfectly with the rain-whipped Saturday. In the library with its coffered ceiling and dark chocolate leather couch, he scanned the shelves.

Novels, biographies, how-to's, poetry, books on gardening, animal husbandry, yoga—apparently Gran *really* got into the practice—an old book on etiquette, and a section of books centered on Whiskey

Beach. A couple of novels, he noted, which might be interesting, histories, lore, a scattering of those written about the Landons. And several referencing pirates and legends.

On impulse he drew out a slim leather-bound volume titled *Calypso: Doomed Treasures*.

Considering the trench in the basement, it seemed apt enough.

Stretched out on the couch, fire blazing, Eli munched on cookies and read. The old book, published at the turn of the twentieth century, included illustrations, maps, biographical snippets of whomever the author deemed a major player. Enjoying himself, Eli delved into the fateful last voyage of the *Calypso*, captained by the not-very-infamous pirate and smuggler Nathanial Broome.

The book carved him as handsome, dashing, full of derring-do, which was probably a crock for any who didn't subscribe to the Errol Flynn or Johnny Depp school of pirates.

He read of the battle at sea between the *Calypso* and the *Santa Caterina* described in an adventurous, bloodless style that made him suspect, perhaps unfairly, the author had been a woman writing under the masculine nom de plume Charles G. Haversham.

The boarding and sinking of the *Santa Caterina*, the pillaging of its stores, the killing of most of its crew turned into high-seas adventure, with hefty doses of romance. Esmeralda's Dowry, according to Haversham, had been magically imbued with its mistress's loving heart so the jewels could be held only by one who'd found true love.

"Seriously?" Eli ate another cookie. He might've put the book down for a different selection, but the author had so obviously enjoyed the writing, and the style proved ridiculously entertaining, and took him into pockets of the legend he'd never heard before.

He didn't have to believe in the transformative power of love—as transmitted in this case by magical diamonds and rubies—to enjoy the telling of it. And he appreciated the consistency of the romantic bent in the author's contention that rather than a lowly seaman surviving the fateful wreck of the *Calypso*—with the treasure—it had been the dashingly romantic Captain Broome.

He read the entire book to its tragic (yet romantic) conclusion, then paged back to study the illustrations again. Warmed by the fire, he dropped into a cookie coma with the book on his chest. He dreamed of sea battles, of pirates, of glinting jewels, of a young woman's open heart and of betrayal, redemption and death.

And of Lindsay, lying in the trench in Bluff House's basement, the stone and dirt stained with her blood. Of himself standing over her, pickax in hand.

He woke in a sweat, the fire burned to a red simmer, his body stiff. Queasy, shaken, he dragged himself off the couch, out of the library. The dream, that final image, held so strong, so clear in his mind, he went down to the basement, walked through the maze of rooms. And he stood over the trench to be sure his dead wife wasn't there.

Stupid, he told himself. Just stupid to feel the need to check out the impossible because of the delusion of a dream brought on by a silly book and too many cookies. Equally stupid to think—hope—that because he hadn't dreamed of Lindsay in a few nights' running he was done with it.

However foolish it was, his earlier optimism and energy faded like chalk in the rain. He needed to go back up, find something to do before he let the dark close around him. God, he didn't want to fight his way back into the light again.

Maybe he'd fill in the trench, he told himself as he started back. He'd check with Vinnie first, then he'd fill it in. Make it go away, and screw whoever had come into Bluff House on their idiotic treasure hunt.

He nursed that little spark of anger—so much better than depression—fanning it as he continued back. Letting it grow and heat against whoever had violated his family home.

He was through being violated, through accepting that someone could have come into his home—or what had been his—killed his wife and left him to hang for it. Through accepting anyone might have come into Bluff House and had anything to do with his grandmother's fall.

He was through feeling victimized.

He stepped up into the kitchen, and stopped dead.

Abra stood, her phone in one hand, and a really big kitchen knife in the other.

"I really hope you're thinking of slicing some giant carrots with that."

"Oh God! Eli." She dropped the knife on the counter, where it clattered. "I came in, and the door to the basement was open. You didn't answer when I called out. Then I heard someone, and . . . I panicked."

"Panicking would be running. Sensible panicking would be running and calling the police. Standing there with a knife isn't sensible or panic."

"It felt like both. I need . . . Can I . . . Never mind." She simply got a glass, got a bottle of wine from the refrigerator. After drawing out its jeweled stopper, she poured it like breakfast juice.

"I scared you. I'm sorry." Her hands shook, he noted. "But going downstairs may happen from time to time."

"I know. It's not that. It's that on top of . . ." She took a long drink, a long breath. "Eli, they found Kirby Duncan."

"Good." His earlier anger could round back again, and this time with a target. "I want to talk to the son of a bitch."

"You can't. They found his body. Eli, they found his body caught in the rocks below the lighthouse. I saw the police, I saw all these people over there, so I went out. And . . . he's dead."

"How?"

"I don't know. Maybe he fell."

"That's a little too easy, isn't it?" They'd come for him again, he thought. The police, with questions. No getting around it.

"No one's going to think you had anything to do with it."

He shook his head, unsurprised she'd read his thoughts. He stepped forward, took the glass, took a long drink of his own. "Sure they will. But this time, I'll be prepared for it. You came to tell me so I would be."

"No one who knows you will think you had anything to do with it."

"Maybe not." He handed her back the glass. "But it's going to fuel the beast. Accused murderer connected to victim of another death. Plenty of dirt to throw, and some of it's going to hit you if you don't keep your distance."

"The hell with that." Her eyes fired at him. The color distress had washed out of her face surged back. "And don't insult me that way again."

"It's not an insult, it's a warning."

"The hell with that, too. I want to know what you're going to do if you believe some people will think you had anything to do with this, if you believe dirt's going to be tossed at you."

"I don't know yet." But he would. This time he would. "Nobody's going to chase me out of Bluff House or away from Whiskey Beach. I stay until I'm ready to go."

"That's good enough. Why don't I fix us some food?"

"No, thanks. I ate the cookies."

She glanced at the plate on the island, and her jaw dropped as she counted a lonely six cookies. "Good God, Eli, there were two dozen. You should be sick."

"Maybe a little. Go on home, Abra. You shouldn't be here when the cops come. No telling when, but soon enough."

"We can talk to them together."

"Better not. I'm going to call my lawyer, just to let him know. Lock your doors."

"All right, fine. I'll be back tomorrow. I'd like you to call me if anything happens."

"I can handle it."

"I think you can." She angled her head. "What happened, Eli?"

"I had a good day, mostly. There's been more of them lately. I can deal with this."

"Then I'll see you tomorrow." She set the glass aside, laid her hands on his face. "Eventually you're going to ask me to stay. I like wondering what I'm going to do about that." She brushed his lips with hers, then pulled up her hoodie against the rain and left.

He liked wondering, too, he realized. And sooner or later, the timing just had to get better.

Light

Hope is the thing with feathers—
That perches on the soul— And
sings the tune without the words—
And never stops—at all—
—EMILY DICKINSON

Eleven

He rose at dawn, after pulling out of a nasty dream where he looked down at a broken, bloody, staring Lindsay on the rocks below Whiskey Beach Light.

He didn't need a shrink to buy him a clue into his subconscious on that one.

He didn't need a personal trainer to tell him every bone, every muscle, every freaking cell in his body hurt because he'd overdone the pumping iron the day before.

Since there was no one around to hear, he whimpered a little as he dragged himself to the shower, hoping the hot water would pound out some of the aches.

He sweetened the pot with three Motrin.

He went down to make coffee, drank it while dealing with e-mail. Time, he figured, for another update to his family. He wished he could realistically edit out any reference to break-ins and dead bodies, but at this point, better they hear it from him than elsewhere.

Word always traveled. Ugly words traveled fast.

He took care with the delivery, assured them all the house was secure. If he glossed over the death of a Boston PI, he thought he was entitled. For Christ's sake, he'd never even laid eyes on the man. Deliberately he left the impression of an accident. It *could* have been an accident.

He didn't believe that for one quick minute, but why worry the family?

He segued into progress on his book, the weather, made some jokes about the book he'd read on the *Calypso* and the dowry.

He read it over twice, decided weaving

the bad news through the center, book-
ending it with light and positive, equaled
the best framework. Hit send.

Remembering his sister, and their bargain, he wrote another e-mail just to Tricia.

> Look, I'm not editing . . . very much.
> The house is secure, and the local
> cops are on it. At this point it looks
> like some asshole's been digging for
> mythical treasure. I don't know what
> happened to the guy from Boston,
> whether he fell, jumped, or got tossed
> over the cliff by Captain Broome's
> vengeful ghost.
>
> I'm okay here. Better than okay. And
> when the cops come around—and I
> know they will—I'll deal with it. I'm
> ready to.
>
> Now, stop scowling at the screen,
> and I know you are. Go find somebody
> else to worry about.

That would do it, he decided. She'd be a
little annoyed, a little amused, and hopefully trust he'd told her the truth.

With a second cup of coffee and a

bagel at his desk, he opened the file on his work in progress, and let himself slide back into the story while the sun climbed over the sea.

He'd switched to Mountain Dew, and the last two cookies, when the doorbell no one ever used echoed its first notes from "Ode to Joy"— a favorite of his grandmother's.

Taking his time, he shut down his work, stuck the half-finished soft drink in the office fridge, then headed down as the notes rang out a second time.

He'd expected the cop at his door. He hadn't expected two of them, or the unhappily familiar face of Detective Art Wolfe from Boston.

The younger one—military haircut, solidly square face, placid blue eyes and a gym rat's body—held up his badge. "Eli Landon."

"Yeah."

"I'm Detective Corbett with the Essex County Sheriff's Department. I believe you know Detective Wolfe."

"Yeah, we've met."

"We'd like to come in and speak with you."

"All right."

Directly against his lawyer's advice, he stepped back to let them in. He'd already made the decision, and hell, he'd been a lawyer himself. He understood the idea behind "Don't say anything, call me, refer all questions to me."

But he couldn't live that way. He couldn't, and wouldn't, keep living that way.

So he led them into the big parlor.

He'd built a fire earlier, in anticipation of just this. It simmered low now, adding warmth and atmosphere to a room comfortable with its art and antiques. One where the high tray ceiling welcomed the light spilling through the tall windows, and the view of the front garden where hardy green spears of daffodils waved and a single brave yellow bloom trumpeted.

He felt a bit like that himself. Ready to face what came and show his true colors.

"Some house," Corbett commented. "I've seen it from the outside, and it sure makes a statement. Makes one on the inside, too."

"Home's where you hang your hat. If

you've got one. We might as well sit down."

He took an internal scan of himself as he did. His palms weren't damp, his heart wasn't racing, his throat wasn't dry. All good signs.

And still, looking into that bulldog set of Wolfe's face, those hard, flat brown eyes kept him wary.

"We appreciate the time, Mr. Landon." Corbett did a scan of his own, of the room, of Eli, as he took a chair. "You might have heard we've had an incident."

"I heard a body was found near the lighthouse yesterday."

"That's correct. I believe you were acquainted with the deceased. Kirby Duncan."

"No, I wasn't. I never met him."

"But you knew of him."

"I know he said he was a private investigator out of Boston, and he was asking questions about me."

Corbett took out a notebook, as much a prop as a tool, Eli knew.

"Isn't it true you stated to the police you believed Kirby Duncan had broken into this house on Thursday night?"

"He was my first thought when I learned about the break-in, and I gave his name to the responding officer. That's Deputy Vincent Hanson." As you damn well know. "However, the woman who was attacked during the break-in, who had met and spoken with Duncan earlier, stated unequivocally that it wasn't Duncan, as the man who grabbed her had a taller, leaner build. Added to that, when Deputy Hanson spoke with Duncan that night, Duncan produced receipts that proved he was in Boston at the time of the break-in."

"Must've pissed you off, him coming here, stirring things up."

Eli shifted his gaze to Wolfe. There'd be no polite Q&A here, Eli thought. "I wasn't happy about it, but more, I wondered who hired him to come here, follow me around, ask questions."

"Easy answer is somebody interested in finding out what you're up to."

"And the easy answer to that is I'm up to adjusting, working, taking care of Bluff House while my grandmother recuperates. Since Duncan wouldn't have had any more than that to report to his client or clients, I have to figure they were wasting their money. But that's their choice."

"Your wife's homicide investigation's still open, Landon. You're still on the list."

"Oh, I'm aware. Just as I'm aware it would be neat and convenient if you could tie me to a second homicide investigation."

"Who said anything about a second murder?"

Smug bastard, Eli thought, but kept his tone even. "You're a murder cop. If you believed Duncan's death was an accident, you wouldn't be here. That means it's either murder or a suspicious death. I used to be a criminal attorney. I know how this works."

"Yeah. Yeah, you know all the ins and outs."

Corbett held up a hand. "Can you verify your whereabouts, Mr. Landon, between midnight and five Friday morning?"

"Friday morning? I went into Boston Thursday. I was at my parents' when I got the call about the break-in. I drove straight back. I think I got here about eleven-thirty, before midnight anyway. I'm not sure of the exact time. I went to check on Abra—

Abra Walsh, the woman who was assaulted in Bluff House."

"What was she doing in the house when you weren't?" Wolfe demanded. "Are you sleeping with her?"

"And how, exactly, is my sex life relevant to this inquiry?"

"Apologies, Mr. Landon." Corbett's warning glance at Wolfe, while subtle, held a charge. "Can you tell us why Ms. Walsh was in the house at that time?"

"She cleans here, and has for my grandmother for a couple years. She'd been in that day and couldn't remember if she'd closed all the windows. We had a storm. I imagine you've already spoken to her, but I'll take you through it. Knowing I was in Boston, she came down to check the windows and drop off some stew she'd made for me. Someone grabbed her from behind—our power was out, so it was dark. She managed to get away, drove to her friends' house— her next-door neighbors, Mike and Maureen O'Malley. Mike contacted me, and the police. I left Boston immediately after Mike called, and drove back to Whiskey Beach."

"Arriving sometime between eleven-thirty and midnight."

"That's right. Abra was shaken up, and as she'd injured her assailant in her struggle to get away, she had the assailant's blood on her clothes. The responding officers took her clothes in evidence. I spent some time at the O'Malleys' before coming here. Abra came with me. We met Deputy Hanson."

"A friend of yours," Wolfe put in.

"I knew Vinnie when we were teenagers, into our twenties. I haven't seen him for a number of years." Eli let the implication go, kept his voice even. "The police who responded found the power had been cut, the alarm deactivated. At that time I couldn't find anything missing or out of place. I told Deputy Hanson about Kirby Duncan, and as I previously stated, Ms. Walsh described her attacker as a man with a different body type. Being thorough, Deputy Hanson indicated he would interview Duncan, who was, I believe, staying at the Surfside B-and-B. Again, I don't know what time, exactly, Deputy Hanson left. My guess would be around twelve-thirty or a little before."

Too bad, Eli thought, he hadn't logged the times.

"When he did, I went, accompanied by Ms. Walsh, into the basement. We have an unreliable generator, and I'd hoped to get some power on. When we were downstairs, and I was hunting around for tools, I found, in the oldest section of the basement, a large trench. There were still tools, which the police have since taken into evidence—picks, shovels, that kind of thing. It's clear whoever broke in had done so before."

"To dig a trench in the basement?" Corbett suggested.

"If you've been around Whiskey Beach for any amount of time, you'd have heard about the legend—the dowry, the treasure. For every person who believes it's bullshit, there's another five who believe it's gospel. I can't swear to the purpose of the break-in, the excavation, but it's a pretty educated guess somebody figured they'd unearth a fortune in jewels."

"You could've dug it yourself."

This time Eli barely spared Wolfe a glance. "I wouldn't have to break into a house I'm already living in, and I'd be pretty stupid to show the trench to Abra or the cops if I'd been spending my time digging. In any case, we were down there awhile. I managed to get the generator going for emergency power. When we came up, I built a fire. It was cold in here, and Abra was still upset. We had some wine, sat in here. She fell asleep on the couch. I do know it was about two in the morning when I went upstairs. I got up about seven-thirty, maybe closer to eight the next morning. She'd gone, left an omelet in the warming drawer. She feeds people, can't seem to help it. I don't know what time she left."

"So you don't have an alibi."

"No," he said to Wolfe. "By your standards I guess I don't. Exactly why do you think I killed him?"

"No one's accusing you, Mr. Landon," Corbett began.

"You're sitting here asking for my whereabouts. The head investigator from my wife's murder is with you. You don't have to accuse me to let me know I'm a suspect. I'm wondering about my motive."

"Duncan was a solid investigator. He was investigating you, and you knew it. And all of his records on that investigation are missing."

"You know him." Eli nodded at Wolfe. "Odds are he was a cop at some time. You knew him. Did you hire him?"

"We're asking the questions, Mr. Landon."

Eli swung back to Corbett. "Why don't you ask why the hell I'd kill somebody I never met."

"He could've dug up some evidence on you," Wolfe began. "Could've made you nervous."

"He dug up evidence on me in Whiskey Beach on a crime I didn't commit in Boston? Where the hell is it? A solid investigator keeps records, makes backups. Where's the evidence?"

"A smart lawyer who knows the ins and outs would make sure he destroyed that evidence. You took his keys, drove to Boston, walked right into his office and got rid of his records, his computer files, the works. Did the same at his apartment."

"His office and apartment in Boston were rifled?" Eli sat back. "That's interesting."

"You had the time, the opportunity, the motive."

"In your mind, because you're so damn sure I killed Lindsay, I had to have done this." Eli continued before Wolfe could speak. "So, walk it through. He either agreed to meet me at the lighthouse in the middle of the night—in the rain—or I somehow lured him there, and that's after he dug up evidence that proves I already killed once. It also means I snuck out of the house while Abra was sleeping—not impossible, I agree. I then killed Duncan, went to the B-and-B, snuck in there, got all his things, took them and his car. I assume I drove his car back to Boston, went to his office and apartment, took care of that. Then drove back. It would be stupid to drive his car back here, but how else do I get back? Then I have to ditch his car somewhere, walk back to Bluff House, get back inside without Abra knowing I ever left."

He knew better than to appeal to Wolfe,

so turned to Corbett. "For God's sake. Just looking at the logistics, the timing, I'd've needed some incredible luck to get all that done before Abra got up to make a goddamn omelet."

"Maybe you didn't do it alone."

Now Eli felt his temper snap, and rounded on Wolfe. "You're going to drag Abra into this? A woman I've only known a few weeks suddenly decides to help me commit murder? Jesus Christ."

"You say a few weeks. Duncan was working the case here, and here's where he found enough to be a threat. How long have you been banging the *housekeeper*, Landon? Screwing around on your wife, she finds out. It just gives you another reason to kill her."

The anger he'd managed to hold at a steady simmer boiled over. "You want to come after me again, you come. But you leave her out of it."

"Or what? Are you going to try for me next?"

"Detective Wolfe." Corbett snapped the words out.

"You think you got away with it once,

so you figure you can get away with it again." Ignoring Corbett, Wolfe slapped his hands on his thighs, leaned forward.

Close in, Eli thought, the way he liked to crowd into personal space in interviews.

"Yeah, I knew Duncan. He was a friend of mine. I'm making it my mission in life to bring you down for him. You won't slip through this time. Everything you and the woman do, have done, think about doing, I'll know. And when I bring you down, you'll stay down."

"Threats and harassment," Eli said, oddly calm again. "That should give my attorney an excellent springboard. I took it before, and I let the life I had go down the drain. I won't take it again. I've answered your questions. You'll need to go through my lawyers now." He got to his feet. "I want you out of my house."

"Your grandmother's house."

Eli nodded. "I stand corrected. I want you out of my grandmother's house."

"Mr. Landon." Corbett got to his feet. "I apologize if you feel threatened or harassed."

Eli simply stared. "Really? If?"

"The fact is, due to the connection, due to the victim's purpose here in Whiskey Beach, you're a person of interest. I'd like to ask if you own a gun."

"A gun? No. No, I don't."

"Is there a gun in the house?"

"I couldn't say." Now he smiled. "It's my grandmother's house."

"We'll get a warrant," Wolfe put in.

"Then get one. You'll need one to get back in this house because I'm done being badgered and hounded by you." He walked out, to the door, opened it. "We're done."

"Keep thinking that," Wolfe muttered as he strode out.

"I appreciate your time," Corbett said.

"Good because I'm finished giving it." Eli firmly closed the door. Then allowed his hands to ball into fists.

Corbett waited until he and Wolfe were in the car. "God damn it! What the fuck were you doing?"

"He did it, and he's not getting away with it again."

"For fuck's sake." Infuriated, Corbett stomped on the gas. "Even if he had motive, which we don't know, can't prove, his opportunity is below nil. He gets Duncan up to the lighthouse in the middle of the damn night, shoots him, shoves him off the cliff, then pulls off the rest? The way he spelled it out's exactly right."

"Not if the woman's part of it. She could've lured Duncan up there, then she follows Landon into Boston, drives him back, sits as his alibi."

"That's bullshit. Goddamn bullshit. I don't know her, but she came off clean and up front. So do her neighbors. And I do know Vinnie Hanson. He's a good cop. He vouches for both of them. It went down just the way they said. The break-in, the goddamn trench, the timing."

"Landon's got money. Money buys a lot of vouches."

"Be damn careful, Wolfe. You're here because we invited you. We can rescind the invitation, and that's exactly what I'm going to recommend. You're fucking obsessed, and you just screwed any chance I have of getting Landon to cooperate."

"He killed his wife. He killed Duncan. Cooperation from him's bullshit."

"You've had a year to pin him for the

wife, and you haven't. Duncan's a hell of
a bigger reach. If you weren't so dug in,
you'd be asking yourself who hired Duncan, why, and where the hell they were
between midnight and five on Friday
morning. You'd be asking yourself who
broke into that house while Landon was
in Boston, and how they knew he was in
Boston."

"One doesn't have dick to do with the
other."

Corbett only shook his head. "Obsessed," he repeated under his breath.

Inside the house, Eli went directly upstairs, turned into the south wing and into
what he'd always thought of as the me-
mento room. Various cases held bits and
pieces belonging to ancestors. A pair of
lace gloves, a music box with a jeweled
butterfly, a pair of ornate silver spurs.
Mixed together in what he considered
charming and unstudied displays were
three leather-bound diaries, military med-
als, a wonderful brass sextant, a marble
mortar and pestle, a pair of satin button

shoes and other interesting Landon debris.

Including a case of antique guns. Locked, he noted with considerable relief, as always. The shotguns, a beautifully preserved Henry rifle, the fascinating pearl-handled derringer, the Georgian-style dueling pistols, flintlocks, a tough-looking Colt .45.

He didn't relax until he'd confirmed every space in the custom-made cabinet held its weapon.

All present and accounted for, he thought. At least he could be confident none of the Landon guns had killed Kirby Duncan. To his knowledge none had been fired in his lifetime, and likely for a generation prior. Too valuable for target practice or sport, he mused, remembering his grandfather allowing a thrilled eight-year-old Eli a chance to hold one of the flint-locks while he explained its history.

Valuable, Eli thought again as he wandered the room. The dueling pistols alone were worth thousands. And easily trans-portable, easily sold to a collector. A locked glass-fronted case would hardly stop a thief, yet whoever had dug in the basement hadn't taken the bird in the hand.

Hadn't known about them? Didn't know the layout and history of the house well enough? Besides the guns—and there had to be six figures, easily, inside that case—the house contained countless valuable, portable items.

His grandmother would have noticed, eventually. But there'd been a decent window of time between her accident and when he himself had moved in. But if and when the intruder had used that window he'd apparently kept his focus on the basement.

Focused, Eli thought again. So it wasn't simply about money, or why not take what came easily to hand? It was about *treasure*.

What kind of sense did that make? he wondered. You could spend one night hauling out a few million in art, memorabilia, collectibles, silver—Jesus, his great-uncle's extensive stamp collection on display in the library. Or you could spend God knew how many nights hacking away at the basement floor with hand tools for a legend.

More than money, then, he thought again as he prowled through the house, taking a speculative mental scan of easily portable valuables. Was it the thrill? The true belief in treasure beyond price?

Was it an obsession, like Wolfe's obsession with him?

The idea took him back to the basement to take a closer study of the intruder's work. On impulse, he stepped down into the trench, found it nearly waist-high in some parts. To his eye it looked as though the work started in the center of the area, then moved out in a kind of grid. North, south, east, west.

Like compass points? How the hell would he know?

He climbed out again, pulled out his phone to take photos from several angles. The cops had pictures, but now he had his own.

For whatever reason, it made him feel proactive. He liked the sensation of doing something. Anything.

To add to it, he went back up, took the

brass telescope on its mahogany stand—
a gift to his grandmother—out onto the
terrace. Proactive meant informed. Maybe
it wasn't the best time for him to take a
hike or drive to the lighthouse, but that
didn't mean he couldn't see.

He aimed, focused, adjusted until he
had a clear view of the yellow police tape.
They'd blocked off the entire area, lighthouse included. He noted a few people
behind the tape—the curious, and a couple of official-looking vehicles.

He turned the scope, aimed down,
watched what he assumed were crime-
scene techs working on the rocks, and
getting soaked despite their protective
gear.

A long drop, he thought, using the
scope to judge the distance from the bluff
to the rocks below. In all likelihood the fall
would've been enough to kill Duncan.
But shooting him first guaranteed it.

Why? What had he known, seen, done?

And how was it connected to Lindsay's
death? Logically, there had to be some
connection. He didn't believe Wolfe had
that part wrong. Unless the whole thing

was as illogical as digging in a basement for pirate treasure, the murders were connected.

Which opened the possibility Duncan's murder was connected to the intruder.

Again, why? What had he known, seen, done?

A puzzle. In his other life, he'd enjoyed puzzles. Maybe it was time to find out if he still had an aptitude for them.

He left the telescope on the terrace, went back upstairs for a legal pad, a pen. This time on his pass through the kitchen he did slap a sandwich together and, what the hell, added a beer. He took it all to the library, lit the fire and sat down at his great-grandfather's magnificent old desk.

He thought to start with Lindsay's death, but realized that wasn't the beginning—not really. He'd considered their first year of marriage an adjustment period. Ups and down, lateral moves, but a great deal of focus, on both sides, on outfitting and decorating the new house.

Things had begun to change between them, if he were honest, within months of moving into the house.

She'd decided she wanted more time before starting a family, and fair enough. He'd put a great deal of time and energy into his work. She'd wanted him to make full partner, and he felt he was on track for that.

She'd enjoyed the entertaining, the being entertained, and she'd had her own career path and social network. Still, they'd argued, increasingly, over his workload, or conflicts between his priorities and hers. Naturally enough, if he continued to be honest. Sixty-hour workweeks were more common than not, and as a criminal attorney he'd put in plenty of all-nighters.

She'd enjoyed the benefits, but had begun to resent what earned them. He'd appreciated her success in her own career, but had begun to resent the conflicts of interest.

At the base? He admitted they hadn't loved each other enough, not for the long haul.

Add in her intolerance—and that was a fair word—for his grandmother, for his affection for Bluff House and Whiskey Beach, and the erosion just quickened.

And he could see now that even in that first year of marriage, an emotional crack had formed between them, one that had steadily widened until neither of them had the means or desire to bridge the gap.

And hadn't he resented Lindsay for his own decision to limit, then to end, his visits to Bluff House? He wanted to save his marriage, but more out of principle than for love of his wife.

That was just sad, he thought.

Still, he hadn't cheated, so points for him.

He'd spent a lot of time trying to calculate when her infidelity had begun. Conclusion? Not quite two years into the marriage, when she'd claimed to be working late, when she'd started to take solo weekend trips to *recharge*, when their sex life had gone to hell.

He wrote down the approximate date, her name, her closest friends, family members, coworkers. Then drew a line from one, Eden Suskind. Both casual friend and coworker, and the wife of Justin Suskind, Lindsay's lover at the time of her death.

Eli circled Justin Suskind's name before continuing his notes.

Eden stood as her cheating husband's alibi for the night of Lindsay's murder. He'd hardly had a motive in any case. All evidence pointed to his plans to take her on a romantic getaway in Maine at what had proven to be a favorite hotel.

His wife certainly had no reason to lie for him, and had been humiliated and devastated when the affair came to light.

Eli's investigator had pursued the possibility of an ex-lover or a second one, one who'd confronted Lindsay and killed her in a fit of temper and passion. But that seed hadn't borne fruit.

Yet, Eli reminded himself.

She'd let someone into the house that night. No forced entry, no signs of struggle. Her phone and e-mail records—home and work—had shown no communications with anyone who hadn't been cleared. Then again, Wolfe had been focused on him, and his investigator could have missed something. Someone.

Dutifully, Eli wrote down all the names

he remembered, right down to her hairdresser.

At the end of two hours, he'd filled several pages of the tablet, had cross-references, unanswered questions, two assaults, if he counted his grandmother's fall, and a second murder.

He'd take a walk, he decided, let it simmer.

He felt good, he realized. Despite—maybe even because of—the muscle aches, he felt damn good. Because he knew as he walked out of the library he'd never let himself be railroaded a second time.

Kirby Duncan's killer had done him a horrible kind of favor.

Twelve

Abra rang the bell first as much for manners as the need for a little assistance. When no one answered, she dug out her house key, unlocked the door, then maneuvered her massage table inside. An automatic glance at the alarm panel and its blinking light had her muttering the new code as she punched it in.

"Eli! Are you up there? I could use a little help here."

After silence, she huffed out a breath, used her table to prop the door open before heading back to her car for the market bags.

She carted them inside, dumped them, muscled her table and tote into the big parlor. Went back for more market bags, carried them into the kitchen.

After she'd put away the fresh groceries, pinned the market receipt to the little bulletin board, she unpacked the container of potato and ham soup she'd made that afternoon, the beer bread she'd baked and, since he apparently had a taste for them, the rest of her chocolate chip cookies.

Rather than hunt him down, she walked back, set up her table, arranged the candles she'd chosen, stirred up the fire, then added a log. Maybe he intended to make an excuse about not wanting or needing his scheduled massage, but he'd have a hard time with that since she had everything in place.

Satisfied with that, she wandered upstairs on the off chance he was too engrossed in his work to hear her, taking a serious nap, in the shower, in the gym.

She didn't find him, but did find his method of making the bed was hauling up the duvet. She fluffed it, and the pillows—a tidy bed was a restful bed to her way of thinking—folded the sweater he'd dropped on a chair, tossed the socks on the floor beside it in the hamper.

Wandering out, she tried the gym, and took the yoga mat stretched out on the floor as a positive sign. Curious, she poked through his wing of the second floor, then went down again to look around the first. She spotted the legal pad, the empty plate and beer bottle (at least he'd used a coaster) on the fabulous old desk.

"What are you up to, Eli?" She picked up the dish, the bottle as she read the first page of his notes. "Now this is interesting."

She didn't know all the names, but followed the lines connecting them, the arrows, the scribbled notes. A few clever sketches scattered through the notes. He had his grandmother's hand, she realized, recognizing one of Detective Wolfe with devil horns and a sharp-toothed snarl.

As she paged through—he'd obviously spent some time on this, she mused—

she found her own name, its connection to Hester, to him, to Vinnie and to Duncan Kirby.

And a sketch of her, too, delighting her. He'd drawn her lounging on the sand at water's edge, a mermaid's tail a serpentine curl from her waist.

She trailed her fingertip along the tail before reading on.

He'd done a timeline of the night of Duncan's death, one that seemed pretty accurate to her own memory of events. And he'd listed the death as between midnight and five a.m.

So the police had talked to him, as they had to her.

That couldn't have been pleasant. Since his car was out front, he'd be on foot. She'd made soup, baked bread, done a short yoga practice to calm herself down after the police visit. She suspected Eli had vented his tension into the notes. And was likely walking off the rest.

Good for him.

She carried the dish and bottle to the kitchen, then stepped out onto the terrace. Surprised to see the telescope, she moved to it. When she looked through the eyepiece, the lighthouse filled her view.

She couldn't blame him for that. In fact it made her wish she had a telescope of her own. Hugging her arms against the chill, she stepped to the edge of the terrace to scan the beach.

And there he was, she noted, hands in pockets, shoulders hunched a bit against the wind. She watched until she saw him veer toward the beach steps.

She went back inside, poured two glasses of wine, then carried them both to the door to meet him.

"Gorgeous day, isn't it?" She passed him a glass. "You can almost smell the leading edge of spring if you try hard enough."

"Spring? My ears are frozen."

"They wouldn't be if you'd worn a hat. I've got the fire built up again in the main parlor."

But his gaze had already landed on the kitchen counter. "You brought more cookies."

"They're for later." Deliberately she stepped over to block him. "After wine, conversation, massage, then the really excellent ham and potato soup and beer bread I made this afternoon."

"You made soup and bread."

"I considered it therapy after dealing with the police. You reap the rewards. They came here, too."

"Yeah, they were here."

"You can tell me about that while we drink this wine. Or do you want me to go first?"

"Chronological order." He stripped off his jacket, tossed it on a kitchen stool. "What?" he said when she just stared at him, eyebrows lifted.

"Didn't your mother teach you to hang up your things?"

"For Christ's sake," he muttered, but he snatched the jacket up, walked to the laundry room to tag it on a peg. "Better?"

"In fact, perfect. Chronological puts me first." On impulse she grabbed the bottle of wine. "In case," she added as she started toward the big parlor.

"You set this up?" he said when he saw the massage table.

"I did, and get the weird thoughts out of your head. A massage is a massage, sex is sex. You may get one with the other, but not when I'm charging you. And I am."

"For the massage or sex, because I should know the rates going in."

"You're a funny guy when you're not brooding." She sat on the sofa, curled up her legs. "So, basically, I had to take the two detectives, one local, one Boston, through what happened here on Thursday night when I initially came in to check the windows, backtrack to my conversation with Duncan in the church basement. Toggle back to what time you came back from Boston, meeting me at Mike and Maureen's, coming here to talk to Vinnie. What I said to him, what you said, what he said—all of which you already know. Going down to the basement, ultimately finding the big hole, and verifying I stayed over, crashing on this very spot. What time I got up, which was about six. At which time I considered going upstairs and crawling into bed with you, though I didn't see the need to tell them that."

"You didn't see the need, apparently, to tell me either until now."

"No, I didn't. You were dead asleep. I did go up," she added.

His eyes narrowed. "You came upstairs that morning?"

"I did. I woke a little uneasy—residual stress, I guess. And really grateful I wasn't alone, but with all of the night before playing around in my head so I *felt* alone down here. I went to see if you were, by any chance, awake, and you weren't. I debated waking you up, decided against. The fact was, seeing you up there helped me not feel alone down here."

"You should've woken me. Depending on how you did, you could've stayed up there, or I'd've come down here with you so you wouldn't have been alone."

"Hindsight. I did tell the police I went upstairs early, saw you were still sleeping, so just came back downstairs. I got the very clear impression your Detective Wolfe thinks I'm a big ho and a skanky liar."

"He's not my Detective Wolfe."

"He thinks he is." Abra took a sip of wine. "I ran it through for them. I came back down, made coffee, ate some fruit, cut up some melon, pineapple and so on for you, made an omelet, left it on warm,

wrote you a note, went home and meditated before I changed for an early class."

"They knew coming in here I couldn't
have killed Duncan, then driven into Boston, searched his office and apartment,
driven back."

"His office? In Boston? What's all
that?"

"Apparently somebody tossed Duncan's office and apartment in Boston,
cleaned out his records, his computers.
Which points to his client being his killer,
unless you're convinced I killed him. But
they talked to you, knew you saw me here
at nearly two in the morning and around
six in the morning. Not just hard for me to
pull all that off in four hours—not possible
for me to pull it off. They knew there
wasn't enough time."

"That depends." She took another
drink. "If you're Wolfe and I'm a big,
skanky lying ho, that puts me on the slippery slope to co-murderer."

"Jesus Christ." Eli set his glass down
to press the heels of his hands to his
eyes. "I'm sorry."

"Oh, shut up. You're not insinuating I'm

a big, skanky lying ho co-murderer. Wolfe doesn't believe he can be wrong about you killing Lindsay, which means you had to have killed Duncan, which means I'm a big, skanky and so forth. I've known people like him. They absolutely, without question, believe they're right, so everything that calls that rightness into doubt is a lie, an evasion, a mistake."

She slugged down some wine. "People like that make me . . . impatient."

"Impatient?"

"Yes, right before they piss me off. The other detective, Corbett, he wasn't buying it. He was careful, but he wasn't buying I colluded with you to kill Duncan, or very much interested in Wolfe's line of questioning leading to us having not only met long before you came back to Whiskey Beach, but carrying on a hot, sexy, secret affair, which naturally means we're both complicit in Lindsay's death."

She shifted, unconsciously nearly mirroring the mermaid pose. "I told him, frankly, I haven't decided if I'm going to have hot sex with you, but I'm leaning toward it, and if I do, it wouldn't be secret and wouldn't necessarily qualify as an affair, or not as he termed it, as neither of us is married or involved with someone else."

"You told them . . ." Eli just sighed, picked up his wine again.

"Well, he made me impatient then pissed me off. Seriously pissed me off, and I've got a pretty high temper threshold. Suddenly I'm a liar, a cheat, a home wrecker, a tramp *and* a murderer. All because he can't accept he pushed the wrong buttons and you didn't kill anyone.

"Asshole." She topped off her wine, offered Eli the bottle. He only shook his head. "So. Your turn."

"Not much to add. I gave them the rundown, which would've run parallel to yours, and Vinnie's—who Wolfe may think is a dirty cop to go along with my other friend, the skanky, lying ho."

"And co-murderer," Abra reminded him with a lift of her glass.

"You take it well."

"Now, after peeling and dicing potatoes, and drinking a glass of wine. But back up, someone got into Duncan's office and apartment in Boston and now there's no record of his clients, who might have hired him to investigate you. And all his things were cleaned out of the B-and-B. So it's a very logical leap to that client. The police have to make that leap."

"Not if it's Wolfe. I'm his white fucking whale."

"I hated that book. Anyway, nobody who knows Vinnie is going to see dirty cop. And as we didn't know each other until you moved here, it can't be proven otherwise. Add to that my sex fast, and it's really hard to box me as a big ho. All of that just weighs on your side, Eli."

"I'm not worried about it. Not worried," he insisted when she just lifted those eyebrows again. "That's not the response. I'm interested. It's been a long time since I've been interested in anything outside of writing, but I'm interested in figuring this out."

"Good. Everyone should have a hobby."

"Is that sarcasm?"

"Not really. You're not a cop or an investigator, but you are a legitimately interested party. And now, so am I. We have a hobby to share. Full disclosure. I saw your notes in the library."

"Okay."

"If you have something you don't want me to see—such as that fabulous sketch of Mermaid Me, which I'd love if you replicated on good paper so I could have it—you need to put it away. I have a key, and I intend to keep using it. I was looking around for you."

"Okay." He did feel a little weird about the sketch. "Sometimes doodling helps me think."

"That wasn't doodling, it was drawing. Doodling's what I do, and it looks like half-ass balloon animals. I liked Devil Vampire Wolfe, too."

"That one had some potential."

"I thought so, and drawing did help you think. The cast of characters, the connections between them, or among them, the timelines and factors, all there, all logical. That all seems like a good start. I think I'm going to make notes of my own."

He considered a moment. "He'll look at you. Wolfe will. And when he does he won't be able to find any contact between us before I moved in here. He also won't be able to find anything that weighs on the side of you being a lying, murdering, skanky ho."

"How do you know?" She smiled at him. "I haven't told you my story yet. Maybe I'm a recovering skanky ho with murderous tendencies."

"Tell me your story and I'll be the judge."

"I will. Later. Now it's time for your massage."

He gave the table an uneasy glance.

"Your honor is safe with me," she said as she rose. "This isn't foreplay."

"I keep thinking about sleeping with you." Actually, he kept thinking about tearing her clothes off and riding her like a horny stallion, but that seemed . . . indelicate.

"I'd be disappointed if you didn't, but that's not going to happen during the next hour. Strip it off, get on the table—faceup. I'm going to go wash up."

"You're bossy."

"I can be, and while that's a flaw and I do work on it, I wouldn't want to be perfect. I'd bore myself." She trailed a hand over his arm as she walked out of the room.

Since it didn't seem time to tear her clothes off, he took off his own.

It was weird, being naked under the sheet. And weirder yet when she came back, turned on her nature music, lit candles.

Then those magic fingers started on his neck, the top of his shoulders, and he had to ask himself if it was weird when sex slid to the back of his mind.

"Stop thinking so hard," she told him. "Let it go."

He thought about not thinking. He thought about thinking about something else. He tried using his book, but the problems of his characters oozed away along with his muscle aches.

While he tried not to think, or to think about something else or use his book as an escape, she released knots, soothed aches, melted away hot little pockets of tension.

He rolled over when she told him to, and decided she could solve all the problems of wars, economy, bitter battles, by just getting the key players on her table for an hour.

"You've been working out."

Her voice stroked as expertly as her hands.

"Yeah, some."

"I can feel it. But your back's a maze of tension, sweetie."

He tried to think of the last time anyone, including his mother, had called him sweetie.

"It's been an interesting few days."

"*Mmm*. I'm going to show you some stretches, some tension relievers. You can take a couple of minutes to do them whenever you get up from the keyboard."

She pulled, pressed, twisted, tugged, ground, then rubbed every little shock away until he lay limp as water.

"How're you doing?" she asked when she smoothed the sheet over him.

"I think I saw God."

"How did she look?"

He let out a muffled laugh. "Pretty hot, actually."

"I always suspected that. Take your time getting up. I'll be back in a couple minutes."

He'd managed to sit up, mostly wrap the sheet around the important parts, when she walked back in with a glass of water.

"Drink it all." She cupped his hands around it, then brushed his hair away from his forehead. "You look relaxed."

"There's a word between 'relaxed' and 'unconscious.' I can't think of it now, but that's where I am."

"It's a good place. I'll be in the kitchen."

"Abra." He took her hand. "It sounds weak and clichéd, but I'm going to say it anyway. You have a gift."

She smiled, beautifully. "It doesn't sound weak and clichéd to me. Take your time."

When he came in she had the soup warming on the stove, and a glass of wine in her hand. "Hungry?"

"I wasn't, but that smells pretty damn good."

"Are you up for another walk on the beach first?"

"I could be."

"Good. The light's so soft and pretty this time of day. We'll work up an appetite." She led the way into the laundry for jackets, zipped up her own hoodie.

"I used the telescope earlier," she told him as they stepped outside. "It's a good spot for it."

"I saw some crime-scene techs poking around by the lighthouse."

"We don't have murder as a rule in Whiskey Beach, and fatal accidents don't draw tourists. It's important to be thorough. And the more thorough they are, the better it is for you."

"Maybe so, but I'm connected. Somehow. The local cop asked if there were guns in the house. I hedged because I had this sudden thought that maybe whoever broke in took something out of the gun collection to shoot Duncan."

"God. I never thought of that."

"You've never been the prime suspect in a murder investigation. Anyway, they're all there, in place, locked in their cases. When they get the search warrant, and they will, they may take them in for testing. But they'll already know none of the weapons in Bluff House killed Duncan."

"Because they'll know what kind of caliber was used, and maybe even what kind of gun. I've watched my share of

CSI-type TV," she added. "They're all antique-type guns in there. I doubt Duncan was shot with a musket or a dueling pistol."

"Odds are low."

"Regardless, we're undoing our earlier work talking about cops and murder." She shook her hair back when they reached the base of the beach steps, lifted her face to the softening blue of the evening sky. "Do you want to know why I moved to Whiskey Beach? Why it's my place?"

"Yeah, I do."

"I'm going to tell you. It's a good beach-walking story, though I have to start back a ways, to give you the background."

"One question first, because I've been trying to figure it out. What did you do before you came here and started your massage/yoga/jewelry-making/house-cleaning business?"

"You mean professionally? I was the marketing director for a nonprofit out of D.C."

He looked at her—rings on her fingers, hair flying everywhere. "Okay, that one didn't make the top ten on my list."

She gave him an elbow poke. "I have an MBA from Northwestern."

"Seriously?"

"Deadly serious, and I'm jumping ahead. My mother is an amazing woman. An incredibly smart, dedicated, brave, *involved* woman. She had me while she was in grad school, and my father decided it was all more than he signed on for, so they split when I was about two. He's not really a part of my life."

"I'm sorry."

"So was I for a while, but I got over it. My mother's a human rights attorney. We traveled a lot. She took me with her whenever she could. When she couldn't, I stayed with my aunt—her sister—or my maternal grandparents. But for the most part I went with her. I got a hell of an education and worldview."

"Wait a minute. Wait." The sudden flash had him gaping at her. "Is your mother Jane Walsh?"

"Yes. You know her?"

"Of. Jesus Christ, Jane Walsh? She won the Nobel Peace Prize."

"I said she was an amazing woman. I wanted to be her when I grew up, but who wouldn't?" Abra lifted her arms high for a moment, closed her eyes to welcome the wind. "She's one in a million. One in tens of millions from my point of view. She taught me love and compassion, courage and justice. Initially I thought to follow directly in her footsteps, get a law degree, but God, it so wasn't for me."

"Was she disappointed?"

"No. Another very essential lesson she taught me was to follow your own mind and heart." As they walked, she wound her arm with his. "Was your father disappointed you didn't follow his?"

"No. We're both lucky there."

"Yes, we are. So I went for the MBA, tailored toward working in the nonprofit sector. I was good at it."

"I bet you were."

"I felt I was making a contribution, and maybe it didn't always feel like the perfect fit, but close enough. I liked the work, I liked my life, my circle of friends. I met Derrick at a fund-raiser I spearheaded. Another lawyer. I must be drawn to the field."

She paused to look out over the sea.

"God, it's beautiful here. I look at the sea every day and think how lucky I am to be here, to see this, to feel it. My mother's in Afghanistan right now, working with and for Afghani women. And I know we're both exactly where we're meant to be, doing what we're meant to do. But a few years ago, I was in D.C., with a closetful of professional suits, an overloaded desk, a crowded appointment book, and Derrick seemed like the right choice at the right time."

"But he wasn't."

"In some strange way, he was. Smart, charming, intense, ambitious. He understood my work, I understood his. The sex was satisfying, the conversations interesting. The first time he hit me, I let myself believe it was a terrible mistake, an aberration, just a bad moment resulting from stress."

Because she felt Eli stiffen, she rubbed her free hand on the arm wound with hers. "I saw his temper as passion, and his possessiveness as a kind of flattery. The second time he hit me, I left because once might be a terrible mistake, but twice is the start of a pattern."

Reaching over, he closed his hand over the one she'd laid on his arm. "Some people don't see the pattern when they're in it."

"I know. I talked to a lot of women in support groups, and understand how you can be persuaded to accept the apology, or begin to believe you deserve the abuse. I got out, and quickly."

"You didn't report it."

Now she sighed. "No, I didn't. I wanted the leaving to be enough. Why damage his career or put myself into a scandal? I took a short leave of absence rather than explain the black eye to coworkers and friends, and I came here for a week."

"To Whiskey Beach?"

"Yeah. I'd come here with my mother years ago, then again with my aunt and her family. I had good memories here, so I rented a cottage and walked the beach, gave myself the time, I thought, to heal."

"You didn't tell anyone?"

"Not then. I'd made a mistake, and told myself I'd fixed the mistake and to get on with my life. And, as foolish as it was, I was embarrassed. After my leave, I went back to work, but nothing seemed exactly right. Friends started asking what was going on, that Derrick had contacted them, told them I'd had a breakdown, which put me in what I considered the humiliating position of telling them he'd hit me, and I'd left him."

"But he'd planted seeds."

She glanced up at him. "It's another pattern, isn't it? Yes, he'd planted seeds, enough some sprouted. He knew a lot of people, and he was smart, and he was angry. He dropped little hints here and there about me being unstable. And he stalked me. The thing about being a stal-kee is not always knowing it's happening. I didn't. Not until I started dating again, casually. Very casually. Look."

She pointed to a pelican, soaring out over the water, then his fast dive for his evening meal.

"I try to feel sorry for the fish, but I just love watching the pelicans. They have the oddest shape, and it strikes me as ungainly—like a moose—then they com-pact that way and dive down like a spear."

Eli turned her to face him. "He hurt you again."

"Oh God, yes. In more ways than one. I should finish it. No need for all the minute details. My boss got anonymous notes about my behavior, my supposed abuse of drugs, alcohol, sex, my using sex to influence donors. Enough of them he eventually called me in, questioned me. And again I had to humiliate myself— or so it felt at the time—by telling him about Derrick. My superior spoke with his superior, and all hell broke loose."

Now she took a long, careful breath. "Nasty little things at first. Having my tires slashed, my car keyed. My phone ringing in the middle of the night, repeatedly, with hang ups, finding someone canceled my reservations for lunch or dinner. My computers, work and home, were hacked. The man I was seeing casually had his car windows smashed, and anonymous complaints—ugly ones—sent to his boss. We stopped seeing each other. It wasn't serious, and it seemed easier."

"What did the cops do?"

"They talked to him, and he denied everything. He's very convincing. He told them he'd ended things with me because

I was too possessive and had gotten violent. He claimed to be worried about me
and hoped I'd get help."

"A decent cop should've seen through
that."

"I think they did, but they couldn't
prove he'd done any of it. It kept going,
little things, bigger things, for over three
months. I was on edge all the time, and
my work was suffering. He started to
show up at restaurants where I'd be having lunch or dinner. Or I'd look out my
apartment window and see his car drive
by, or think I did. We ran in similar circles, lived and worked in the same
general area, so because he never approached me the police couldn't do anything about it.

"I snapped one day when he strolled
into the place where I was having lunch
with a coworker. I marched over, told him
to leave me the hell alone, called him
names, created a terrible scene until the
woman I worked with got me out."

"He broke you down," Eli stated.

"Completely. He stayed absolutely
calm through it, or I thought he did. And
that night he broke into my apartment.

He was waiting for me when I came home. He was out of control, completely out of control. I fought back, but he was stronger. He had a knife—one of mine from my kitchen—and I thought he'd kill me. I tried to get out, but he caught me, and we struggled. He cut me."

Eli stopped walking, turned to take both of her hands.

"Along my ribs. I still don't know if it was an accident or he meant to, but I thought I'd be dead, any second, and started screaming. Instead of the knife, he used his fists. He beat me, he choked me, and he was raping me when my neighbors broke in. They'd heard me screaming and called the police, but thank God they didn't wait for the cops. I think he might've killed me, with his bare hands, if they hadn't stopped him when they did."

His arms came around her, and she leaned into him. She thought a lot of men backed off when they heard the word "rape." But not Eli.

She turned to walk again, comforted by his arm around her waist. "I had more than a black eye this time. My mother had been in Africa and came straight back. You'd know all about the process—the tests, the interviews with the police, the counselors, the lawyers. It's horrible, that reliving of it, and I was angry to be viewed as a victim. Until I learned to accept I was a victim, but I didn't have to stay one. In the end I was grateful they worked out a plea so I didn't have to go through it all again in a trial. He went to prison, and my mother took me to this place in the country—a friend's summer house in the Laurel Highlands. She gave me space, but not too much. She gave me time—long quiet walks, long crying jags, midnight baking sessions with tequila shots. God, oh God, she's the most wonderful woman."

"I'd like to meet her."

"Maybe you will. She gave me a month, and then she asked me what I wanted to do with my life. The stars are coming out. We should walk back."

They turned, walking now with the evening breeze at their backs. "What did you tell her?"

"I told her I wanted to live at the beach. I wanted to see the ocean every day. I told her I wanted to help people, but I couldn't face going back to an office, going back to appointments and meetings and strategy sessions. I blubbered because I was sure she'd be disappointed in me. I had the education, the skills, the experience to make a difference. I had been making a difference, and now I just wanted to see the ocean every day."

"You were wrong. About her being disappointed."

"I was wrong. She said I should find my place, and I should live my life in a way that satisfied me, that made me happy. So I came here, and I found ways to make myself happy and satisfied. I might not be here, doing what I really love, if Derrick hadn't broken me."

"He didn't break you. I don't believe in fate, in destiny, in absolutes, but sometimes it smacks you in the face. You're where you're meant to be because you're meant to be here. I think you'd have found your way."

"That's a nice thought." She stood on the bottom beach step, turned to him, laid her hands on his shoulders. "I have been happy here, and more open here than I ever was before. I made a very deliberate decision a year or so ago to go on my sexual fast because, though I'd met some very nice men, none of them fulfilled that part of me that may have been damaged more than I admitted. It's a lot to lay on you, Eli, but I'd really appreciate it if you'd help me break my fast."

"Now?"

"I was thinking now would be good." She leaned in to kiss him. "If you wouldn't mind."

"Well, you did make soup."

"And bread," she reminded him.

"It seems like the least I can do. We ought to go in the house first."

He cleared his throat as they started up the steps. "Ah, I'm going to have to make a quick trip to the village. I didn't bring any protection. I haven't been thinking much about sex until recently."

"No problem, and no need for the trip. I put a box of condoms in your bedroom the other day. I've been thinking about sex recently."

He let out a breath. "You're the best housekeeper I've ever had."

"Oh, Eli, you haven't seen anything yet."

Thirteen

Out of practice, he thought with some nerves as they climbed the beach steps, and he wasn't entirely convinced sex was like riding a damn bike.

Sure, the basics remained the basics, but the process required *moves*, technique, timing, finesse, tone. He liked to think he'd been pretty good at it once. Nobody'd complained, including Lindsay.

Still.

"We're going to stop thinking about it," Abra announced when they reached the door. "I'm messing up my head, and I'll lay odds you're messing up yours."

"Maybe."

"So let's stop thinking."

She peeled off her hoodie, hung it on a peg, then grabbed his jacket, yanked it off his shoulders as she pulled herself in, as she fixed her mouth on his.

His brain didn't explode out of the top of his head, but it sure as hell banged around in there.

"That's how it works," she said as she tugged his jacket off, hung it up.

"Yeah, it's coming back to me." He grabbed her hand, pulled her along with him. "I don't want to do this in the laundry room, or on the kitchen floor. And they're both looking pretty good to me right now."

With a laugh, she spun into him, took his mouth again as she flipped open buttons on his shirt. "No reason not to get started on the way."

"That's a point." She wore a soft blue pullover, or did until he yanked it up and off, tossed it behind them as they arrowed toward the stairs.

She pulled at his belt; he dragged at

the skinny white tank she wore under the pullover. And both of them tripped on the base of the stairs.

They teetered, groped.

"Maybe we'd better get up there," she managed.

"Good idea." He grabbed her hand again.

They raced up—like a couple of kids, he'd think later, running toward the big, shiny gift under the Christmas tree. Except most kids didn't try to rip each other's clothes off while they ran.

Out of breath, he finally stripped off her white tank as they hurtled into the bedroom.

"Oh God, look at you."

"Look later." She slid his belt free, let it fall to the floor with a clunk.

He knew they couldn't dive into the bed, not literally, but he figured they came pretty damn close. He forgot about moves, timing, technique. He sure as hell forgot finesse. But she didn't seem to mind.

He wanted those soft, pretty breasts in his hands—the femininity of the shape, the smoothness of skin. He wanted his mouth on them—the leap of her heart against his lips and tongue, the grip of her hand in his hair as she pressed him against her.

As her body bowed up to his like an offering.

He gorged himself on the scent of her, that goddess-of-the-sea scent that brought mermaids and sirens to his mind. That sleek, sculpted body vibrated with energy, infused his own.

As they rolled over the bed, grasping, groaning, he felt he could do anything, be anything, have anything.

She yearned. She ached. Everything felt frantic, fast, fabulous. His hands on her body, hers on his. She knew the lines of him, the shape, but now she could take, now she could *feel*—not to soothe or comfort, but to ignite.

She wanted to fire him, and have the blaze consume them both.

All the needs, good, strong, healthy needs, she'd locked away broke free in a crazed stampede that trampled any thought of restraint or caution.

She couldn't get enough, ravaged his mouth in her quest to feed and fill. But the hunger only grew keener, like a blade whetted on a speeding wheel. She all but clawed her way on top of him to sink her teeth into his shoulder, lost her breath as he flipped her back again and found her white-hot center with his fingers.

The orgasm ripped through her, a glorious shock. Dazzled and drugged with it, she groped for him.

"God. God. Please. Now."

Thank you, Jesus, he thought, because it *had* to be now. When he drove himself into her, the earth didn't simply move. It quaked.

The world shook; the air thundered. And his body lit up, then erupted with triumph and pleasure, with a desperate, dizzying demand for more.

She clung to him, arms and legs locked in the wild ride full of sound and speed. Fast, rhythmic slaps of flesh to heat-slicked flesh, the crazed creak of the bed, the pants of labored breath overrode the lazy beat of the sea to shore whispering at the windows.

He felt himself fall away, just fall away into that whirl of sound, into the rush, into the stupefying pleasure.

Into her.

He'd have sworn he flew, too far, too high, into a moment of exquisite pain, before he just emptied.

They didn't move. It had gone dark sometime during the race to the bedroom and the sprint to the finish line, but he wasn't entirely sure he hadn't been struck blind.

Better to stay just as he was for the time being. Besides, the sensation of her body beneath his, sleek and toned and absolutely still, felt so damn good. Though she'd gone lax, her heart continued to rage against his. The rapid beat made him feel like a god.

"And I wasn't sure I'd pull it off."

"Oh, you pulled it way off. I may never get it on again."

He blinked. "Did I say that out loud?"

The laugh rumbled in her throat. "I won't hold it against you. I wasn't sure either of us would pull it off. I feel like I must be glowing. I can't understand why I'm not illuminating the whole room like a torch."

"I think we went blind."

When she felt him shift, Abra opened

her eyes, looked into the glint of his. "No, I can see you. It's just dark. There's only a quarter moon tonight."

"I feel like I landed on it."

"A trip to the moon." It made her smile as she brushed at his hair. "I like it. All I need now is some water, before I die of thirst, and maybe some food before we try for the return trip."

"I can supply the water. I keep some in the . . ." He rolled over, reached out for the nightstand, and ended up on the floor. "What the hell!"

"Are you okay?" She scrambled to the edge of the bed to stare down at him. "Why are you on the floor?"

"I don't know."

"Where's the lamp? Where's the night-stand?"

"I don't know. Did we end up in an alternate universe?" He rubbed his hip as he got to his feet, and stood straining to see while his eyes adjusted to the dark. "Something's not right. The terrace doors are supposed to be over there, but they're over there. And the . . . Wait a minute."

Cautious, he moved in the darkened room, cursed when his toe stubbed against a chair, skirted it, then groped for the bedside lamp.

The light flashed on.

"Why am I over here?" she asked him.

"Because the bed's over there. It was over here. Now it's over there and turned sideways."

"We moved the bed?"

"It was over here," he repeated, then walked back to her. "Now it's over here." He got back in as she sat up beside him. Both of them sat, studying the empty space between the two nightstands.

"That's a lot of pent-up sexual energy," she decided.

"I'd say massive amounts. Has this ever happened to you before?"

"It's a first."

"Me, too." He turned, grinned at her. "I'm going to mark it down on the calendar."

Laughing, she twined her arms around his neck. "Let's leave it here for now, see if we can move it back again later."

"There are a lot of other beds in this house. We could experiment. I think . . . Shit. Shit. Pent-up sexual energy. Abra, the bed's here, the nightstands, and the condoms are over there. I didn't think. I couldn't think."

"We're okay. I'm on birth control. How long have you been storing up your sexual energy?"

"Some over a year."

"Same here. I think that area of safety's covered, so to speak. Why don't we hydrate, eat, then see what else we can move?"

"I really like the way your mind works."

She was right about the soup. It was exceptional. He'd begun to think she was very rarely wrong about anything.

They sat at the kitchen island, he in flannel pants and a sweatshirt, Abra in one of his grandmother's robes. Eating soup, hunks of bread, drinking wine, talking about movies she claimed he had to see or books they'd both read.

He told her about his find in the house's library. "It's interesting, definitely written by a woman with a male pseudonym."

"That sounds biased and a little snarky."

"Not meant that way," he claimed.

"*Writer*'s a word without gender. But this struck me as female, especially given the era it was written in. It's a little flowery, definitely romantic. I liked it, even if it should've been labeled fiction."

"I'd like to be the judge of that. Can I borrow it?"

"Sure. I thought, given the trench, I'd take a pass through the library here, read what we've got on the legend, the *Calypso*, on Nathanial Broome and my ancestor Violeta."

"Now that's a project I can get behind. I always meant to ask Hester if I could borrow some of the books, but never did. I tend toward fiction or self-help."

Since he considered her one of the most self-aware and contented women he'd ever met, he had to ask, "What help does your self need?"

"Depends on the day. But when I first moved here I still felt a little unsteady. I read a lot of books on finding balance, dealing with trauma."

He laid a hand over hers. "I don't want to bring back bad memories, but I want to ask how long he got."

"Twenty years. The prosecutor was pushing for rape, battery, attempted murder, and he would've faced life. So they pleaded it down to aggravated sexual assault, adding in the knife, and held to the maximum. I didn't think he'd take it, but—"

"Factor in the stalking, the premeditation in breaking into your place, eyewitnesses in your neighbors. He was smart to take it. How are you about the twenty?"

"I'm good with it. Satisfied with it. When he comes up for parole, I intend to go in, speak to the board. I intend to take the photos of me after the assault. I like to think it's not vindictive, but—"

"It's not."

"I don't really care if it is, and I've made peace with my own needs on it. I do know I feel lighter with him in prison, and I'll do what I can to keep him there. Away from me, away from someone else he might focus on. So I found my balance, and every now and then I like a little boost, or something that opens me up to a different way of thinking."

With a smile, she spooned up more soup. "How's your balance, Eli?"

"Right now I feel like I could do hand-springs across a tightrope."

She laughed into her wine. "Sex is the best invention."

"No argument here."

"Maybe you should write some sex into your book, unless you think it's too female and flowery."

"I sense a challenge."

"Wouldn't you like your hero to find his balance in the end?" She leaned over, brushed her lips lightly to his. "I'd love to help you with your research."

"I'd be a fool to say no." Eyes on hers, he slid his hand up her thigh. "The kitchen floor still looks good."

"We should see how it feels."

As she angled toward him, the doorbell chimed.

"Damn it. Hold that thought."

He found Vinnie at the door, and real-ized he hadn't hit balance when the sight of a cop, even an old friend, still made his heart lurch.

"Hey, Vinnie."

"Eli. I had a call out this way, and was heading back in since my shift's up. I wanted to stop by to . . . Oh, hi, Abs."

"Hi, Vinnie." She stepped up beside Eli. "Come in out of the cold."

"Oh, well . . . bad timing. I can talk to you tomorrow, Eli."

"Come on in, Vinnie. We were just having some soup Abra made."

"Do you want a bowl?" she asked him.

"No. Thanks. No. Ah, I had a dinner break a couple hours ago, and . . ."

"I've got Eli on twice-weekly massages," Abra said easily. "And I'm making sure he eats, which is something he's been neglecting. And we're having sex. That's a new development."

"Okay. Jesus, Abra. Man."

"Why don't you go in and sit down with Eli? I'll get you some coffee."

"I don't want to get in the way."

"Too late," Abra said as she walked off.

Eli just grinned after her. "She's amazing."

"Yeah, well. Look, Eli, I like you. At least I liked you back in the day, and I'm inclined to like you now. Just don't mess up with her."

"I'll be working hard not to. We might as well go in and sit down." He turned toward the parlor, stopped when Vinnie studied the massage table. "She won't take no."

"Not on much." Vinnie hooked his thumbs in his uniform belt. "Anyway, Eli, I know Detectives Corbett and Wolfe came to see you."

"Yeah, we had an interesting chat earlier."

"Corbett's straight and smart—and thorough. I don't know Wolfe, but it's pretty clear he's got his teeth in this bone, and he's not giving it up."

"He's had his teeth in me for a year." Eli dropped down on the sofa. "I've got the scars."

"He's going to chomp them into Abra now, and into me."

"I'm sorry, Vinnie."

Vinnie shook his head, lowered to a chair. "I'm not looking for sorry. But I figured you should know he's going to do what he can to discredit Abra as your alibi, and take a swing at me as I play into it."

"He's a bully." Abra walked in with a mug of coffee. "A dangerous one, I think."

Vinnie took the coffee, stared into it.

"He's a hard-nosed, experienced cop with a pretty solid rep. My take? Coming up against you, Eli, when his gut and the circumstantial says you're guilty as black-eyed sin, then not being able to prove it's got him pissed."

"I can't be guilty of murder just to keep his record clear."

"He knew Duncan."

"I got that."

"I haven't looked deep, but my sense is they knew each other pretty well. So now he's got more motivation to break you down. And this time, you've got an alibi."

"Which would be me."

"And you," Vinnie said to Abra, "he's going to see as a liar, protecting your . . ."

"The word these days is 'lover,'" Abra put in. "He can try to discredit me. He's doomed to failure. And I can see on your face you're thinking it was easier, clearer when I wasn't sleeping with Eli. I've—We've complicated things. But the truth's still the truth, Vinnie."

"I just want you to know he's going to stir things up. He'll dig. He's already dug as far as can be dug with Eli, so you need to expect him to do the same on you, Abs."

"It doesn't worry me. Eli knows about Derrick, Vinnie."

"Okay." With a nod, Vinnie drank some coffee. "I don't want you worried. Just prepared."

"I appreciate it."

"Have they run ballistics?" Eli asked him.

"I can't give you details of the investigation." Vinnie shrugged, drank more coffee. "Your grandmother's got a nice antique gun collection upstairs. She let me see it once. I don't recall any .32 calibers up there."

"No," Eli said just as casually. "Nothing like that in the collection, or in the house."

"Well . . . I'd better get going. Thanks for the coffee, Abra."

"Anytime."

Eli rose to walk him to the door. "I appreciate you coming by like this, Vinnie. I won't forget it."

"You look out for her. She knows just how vicious people can be, but she's still inclined to think they won't be. Stay out of trouble."

I thought I was, Eli mused. But trouble had a way of wiggling its way through the smallest opening.

When he stepped back into the parlor, she straightened from adding a log to the fire. Then she turned, flames licking and rising behind her back.

"However it happened," he began, "whoever's to blame, you being here, being with me, puts you in the crosshairs. Your personal life, what happened to you, choices you've made, your work, your family, your friends—all of everything is going to be turned over, dug into, examined, talked about. You've been through something like this once, and you put it behind you. But staying here will put it in front of you again."

"That's true. And?"

"You should take some time to think about that, to decide if you really want to put yourself under that kind of scrutiny."

Her gaze stayed calm and quiet on his. "Which means you don't think I have thought about it, and doesn't say much for your opinion of my sense of self or my ability to reason out consequences for actions."

"That's not what I meant."

"You're not going to save me from myself, Eli. I do fine in that area. I'm not opposed to you looking out for me because I believe, strongly, people should look out for each other, but Vinnie's wrong. Voices carry in empty houses, and I have excellent hearing," she pointed out. "I do know how vicious people can be, but I'm not inclined to think they won't be. I'm inclined to hope they won't be, and that's very different."

"They usually are, given half a chance."

"It's a shame you feel that way, but given what's happened, what's happening now, it's hard to blame you. Still, we could have an interesting debate on that subject sometime. But right now, do you want to know what I think?"

"Yeah, I do."

"I think while the kitchen floor looks good, that couch looks even better. Want to try it out and see?"

"Yeah." He walked toward her. "I do."

She stayed. When they finally made it back to bed, finally exhausted themselves, she learned he wasn't a snuggler. But he earned half a point rather than a full one in her score book by not objecting to snuggling.

She woke in light like a gray pearl, when he shifted to ease away from her. "Mmm. You getting up?"

"Yeah. Sorry I woke you."

"It's okay." But she curled around him again. "What time is it?"

"About six. You should go back to sleep."

"I have an eight-o'clock class." She nuzzled at his throat. "What's on your plate?"

"Usually coffee and work." But he could adjust that, he thought, and ran a hand down her long, bare back.

"Then you have time to join me for a short morning stretch and I'll fix you breakfast as a reward before I go."

"We can stretch right here."

She didn't object when he rolled over, slipped inside her. Instead, she sighed deep, smiled into his eyes. "A wonderful way to salute the sun."

Slow and easy, like floating on a quiet sea. The lazy counterpoint to the night's rush and thunder slid through her like the sunrise, like that promise of the fresh and the new and the hopeful.

She could see him now, the lines of his face, the clarity of his eyes with the dark trouble still shadowed in them.

Her nature urged her to banish shadows, to bring the light. So she gave herself to him for his pleasure, for her own. She took that gentle ride up the crest, down again, and watched for a moment, for their moment, that light burn through.

She lay with him, wrapped around him, and basked in that moment.

"You should think about me today."

He turned his head to brush his lips against her throat. "I think the odds are pretty good on that."

"Deliberately think of me today," she amended. "Say around noon. And I'll deliberately think of you. We'll send strong, positive, sexy thoughts into the universe."

He lifted his head. "Sexy thoughts into the universe."

"It couldn't hurt. Where do writers and artists and inventors and all the creative people get their ideas?" She lifted her hands, circled her index fingers in the air.

"Is that where they come from?"

"They're out there." Lowering her hands, she ran her fingers in a firm line down his spine, up again. "People have to open up, reach for them. Positive or negative thoughts, it's up to you. One of the ways to grab the good ones is to start the day opening up."

"I think we accomplished that."

"Step two." She nudged him aside, made a dash toward the bathroom. "See if you can hunt me up a pair of sweat-pants or shorts. Drawstrings would work. I'm using one of the spare toothbrushes stocked in the cabinet in here."

"Okay." She'd know more about the amenities than he did, he figured, as she'd probably put them in there.

He found a pair of shorts with a draw-string and dragged on a pair of sweats himself.

"They're going to be too big," he told her when she came out.

"I'll make do." She pulled them on,

began adjusting them. "You can meet me in the gym."

"Oh. I really—"

"We've spent considerable time naked and intimate, Eli."

Hard to argue when she stood there in his shorts, naked from the waist up.

"I think breathing and stretching comes pretty low on the list of embarrassments." She grabbed her white tank, wiggled into it. "I need a hair tie—got one in my bag. In the gym," she repeated, and left him.

Maybe he stalled a little. It wasn't embarrassment, he told himself. He just preferred starting the day with coffee, like normal people.

But he found her in the gym, sitting cross-legged on one of the two yoga mats she'd laid out, her hands on her knees, her eyes closed.

She should've looked ridiculous in his shorts. So why did she look sexy, and peaceful, and just exactly right?

Eyes still closed, she reached over and patted the second mat. "Sit down, be comfortable. Take a couple minutes to breathe."

"I usually breathe all day. At night, too."

Her lips curved a little. "Conscious breathing now. In through the nose—expanding the belly like blowing up a balloon, out through the nose, deflating the balloon. Long, deep, even breaths. Belly rises and falls. Relax your mind."

He didn't think he was very good at relaxing his mind, unless he was writing. And that wasn't relaxing it but using it. He'd get coffee quicker if he breathed, though.

"Now, inhale your arms up till your palms touch, exhale them down. Inhale up"—she continued in that quiet, soothing voice—"exhale down."

She had him stretch over his crossed legs, from side to side. Over one extended leg, the other, over both. He relaxed into it, a little. Until she told him to stand at the front of his mat.

Then she smiled at him, the day dawning behind the window at her back. If she'd asked him to twist his body into a pretzel, he'd have given it a shot.

Instead she had him repeat vertically what they'd done on the floor. Just breathing, reaching, bending, with a few variations of lunges, all as slow and easy as their morning lovemaking.

In the end she had him lie on his back, palms up, eyes closed. She spoke of letting go, of inhaling light, exhaling dark, while she rubbed his temples with her fingertips.

By the time she brought him back, had him sitting again, bending forward to—as she called it—seal his practice, he felt like he'd had a little nap, in a warm sea.

"Nice." She gave him a pat on the knee. "Ready for breakfast?"

He looked into her eyes. "They don't pay you enough."

"Who?"

"Whoever comes to your classes."

"You don't know what I charge for my classes."

"It isn't enough."

"I charge more for private lessons." Grinning, she walked her fingers up his arm. "Interested?"

"Well . . ."

"Think about it," she said as she rose. "And for now, do those neck stretches I showed you every couple hours when you're at the keyboard. Those and the shoulder rolls for now," she continued as they started downstairs. "Since I'm smelling spring, I'm thinking spring omelet. You can make the coffee."

"You don't have to go to the trouble. You have a class."

"I've got time, especially if I can come back for my massage equipment when I bring the groceries and do the house."

"It feels—I feel—a little weird having you take care of the house, and cook, and everything when we're sleeping together."

She opened the refrigerator, began taking out what she wanted. "Are you firing me?"

"No! I just think it feels like taking advantage."

She got a cutting board, a knife. "Who initiated sex?"

"Technically you did, but only because you beat me to it."

"That's nice to hear." After washing the asparagus and mushrooms, she brought them to the board to slice. "I like working here. I love the house. I love cooking, and I get a lot of satisfaction seeing my cooking work for you. You've put on a little healthy weight since you've been eating it. I like sex with you. Why don't we say if any of those things change, I'll let you know, and we'll deal with it. If you decide you don't like how I take care of the house, or cook, or don't want to have sex with me, you let me know, and we'll deal with it. Fair enough?"

"More than."

"Good." She got out a frying pan, olive oil. Smiled. "How about that coffee?"

Fourteen

He couldn't call time with Abra a routine, but he supposed they developed a kind of pattern over the next few days.

She cooked, either at Bluff House or her cottage. They walked the beach, and he, too, began to smell spring.

He grew accustomed to having food put in front of him, to having a house filled with flowers, candles, her scent, her voice.

Her.

His work progressed to the point where he began to think he actually had something other than an escape from his own head.

He read, he worked, he dragged himself into his grandmother's gym. And for a few precious days even the idea of murder seemed to belong to another world.

Then Detective Corbett came to his door, with a team of cops and a search warrant.

"We have a warrant to search the premises, any outbuildings and vehicles."

Stomach knotted, Eli took the warrant, skimmed it. "Then I guess you'd better get started. It's a big house."

He stepped back, spotted Wolfe. Saying nothing, Eli walked out, grabbed the kitchen phone and took it out to the terrace to call his lawyer. Better safe—he'd learned that the hard way—than sorry.

Yeah, he could smell spring, he thought when he'd finished the call. But spring brought storms just like winter. He'd just have to ride this one out like the rest.

Corbett came out. "That's quite a collection of guns upstairs."

"It is. And unloaded, unfired, as far as I know, for at least a generation."

"I'd appreciate the keys to the cases."

"All right." Eli went inside, wound through to the library and the drawer in his grandfather's desk. "You know damn well none of those guns fired the shot that killed Duncan."

"Then you don't have a problem."

"I've got a problem as long as Wolfe ignores evidence, timelines, witness statements and everything else but me." Eli handed over the keys.

Corbett's face remained impassive. "I appreciate the cooperation."

"Detective," Eli said as Corbett turned to go. "When you finish with this, find nothing? If you come back without real evidence, real motive, actual probable cause, I'm going to file suit against your department and the BPD for harassment."

Now Corbett's eyes flicked just a touch of heat. "That sounds like a threat."

"You know it's not. What it is, it's enough. It's way past enough."

"I'm doing my job, Mr. Landon. If you've got nothing to hide, the more thoroughly I do it, the sooner you're in the clear."

"Tell that to someone who hasn't been hounded for more than a year."

Eli walked out, got a jacket. He knew he shouldn't leave the house, but he couldn't stomach watching them go through Bluff House, through his things, through his family's things. Not again.

Instead he went to the beach, watched the water, the birds, the kids he realized must be on spring break.

His mother wanted him to come home for Easter dinner. He'd intended to go, to ask Abra to come with him. He'd been ready for it, primed for it—the family event, with Abra in it, the big ham Alice would bake and his mother would insist on glazing herself. The baskets, the candy, the colored eggs.

The tradition of it. And the comfort of it.

But now . . . It seemed smarter to stay put, to stay out of everyone's way, everyone's life, until the police found Duncan's killer.

Lindsay's killer.

Or his own investigator found something that turned at least one key in one lock.

Not that that angle was going anywhere yet.

He looked up at Laughing Gull Cottage. Where was Abra? he wondered.

Teaching a class? Running errands for a client or cleaning a home? Tucked into her own kitchen cooking, or in the little room she used for making earrings and pendants?

He'd been crazy to get involved with her, to drag her into this mess. Or, more accurately, let her push her way into it.

She had things in Bluff House. Clothes, shampoo, a hairbrush—little bits of intimacy. His stomach clenched into angry knots as he pictured the police pawing through what was hers because she'd left it in what was his.

He knew the comments, the smirks, the speculation—and worse, the guilt by association that would root in Wolfe's brain.

They'd search her house next if they could get a judge to sign off.

The thought galled him, infuriated him and sent him back to the house for the phone he hadn't thought to take with him.

Once again he took it out to the terrace, and once again contacted his lawyer.

"Change your mind?" Neal said when he came on the line. "I can be there in a couple hours."

"No, no point. Listen, I'm involved, on a personal level, with Abra Walsh."

"I already knew that, unless you're about to tell me you're sleeping with her."

"That's what I'm telling you."

He expected the sigh, and wasn't disappointed. "All right, Eli. Since when?"

"A few days ago. I understand about perception, Neal, so don't bother. The facts remain the facts. I'm asking for you to keep an ear to the ground in case Wolfe pushes for a search warrant for her place. Laughing Gull Cottage. She rents, but I can find out the owner if you need it. I don't want her hassled over this. She isn't part of it."

"She's your alibi, Eli. The cops have squat on you for Duncan, but she's a big part of the reason they have squat. It wouldn't hurt for her to get her own lawyer. She knows how it works."

His body, his voice stiffened. "Excuse me?"

"Eli, you're my client. She's your alibi. Wolfe insinuated the two of you were lovers when Lindsay was alive. Do you think I didn't run background on her? Exactly as you'd have done in my place? She's clean, she's smart, and from all accounts, she can hold her own. There sure as hell isn't a law against the two of you having a relationship, so relax. If they take a pass at her, she'll come through it. But she should get a lawyer. I'm not telling you anything you don't know. Is there anything you're not telling me?"

"No. She brought me some damn stew, Neal, and ended up getting attacked and tossed in the middle of a murder investigation. I want to do something. God damn it, I want to do something besides just standing here."

"You did. You called me. I reached out to a contact on the BPD. Wolfe pushed and pushed hard for this warrant. He's about used up his currency where you're concerned. Let this play out, Eli. It's going nowhere. And the Piedmonts' suit has throttled back to a few mutters to reporters who bother to listen to them these days."

"There are cops swarming all over my grandmother's house. It's hard to shrug that off."

"Let it play out," Neal repeated. "Then close the door. If they push again, they're going to get slapped with a suit. Trust me, Eli, the brass doesn't want that—the wrangling or the publicity. They'll shut Wolfe down. Let me know when they're out of there."

"Sure."

Eli hung up. Maybe his superiors would shut Wolfe down, officially. But Eli didn't believe for a moment that would stop him.

Because of an emergency call for a grocery run due to a preschooler with strep, Abra arrived a bit later than she liked for her church-basement yoga class.

She dashed in. "Sorry! Natalie's kid's down with strep, and she needed some supplies. She won't make it to class, obviously."

Even as she set down her mat, her tote, the vibes hit her. She caught the speculative looks, and more, the furious flush on Maureen's face.

"Something up?" she said, casually enough, as she unzipped her hoodie.

"There's police—a lot of police—at Bluff House. Don't give me that look, Maureen," Heather snapped. "I didn't make it up. I saw them. I think they must be arresting Eli Landon for killing that poor man. And maybe for his wife, too."

"A bunch of police?" Abra repeated as calmly as possible.

"Oh, at least a dozen. Maybe more. I slowed down when I drove by, saw police going in and out."

"So you think they'd send a dozen, or more, cops to arrest one man? Did they bring in a SWAT team, too?"

"I understand you'd be defensive." Heather's voice dripped with sugary sympathy. "Considering your relationship."

"Are you considering that?"

"Well, for heaven's sake, Abra, it's not like you've been making a secret of it. People have seen your car parked there late at night or early in the morning."

"So wondering why it takes a platoon

of cops to arrest one man—one, since I happened to be with him, I know didn't kill *that poor man*—is defensive because Eli and I are sleeping together?"

"I'm not criticizing you, honey."

"Oh, bullshit!" Maureen exploded. "You've been standing around here pretending to feel sorry for Abra while gleefully questioning her judgment. And you've already arrested, tried and convicted Eli without knowing *dick* about *squat*."

"I'm not the one suspected of murder—*twice*—or with police in my house. I don't blame Abra, but—"

"Why don't you stop right there," Abra advised. "I don't blame you either, Heather, for gossiping or for jumping to conclusions about someone you don't even know. For now, let's consider this a no-blame area, and we can get started."

"All I did was say what I saw with my own eyes." And now those eyes brimmed with tears. "I have children. I'm allowed to be concerned we may have a murderer living right here in Whiskey Beach."

"We're all concerned." Greta Parrish patted Heather's shoulder. "Especially

since we don't know who killed that detective from the city, or why. I think we're
better off sticking together than we are
pointing fingers."

"I wasn't pointing fingers. There are
police at Bluff House. That PI was from
Boston, where Eli Landon's from, and
somebody shot him here, where Eli
Landon *is*. I have every right to talk about
it, and to be worried about my family."

Choking on tears, Heather grabbed her
things and fled.

"Now she's the victim," Maureen
sighed.

"Okay, Maureen. Okay." Abra drew a
long breath. "Let's just clear the air.
Heather's upset. Someone was killed.
We're all upset and concerned. I know Eli
wasn't responsible, because I was with
him the night it happened. He can't be in
two places at once. My personal life is
my business unless I choose to share it.
If anyone's uncomfortable with my personal choices, that's fine. If anyone wants
to cancel their classes with me, I'll issue
refunds, no problem. Otherwise let's take
seats on our mats for a minute, and
breathe."

She unrolled her own mat, sat. When the others did the same, the fist clenched in her belly loosened a little.

Though she couldn't find her center, her balance, her own sense of calm, she took the class through the hour.

Maureen lingered after the class ended. Abra expected no less.

"Your place or mine?" Maureen asked.

"Mine. I have a cleaning job in an hour, I need to change."

"Good. You can give me a lift. I walked."

"Sundaes last night?"

"Toaster Strudel this morning. I shouldn't have them in the house, but I'm weak."

"Prepare to be weaker," Abra warned as they walked out together. "I made brownies."

"Damn you."

They piled into the car. "I'm trying to consider the source."

"The source is an idiot."

Abra sighed. "She can be, but so can we all."

"Idiot is Heather's default."

"No, gossiping is her default, and you and I both enjoy it from time to time. And

occasionally between times. I'm also trying to remember she does have kids, and
tends to be overprotective by my gauge.
But I don't have kids."

"I do, and she's way over the top. She'd
put GPS implants in her kids if she could
get away with it. Don't sit there being tolerant and understanding. She crossed a
line. Everybody, including her best bud,
Winnie, knew it. Jesus, Abra, she was
gloating about seeing police at Bluff
House."

"I know it. I know it." Abra pulled up at
the cottage with a squeal of brakes.
"Most of the gloat was because she got
to announce it, but there was plenty left
over for Eli's misery. I'm *not* tolerant and
understanding." She shoved out of the
car, snatched her bag, heaved the door
shut. "I'm pissed."

"Good. Me, too. Let's eat a whole
bunch of brownies."

"I want to go down there," Abra said as
they walked to the door. "But I'm afraid
I'll just make it harder for him. And I want
to go hunt down Heather and give her
one good bitch slap, and that would only
make me feel crappy after."

"Yeah, but it'd feel good doing it."

"It really would." Leaving her bag by the door, Abra walked straight to the kitchen, pulled the clear wrap off a plate of brownies.

"What if I bitch-slapped her and you just watched?" At home, Maureen grabbed napkins while Abra put on the kettle. "Would you still feel crappy?"

"Probably." Abra grabbed a brownie, bit in while she gestured with her free hand. "She thinks I'm lying about being with Eli when Duncan was killed. She had that 'You poor, deluded thing, I'm worried about you' look on her face."

"I *hate* that look." In solidarity, Maureen bit into her own brownie. "It's superior, fake and infuriating."

"If she thinks I'm lying, maybe the police do, too. That worries me a lot more."

"They've got no reason to think you're lying."

"I'm sleeping with him."

"You weren't when this happened."

"I am now." She took another bite of brownie before dealing with the tea. "I like sleeping with him."

"I suspected that was why you're doing so much of it."

"He's good in bed."

"You're bordering on bragging, but under the circumstances, continue."

With a half laugh, Abra moved her vase of baby iris from the center of her kitchen table to the stone-colored counter, then set down the teacups. "It's really great sex."

"Unsubstantiated. Provide an example."

"We moved the bed."

"People often move beds, couches, tables. It's called rearranging the furniture."

"While we were in it, having sex."

"That can happen."

Abra shook her head, got up for a pen. "Here's the bed," she said as she sketched. "Against this wall—the first time we had sex. And when we finished having sex, the bed was over here." She drew a line, curved it, sketched in the bed. "From there, to there, and turned sideways."

Munching brownie, Maureen studied the napkin. "You're making that up."

With a grin, Abra swiped a finger over her heart.

"Is it on wheels?"

"No, it's not on wheels. The power of repressed sexual energy unleashed is an awesome thing."

"Now I'm jealous, but I can flip that by knowing, without doubt, Heather has never moved the bed."

"I'll tell you what really pissed me off. Her acting like I'm as reckless as one of those women who write to serial killers in prison. The ones who fall in love with some guy who strangled six women with shoelaces. I don't know how Eli deals with it, I swear, how he deals with that cloud of suspicion constantly over his head."

"It must be easier for him now, having you."

"I hope so." Abra breathed again. "I hope so. I have feelings for him."

"Are you in love with him?" Abruptly concerned, Maureen licked chocolate from her thumb. "It's only been a few weeks, Abra."

"I'm not saying I'm in love with him. I'm not saying I'm not. I'm saying I have feelings for him. I had them the first time I met him, though I think that was mostly sympathy. He looked so wrecked, so tired, so sad—and with this awful anger under it that must be terrible to hold in, day after day. And as I've gotten to know him, there's still sympathy, but there's respect, too. It takes a lot of courage, a lot of spine to get through what he's been through. There's attraction, obviously, and affection."

"I felt like he relaxed and enjoyed himself the night we hung out at the pub."

"He needs people, and I think even with his family, he's felt alone for a long time." Being alone was, in Abra's opinion, sporadically necessary for recharging self. Being lonely was a state she pitied, and wanted to fix. "I've watched him relaxing and enjoying a little bit more all the time. He's got humor and a really good heart. I'm worried about him now."

"Why do you think all those cops are at Bluff House?"

"If Heather wasn't exaggerating, I think they must've gotten a search warrant. I told you before that Detective Wolfe is convinced Eli killed Lindsay. He's obsessed with proving it. And now with proving he killed again."

"They have to *dis*prove you to do that." Maureen reached over for Abra's hand. "They're going to question you again, aren't they?"

"I'm pretty sure of it. Maybe you and Mike, too."

"We'll handle it. And we'll all handle gossips like Heather, too. I wonder if she'll come to your next class here, at the cottage."

"If she does, no bitch-slapping."

"Spoilsport. Just for that, I'm taking a brownie for the road. If you need me, you call me. I'll be home for the rest of the day. I've got to get some paperwork done before the kids get home."

"Thanks." Abra moved in for a hug as they rose. "For being just the right antidote to the idiot."

When Maureen left, she went to her bedroom to change. Two brownies before noon made her feel just a little bit sick, but she'd get over it. And once she finished work for the day, she was going to Eli. For better or worse.

It took hours. When they'd cleared his office, Eli retreated to it while cops swarmed the house. Once he'd put his things back in order, he'd busied himself with calls, e-mails, neglected paperwork.

He'd hated calling his father, but trouble had a way of leaking. Better the family hear directly than through other means. He didn't bother playing it down, his father was too smart for that. But at least he could reassure him and, through him, the rest of the family.

The cops would find nothing because there was nothing to find.

He couldn't bring himself to write, not with the police, metaphorically at least, breathing down his neck. He shifted into research instead, eating away at the day by shifting from book research to research on Esmeralda's Dowry.

He turned at the rap on the doorjamb. He acknowledged Corbett by swiveling the chair around, but didn't get up, didn't speak.

"We're wrapping it up."

"All right."

"About that digging in the basement."

"What about it?"

"That's a hell of a trench down there." Corbett waited a beat, but Eli didn't respond. "No clue who's responsible?"

"If I had a clue I'd have told Deputy Hanson."

"It's his theory and, I'm told, yours, that whoever broke in the night Duncan was killed dug it. And since he sure as hell didn't do all that in one night, it wasn't the first time he'd gotten in."

"It's a theory."

Irritation flicked over Corbett's face before he stepped in, closed the door at his back. "Look, Wolfe's on his way back to Boston. If he comes back, unless he comes back with conclusive evidence against you, he's on his own. There's nothing tying you to Duncan's murder at this time. The only connection is, person or persons unknown hired him to report on your movements. I don't see you for it, for all the reasons discussed in our last meeting. Added to it, I've got no reason to doubt Abra Walsh's word, even though my investigative powers tell me she's spent a few nights here since, and not on the sofa downstairs."

"Last I checked sex between consenting adults was still legal in Massachusetts."

"And thank God for that. What I'm telling you is you're not on my radar for this. The problem is nobody's on my radar for this. Yet. What I've got is a break-in, an assault and a murder, in the same night. That makes me wonder. So if you do get a clue who's been digging down there, it'd be in your best interest to let me know."

He turned for the door, paused, turned back to face Eli. "I'd be pissed off if I had a bunch of cops going through my house all day. I'm going to tell you I handpicked them. If we didn't find anything, there's nothing to find. And I should further add that even though they were careful, this is a damn big house with a hell of a lot of stuff. Some of it may not be back in place."

Eli hesitated as Corbett opened the door, then took the leap. "I think whoever dug that trench either pushed my grandmother on the stairs or caused her to fall. Then left her there."

Corbett stepped back, shut the door again. "I've given that some thought myself." Without waiting for the invitation, he crossed over, sat down. "She doesn't remember anything?"

"No. She can't even remember getting up, coming downstairs. The head trauma . . . the doctors say it's not unusual. Maybe she'll remember, maybe not. Maybe parts, maybe all, maybe none. She could've died, and probably would have if Abra hadn't found her. Shooting a PI's not a far reach from pushing an old lady down the stairs and leaving her to die. This is her place, her heart's here, and she may never be able to live here, at least not on her own, again. I want to know who's responsible for that."

"Tell me where you were that night, the night she fell."

"Jesus Christ."

"Let's be thorough, Mr. Landon. Do you remember?"

"Yeah, I remember, because I'll never forget the look on my mother's face the next morning when she came in to tell me, after Abra called the house. I wasn't sleeping well. I hadn't slept well since . . .

in a long time. I moved in with my parents a few weeks after Lindsay's murder, so I was there the night of my grandmother's accident. My father and I ended up playing gin and drinking beer until about two. I guess I could've hauled my ass up here, tossed my grandmother down the steps, then hauled my ass back to Boston and settled in before my mother came in to tell me Gran was hurt and at the hospital."

Ignoring the comment, Corbett took out his book, made some notes. "There are a lot of valuables in this house."

"I know it, and I can't understand it. There's plenty you could basically stuff in your pockets and make a nice profit. But he spends hours, days, hacking at the basement floor."

"Esmeralda's Dowry."

"It's all I can come up with."

"Well, it's interesting. Any objection, if her doctors clear it, if I talk to your grandmother?"

"I don't want her upset, that's all. I don't want my family dragged through another mess. They've dealt with enough."

"I'll be careful."

"Why do you care?"

"Because I shipped a dead man back to Boston, and as far as I can tell, he was just doing his job. Because somebody broke into this house and might've done more than assault a woman if she hadn't defended herself and gotten away. Because you didn't kill your wife."

Eli started to speak, then whatever had been in his mind just slid away. "What did you say?"

"Do you think I didn't read and review every word of your file? You never changed your story. The wording, the delivery, but never the content. You weren't lying, and if it had been a crime of passion, as speculated, a good criminal defense lawyer—and you had a record of being one—would've covered his tracks a hell of a lot better."

"Wolfe thinks I did."

"Wolfe's gut tells him you did it, and I think he's got a good gut. This time it's wrong. It happens."

"Maybe your gut's wrong."

Corbett smiled thinly. "Whose side are you on here?"

"You're the first cop who's looked me in the face and said I didn't kill Lindsay. It takes some getting used to."

"The prosecutor didn't think you did it either. But you were all they had, and Wolfe was dead sure, so they pushed until they ran out of room."

Corbett rose. "You got a raw deal. You won't get one from me this time around. You've got my number if you think of anything relevant."

"Yeah, I've got it."

"We'll get out of your hair."

Alone, Eli sat back and tried to sort out his mixed feelings.

One cop saw him as innocent, one cop saw him as guilty. It felt good to be believed, to have the words still hanging in the air.

But any way he cut it, he was still stuck in the middle.

Fifteen

She worried how she'd find him. Depressed and brooding? Angry and dismissive?

Whatever his reaction, she couldn't blame him for it. His life had been disrupted, again, his morality questioned, again. And his privacy shattered—not only by the police, but by people like Heather. Again.

She prepared herself to be understanding, which might mean firm and matter-of-fact or supportive and sympathetic.

She didn't expect to find him in the

kitchen working at a cluttered island with a look of exasperation on his face and a bulb of garlic in his hand.

"Well. What's going on here?"

"Chaos. Which is apparently what happens when I try to cook."

She set aside the plate of brownies. "You're cooking?"

"'Try' is the operative word."

She found the trying both sweet and positive. "What are you trying?"

"Some chicken-and-rice thing." He shoved at his hair, scowled down at the mess he'd made. "I got it off the Internet under 'Cooking for Morons.'"

She came around the island, studied the printout of the recipe. "Looks good. Want some help?"

He turned the scowl on her. "Since I qualify as a moron in this area, I should be able to handle it."

"Great. Mind if I get a glass of wine?"

"Go ahead. You can pour me one, too. In a freaking tumbler."

Though she found cooking relaxing, she understood the frustrations of the novice or very sometimes cook. "What inspired this domestic bliss?" she asked as she got out glasses—wineglasses, despite his comment.

His eyes narrowed as she slipped into the butler's pantry for the wine. "Are you looking for a kick in the ass?"

"Actually, I'm looking for a nice pinot grigio," she called out. "Ah, here we go. I hope I'm invited to dinner," she continued as she brought the bottle back to the kitchen. "It's been a while since anyone's cooked for me."

"That was the idea." He watched her uncork the wine she'd very likely stocked herself in the wine cooler. "Is nine-one-one on speed dial?"

"Yes." She gave him a glass, and a friendly kiss on the cheek. "And thank you."

"Don't thank me until we rule out kitchen fire and food poisoning."

Willing to risk both, she sat on a stool, enjoyed her first sip of wine. "When's the last time you cooked anything that didn't come out of a can or a box?"

"Certain smug people smirk at food from cans and boxes."

"We do. Shame on us."

He turned his frown back on the garlic bulb. "I'm supposed to peel and slice this garlic."

"Okay."

When he just stared at her, she shifted, picked up the knife. "I'll demonstrate the procedure."

She tugged off a clove, held it up, then, setting it on the cutting board, gave it a kind of smack with the flat of the knife. The peel slid off, easy as a stripper's breakaway. Once she'd sliced it, she handed him back the rest of the bulb and the knife. "Got it?"

"Yeah." More or less. "We had a cook. When I was growing up, we always had a cook."

"Never too late to learn. You might even like it."

"I don't think that's going to happen. But I ought to be able to follow a recipe for morons."

"I have every faith."

He mimicked her slicing procedure, and felt marginally more hopeful when he didn't cut off a finger. "I know superior amusement when I'm standing in it."

"But it's superior and affectionate

amusement. Affectionate enough I'll teach you a trick."

"What trick?"

"A quick and easy marinade for that chicken."

Fear and loathing of the very idea echoed in his voice. "It doesn't say anything about marinade."

"It should. Hold on a minute." Rising, she went to the walk-in pantry. It gave her a jolt, seeing everything mixed up, out of order, jumbled. Then she remembered the police.

Saying nothing, she picked up a bottle of liquid margarita mix.

"I thought we were drinking wine."

"And so we are. The chicken's going to drink this."

"Where's the tequila?"

She laughed. "Not this time. Actually the chicken I use for tortilla soup drinks tequila, but this one just gets the mixer."

She got out a large bag, slid the chicken inside, dumped the liquid in with it. Sealed the bag, turned it a few times.

"That's it?"

"That's it, that's all."

"That part should've been for morons. I could've done that."

"Next time you will. It's good on fish, too, just FYI."

When she sat again, he went back to focusing on slicing garlic, and not his fingers. "The police were here today, all day, executing a search warrant." He glanced up. "And you already knew."

"That they were here, yes. I assumed the search." Reaching across the island, she brushed her fingers over his wrist. "I'm sorry, Eli."

"After they left I went through a couple of the rooms, put things back together. It started pissing me off again, so I decided to do something else."

"Don't worry about any of that. I'll take care of it."

He only shook his head. He intended to do a couple rooms at a time until the house was back to normal. Bluff House and everything in it were his responsibility now.

"It could've been worse. They could've trashed the place. They were thorough, but I've seen searches before, and they didn't just dump things."

"Fine, points for them, but it's still unfair. It's still wrong."

"Unfair and wrong happen every hour, every day."

"That's a sad and cynical viewpoint."

"Realistic," he corrected.

"The hell with that." Her temper spiked, making her realize it had been in there bubbling all along. "That's just an excuse to do nothing about it."

"Do you have any suggestions on what to do about a duly authorized warrant?"

"Having to accept it isn't the same as accepting it's just the way life goes. I'm not a lawyer, but I was raised by one, and it's pretty damn clear they had to push the envelope and push it hard to get a search warrant. And it's just as clear that Boston cop did the pushing."

"No argument."

"He should be sanctioned. You should sue him for harassment. You should be furious."

"I was. And I talked to my lawyer. If he doesn't back off, we'll talk about a suit."

"Why aren't you still mad?"

"Jesus, Abra, I'm making chicken from a recipe I got off the Internet because going around the house cleaning up cop mess pissed me off all over again, and I needed something to do with the mad. I don't have any more room for the mad."

"Looks like I do, and plenty of it. Just don't tell me unfair and wrong is just the way it goes. The system's not supposed to kick people around, and I'm not naive enough to believe it doesn't sometimes do just that. But I'm human enough to wish it didn't. . . . I need some air."

She shoved up, strode to the terrace doors, and out.

Considering, Eli set down the knife, absently swiped his hands on the hips of his jeans, and followed.

"Not helpful." She waved a hand at him as she paced around the terrace. "None of that was helpful, I know."

"I don't know about that."

"It's been stuck in my gut since I heard, even though I put two enormous brownies in there with it."

He knew the classic female reliance on chocolate, though he'd go for the beer instead. "How did you hear about it?"

"My morning yoga class, one of my students. Gossip's her religion. And that's bitchy. I hate being bitchy. Negative vibes," she added, shaking her arms as if to shake those vibes loose to be carried off by the breeze. "It's just that she's so goddamn self-righteous, so *concerned*, so full of it. The way she talked it was like they'd sent in an assault team to pin down the crazed killer, who I have the bad judgment to sleep with. And she acts like she's just worried for the community, and of course for me as you could smother me in my sleep or bash my head in or—

"Oh God, Eli." She stopped short, appalled. "I'm sorry. I'm sorry. That was stupid. Stupid and bitchy and insensitive—three things I most hate to be. I'm supposed to cheer you up or support you—or both. Instead I'm snapping and slapping at you, and saying horrible and stupid things. I'll stop. Or I'll go and take my crappy mood with me."

Anger and frustration flushed her face, he noted. Horrified apology lived in her eyes. And the breeze from the sea streamed through her hair so the wild curls danced.

"You know, my family, and the friends I

have left, don't talk about it. I feel them creeping around it like it's a . . . not an elephant in the room but a fucking T. rex. Sometimes I felt it would swallow me whole. But they crept around it, didn't want to talk about it any more than was absolutely necessary.

"'Don't upset Eli, don't make him think about it, don't depress him.' It was damn depressing knowing they couldn't or wouldn't tell me how they felt, what they thought other than the 'It'll all be fine, we're behind you.' I appreciated knowing they'd stand up for me, but the screaming silence of that T. rex, and what they felt inside, almost buried me."

"They love you," Abra began. "They were scared for you."

"I know it. I didn't just come here because Gran needed someone in the house. I'd already decided I had to get out of my parents' place, find a place—I couldn't or hadn't drummed up the energy to do it, but I knew I had to get away from that creeping silence—for myself and for them."

She understood exactly. A lot of people had crept around her after Derrick had attacked her. Afraid to say the wrong thing, afraid to say anything at all.

"It's been a terrible ordeal for all of you."

"And back again because today I had to tell them what was going on before they heard about it from somebody else."

Sympathy rolled through her again. She hadn't thought of that part. "It was hard to do."

"Had to be done. I played it down, so I guess that's the Landon way of handling things. You're the first one who's said what you think, what you're feeling, without filters. The first one who doesn't pretend that T. rex isn't right here, that somebody beat Lindsay's head in, and plenty think it was me."

"Thoughts and feelings and the passionate expressing of same were big in my house."

"Who'd have guessed?"

That teased out a wisp of a smile. "I wasn't going to say anything, but I must have used up my quota of restraint today when I didn't knock Heather on her butt."

"Tough girl."

"I know tai chi." She deliberately rose up on one leg in the Crane.

"I thought that was kung fu."

"Both are martial arts, so watch it. I'm not so mad anymore."

"Me, either."

She walked to him, linked her arms around his neck. "Let's make a deal."

"All right."

"Thoughts and feelings on the table, whenever necessary. And if a dinosaur walks into the room, we won't ignore it."

"Like cooking, you're going to be better at it than I am, but I'll give it a shot."

"Good enough. We should go back in so I can watch you cook."

"Okay. Now that we've . . . set the table, there are some things I should say."

He led the way back in. At the island, he picked up a pepper, studied it as he tried to figure out how to cut it.

"I'll demonstrate again."

While she topped, cored, sliced, he picked up his wine. "Corbett knows I didn't kill Lindsay."

"What?" Her head shot up, her hand stilled on the knife. "Did he say that to you?"

"Yeah. I've got no reason to think he's bullshitting me. He said he read the files, looked at everything, and he knows I didn't kill her."

"I've just completely changed my mind about him." She reached across to take Eli's hand for a moment. "No wonder you weren't as mad as I was."

"It lifted something. There's still plenty there, but it lifted some of it."

He tried his hand at slicing as he told her what Corbett had said.

"So he thinks it's possible, too, that whoever was in the house that night was in the house when Hester fell. And also possible that person shot Duncan."

"I think it's an angle he'll work. My lawyer would kick my ass, and rightfully, if he knew how I'd talked to Corbett, what I told him. But—"

"Sometimes you have to trust."

"I don't know about trust, but he's in the best position to find Duncan's killer, and if and when, we're going to get some answers."

He set the green pepper aside, picked up the red. "Meanwhile, there's someone out there who wants in this house, someone who's already attacked you, and may have hurt my grandmother. There's someone out there who's killed a man. Maybe it's the same person. Maybe it's a partner, or a competitor."

"Competitor?"

"A lot of people believe Esmeralda's Dowry exists. When treasure hunters found the wreck of the *Calypso* some thirty years ago, they didn't find the dowry. Haven't found it yet, and more have looked. Then again, there's no solid, corroborated evidence the dowry was on the ship when it wrecked on Whiskey Beach, or was ever on it. For all we know, it went down with the family's trusted liaison when the *Calypso* attacked the *Santa Caterina*. Or the liaison absconded with the dowry and lived fat and rich in the West Indies."

"Absconded. That sounds so classy."

"I'm a classy guy," he said, and finished the pepper. "Most of it's rumor, and a lot of rumors conflict. But anyone who'd go to the trouble this guy has, who'd kill, is a true believer."

"You think he'll try to get back in, while you're in the house?"

"I think he's taking some time, waiting for everything to settle down some. Then yeah, he's got to get back to it. That's one thing. The other is there are people in the village, people you know, you work for, you give classes to, who—like what's her name—are going to believe I did it, or at least wonder. That puts you in the middle—of possible harm, of certain gossip. I don't want you there."

"You can't control what other people say and do. And I think I've already proven I can defend myself in the possible-harm category."

"He didn't have a gun—or didn't think he needed to use it. Then."

She nodded. She couldn't deny the idea unnerved her, but she'd decided long before not to live her life in fear. "Killing me, or both of us, for that matter, in our sleep, or when I'm scrubbing the floor, only brings the cops in, again. I'd think that would be the last thing he wants. He needs to avoid attention, not only to himself but to Bluff House."

"That's logical. I'm looking at the big picture, and he hasn't used a lot of logic so far. I don't want you hurt. And I don't want you dealing with anything like you dealt with this morning again because you're involved with me."

Eyeing him coolly, she took a slow sip of wine. "Are you cooking me a farewell dinner, Eli?"

"I think it's better all around if we take a break."

" 'It's not you, it's me'—is that the next line?"

"Look. It's because I . . . because you matter to me. You've got some of your things in the house, and cops pawed through them today. Corbett may believe me, but Wolfe doesn't—and he won't stop. He'll do everything he can to discredit you, because it's your statement that takes me out of the equation in Duncan's murder."

"He'll do that whether or not I'm with you."

For a moment she considered how she felt about being protected—from harm, from ugly talk. She decided she felt fine about it, even if she didn't intend to allow it.

"I appreciate your position. You think you need to protect me, to shield me from harm, from gossip, from police scrutiny, and I find I like being with a man who would try to do that. But the fact is, Eli, I've already been through all of it, and more, once in my life. I'm not going to give up what I want on the chance I may go through some of it again. You matter to me, too."

She lifted her wine as she studied him. "I'd say we're at an impasse on this, except for one thing."

"What thing?"

"It's going to depend on how you answer the question. Which is, do you believe women should get equal pay for equal work?"

"What? Yes. Why?"

"Good, because this discussion would veer off into another avenue if you'd said no. Do you also believe women have the right of choice?"

"Jesus." He dragged a hand through his hair. "Yes." He saw exactly where she was taking him, and began to work on a rebuttal in his head.

"Excellent. That saves a long, heated debate. Rights come with responsibilities. It's my choice how I live my life, who

I'm with, who I care for. It's my right to make those choices, and I take the responsibility."

Her eyes narrowed on his face. "Oh, go right ahead."

"And what?"

"Raised by a lawyer," she reminded him. "I can *see* Mr. Harvard Law thinking through how to make a complicated argument to tangle up all my points. So go ahead. You can even throw out a couple of 'wherefores.' It won't make any difference. My mind's made up."

He shifted gears. "Do you understand how much I'll worry?"

Abra tipped her chin down, and those narrowed eyes went steely.

"That always works for my mother," he pleaded.

"You're not my mother," she reminded him. "Plus you don't have mother-power. You're stuck with me, Eli. If you cut me loose, it has to be because you don't want me, or you want someone else, or something else. If I walk away, it has to be for the same reasons."

Feelings on the table, he thought. "Lindsay didn't matter anymore, but every day I regret I couldn't do anything to stop what happened to her."

"She mattered once, and she didn't deserve to die that way. You'd have protected her if you could." She rose, went to him, slid her arms around his waist.

"I'm not Lindsay. You and I are going to look out for each other. We're both smart. We'll figure it out."

He drew her in, stood with his cheek pressed to hers. He wouldn't let anything happen to her. He didn't know how he would keep that unspoken promise to her, to himself, but he'd do whatever he needed to do to keep it.

"Smart? I'm following a recipe for morons."

"It's your first day on the job."

"I'm supposed to cube that chicken. What the hell does that mean?"

She drew back, then moved in again for a long, satisfying kiss. "Once again, I'll demonstrate."

She was in and out of the house. Early classes, cleaning jobs—his included—

marketing, private lessons, tarot readings for a birthday party.

He barely knew she was there when he was working, yet when she wasn't, he knew it acutely. The energy—he was starting to think like her—of the house seemed to wane without her in it.

They walked on the beach, and though he'd firmly decided cooking would never be a form of relaxation for him, he pitched in to help now and then.

He had a hard time imagining the house without her. Imagining his days, his nights without her.

Still, when she urged him to come the next night she worked at the bar, he made excuses.

He did want to continue researching the dowry, the ship, he reminded himself. He carried books out to the terrace to read there while he still had enough light, and settled down near the big terra-cotta pots Abra had planted with purple and yellow pansies.

As his grandmother did, he remembered, every spring.

They'd take the cool nights, even a frost

if they got another. And that was likely, he thought, despite the blessed warm spell they'd enjoyed the last few days.

People had flocked to the beach to take advantage. He'd even spotted Vinnie through his telescope, riding waves with the same flash and verve he'd had as a teenager.

The warm, the flowers, the voices carried on the wind, and the cheerful blue of the sea nearly lulled him into thinking everything was normal and settled and right.

It made him wonder what life would be like if all that were true. If he made his home here, did his work here, reclaimed his roots here without the nagging weight still chained around his waist.

Abra flitting in and out of the house, filling it with flowers, candles, smiles. With heat and light and a promise he didn't know he could ever make, ever keep.

Thoughts and feelings on the table, he remembered. But he didn't know how to describe what he felt with her or for her. Wasn't at all sure what to do with those feelings.

But he did know he was happier with her than he'd ever been without her. Happier than he'd ever believed he could be, despite everything.

He thought of her—high heels, short black skirt, snug white shirt, gliding around the noisy bar with her tray.

He wouldn't mind a beer, some noise, or seeing her quick smile when he walked in.

Then he reminded himself he'd neglected the research over the last couple of days, and buckled down to it.

Not that he saw what possible use it could be, reading stories—for what else were they but stories?—of pirates and treasure, of ill-fated lovers and violent death.

But the hell of it was, it was the only clear channel he had to real death, and maybe, just maybe, some remote chance of clearing his name.

He read for an hour before the light started to go. He rose, wandered to the edge of the terrace to watch the sea and sky blur together, watched a young family—man, woman, two small boys— walk along the surf, with the boys, legs pumping in shorts, dashing into the shallows and out again, quick as crabs.

Maybe he'd have that beer after all, take a short break, then put in another hour on the notes he'd taken, both on the legend and on his twisty reality.

Gathering everything, he stepped back into the house, then dumped everything to answer the phone. He saw his parents' home number on the readout, and as it always did these days, his heart jumped at the fear his grandmother had fallen again. Or worse.

Still, he put as much cheer into his voice as possible. "Hi."

"Hi yourself." He relaxed again at the easy tone of his mother's voice. "I know it's a little late."

"It's not even nine, Mom. And not a school night."

He heard the smile in her voice. "Don't put off your homework till Sunday night. How are you, Eli?"

"Good. I was just reading a book on Esmeralda's Dowry."

"Yo ho!"

"How's Gran? And Dad? Tricia?"

"Everyone's fine. Your gran's looking

more like herself every day. She still tires quicker than I'd like, and I know she has some discomfort, especially after her therapy, but we should all be so tough at her age."

"Amen."

"She's really looking forward to seeing you for Easter."

He winced. "Mom, I don't think I can make it."

"Oh, Eli."

"I don't like leaving the house empty for that long."

"You haven't had any more trouble?"

"No. But I'm right here. If the police have any leads on who broke in, they're not saying. So it's just not smart to leave it empty for a day or two."

"Maybe we should lock the place up, hire a guard until they catch whoever's breaking in."

"Mom. There's always a Landon at Bluff House."

"God, you sound just like your grand-mother."

"I'm sorry. Really." He knew just how much holiday traditions meant to his mother, and had let her down there too many times already. "I needed a place, and she gave it to me. I need to take care of it."

She let out a sigh. "All right. You can't come to Boston. We'll come to Whiskey Beach."

"What?"

"There's no reason we can't come there. Hester would love it—and we'll make sure her doctors clear it. Your sister and her family would love it, too. It's past time we had the whole family together for a holiday at Bluff House."

His first reaction had been panic. Now it shifted. She was right, past time. "I hope like hell you don't want me to bake a ham."

"I'll take care of that, and whatever else. We'll let Selina hunt eggs—oh, remember how you and Tricia used to love doing that? We'll come up Saturday afternoon. This is better. Better than you coming here. I should've thought of it in the first place."

"I'm glad you thought of it. Ah, listen, I'd like Abra to come, too."

"That would be perfect. Hester especially would want to see her. You know she calls every couple of days to talk to your gran. We'd love to have her."

"Okay, good, because I'm actually seeing her."

There was a pause, long and buzzing. "*Seeing* seeing?"

"Yeah."

"Oh, Eli, that's wonderful! That's so, so good to hear. We love Abra, and—"

"Mom, it's not like . . . It's just seeing. Seeing."

"I'm allowed to be happy. You haven't . . . It's been a long time since you had someone in your life. And we're especially fond of Abra. I love you, Eli."

Something in the tone had his stomach jittering. "I know. I love you, too."

"I want you to have your life back. I want you to be happy again. I miss my boy. I miss seeing you happy."

He heard the tears, closed his eyes. "I'm getting it back. I feel more myself here than I have in a long time. Hey, I've put on ten pounds."

When she burst into tears, the panic returned. "Mom, don't cry. Please."

"It's happy. It's just happy. I can't wait to see you for myself. I'm going to go tell your father, Hester, and call Tricia. We'll bring a feast. Don't worry about a thing. Just keep taking care of yourself."

When he hung up he just stood for a moment getting his bearings. Ready or not, his family was coming to Bluff House. And his mother's "Don't worry about a thing" wouldn't cut it.

He knew damn well his grandmother would expect Bluff House to shine, and he couldn't dump all that on Abra.

He'd figure it out. He had better than a week to figure it out. He'd make a list.

Later, he decided. Now, he discovered, he really did want that beer. And he wanted it in a noisy bar. With Abra.

So, he'd grab a shower, and maybe he'd walk to the village. That way she could drive them both back after her shift.

He headed for the steps, realized he wore a grin. Yeah, he thought, he felt more like himself than he had in a very long time.

Sixteen

Abra wound her way through tables, busing empties, taking orders and checking IDs as the Boston-born band pulled in a hefty share of the college crowd. Following bar policy, she rewarded each party's designated driver—when they had one—with free non-alcoholic drinks through the night.

Otherwise, tonight's crowd leaned heavy on beer and wine. She kept her tables happy—casually flirting with guys, complimenting girls on hair or shoes, laughing at jokes, quick conversations with familiar faces. She enjoyed the work, the noise and the hustle. She liked the people-watching, the speculating.

The stone-cold-sober DD from her table of five channeled any desire he might have had for beer into hitting on a nearby table of girls, particularly the milk-skinned redhead. From her reaction, the way the two of them danced, the whispers when the girl group trooped off as a pack for the ladies', Abra figured the DD might just get lucky later.

She served a round to a pair of couples—she cleaned for one set—and was pleased to see earrings she'd made dangling from both women's earlobes.

Boosted, she made her way to the back table, and its single occupant. No familiar face here, and not by her gauge a particularly happy one. Anyone who sat alone at the back of a bar nursing tonic and lime didn't project happiness.

"How's it going back here?"

She got a long stare and a tap on the now empty glass in answer.

"Tonic with lime. I'll take care of that. Can I get you anything else? We're famous for our nachos."

When all she got was a shake of the

head, she took the empty, tried an easy smile. "I'll get right back to you."

Thinking the likelihood strong that the tonic-and-lime would be a lousy tipper, she headed back to the bar.

Risky, he thought. Risky coming in here, getting so close to her. But he'd been reasonably sure she hadn't seen him that night in Bluff House. Now as she looked him right in the eye without a single flicker of recognition, he could be absolutely sure. And rewards, God knew, took risk.

He'd wanted to watch her, to see how she behaved—and he'd hoped Landon would be there, opening up a fresh opportunity to get back into the house.

But then he'd hoped the police would take Landon in for questioning. He'd needed only a small opening to get in, plant the gun, make an anonymous call.

Now, they'd searched the place, so planting the gun in Bluff House wouldn't work. But there was always another avenue. The woman might be the best route.

She could be his way back into Bluff House. He needed to think about that.

He *had* to get back in, finish his search. The dowry was there; he believed it with every fiber of his being. He'd already risked so much, lost so much.

No going back, he reminded himself. He'd killed now, and found it a great deal easier than he'd expected. Just the press of a finger on the trigger, hardly any effort at all. Logically, it would be easier the next time, if a next time proved necessary.

In fact, he might enjoy killing Landon. But it had to look like an accident, or suicide. Nothing that made the police, or the media, or anyone, question Landon's guilt.

Because he knew, without doubt, Eli Landon had killed Lindsay.

He could use that, and already imagined forcing Landon to write out a confession before he died. Spilling that blue Landon blood as the coward begged for his life. Yes, he found he wanted that more than he'd realized.

An eye for an eye? And more.

Landon deserved to pay; he deserved to die. Making that happen would be nearly as rich a reward as Esmeralda's Dowry.

When he saw Eli walk in, the rise of rage nearly choked him. The red-hot haze of it blurred his vision, urged him to reach for the gun holstered at his back, the same gun he'd used to kill Kirby Duncan. He could see, actually see the bullets punching into the Landon bastard's body. The blood gushing as he fell.

His hands trembled with the need to end the man he hated above all else.

Accident or suicide. He repeated the words over and over in his head in a struggle to regain control, to calm his killing fury. The effort popped beads of sweat on his forehead as he fought to consider his options.

At the bar Abra waited for her drink orders and chatted with her favorite village character. Short, stocky, with a monk's ring of wispy white hair, Stoney Tribbet worked on his second beer and a bump of the night. Stoney rarely missed a Friday night at the pub. He claimed he liked the music, and the pretty girls.

He'd be eighty-two that summer, and he'd spent every year of it—except for a stint in the army in Korea—in Whiskey Beach.

"I'll build you your own yoga studio when you marry me," he told her.

"With a juice bar?"

"If that's what it takes."

"I'm going to have to think about that, Stoney, because it's pretty tempting. Especially since it comes with you."

His weathered map of a face went pink under its permanent tan. "Now we're talking."

Abra gave him a kiss on his grizzled cheek, then lit up when she saw Eli.

"I didn't expect you to come in."

Stoney turned on his stool, gave Eli the hard eye, then it softened. "Now that's a Landon if I ever saw one. Are you Hester's grandboy?"

"Yes, sir."

"Stoney Tribbet, Eli Landon."

Stoney shot out a hand. "I knew your grandpa—you got his eyes. We had some adventures together back a ways. Some long ways."

"Eli, why don't you keep Stoney company while I get these drinks served?"

"Sure." Due to the current lack of a stool, Eli leaned on the bar. "Can I buy you a drink?"

"Looks like I've got one here. Belly up, boy, and I'll buy you one. You know your grandpa and I both had our eye on the same girl once upon a time."

He tried to picture his tall, lanky grandfather and this fireplug of a man on adventures, and competing for the same woman.

A tough picture to mind-sketch.

"Is that so?"

"Rock-solid truth. Then he went off to Boston to school, and I scooped her up. He got Harvard and Hester, and I got Mary. We agreed we both couldn't have done better. What're you drinking?"

"I'll have what you're having."

Pleased two of her favorite people were sharing drinks and conversation, Abra snaked her way through to deliver orders. As she moved toward the back, she saw the empty table, and the bills tossed on it.

Odd, she thought, putting the money on her tray. It looked like her solo had changed his mind about another tonic and lime.

At the bar Eli settled in, snagging a stool when an ass lifted off one, listening

to stories—some he assumed were exaggerated for effect—about his grandfather as a boy and young man.

"He rode that motorcycle hell for
leather. Gave the locals a fit."

"My grandfather. On a motorcycle."

"Most usually with a pretty girl in the
sidecar." Eyes twinkling, Stoney slurped
through the head of his beer. "I thought
he'd win Mary because of that motorcycle. She loved riding. The best I could
offer back then were the handlebars of
my bike. We'd've been about sixteen
then. Used to have the best damn bon-
fires down on the beach. With whiskey Eli
nipped from his father's cabinet."

Now Eli tried to picture the man he'd
been named for driving a motorcycle with
a sidecar, and pilfering his own father's
liquor supply.

Either the image came more naturally,
or the beer helped it along.

"They threw some big parties at Bluff
House," Stoney told him. "Fancy people
would come up from Boston, New York,
Phillydelphia and where-not. They'd have
the house lit up like a Roman candle, with

people gliding along the terraces in their white tuxes and evening gowns.

"Made a hell of a picture," Stoney said, and downed his bump.

"Yeah. I bet it did."

Chinese lanterns, silver candelabras, big urns of tropical flowers—and the people in their Gatsby elegance.

"Eli, he'd slip out, get one of the servants to bring down food and French champagne. I'm pretty sure his parents knew about it. We'd have our own party on the beach, and Eli, he'd go back and forth between. He was good at that, if you take my meaning. Good at being between. Rich and fancy, and everyday. First time I saw Hester, he brought her down from a party. She was in a long white dress. Had a laugh in her, always did. One look at her, and I knew Mary was mine. Eli couldn't take his eyes off Hester Hawkin."

"Even as a kid I knew they were happy together."

"So they were." Nodding sagely, Stoney banged a hand on the bar, his signal for another round.

"You know, Eli and I married our girls within a couple months of each other. Stayed friendly, too. He lent me the money to start my carpentry business. Wouldn't take no when he heard I was going to go to the bank for a loan to get it going."

"You've lived here all your life."

"Ayah. I was born here, figuring on dying here in another twenty, thirty years." He grinned over the dregs of his beer. "I did a lot of work in Bluff House over the years. Been retired awhile, but when Hester got it in her head to refit that room up on the second floor for a gym, she brought the plans to me to look over. I'm glad she's doing better. Whiskey Beach isn't the same without her in Bluff House."

"It's not. You know the house pretty well."

"I'd say as well as those who've lived there. Did some plumbing for them on the side. No plumbing license, but I've got handy hands. Always did."

"What do you think about Esmeralda's Dowry?"

He snorted. "I think if there ever was such a thing, it's long gone. Don't tell me you're looking for it. If you are, you've got your grandfather's eyes but not his good sense."

"I'm not. But somebody is."

"Do tell."

Sometimes, Eli thought, the way to get information was to give it. He did tell.

Stoney pulled on his bottom lip and considered. "What the hell could you bury in that basement? The floor's as much stone as dirt. There are better places to hide a treasure, if you're hiding it. Not too bright to think it's in the house in the first place. Generations of people living there—servants, workmen like me and my crew. Plenty of us have been over every inch of that place at one time or another, including the servants' passages."

"Servants' passages?"

"Long before your time. Used to be staircases behind the walls, and ways for the servants to get up and down without running into family or guests. One of the first things Hester did once they took over the house was have them closed up. Eli made the mistake of telling her how kids had gotten lost and locked in behind the walls. He made half of it up, I expect, that was his way to a good story. But she put her foot down. I closed them up myself, me and three I hired on for the job. What she didn't close off she opened up—the breakfast room, another bed and bath on the second floor."

"I had no idea."

"She was carrying your father when we did the work. Everybody who's lived in Bluff House put their stamp on it one way or the other. What are you planning?"

"I haven't thought about it. It's my grandmother's house."

Stoney smiled, nodded. "Bring her back home."

"That I am planning on. Maybe you could give me a better idea where those passages were."

"Can do better." Stoney picked up a bar napkin, rooted a pencil out of his pocket. "My hands aren't as handy as they once were, but nothing's wrong with my brain cells or memory."

They closed the place down. Though Stoney outdrank him two for one, Eli was damn glad he wouldn't drive home. And just as glad when Stoney told him he was on foot.

"We'll give you a lift," Eli told him.

"No need for that. I barely live a Stoney's throw from here." He cackled at his own joke. "And it looks to me like I've got another Landon eyeing my girl."

"I don't know if this one can fix my screen door." Abra tucked her arm through Stoney's. "I'll take Eli's keys and drive all three of us home."

"I didn't bring my car. I figured I'd ride home with you."

"I walked."

Eli frowned down at her high black heels. "In those?"

"No. In these." She pulled a pair of green Crocs out of her bag. "And it looks like I'm putting them back on because we're all walking home."

She changed her shoes, zipped into a jacket. When they stepped outside she took each man by the hand. "Looks like I won tonight's jackpot. Two handsome men."

Both of whom, she thought as they walked, were just a little bit drunk.

Over his objections, they detoured to walk Stoney to the door of his trim little house. The sound of high-pitched barking sounded before they were within two yards.

"All right, Prissy! All right!"

The barks turned to excited whines. "The old girl's half blind," Stoney said, "but she's got her hearing. Nobody gets past old Prissy. You two go on now. Go do what healthy young people ought to be doing on a Friday night."

"I'll see you Tuesday." Abra kissed his cheek.

They strolled away, but waited until the lights switched on before veering back toward the shore road. "Tuesday?" Eli asked.

"I clean for him every other Tuesday." She hitched her bag more securely on her shoulder. "He and his Mary, I never got to meet her. She died five years ago. They had three kids. A son and two daughters. The son's in Portland—Maine—one of the daughters lives in Seattle. The closest one is in D.C., but they manage to visit him pretty regularly. And there's grandchildren, too. There are eight, and five great-grandchildren so far. He can take care of himself, but it doesn't hurt to have somebody right here looking in from time to time."

"So you clean his place every other week."

"And run errands. He doesn't do much driving anymore. His next-door neighbor has a kid about ten who's crazy about Stoney, so he rarely gets a day when somebody's not dropping in or calling. I'm fairly crazy about him myself. If I marry him, he's promised to build me my own yoga studio."

"I could . . ." Eli considered his carpentry skills. "I could have a yoga studio built for you."

On a flutter of eyelashes, she tipped her face up to his. "Is that a proposal?"

"What?"

She laughed, curled her arm through his. "I should've warned you Stoney has an impressive capacity for alcohol. He likes to say he was reared on the whiskey of Whiskey Beach."

"We were switching off. He bought the first round, so I bought the second. Then he bought a third, and I felt obligated. I don't quite remember how many times I felt obligated. There's an awful lot of fresh air out here."

"There is." She tightened her hold when he weaved a bit. "And gravity, too. This place is lousy with air and gravity. We should get inside. My place is closer."

"Yeah, we could . . . except I don't like leaving the house empty. It feels wrong."

With a nod, she forgot the shorter walk. "It's good for you to walk in the fresh air and gravity anyway. I'm glad you came in tonight."

"I wasn't going to, but I kept thinking about you. Then there was the whole Easter thing happening."

"The Easter Bunny came already?"

"What? No." Now he laughed, the sound rolling down the empty street. "He hasn't finished laying the eggs yet."

"Eli, the Easter Chicken lays the eggs. The bunny hides them."

"Whatever, they're doing it at Bluff House this year."

"They are?" She glanced at her cottage as they passed, but didn't think she should run in for a quick change of clothes. She might come out and find him curled up asleep in the middle of the road.

"That's what my mother said. They're all coming up on Saturday."

"That's great. Hester's able to travel?"

"She's going to talk to the doctor first, but it looks good for it. The whole bunch of them. There's stuff I have to do first. I can't think what it is right now, except I don't have to bake a ham. But you have to come."

"I'll drop in, sure. I'd love to see them, Hester especially."

"No." While he felt slightly steadier with the sea breeze blowing, Eli had a sudden, wicked craving for potato chips. Or pretzels. Or just about anything that would sop up some of the excess beer in his belly.

"You have to be there," he continued, "for the thing. Easter. I thought I should tell my mother we were seeing each other so it wouldn't be weird. Then it got weird, like I'd won a blue ribbon or something, then she started crying."

"Oh, Eli."

"She said happy crying, which I don't get, but women do." He glanced down at her for verification.

"Yes, we do."

"So it's probably going to be weird, but you have to come anyway. I need to buy stuff. And things."

"I'll put stuff and things on the list."

"Okay." He weaved again. "It's not the beer, it's the bumps. . . . My grandfather used to drive a motorcycle with a sidecar. I didn't know that. It seems like I should have. I didn't know there used to be servants' passages in the house. There's too much I don't know. Look at it."

Bluff House stood silhouetted in starlight, illuminated from within. "I've taken it for granted."

"I don't think that's true."

"Too much of it. I haven't paid attention, especially in the last few years. Too wrapped up in my own stuff, and couldn't seem to roll my way out of it. I need to do better."

"Then you will."

He stopped a moment, smiled at her. "I'm a little drunk. You look amazing."

"I look amazing because you're a little drunk?"

"No. Some of it's just knowing who you are and being good with it, doing what you do, and, well, being happy doing it.

And some of it's those sea-witch eyes and that sexy mouth with that little mole right there. Lindsay was beautiful. She took your breath away."

A little drunk, Abra reminded herself. Allowances could be made. "I know."

"But she, I think, she didn't really know who she was, and wasn't good with it. She wasn't happy. I didn't make her happy."

"Everyone has to make themselves happy first."

"Now you remember."

"I remember." He leaned down to kiss her, there in the shadows of the great house under a sky mad with stars. "I need to sober up some because I want to make love with you, and I want to be sure I remember that, too."

"Then let's make it unforgettable."

The minute they were inside and he'd punched in the alarm code, he pulled her against him.

She welcomed his mouth, his hands, but eased away. "First things first," she said, drawing him through the house. "What you need is a big glass of water and a couple aspirin. Hydration and hangover anticipation. And I'm going to have a glass of wine so you're not so far ahead of me."

"Fair enough. I really want to tear your clothes off." He blocked her, shoved her back against the counter. "Just tear them off because I know what's under them, and it drives me crazy."

"Looks like we're going to get to the kitchen floor this time." With his teeth at her throat, she dropped her head back. "I think it's going to live up to the hype."

"Just let me . . . wait."

"Oh, sure, now it's wait after you've—"

"Wait." He set her aside, his face stony now. She followed his gaze to the alarm panel.

"How did you manage to smudge that up? I'll clean it tomorrow," she said, reaching for him.

"I didn't." He stepped over, examined the door. "I think the door's been forced. Don't touch anything," he snapped when she went to him. "Call the police. Now."

She dug into her bag, then her hands froze when he pulled a knife out of the block. "Oh God, Eli."

"If there's any trouble, you run. Do you

hear me? You go out that door and you run, and don't stop until you're safe."

"No, and now you wait." She punched numbers on the phone. "Vinnie, it's Abra. Eli and I just got back to Bluff House. We think someone's broken in. We don't know if he's still here. In the kitchen. Yes. Yes. Okay. He's coming," she told Eli. "He's calling it in on the way. He wants us to stay right where we are. If we see or hear anything, we go out, and get gone."

Her heart picked up another speed when she saw Eli's gaze turn toward the basement door. "If you go down there, I go down there."

Ignoring her, he walked to the door, turned the knob. "It's locked from this side. The way I left it." Still holding the knife, he walked to the back door, un-locked it, opened it, then crouched.

"Fresh marks here. Back door, facing the beach at night. Nobody to see. He had to know I wasn't here. How did he know?"

"He must be watching the house. He must have seen you leave."

"On foot," Eli remembered. "If I'd just been taking a walk, I might have been gone for ten, fifteen minutes. It's a lot of risk."

"He might've followed you, seen you go into the bar. A calculated risk that he'd have more time."

"Maybe."

"The alarm pad." Still wary, Abra edged a bit closer. "I've seen that somewhere— TV, movies—I thought it was just made up. Spraying something on the pad so the oil from fingerprints comes up. You know what numbers have been pressed. Then a computer thing runs different patterns until it breaks the code."

"Something like that. It's how he might've gotten in before, when my grandmother was here. He could've gotten her keys, made copies. Just let himself the fuck in after that. But he didn't know we'd changed the code, so he cut the power the last time when the old code didn't work."

"That makes him stupid."

"Maybe desperate or panicked. Maybe just pissed off."

"You want to go down there. I can see it. You want to know if he started digging again. Vinnie will be here any minute."

If he went down and she came with him, and anything happened, he'd be responsible. If he went down and she stayed put, and anything happened, he'd be responsible.

So, Eli concluded, he was stuck.

"I was gone about three hours. God damn it, I gave him a nice, big window."

"What are you supposed to do? Pull a Miss Havisham and never leave the house?"

"The alarm system sure isn't doing any good. We're going to have to beef that up."

"Or something." She heard the wail of sirens. "That's Vinnie."

Eli slid the knife back into the block. "Let's go let him in."

Cops swarmed his house again. He was getting used to it. He drank coffee, and walked the house with them, starting with the basement.

"Determined bastard," Vinnie remarked as they studied the trench. "He got another couple feet in. He must've brought in more tools, and took them away with him this time."

Eli glanced around to make sure Abra hadn't come down. "I think he's crazy."

"Well, he ain't smart."

"No, Vinnie, I think he's crazy. He'd risk breaking in, again, to spend a couple hours hacking at this floor? There's nothing here. I talked to Stoney Tribbet tonight."

"Now there's a character."

"He is, and he also said something that makes clear sense. Why would anyone bury anything here? It's damn hard dirt and rock, or a lot of it is. It's why we never bothered to lay concrete. If you bury something—excluding a body—don't you usually intend to dig it back up, at some point?"

"Most likely."

"Then why make it so damn much work? Bury it in the garden, plant a fucking bush over it. Out front where the ground's softer, or where it's mostly sand. Or don't bury it at all, but hide it under floorboards, behind a wall. If I'm looking for the damn treasure, I'm not going to use a pick and shovel down here. Or if I'm crazy enough to believe it's here, I'm going to wait until I know the house is empty for a couple days—like it is when my grandmother visits Boston—and I'm going to go at it with a jackhammer."

"I'm not going to argue, but this is what it is. I'm going to let Corbett know about this, and we'll increase the patrol. We're going to make noise about the extra patrols." Vinnie added, "If he's in the area, he'll hear about it. It should give him second thoughts about trying this again."

Eli doubted second thoughts would stop anyone willing to risk so much for a legend.

Seventeen

In the morning, Abra returned to Bluff House from her tai chi class via the market, then detoured for a secondary stop. She couldn't guarantee Eli's reaction to what she'd picked up, but she had a pretty good idea what it would be—initially.

They'd work around it. Or, she admitted, she'd work around him. Not entirely fair, and she really hated to manipulate. But in this case, she firmly believed it was for the best.

She gauged her time as she unloaded the car. She had not only her regular cleaning on the slate, but the reordering after the police search. But no reason she couldn't get it all done, maybe throw a meal together, then get home for her in-house yoga class.

It was all about prioritizing.

She stepped inside, instantly recalculated everything as instead of working in his office, Eli stood at the counter pouring coffee.

"I thought you'd be working."

"I was. Am. I needed a walk around to think through . . ." He trailed off as he turned and looked down at the big brown dog currently sniffing at his pants leg. "What's this?"

"That's Barbie."

"Barbie? Seriously?" Automatically, he scratched the wide head between the ears.

"I know. Barbie's blond and busty, but dogs don't really get to choose their names." She watched him out of the corner of her eye as she put groceries away. He'd stopped what he was doing to pet the dog, and had that easy appreciation on his face people who enjoy dogs tend to wear around them.

So far, so good.

"Well, she's pretty. Yeah, you're pretty," he said, rubbing as Barbie murmured in her throat and leaned against him. "You're dog-sitting?"

"Not exactly. Barbie's a sweetheart. She's four. Her owner died a couple of weeks ago. The owner's daughter tried to take the dog, but her husband's allergic. There's a grandson, but he lives in an apartment with a no-pet clause. So poor Barbie lost her best pal, and couldn't go with family. She's been fostered for the last week or so while the local organization tries to find her a good home. She's been really well trained, she's healthy, she's spayed. But people usually want puppies, so an older dog takes a bit longer to place, especially since they're trying to stick with Whiskey Beach. It's her beach."

"Beach Dog Barbie?" He grinned, crouching as Barbie rolled over to have her belly rubbed.

Nearly there, Abra calculated. " 'Beach Bitch Barbie' would've given you the alliteration, and have been accurate. But she's so sweet, it's hard to use the B word. Actually, I thought of taking her myself. I volunteer off and on at the shelter. But with my schedule I'm just not home enough. It didn't seem fair when she's used to companionship. She's a Chesapeake Bay retriever with a little something else mixed in. Retrievers love being around people."

Abra closed the last cupboard, smiled. "She really likes you. You like dogs."

"Sure. We always had a dog growing up. In fact, I imagine my family will bring . . ." He straightened as if shot out of a rubber band. "Wait a minute."

"You work at home."

"I'm not looking for a dog."

"Sometimes the best things you get you weren't looking for. And she comes with a strong plus."

"What?"

"Barbie? Speak!"

Sitting again, the dog lifted her head, obligingly sent out two cheerful barks.

"She does tricks."

"She barks, Eli. I actually got the idea thinking about how Stoney's dog barked when we walked him home. Someone's been getting into the house, past your high-tech alarm. So go low-tech. Barking dogs deter break-ins. You can Google it."

"You think I should foster a dog be-cause she barks on command?"

"She barks when she hears anyone coming to the door, and stops barking on command. It's in her bio."

"Her bio? Are you kidding me?"

"I'm not."

"Most dogs bark," he argued. "With or without bios and head shots or whatever else she has. It's not a qualified reason to foster a dog."

"I think you could try fostering each other for now. Because she barks, and needs a home in Whiskey Beach, and you'd be company for each other."

"Dogs need to be fed and watered and walked. They need a vet, equipment, at-tention."

"All true. She comes with bowls, food, toys, her leash, her medical records—she's up-to-date there. She was raised from a pup by a man in his eighties, and she's very well behaved, as you can see for yourself. The thing is she really loves men, is happier around men as she bonded with one as a pup. She loves playing fetch and tug, she's great with kids, and she barks. If you needed or wanted to go out for a couple hours, someone would be in the house."

"She's not someone. She's a dog."

"Hence the barking. Listen, why don't you try it for a few days, see how it goes? If it just doesn't work, I'll take her, or I'll talk Maureen into taking her. She's a soft touch."

The dog sat like a lady, watching him with big brown eyes, her head slightly cocked as if asking: Okay, what's it going to be?

And Eli felt himself sinking. "A guy shouldn't have a dog named Barbie."

Victory, Abra concluded, and stepped to him. "No one will hold that against you."

Barbie nuzzled her nose at his hand, politely.

Sinking fast.

"A couple of days."

"Fair enough. I'll go out and get her things. I thought I'd start upstairs today, work my way down. I won't vacuum up there until you take another break."

"Fine. You know this was an ambush. And you know I know you know."

"I do." She took his face in her hands. "It was, and I do know." She laid her lips on his, soft and lingering. "I'll have to find a way to make it up to you."

"That's pandering."

"It *is!*" She laughed and kissed him again. "Now I have to make it up to you twice. Go on back up to work," she suggested as she started out. "I'll show Barbie around."

Eli studied the dog; the dog studied Eli. Then she lifted a paw in invitation. Only a heartless man would have refused to take the offered paw in his for a shake. "It looks like I've got a dog named Barbie. For a couple days."

When he started out, Barbie fell in at his heel, tail wagging enthusiastically. "I guess you're coming with me."

She followed him up, into his office. When he sat she moved up to sniff at his keyboard. Then she wandered off, her toenails clicking lightly on the hardwood.

Okay, Eli thought, so she wasn't pushy. A point for Barbie.

He worked through the morning, then sat back, held an internal debate before taking the plunge.

He e-mailed his agent, a woman who'd stuck with him since his law school days, to tell her he thought he had enough for her to take a look. Struggling to ignore all the whining voices in his head, he attached the first five chapters. Hit send.

"Done it now," he said, and sighed.

And since he had, he wanted to get out of the house, away from those whining voices.

He stood up, and nearly tripped over the dog.

Sometime during the last couple of hours, she'd come in silent as a ghost, to curl up behind his chair.

Now she lifted her gaze to his, bumped her tail politely on the floor.

"I guess you're a pretty good dog."

The tail picked up its beat.

"Want to go for a walk on the beach?"

He didn't know the key word, or if she just understood whole sentences, but she scrambled to her feet, a gleaming joy in her eyes. It wasn't just her tail wagging now, but her whole body.

"I'll take that as a yes."

She trotted downstairs with him, gave another wiggle when he picked up the leash Abra had left on the counter, then added a happy yip when they stepped into the laundry room where Abra was unloading the dryer.

"Hey there, how's it going?" Abra set the laundry in the basket to give Barbie a rub. "Good day so far?"

"I was going to take a walk. She opted to come." He pulled a jacket off the peg. "Why don't you?"

"I'd love it, but I'm on a schedule today."

"Your boss says you can take a break."

She laughed at him. "I'm my own boss—you just pay me. Go bond with Barbie. You can have some lunch when you get back. Oh, take this." She plucked a red ball out of a basket of dog toys on the washing machine. "She likes to fetch."

"Right."

She was right, too, about being her own boss, he thought. He liked and admired that about her, her ability to find and do work that satisfied her on so many levels. Once he'd thought he'd found that with the law, and his writing served as a kind of creative perk.

Now he was all in, and his life—on so

many levels—depended on the reaction of a woman in New York with a colorful collection of cheaters, a broad Brooklyn accent and a sharply critical eye.

Not going to think about it, he told himself as he led Barbie down the beach steps. And because he couldn't stop thinking about it as they walked, as the dog trotted and wiggled with joy, he stopped and scanned the beach.

Technically, she should stay on the leash, but hell, nobody, or hardly anybody, was out there.

He unclipped her, pulled the ball out of his pocket and winged it.

She charged, sand kicking, legs blurring. She clamped the ball in her teeth, raced back to him and dropped it at his feet. He winged it again, and again. Lost count of the number of times. When he timed it right, she was fast and accurate enough to leap, snatch the ball out of the air.

And each time she did, trotted back to drop it at his feet, they just grinned at each other.

She didn't chase the birds, thankfully, though she did give them longing looks.

He argued with himself, but curiosity and the little boy inside him won. He hurled the ball over the water to see how she'd react.

She gave a bark of sheer, unmistakable delight and roared into the sea.

She swam like—well, a retriever, he decided, laughing all the way down in his gut until he had to brace his hands on his thighs. She swam back to shore, red ball in her teeth, wild happiness beaming from her big brown eyes.

She dropped the ball at his feet again, shook herself. Soaked him.

"What the hell?" He threw it out over the water again.

He stayed out longer than he'd planned, and his pitching arm felt like overcooked spaghetti. But man and dog were relaxed and pleased with themselves when they walked back into Bluff House.

On the kitchen island sat a clear-wrapped plate holding a cold-cut sandwich on a long roll, two pickle spears and a scoop of pasta salad. Beside it lay a Milk-Bone.

The sticky note read:

Guess which is whose.

"Funny. I guess we eat."

He picked up the dog biscuit. The minute she spotted it, Barbie dropped her butt to the floor while the look in her eyes went slightly crazed. Like a crack addict, he thought, about to take the pipe.

"Damn it, Barbie. You're a good dog."

He went out on the deck and ate lunch in the sun with the dog sprawled contentedly by his chair.

His life, he decided, if you didn't count murder, break-ins and clouds of suspicion, was pretty damn good right at the moment.

When he went back upstairs, he heard Abra singing. He poked his head into his bedroom first and, since the dog walked right in to explore, went over to see what towel art she'd left on the bed.

Unmistakably a dog, he thought. Especially since she'd fashioned a heart out of a Post-it. On it, she'd written:

BARBIE LOVES ELI

He glanced over, saw Abra had brought up a wide brown cushion. It sat on the floor near the terrace doors. Obviously, the way the dog snuggled into it, it had served as her bed before.

"Yeah, sure, make yourself at home."

He left the dog to follow the singing.

In his grandmother's bedroom, she had the terrace doors opened wide, though it was a bit cool yet. He saw the duvet clothespinned to some sort of portable pole flapping in the breeze.

And though Hester wasn't there, a little vase of wild violets stood on the nightstand.

A small thing, Eli thought. Abra was good at small things that made big differences.

"Hi. How was your walk?" She picked up a pillow, shook it out of its case.

"Nice. The dog likes to swim."

She'd noticed as she'd watched them from the terrace, and as she'd watched, her heart had simply glowed—and melted.

"It's a perk for her, being right on the beach."

"Yeah. She's in on her bed, taking a nap."

"Swimming wears you out."

"Yeah," he said again as he skirted the bed to her side. "What are you doing?"

"I thought since your family's coming I'd air out the linens so they'll be nice and fresh."

"Good thinking. They look nice and fresh already."

He backed her up until she fell on the bed under him.

"Eli. My schedule."

"You're your own boss," he reminded her. "You can adjust the schedule."

She accepted defeat when his hands and mouth got busy, but tried a token protest. "I could. But should I?"

He lifted his head briefly to pull off her tank. "I'm keeping the dog. No less of an ambush," he said when her eyes lit up. "So you still have to make it up to me."

"When you put it that way."

Rearing up, she tugged off his shirt. "Somebody's been working out." She trailed her tongue over his chest.

"Some."

"And eating his protein." She wrapped her legs around his waist, stretched up, canted forward until she had him on his back. "I'm supposed to be cleaning your house, earning my pay, not getting naked with you in this gorgeous old bed."

"You can call me Mr. Landon, if that helps ease your conscience."

Her laugh was warm against his skin. "I think my conscience can be flexible in this case."

So was she, he thought, flexible. Those long arms, long legs, the long torso. All so smooth and fluid as she moved over him, as all that wild hair feathered over his skin.

Muscles he'd begun to recognize again bunched and tensed as she glided her lips over him, as her skilled hands pressed, kneaded, stroked. Arousing, soothing, seducing the already seduced.

Naked in bed. That's how he wanted her.

He peeled the snug, stretchy pants over her hips, down her legs, exploring her inch by inch all the way to her ankles. And up again over the taut curve of calf, the delicate back of her knee, along the firm length of her thigh to that hot, damp core.

She arched, a hand digging into the sheet, fisting there as pleasure struck and quivered. And it built, built, built until she broke, until she cartwheeled into the tumble of sensations.

She levered up, dragging him to her, latching her arms around him when they knelt body-to-body on the bed.

Heat flooded her, sent even her blood to sizzling under her skin as the breeze whipped in the open doors to flow over them.

It danced through her hair, he thought, and the sun streamed over her like molten gold. They might've been on some lost island with the relentless voice of the sea, the tang of it on the air, the mocking laugh of gulls winging across the blue bowl of sky.

Now those limbs wrapped around him—demand, invitation, plea. He took what she offered, gave what she asked. His body plunged to hers while lips met in unsated appetite.

Faster, stronger, with her head flung back and his mouth on her throat where her pulse beat in mad time.

Then she cried out his name, just his name, and he felt even his slippery hold on control snap loose.

———

He lay facedown, she faceup, and both struggled for breath. With her eyes closed, Abra slid her hand over, found his arm, trailed down until she could link fingers with him.

"That was a hell of an afternoon break."

"My new favorite kind," he mumbled, his voice muffled against the mattress.

"I really have to get up and get back to work."

"Let me write an excuse note to your boss."

"She won't buy it. She's really strict."

Now he turned his head and studied her profile with sleepy eyes. "No, she's not."

"You don't work for her." She curled toward him now. "She can be a total bitch."

"I'm going to tell her you said that."

"Better not. She might fire me, then who'd clean the house?"

"That's a point." He draped an arm around her. "I'll help you deal with the rest of the house."

She started to decline, quickly and

gently. She had a routine, and he'd be in her way. But she let it go—for now. "Why aren't you doing your own work?"

"I'm taking the rest of the day off."

"Dog love?"

"No." He trailed his fingers through her hair before he sat up. "I have enough finished and polished up to send to my agent. So I did."

"That's great." She popped up beside him. "Isn't it?"

"I guess I'll find out in the next few days."

"Let me read it." When he shook his head, she rolled her eyes.

"Okay, I get that, more or less. How about letting me read one scene? Just one. A page?"

"Maybe. Maybe later." Evade now, he thought, as she had a sneaky way of talking him into things. Like a dog. "I'll ply you with wine first so you're mildly impaired."

"I can't get mildly impaired tonight. I have a yoga class at home."

"Sometime. Later. I'll help you get some of the stuff the cops jumbled up put back."

"Okay, you can strip the bed, that's basic."

Even as she rolled out of it, the dog let out a trio of warning barks.

"Perfect," Eli muttered, grabbed his pants. He heard the dog charge down the steps, barking like a hound out of hell.

"You win that one." He dragged on his shirt. "And you're naked."

"I'll take care of that."

"Too bad. Naked housekeeping might've been fun."

She grinned as he hurried out, as he called to the dog.

Eli Landon, she thought, was coming back strong.

Downstairs he ordered the dog to stop. She surprised him by doing just that, butt sitting right by his side as he opened the door.

He tried to block that first, automatic strike of panic when he saw cops. Pushed back against the dark cloud that habitually followed.

Not Wolfe at least, he thought.

"Detective Corbett, Vinnie."

"Nice dog," Corbett began.

"Hey, is that Barbie?" When the dog immediately reacted with a greeting woof and wagging tail, Vinnie bent down to pet her. "You've got Barbie, Mr. Bridle's dog. He died in his sleep a couple weeks ago. The neighbor came to check on him as she did most days, and found Barbie here guarding the bed. She's a good dog, she is."

As if remembering himself, Vinnie straightened. "Sorry. I'm just glad to see her in a good home. She's a great dog."

"Pretty girl," Corbett commented. "Do you have a few minutes, Mr. Landon?"

"I get that question from cops a lot." But he stepped back to let them in.

"Deputy Hanson told me about the latest break-in so I asked him to come with me to speak to you. Have you had a chance to go through the house thoroughly, check for anything missing or out of place?"

"Things were already out of place from the search. We've been putting it back together, and so far I haven't found anything missing. He's not a thief, not in the classic sense anyway."

"I have your statement from last night, but I wonder if you could go over your activities yesterday evening for me."

Corbett looked up as Abra, fully dressed, walked downstairs with a laundry basket. "Ms. Walsh."

"Detective. Hi, Vinnie. Cleaning day. Can I get you coffee? A cold drink?"

"No, but thanks." Corbett shifted his stance. "You were with Mr. Landon when the break-in was discovered?"

"That's right. I work at the Village Pub on most Friday nights. Eli came up— when was that?—nine-thirty or so, I guess. He and Stoney Tribbet hung out at the bar swapping lies."

"Stoney's a local character," Vinnie explained.

"We stayed till closing," Eli continued. "Abra and I walked Stoney home, then walked back here."

"Deputy Hanson logged your call to him at one-forty-three."

"That's right. We went into the kitchen, and I saw the alarm pad smudged, then checked the door and found fresh jimmy marks. And yeah, I've changed the code. Again."

"And added backup," Abra said, giving Barbie a rub.

"Did you see any cars you didn't recognize, anyone either on the beach or on the street?"

"No, but then I wasn't looking for any. I'd been outside earlier, doing some research, reading on the back terrace. I didn't notice anything or anyone. I hadn't planned on going to the bar. I didn't tell anyone I was going. It was impulse."

"Do you tend to go in on Friday nights?"

"I've only been in there once before."

"Did you see anyone in the bar who struck you in any way? Anyone who seemed to be acting unusual?"

"No."

"I'm going to put this load in," Abra began. She took two steps away, turned back. "Tonic and lime."

"I'm sorry."

"It's nothing. I'm sure it's nothing, but I did serve a table of one, a man I didn't recognize. He sat in the back, alone, drank tonic and lime. He ordered three, but he didn't stay for the third."

"Why unusual?" Corbett asked her.

"Most people who come in come with

friends or to see them, or if they're just passing through, they'd likely have a beer or a glass of wine. Still, maybe he just doesn't drink, and he just wanted to hear the band. They're good. But . . ."

"Go on," Corbett prompted.

"It's just that, now that I'm playing it back, he left right after Eli came in. I'd taken his order, added it to the others and gone to the bar to put it in. I stood there a couple minutes—if that—talking to Stoney. I was facing the main door, so I saw Eli come in. I introduced them, then picked up my orders. And when I went back I saw he'd gone, and just left money on the table."

"I know the bar." Corbett's eyes narrowed as he thought of it. "There's another exit, but you have to go through the kitchen."

"That's right. I don't think I'd have seen him leave if he left after Eli came in because I'd shifted—you know—so I wasn't facing the door. Unless he went through the kitchen, he left between the time Eli got there and I went to take him his drink. Either way, he left about five minutes after he ordered the tonic."

"Do you remember what he looked like?"

"God. In vague terms. White, late thirties, I think. Brown hair, or dark blond—the light's dim in there—and longish, over the collar. I couldn't tell you his eye color. I don't really know his build as he was sitting. He had wide hands. I might remember more if I just clear my mind."

"Will you work with a police artist?"

"Well, yes, but . . . Do you really think that could be the man who broke in here?"

"It's worth pursuing."

"I'm sorry." She looked from Eli to Vinnie. "I didn't think of it last night."

"That's why we do follow-ups," Vinnie told her.

"I don't know how much help I'll be. You know the lighting in there, especially when they have music. And he was sitting in a back corner where it's darker yet."

"What did he say to you, talk about?" Corbett asked.

"Not much. Tonic and lime. I asked if he was meeting anyone because chairs get to be a premium on the weekends.

He just repeated the order. Not the friendly sort."

"We'll arrange the artist when it's a good time for you. We'll be in touch." Since Barbie was sniffing at his shoes, Corbett leaned down to rub her head. "Oh, and the dog's a good idea. A big dog barking inside a house makes a lot of B-and-E men think twice."

When Eli let them out, Abra stood there, the basket of laundry on her hip. "I'm sorry, Eli."

"For what?"

"If I'd remembered that guy last night, we might already have a sketch. And I'm already sorry because I don't know how well I can describe him. I really didn't pay close attention to his face after it was clear he wanted to be left alone."

"We don't even know if he has any part in this. And if he does, however vaguely you remember, it's more than we had."

"I'm going to meditate later, see if I can clear things out, pull it back. And don't dis meditation."

"I didn't say a word."

"You thought several. I'm going to put this laundry in." She checked the time.

"I'm definitely behind schedule. I'll just take some time tomorrow to do the bedrooms I didn't get to today. I'll finish your grandmother's, and get what I can get done by five. I have things to do at home before class."

"Will you come back after class?"

"I really have things I've neglected, and I'm going to want my own empty house—without your doubting vibes—to meditate. Plus, you and Barbie need to finish bonding. I'll be back tomorrow. Gotta get this load in," she repeated, and hurried off.

"Just you and me, Barbie," Eli told her. Probably for the best. He was getting just a little too used to having Abra there. Probably better for both of them to have some time, some space.

But it didn't really feel better.

Eighteen

Blocked, Abra decided. She was blocked, that had to be the answer. She'd meditated, worked with the police artist, tried active dreaming—which she wasn't very good at—and still the time, effort and skill of the artist produced a sketch that could be nearly any man between thirty and forty.

Any man, she thought, studying her copy of the sketch yet again, with a thin face, long, somewhat shaggy medium brown hair and thin lips.

She couldn't swear to the lips, if it

came to that. Had they really been thin or had she projected thin lips because he'd struck her as such a tight-ass?

So much for her powers of observation, she decided in disgust, which she'd considered above average before this.

Of course, there wasn't any proof her tight-assed, tonic-and-lime-drinking customer had anything to do with anything. But still.

Nothing to be done about it, at least until after the holiday weekend. She added the last little silver ball to finish the pair of citrine and silver dangle earrings. As she filled out the description card, she imagined Eli's family already on their way.

That was one good thing. Another? The house hit "family holiday" perfectly on her scale. At least fussing with that had taken her mind off her pitiful failure with the artist.

She wanted progress, as she took off the glasses she wore for close-up work and reading. She admitted she'd hoped to play a part in identifying the intruder and potential murderer, in helping Eli resolve his problems, with the little rush of solving a mystery. She wanted to make it all neat and tidy when she knew, absolutely, life was anything but.

Now she couldn't shake off the nagging sense of annoyance, and the underlying sense of unease.

At least her new jewelry stock turned out well, if she did say so herself. But her hope that the creative energy would unblock the block fell short.

She straightened up her worktable in her tiny second bedroom, put her tools and supplies away in their labeled bins. She'd take the new stock into the gift shop, and maybe buy herself a little something with the profits.

She opted to walk, to give herself a chance to admire the play of daffodils and hyacinths cheerfully showing off their blooms, the colorful Easter eggs dangling from tree branches, the bright pop of forsythia.

She always loved the birth of a new season, whether it was the first spear of green in spring or the first drift of snow in winter. But today anxiety plagued her so she wished she'd stopped at Maureen's,

talked her friend into going into the village with her.

It was stupid to feel she was being
watched. Just a residual reaction to what
had happened at Bluff House. And the
lighthouse, she thought as she turned to
study its sturdy white lance. No one was
following her, though she couldn't resist
a look over her shoulder, or the rising chill
up her spine.

She knew these houses, knew most of
the people in them, or who owned them.
She passed Surfside Bed & Breakfast,
fought off a dragging dread and a sudden urge to turn around, run back home.

She wouldn't be chased away by her
own silly thoughts. Wouldn't deny herself
the pleasure of her walks in the place
she'd made her home.

And she wouldn't think of being
grabbed from behind in a dark, empty
house.

The sun shone, birds called, holiday
traffic chugged by.

But she let out a relieved breath when
she entered the main village with its
shops and restaurants, and people.

It pleased her to see customers milling around the window of the gift shop. Tourists taking their holiday at the beach, families like Eli's spending the weekend. She started to go inside, then saw Heather behind the counter.

She stepped back, started to walk on. "Crap," she muttered. "Just crap."

She hadn't seen the shop clerk since Heather had run out of yoga class in tears. Heather hadn't made the in-home practice, nor the next on her schedule. And inside, Abra harbored enough anger and resentment to prevent her from calling to check.

Negative energy, she told herself, and stopped. Time to expel it, rebalance her chi. And maybe she'd break that block after all.

In any case, Heather was who she was. There was no point in hoarding bad feelings, on either side.

She made herself walk back, step inside. Good smells, pretty light, the strong sense of local arts and crafts. Take that mood, she ordered herself, and go with it.

She waved casually to the other clerk, noted the woman's slight wince as she continued to wait on a customer. No doubt Heather had unloaded her perceived slights on her coworkers.

Who could blame her, really?

Deliberately, Abra made her way back to Heather, waited patiently as she was studiously ignored. When Heather finished ringing up a sale, Abra stepped forward.

"Hi. Busy today. I just need five minutes. I can wait until you have it."

"I really can't say when that might be. We have customers." Stiff, jaw tight, Heather skirted around the counter and clipped her way to a trio of women.

Temper rose up high enough to actually tickle the base of Abra's throat. She breathed it down again, then impulsively picked up a set of handblown wineglasses she'd admired for weeks but couldn't really afford.

"Excuse me." With a smile plastered on her face, Abra took the glasses over to Heather. "Could you ring me up? I just love these. Aren't they great?" she said to the other women, and got admiring assents even as one of them shifted to pick up a set of champagne flutes by the same artist.

"These would make a wonderful wedding gift."

"Wouldn't they?" All smiles, Abra turned one of her glasses in the light. "I just love the braided stems. You can't go wrong with anything in Buried Treasures," Abra added, beaming toward Heather as she held out the glasses.

"Of course. If you have any questions, just ask," Heather said to the shoppers, then walked back to the counter.

"Now I'm a customer," Abra announced. "First, we've missed you at class."

Jaw still tight, Heather got bubble wrap from under the counter, began to roll it around a glass. "I've been busy."

"We've missed you," Abra repeated, and laid a hand over Heather's. "I'm sorry we argued, and I said things that upset you and hurt your feelings."

"You made it seem like I was just a busybody, and I— The police *were* there."

"I know, and now they're not because he didn't do anything. Someone broke into Bluff House twice, that we're sure of. The first time, whoever it was grabbed me."

"I know. It's just another reason I'm concerned."

"I appreciate your concern, but Eli's not the one who tried to hurt me. He was in Boston. And he's not the one who . . ." She took a quick glance around in case any of the customers were standing close enough to hear. "Who hurt the detective from Boston, because I was with Eli when that happened. Those are facts, Heather, verified by the police."

"They searched Bluff House."

"To be thorough. They may search my cottage."

"Yours?" Shock and genuine concern popped through. "Why? That's ridiculous. That's not right."

Barrier cracked, Abra thought when Heather's voice rang with insult. "Because there's one—just one—cop in Boston who won't accept the facts and the evidence, and he's hounded Eli for a year. Now he's done some hounding in my direction."

"I think that's terrible."

"So do I, but since we've got nothing to hide, let him hound. Our local police are investigating now. I have a lot more faith in them finding out what's happening and who's responsible."

"We take care of our own," Heather said with a nod of civic pride. "Just be careful."

"I will be."

Abra tried not to flinch when Heather rang up the glasses. Bye-bye, cute new yoga outfit. But she dug in her bag for her credit card, and remembered the jewelry.

"I nearly forgot. I made about a dozen pieces." She took them out, set them on the counter, all sealed in their clear bags. "You can take a look at them when you have time, let me know."

"I will. Oh, I love these!" She held up the citrine and silver, the last pieces Abra made. "Little silver moons and stars, then the citrine's like sunlight."

"Those are really nice." The woman with the champagne flutes walked over to the counter.

"Abra's one of our artists. She just brought in some new pieces."

"Aren't we lucky? Oh! Joanna, come look at this necklace. It's so you."

Abra exchanged a smug look with Heather as she handed over her credit card. The way the three women huddled around the new pieces, she might justify a cute new yoga outfit after all.

Thirty minutes later, Abra treated herself to an ice cream cone and walked home in a much more positive state of mind. She'd sold half her new pieces on the spot, and two more from what the store already had in stock. Definitely new outfit time, and she had just the one book-marked on her favorite site.

Plus, she'd *earned* the gorgeous wine-glasses.

First chance, she'd have Eli to the cot-tage for a little wine and candlelight din-ner and use them.

But now, she'd try meditation again. Maybe with some incense this time. Usu-ally she preferred the fresh sea air, but that hadn't been working. Change it up, she decided.

She let herself into the house, enter-tained herself by unwrapping and wash-ing her new glasses before setting them out on display on her kitchen shelves. Admiring them gave her positive outlook another boost.

In anticipation she got a pencil, a pad, the copy of the sketch, set it all by her meditation cushion in her bedroom. Though an average artist at best in her own estimation, she thought she might be able to make any changes or additions that came into her mind right then and there. Already starting her breathing, she went to the closet for the box that held her incense—cones and sticks—and the various holders she'd collected over time.

Maybe the lotus scent, she considered, to open the mind's eye. Really, she should've tried this before.

She got the box off the high shelf, opened it.

And with a strangled gasp, dropped it as if it held a hissing snake.

Her incense rained down, the holders clattered. And the gun thudded on the floor. Instinctively she backed away from it. Her first gut reaction was to run, then logic clicked in.

Whoever had put the gun there wouldn't be waiting in the house for her to find it. They'd put it there, she thought as she let herself breathe, so the police would find it.

That meant, had to mean, whoever had held that gun last had committed murder.

She went straight to the phone.

"Vinnie, I've got a really big problem. Can you come?"

In under ten minutes, she met him at the door. "I didn't know what else to do."

"You did just right. Where is it?"

"In the bedroom. I didn't touch it." She led the way, then stood back while he crouched to examine the gun. "It's a .32."

"Is that the same kind that . . ."

"Yeah." He straightened, took his phone out of his pocket, took several pictures.

"You're not in uniform," she realized. "You weren't even on duty. You were home with your family. I shouldn't—"

"Abs." He turned, took her in for a hug, patting her back like a daddy. "Relax. Corbett's going to want to know about this."

"I swear it's not my gun."

"I know it's not your gun. Nobody's going to think otherwise. Relax," he repeated. "We'll sort this out. Have you got anything cold?"

"Cold?"

"Yeah, a Coke, iced tea, whatever?"

"Oh, sure."

"I could use something cold. Maybe you could go take care of that, and I'll be right out."

He'd given her a chore to calm her down, she knew. So she'd calm down.

She got out a pan, added water, sugar, then set it on heat to dissolve while she juiced lemons.

By the time Vinnie came in, she was pouring her mix into a tall glass pitcher.

"You didn't have to do all that."

"It kept my hands busy."

"Fresh lemonade, from scratch."

"You deserve it. Tell Carla I'm sorry I interrupted your weekend."

"She's married to a cop, Abra. She gets it. Corbett's on his way. He wants to see it in place."

She wanted it, and the death surrounding it, out of her house. "Then you'll take it away."

"Then we'll take it away," he promised. "So go through it with me."

"I went out, walked to the village, spent a little time in the gift shop. I bought an ice cream cone, came home."

As she spoke she poured the lemonade over ice, added a plate of crispy cookies to the table. "I couldn't have been gone more than an hour, an hour and fifteen."

"Did you lock the doors?"

"Yes. I've been careful, or mostly careful, about that since the break-ins at Bluff House."

"When's the last time you looked in that box?"

"I don't use incense often, and I haven't bought any in a while. I end up buying it, not using it, giving it away. And I'm rambling." She took a drink. "I don't know exactly, but I'd say at least a couple weeks. Probably three."

"You spend a lot of time out of the house, a lot of that time at Bluff House."

"Yes. Classes, my cleaning jobs, shopping—for myself and for clients. Errands. And I've been spending most nights with Eli. Whoever killed Kirby Duncan planted it, Vinnie, to try to implicate me."

"That's a pretty sure bet. I'm going to take a look at the doors and windows, okay? Good lemonade," he added. "Good cookies, too."

She stayed where she was rather than dogging him. Going through her cottage couldn't take long. Small-scale, it boasted three bedrooms though the second of the three hardly qualified as a storage closet and served as her craft room. Kitchen, living room, with its sunroom that had been one of its main selling points. Two small baths.

No, it wouldn't take long. She rose, walked to look out on her back deck. Another selling point, that generous outdoor living space. She used it as much as the interior in good weather. Then that view, the jagged curve of the little cape with the lighthouse, the spread of sea and sky.

So much what she wanted, and such a constant comfort and pleasure to her.

Now someone had violated that, and her. Someone had been in her home, walked through her rooms, and left death behind.

She turned when Vinnie came back in,

waited while he looked at the deck door, the back windows.

"You've got windows unlocked back here, and a couple in the front, too."

"I'm an idiot."

"You're not."

"I like to open the house, air it out. I'm a fiend about it." Gripping her own hair, she tugged because it was easier than kicking herself. "I'm surprised I thought to lock any of the windows."

"Couple of threads caught here." He took a picture with his phone. "You got tweezers?"

"Yes. I'll get them."

"Didn't think to bring a kit," he said when she stepped out. "I brought an evidence bag for the gun, but not much else. That should be Corbett," he continued at the knock on the door. "Do you want me to get it?"

"No, I've got it."

Tweezers in hand, she opened the front door. "Detective Corbett, thanks for coming. Vinnie— Deputy Hanson's back in the kitchen. The gun . . . I'll show you."

She led the way to the bedroom. "I

dropped the box—everything—when I saw it inside. I was getting some incense, and it was in there."

"When's the last time you opened the box?"

"I told Vinnie, probably three weeks ago. Um, he took pictures," she said when Corbett took out his camera.

"Now I have my own." He crouched, pulled out a pencil, hooked the trigger guard. "Do you own a gun, Ms. Walsh?"

"I don't. I've never owned a gun. I've never even held a gun. Not even a toy one, really. My mother was firmly anti– war toys, and I liked puzzles and crafts, and . . . I'm rambling. I'm nervous. I don't like having a gun in my house."

"We'll take it with us." Corbett pulled on protective gloves as Vinnie came in.

"Detective, there's some unlocked windows. Abra told me she doesn't always think to lock them. I've got some fibers stuck in one of the rear ones."

"We'll take a look at that. Who's been in the house in the last couple weeks?"

"Oh, I have in-home yoga classes once a week in the evening, so my students.

And my neighbors' kids have been over. Oh my God, the kids. Is that loaded? Is that thing loaded?"

"Yeah, it's loaded."

"What if one of them had come in here and . . . I'm being irrational. They wouldn't come in here and get that box off the top shelf of my closet. But if they had . . ." She closed her eyes.

"Any repairman in for any reason?" Corbett asked as he pulled an evidence bag from his pocket.

"No."

"Landlord, cable company, anything like that?"

"No. My class, the kids."

"Eli Landon?"

Her eyes flashed. Corbett simply studied her. "You told him you know he's innocent."

"I still have to ask the question."

"He hasn't been in the cottage in the last few weeks. He's stuck close to Bluff House since the first break-in. I had to wheedle to get him to leave the house long enough to shop for his family's visit this weekend."

"Okay."

He straightened. "Let's take a look at the fibers."

She waited while they studied them, murmured over them, tweezed them out and bagged them.

"Would you like some lemonade, Detective? I just made it."

"That'd be nice. Then why don't you sit down?"

Something about the way he said it made her palms clammy. She poured the drink, sat down at the table.

"Have you seen anyone hanging around?"

"No. And I haven't seen the man from the bar again. At least I don't think I have. I should recognize him, even though I haven't been much help with the description. It's why I went for the incense. I thought I'd light some, try more meditation. I've been edgy the last few days, and I thought I'd broken through."

"Edgy?"

"With all that's gone on, it's understandable. And . . ." Hell with it. "Someone's watching me."

"You've seen someone?"

"No, but I feel it. It's not my imagination, or I'm nearly positive it's not. I know what it's like to be watched now. You know what happened to me a few years ago."

"Yes, I do."

"And I feel it, and have for several days now."

She glanced toward the window she'd left unlocked, toward her glass deck door and the pots of mixed flowers she'd set up in the sun.

"I'm out of the house a lot, and I've been spending most nights down with Eli. And since I was careless enough not to lock the windows, it would be pitifully easy to get in here, to leave that gun here. But why? I don't understand why here? Why me? Or I do, but it's convoluted. If someone wanted to discredit me, implicate me to cast doubt on Eli's alibi, why not just plant the gun in Bluff House during the break-in?"

"We searched before he could plant it, or he didn't plan on giving it up," Vinnie said. "Sorry, Detective. Out of turn."

"No, it's fine. The last couple days, Wolfe's pushed for a search warrant, for this cottage. His superiors aren't backing him on it, and neither are mine. But he's pushing. He claims he got an anonymous call telling him the caller saw a woman, a woman with long curly hair, walking away from the lighthouse on the night Duncan was murdered."

"I see." A canyon opened up in her belly. "You'd find the gun here. So either I killed Duncan or was an accomplice. Do I need a lawyer?"

"It couldn't hurt, but right now this looks like what it is: a setup. That doesn't mean we don't go through the process."

"All right."

He sampled the lemonade. "Look, Ms. Walsh—Abra. I'm going to tell you how this reads, and how my boss is going to read it. If you had anything to do with Duncan, why the hell didn't you throw that gun off the cliff, especially after we executed the search on Bluff House? Putting it in your bedroom closet with a bunch of incense? That makes you dumb as a bag of hair, and there's nothing that indicates you're dumb as a bag of hair."

Not trusting her voice yet, she nodded.

"You find it, call it in. Coincidentally, the lead detective on Landon's wife's homicide gets a call from an anonymous source—on a prepaid cell that pinged from a local tower—claiming, three weeks after the incident, he saw a woman with your hair and body type walking away from the crime scene on the night in question."

"And Detective Wolfe believes him."

"Maybe he does, maybe he doesn't, but he'd like to hook a search warrant with it. It screams setup, and a clumsy one at that, so I think Wolfe's not buying it, but like I said, he wouldn't mind giving your place a look."

"There's nothing here. Nothing . . . but that gun."

"We'll go through the process. I can get a warrant for a search, but it'd be easier all around if you just gave your permission."

She didn't want it; it made her a little sick inside. But more, she wanted it over. "All right, search, look, do whatever you have to do."

"Good. When we finish, I want you to

make sure this place is locked—including windows."

"Yes, I will. And I think I'll spend the nights either at Bluff House or with my next-door neighbors until . . . for a while."

"Better yet."

"Do you have to tell Eli now?" She dropped her hand when she realized she'd been twisting the smoky quartz pendant she wore—one made in her craft room—around and around on its chain. "It's just his family's coming. They're probably here now for Easter. Something like this is going to upset everyone."

"Until I need to talk to him again, I don't have to tell him anything."

"Good."

"I've called for somebody to come in, check for prints, but—"

"There won't be any. But it's the process."

"That's right."

She got through it. Little house, she thought, didn't take long. She stayed out of the way, stayed outside when she could. This was how Eli had felt, she realized, how he must've felt when the police came, to check, to search, to look for evidence. He must've felt, for that bubble of time, the house wasn't his. His things weren't his things.

Vinnie stepped out. "They're finishing up. Nothing," he told her. "No prints on the window, on the box, on the contents." He gave her back a quick rub. "The search is a formality, Abs. You okaying it without a warrant only adds weight to this being a setup."

"I know."

"Want me to hang out with you awhile?"

"No, you should go home to your family." To dye Easter eggs, she thought, with his little boy. "You didn't have to stay this long."

"I want you to call me, anytime, for anything."

"I will. Count on it. I'm going to put myself together a little and go down to Bluff House. I want to see Hester."

"You give her my best. I can wait until you're ready to go."

"No, I'm fine. Better. It's broad daylight. There are people on the beach. He's got no reason to bother me anyway at this point."

"Keep the doors and windows locked anyway."

"I will."

She walked him out. Her across-the-street neighbor sent her a wave, then went back to digging in his front garden. A couple of boys raced by on bikes.

Too much activity, she assured herself, for anyone to try to get inside. And no reason now to do so.

She got a trash bag, went into the bedroom. Kneeling, she threw everything on the floor away, box and all. She couldn't know what he'd touched. If she could, she'd have thrown everything in the closet away.

Instead, she freshened up her makeup, packed a small bag, included the sketch. After she tidied up the kitchen, she retrieved the strawberry-rhubarb pies she'd made, boxed them up.

She carried them out to her car, went back for her bag, her purse. And when she locked her front door, her heart broke a little.

She loved her little cottage, and didn't know when she'd feel safe in it again.

Nineteen

People, noise, movement filled Bluff House. Eli had forgotten what it was like to have so many voices speaking at once, so many activities rolling over each other, so many questions to answer.

After the initial jolt, he found himself enjoying the company and chaos. Hauling luggage upstairs or bags and platters into the kitchen, watching his niece toddle everywhere—and holding what seemed to be intense conversations with the dog—noting his mother's surprised approval when he pulled out a fancy tray of fruit and cheese to offer as a post-trip snack.

But his biggest pleasure came from seeing his grandmother stand on the terrace, the breeze fluttering her hair as she looked out to sea.

When he slipped out to join her, she leaned against him.

In her beam of sun, the old dog Sadie raised her head, gave a little wag, then went back to sleep.

"Sun warms old bones," Hester said. "Mine and Sadie's. I've missed this."

"I know." He draped an arm around her shoulders. "And I think this has missed you."

"I like to think so. You potted pansies."

"Abra did. I water them."

"Teamwork's a good thing. It's helped knowing you're here, Eli. Not just on the practical level of having someone in the house, but having *you* here. Because I think this has missed you, too."

The familiar vine of guilt and regret wound through him. "I'm sorry I stayed away so long. Sorrier I thought I had to."

"Did you know I hated to sail?"

Pure shock had him gaping down at her. "You? Hester First Mate Landon? I thought you loved it."

"Your grandfather loved it. I had to take a pill to keep my stomach steady. I love the sea, but better when I'm on land looking at it. We sailed together, Eli and I, and I don't regret a single pill, a single minute on the water with him. Marriage is a series of compromises, and at its best, the compromises create a life, a partnership. You compromised, Eli, and that's nothing to apologize for."

"I was going to take you out tomorrow."

She laughed, quick and delighted. "Let's not."

"Why do you keep the boat?"

When she simply looked at him, smiled at him, he understood. For love, he thought, and pressed his lips to her cheek.

She shifted to look him in the eye. "So, you have a dog."

"I guess I do. She needed a place. I can relate."

"A dog's a healthy step." She shifted again to study him more closely, and leaned on her cane. "You look better."

"I hope to hell I do. You look better, Gran."

"I hope to hell I do." She let out another laugh. "We were a couple of wounded warriors, weren't we, young Eli?"

"Healing up now, and coming on strong. Come home, Gran."

She sighed, gave his arm a squeeze before she walked with the aid of her cane to a chair to sit. "I've got more healing to do yet."

"You can heal here. I'll stay with you, as long as you need."

Something shimmered in her eyes. For a moment, he feared tears, but it was light. "Sit," she told him. "I fully intend to come back, but now's not the time. It would be both impractical and unwise to be here when I have all those damn doctors and physical therapists in Boston."

"I can take you in for your appointments." He hadn't realized, not really, until he'd seen her standing on the terrace, her eyes on the sea, how much he wanted her back. "We can arrange for you to have your therapy here."

"God, how much your mind's like mine. I've considered exactly that almost from the moment I woke up in the hospital.

Coming back's one of the main things that got me through. I come from tough stock, and marrying a Landon gave me more. I made those doctors eat crow when I recovered, when I got on my feet again."

"They didn't know Hester Landon."

"They know me now." She sat back. "But I've got a ways to go yet. I need your mother. Oh, I need your father, too. He's a good son, and always has been. But I need Lissa, bless her, for a while longer. I'm on my feet, but I can't stay there as much as I'd like, as much as I will. So I'll stay in Boston until I'm satisfied I'm steady again. And you'll stay here."

"As long as you want."

"Good, because this is exactly where I want you, and always have. I wondered if I'd be the last Landon in Bluff House. The last who'd live in Whiskey Beach. I've asked myself more than once if the reason I never warmed to Lindsay was because she'd keep you in Boston."

"Gran—"

"Well, however selfish and self-serving, it was part of the why. Not the whole, but part. I would have accepted that, or tried, if she'd made you happy—the way Tricia's family, and her work at Landon Whiskey, make her happy."

"She's a whiz at it, isn't she?"

"She takes after your grandfather, and your father. Born and bred for it. You're more like me. Oh, we can handle business when we have to, and we're not fools. But it's art that pulls us."

Reaching over, she patted his hand. "Even when you turned your sights on the law, it was your writing that made you happiest."

"It seemed like too much fun to be a job. And now that it's a job, it's a lot more work. When I practiced law, it felt as if I had something important, something solid. More than daydreaming on paper."

"Is that all there is to it? Daydreaming?"

"No. Lindsay used to call it that." He'd nearly forgotten. "Not harshly, but . . . a handful of short stories wasn't all that impressive."

"She preferred the impressive, and I don't say that harshly. She was who she was. But in that series of compromises, the plain truth is Lindsay rarely pulled her weight. Or not that I could see. People who say not to speak ill of the dead just don't have the spine to say what they think."

"You've got plenty of spine."

He hadn't expected to talk of Lindsay, not here, not with his grandmother. But maybe this was the place to put some of it to rest. "It wasn't all her fault."

"It's rarely only one person's fault."

"I thought we'd take our own steps, meld our strengths, weaknesses, goals. But I married a princess. Her father always called her that. Princess."

"Ah, yes, I recall that now."

"She always got what she wanted. She was raised to believe she could and would—and should. She was naturally charming, incredibly beautiful and absolutely believed her life would be perfect, exactly the way she wanted."

"And life isn't a series of fairy tales, even for a princess."

"I guess not," he agreed. "It turned out life just wasn't perfect with me."

"She was young and spoiled, and given the chance, she may have matured and become less self-involved. She did have charm, and an excellent eye for art, for decor, for fashion. With time she might have made something of that, and of herself. But the blunt truth is, she wasn't your match, or your mate, or the love of your life. You weren't hers."

"No," he admitted, "neither of us made the grade."

"The best that can be said is you both made a mistake. She paid too big a price for that mistake, and I'm sorry for it. She was a young, beautiful woman, and her death was senseless and cruel. It's done."

No, Eli thought, not until who caused it paid.

"I have a question for you," Hester continued. "Are you happy here?"

"I'd be crazy not to be."

"And you work well here?"

"Better than I expected or hoped. For most of this past year writing was more of an escape, a way to get out of my head—or into another part of it. Now it's my work. I want to be good at it. I think being here's helped me with that."

"Because this is your place, Eli. You

belong in Whiskey Beach. Tricia? We all know her life, her family, her home's in Boston." She glanced back, through the terrace doors where Selina sprawled on the floor beside an ecstatic Barbie. "This is a place for her to come, to spend a weekend, a summer break, a winter holiday. It's not home for her, and never was."

"It's your home, Gran."

"You're damn right it is." Her jaw lifted, her eyes went deep and soft as she looked over the heads of fluttering pansies and out to the roll of the sea. "I fell in love with your grandfather on that beach, one heady spring night. I knew he'd be mine, and we'd make our home in this house, raise our children here, live our lives. It's my home, and what's mine I'm free to give."

She turned to Eli now, and those soft eyes went steely. "Unless you tell me, and make me believe, that you don't want it, you can't make your life here, be happy here, I'll be making arrangements to deed it to you."

Stunned, he could only stare at her. "Gran, you can't give me Bluff House."

"I can do exactly as I please, boy." She tapped her finger firmly on his arm. "As I always have and intend to continue to do."

"Gran—"

She tapped her finger again, a warning this time. "Bluff House is a home, and a home needs to be lived in. It's your legacy, and your responsibility. I want to know if you're willing to make it your home, if you're willing to stay, when I'm able to come back, and when I'm gone. Is there somewhere else you'd rather be?"

"No."

"Well then, that's settled. It's a weight off my mind." With a contented sigh, she looked out to sea again.

"Just like that?"

She smiled, reached over to lay a hand on his, gently now. "The dog clinched it."

Even as he laughed, Tricia opened the terrace doors. "If you two can tear yourself away, it's egg-dyeing time."

"Let's get to it. Give me a hand, Eli. I can get down, but I still have trouble getting up."

He helped her to her feet, then just wrapped his arms around her. "I'll take good care of it, I promise you. But come home soon."

"That's the plan."

She'd given him a lot to think about, but dyeing Easter eggs with a toddler—not to mention her very competitive fifty-eight-year-old grandfather—made it difficult to think. So Eli just rolled with it. By the time the doorbell chimed, puddles of dye pooled and splattered the newspaper covering the kitchen island.

With the dog at his side, he opened the door for Abra. She stood with the straps of bags over each shoulder and a covered tray in her hands.

"Sorry, I didn't have enough hands to open it myself."

He just grinned at her, leaned over the tray to kiss her. "I was about to call you." He took the tray, angling so she could get by him. "I thought you'd be here before this—but I did, with great effort and canniness—manage to save some eggs for you."

"Thanks. I just had some things to deal with."

"Is anything wrong?"

"What could be wrong?" She set the bags aside. "Hello, Barbie. Hello." Better to hedge, she decided, than dump distressing news on a family party. "Pies take time."

"Pies?"

"Pies." She took the tray back, walked with him to the back of the house. "From the sound of it, everyone's settled in."

"Like they've been here a week."

"Good or bad?"

"Good. Really good."

She saw that for herself when they stepped into the kitchen. Everyone was spread around the island. Eggs, colored with varying degrees of skill and creativity, sat nesting in crates. She pumped up her smile, tried to put the horrible day behind her as attention turned to her.

"Happy Easter." She hurried over to set down the pies, turned immediately to Hester. After wrapping her arms around Hester, she closed her eyes, swayed a little. "It's so good to see you here. It's so good to see you."

"Let me look at you." Hester drew her back. "I've missed you."

"I need to come visit more often."

"With your schedule? We're going to sit down with a glass of wine for you, and a martini for me, and you're going to fill me in on all the gossip. Because I'm not ashamed to say I've missed that, too."

"You're nearly up-to-date, but I can dig out a few more tidbits for wine. Rob." Abra rose on her toes to embrace Eli's father.

Eli watched her work her way through his family. Hugging came naturally to her, that physical contact, the intimate touch. But seeing her with his family made him realize she was woven through their lives in ways he hadn't understood.

He'd been . . . apart, he thought now. Had taken himself to the side. For too long.

Within minutes she stood hip to hip with his sister, using a wax crayon to draw a design on an undyed egg, and talking about potential names for the new baby.

His father edged him aside. "While they're busy finishing up here, take me down and show me this business in the basement."

It wasn't the most pleasant of tasks, but it needed to be done. They went down, started through. Rob paused beyond the wine cellar.

He stood, a man who'd passed his height, his build—and the Landon eyes—to his son, his hands in the pockets of khakis.

"In my grandmother's day, this whole area was filled with jams, jellies, fruits, vegetables. Bins of potatoes, apples. It always smelled like fall to me in here. Your grandmother continued the tradition, though on a smaller scale. But then the days of the endless and elaborate parties faded off."

"I remember some elaborate parties."

"Nothing like the generation before," Rob said as they moved on. "Hundreds of people, and dozens of them who'd stay for days, even weeks during the season. For that, you needed a lot of idle time, a warehouse of food and drink, and a houseful of servants. My father was a businessman. If he had had a religion, it would have been business as opposed to society."

"I never knew about the servants' passageways. I just heard about them."

"To my great disappointment as a boy, they'd been closed up before I was born. Mom threatened to do the same with parts of the basement. I used to sneak down here with my friends. God knows why."

"I did the same thing."

"You think I didn't know?" Rob chuckled, slapped Eli on the shoulder. Then stopped again when they reached the old section.

"Christ almighty. I know you told me how extensive, but I didn't fully believe it. What kind of madness is this?"

"Treasure fever, I think. Nothing else makes sense."

"You can't grow up in Whiskey Beach and not come across treasure fever, even catch a mild case."

"You?"

"I believed—feverishly—in Esmeralda's Dowry as a teenager. Scoured books, hunted up maps. I took scuba lessons in preparation for a career as a treasure hunter. I grew out of it, but there's still a part that wonders. But this . . . this is senseless. And dangerous. The police have no leads?"

"Not so far, or not that they're sharing with me. Then again, they have a murder on their hands."

Eli had considered this, had weighed the pros and cons of laying it all out for his father. He hadn't known until that moment, he'd decided to do so. "I think they might be connected."

Rob studied his son. "I think we should take those dogs of ours for a walk, and you can tell me why. And how."

Inside, Abra sat with Hester in the morning room.

"This is nice," Abra said. "I've missed this."

"You've kept the house beautifully. I knew you would." She gestured to the pots of flowers on the terrace outside. "Your work, I'm told."

"I got some limited assistance. Eli's not much of a gardener."

"That can change. He's changed since he's been here."

"He needed the time, the space."

"It's more than that. I'm seeing glimpses of who he used to be, mixed with who he's becoming. It does my heart good, Abra."

"He's happier than when he came. He looked so sad, so lost and so angry under it all."

"I know it, and it's more than what happened in the past year. He let too much of himself go before that because he'd made a promise, and keeping promises is important."

"Did he love her? It doesn't feel right to ask him."

"I think he loved parts of her, and he wanted what he thought they could make together, wanted it enough to make the promise."

"A promise is a fearsome thing."

"For some, yes. For people like Eli. And for you. If his marriage had been happy, he might've become someone else yet, some other combination of himself. Someone who could have been content with his work in the law, his life in Boston, and he'd have kept the promise. I would have lost the boy who once thrived in Whiskey Beach, but that would've been fine. The same could be said about you."

"I guess it could."

"Is he seeing people?"

"He likes his solitude, but that goes with the work he's chosen. But yes. He and Mike O'Malley seem to have hit it off, and he's reconnected with Vinnie Hanson."

"Oh, that boy. Who'd have thought that half-naked, surf-riding, pot-smoking lay-about would end up a county deputy?"

"You always liked him, it shows."

"He was so damn affable. I'm glad Eli's reconnected with him, and is friendly with Mike."

"I think Eli makes friends, and keeps them, easily. Oh, and he spent the best part of an evening tossing them back with Stoney at the pub. They *really* hit it off."

"Good God. I hope someone drove him home, and I don't mean Stoney."

"We walked." Abra realized the implications of "we" the instant Hester's brows lifted.

"I wondered." With a curve to her lips, Hester lifted her martini glass. "Lissa seemed very excited you'd join us for the weekend."

"I don't want it to be awkward. Hester, you mean so much to me."

"Why would it be awkward? When I asked Eli to stay here, I hoped he'd find that time and space, find those pieces of himself. And I hoped the two of you would . . . start walking home together."

"Did you?"

"Why wouldn't I? In fact, I intended to meddle, if necessary, once I got fully back on my feet. Are you in love with him?"

Abra took a deep sip of wine. "You move fast."

"I'm old. I can't waste time."

"Old, my ass."

"But not so old I don't notice you haven't answered the question."

"I don't know the answer. I love being with him, and watching him become the way you talked about. I know things are complicated for both of us, so I'm happy with that."

"Complications are part of living." Taking her time, Hester sampled one of the two olives in her glass. "I know some of what's happened here, but not, I think, all. Everyone's too careful around me. I have a blank in my memory, but my mind's perfectly sound."

"Of course it is."

"And the rest of me soon will be. I know someone broke into Bluff House, and that's upsetting. I know someone was killed, and the police searched the house, which is more upsetting."

"The lead detective doesn't consider Eli a suspect," Abra said quickly. "In fact, he doesn't believe he had anything to do with Lindsay's death."

Her face a study of relief and annoyance, Hester sat back. "Why hasn't anybody told me *that*?"

"I imagine they didn't want to upset you with everything that went around it. But as bad as it's been, what's happened has worked Eli up. He's pissed, Hester, seriously pissed, and he's ready to stand up, to fight back. That's a good thing."

"A very good thing." She looked outside, toward the sea. "And this is a very good place to make a stand."

"Sorry to break this up." Lissa walked in, gave the watch on her wrist a tap.

"Oh, it's the warden," Hester announced.

"Hester, you need to rest."

"I'm sitting. I'm drinking an excellent martini. I'm resting."

"We had a deal."

On a huff of breath, Hester downed the rest of her martini. "All right, all right. I'm required to take a nap, just like little Sellie."

"And if you don't, you're as cranky as Sellie when she misses hers."

"My daughter-in-law has no problem insulting me."

"It's why you love me," Lissa said as she helped Hester to her feet.

"One of the many. We'll talk more later," she said to Abra.

Alone, Abra gave herself a moment for depression, for worry. Should she make an excuse and run home? For what? To make sure no one had broken in, left more incriminating evidence?

She had nothing to gain by obsessing, by letting worry nibble away at the corners of her mind. Better off here, she told herself, with people. Better off enjoying the moment.

God knew what might happen next.

Rising, she wandered into the kitchen. She'd like to cook something, she realized, but right now she was guest, not housekeeper, and didn't have free rein.

She should take her things upstairs, put together the little gift bags she'd made for the family.

She needed to keep busy.

She turned when Lissa came back in.

"Hester always complains about the nap, and always sleeps like a rock for an hour."

"She's always been so active and independent."

"Don't I know it. Still, an hour's nap is nothing. When she was first hurt, she was rarely awake for an hour at a time. She beat all the odds, and I shouldn't have expected less. You know, that looks good."

"Let me pour you a glass. I was just poking around, wondering what I could do to help. With dinner. Or anything."

"Oh, I'm going to draft you for dinner

detail. I can hold my own in the kitchen, when our Alice lets me. But I'm no Martha Stewart. You must be a wonderful cook."

"I must?"

"Hester's said so, and I see the evidence myself. Eli's putting weight back on instead of shedding it. I owe you for that."

"I like to cook, and he remembered he liked to eat."

"And he remembered he likes dogs, and walks on the beach, and companionship. I'm grateful, Abra."

"I liked reminding him."

"This shouldn't be awkward. We had a friendly relationship before you and Eli started seeing each other."

"You're right." She let out a breath. "I haven't been involved with anyone in a long time, especially anyone with close family. Truth? I'm so used to doing whatever needs to be done around here, or finding something that could be done. I'm not sure what I should or shouldn't do as a guest."

"Why don't we take 'guest' out of it

and consider we're all family. Hester thinks of you as hers. Eli thinks of you. Why don't we start with that?"

"I'd like that. Then I can stop second-guessing myself."

"I had Max take your things up to Eli's room." Lissa offered an easy smile, and a twinkle. "I didn't see the point in second-guessing."

After a surprised laugh, Abra nodded. "That makes it all simple. Why don't you give me the basics of the weekend's menus, and I'll take assignments?"

"We can do that. But while we've got a minute or so, I'd like you to tell me what, exactly, has gone on. I know Eli's out there, using that sweet dog and poor old Sadie as excuses to give his father all the details he's left out. Protect the women-folk from worrying their pretty heads."

Abra fisted her hands on her hips. "Really?"

"It's not quite that bad, but not that far off. I lived the last year, too, Abra. Every day of it. Every hour. I want to know what's happening with my son."

"Then I'll tell you."

She hoped she'd done the right thing, but to Abra it had been the only thing. Direct questions deserved direct answers. Now, as she trusted Lissa's judgment, both Eli's parents knew the score.

No more hedging or leaving out unpleasant details.

And what was she doing? she asked herself. Wasn't she hedging and leaving out unpleasant details? Eli certainly had a right to know about the planted gun, the police search. Shouldn't she trust him enough for full disclosure?

"There you are." Eli, windblown, smiling, walked in. "Barbie deserted me for my father, and her new best friend, Sadie. I think she's a little too easy."

"Good thing she's spayed. Any handsome hound might seduce her."

"I'm really glad you're here. I told my father the whole shot, all the grim and grisly details. I figured it was time."

"Good, because I just finished doing the same with your mother."

"My—"

"Goose and gander, Eli. She asked me directly. I answered. And she'll worry less knowing than wondering."

"I just wanted her to feel safe and un-burdened here for a couple days."

"I understand. I thought the same, and that's why I didn't— Is that Hester?"

At the shout, Eli was out of the room before Abra finished the question, and moving fast to his grandmother's bed-room.

Close on his heels, Abra hurried in to see Hester, white as the sheets, sitting up in bed. Her breath came too fast, and the hands she reached out to Eli shook.

Abra darted into the bathroom for water.

"It's okay. I'm right here. Take it easy, Gran."

"Here, Hester, drink a little water. Re-member your breathing." Abra's voice was a balm over a wound. "Hold the glass for her, Eli, while I fix the pillows. I want you to relax back now, breathe."

Hester kept one hand gripped on Eli's, sipped slowly before she let Abra ease her back against the pillows.

"I heard a noise."

"I ran upstairs," Eli began. "I wasn't thinking."

"No." Her eyes on Eli's, Hester shook her head. "That night. That night, I heard a noise. I got up because I heard a noise. I remember . . . I remember getting up."

"What kind of noise?"

"Footsteps. I thought . . . but then I thought I was imagining things. Old houses make noise. I'm used to it. The wind, I thought, but it was still, almost still that night. Just the house creaking like an old woman. I thought I'd make some tea, some of that special herbal tea you got for me, Abra. It's soothing. I'd make tea and I'd be able to sleep again. I got up to go downstairs.

"It's in pieces. It's all in pieces."

"It's all right, Gran. You don't have to remember it all."

Her grip tightened. "I saw something. I saw someone. Someone in the house. Did I run? Did I fall? I don't remember."

"Who did you see?"

"I don't know. I'm not sure." Her voice

cracked on it, fragile glass. "I can't see his face. I tried to get downstairs, but he's behind me. I think . . . I think I couldn't go up, so I ran down. I hear him, I hear him coming after me. Then I can't remember anything until I woke up in the hospital. You were there, Eli. You were the first one I saw when I woke up. I knew I'd be all right because I saw you."

"You are all right." He kissed her hand.

"Someone was in the house. I didn't dream it."

"No, you didn't dream it. I won't let him come back, Gran. He won't hurt you again."

"It's you who's in the house now, Eli. You have to protect yourself."

"I will. I promise you. Bluff House is my responsibility now. Trust me."

"More than anyone." She closed her eyes a moment. "Behind the armoire, on the third floor—the big double armoire—there's a mechanism in the molding that opens a panel."

"I thought all the passageways were sealed."

Her breathing leveled, and when she opened her eyes again, they beamed clear. "Yes, most are sealed, but not all. Curious little boys can't move that heavy armoire, or the shelving in the basement, in the old section—where your grandfather had a little workshop for a short time. There's another panel behind the shelving. The rest I had sealed. A compromise."

Now she managed to smile at him. "Your grandfather let me have my way, and I let him have his. So we didn't seal those two, and completely close a Bluff House tradition. I didn't even tell your father, not even when he was old enough not to be foolish."

"Why?"

"His place was Boston. Yours is here. If you need to hide, to get away, use the panels. No one else knows, except Stoney Tribbet, if he remembers."

"He remembers. He drew me a blueprint of where the panels used to be. But he didn't tell me two were still open."

"Loyalty," Hester said simply. "I asked him not to tell anyone."

"All right. Now I know, and you don't have to worry about me."

"I need to see his face, the man who

was in the house that night. I will see it. I'll put the pieces together."

"Why don't I fix you that tea now?" Abra offered.

"It's past time for tea." Hester squared her shoulders. "But you can help me get up, get myself downstairs. Then you can pour me a good glass of whiskey."

Twenty

Twice during the night Eli rose to prowl the house, the dog padding faithfully by his side. He checked doors, windows, the alarm, even slipped out to the main terrace to scan the beach for movement.

Everyone he cared about was sleeping in Bluff House, so he'd take no chances.

What his grandmother remembered changed things. Not the intruder—he'd already believed there was one on the night she fell. But the location. She'd described seeing someone *upstairs*, then running down, or trying to. Not someone on the main floor, someone who had come up from the basement.

That left three options.

His grandmother's mind was confused. Possible, of course, given the trauma she'd suffered. But he didn't think so.

It was also possible they were dealing with two different intruders, either connected or completely separate. He couldn't and wouldn't discount that avenue.

Last, a single intruder, the same one who had broken in and assaulted Abra, the same person who had excavated the old basement. Which posed the question: What had he been looking for upstairs? What had been the purpose?

Once the family left for Boston, he'd go through the house again, room by room, space by space looking for answers from that angle.

Until then, he and Barbie were on guard duty.

He lay wakeful beside Abra, trying to piece it together. An unnamed intruder partnered with Duncan? Move to the "No honor among thieves" theory, and the unnamed kills Duncan, then removes all records associated with him from Duncan's office.

Possible.

Duncan's client, the intruder, hired him. Duncan learns the client's breaking and entering, attacking women. Confronts the client, either threatening to report him to the police or attempting blackmail. And the client kills him and removes the records.

Equally possible.

The intruder or intruders weren't related to Duncan in any way. In doing his job, he discovered them, and was killed.

Possible, too, but unlikely, at least it seemed so at four in the morning.

He tried to shift his mind to his work. At least there were channels and possibilities in his plot he could solve before dawn.

He'd boxed in his main character— with the antagonist, with a woman, with the authorities. With his life in turmoil, he faced conflict and consequences on every level. It all came down to choices. Would he turn left or right? Would he stand still and wait?

Eli considered all three as his mind finally started to fuzz with sleep.

And somewhere in the maze of his subconscious, fiction and reality merged. Eli opened the front door of the house in the Back Bay.

He knew every step, every sound, every thought, but still couldn't make himself change any of it. Just turn around, walk back out into the rain. Just drive away. Instead, he repeated the loop he'd taken the night of Lindsay's murder and revisited in dreams ever since.

He couldn't change it, and yet it changed. He opened a door in the Back Bay and walked into the basement at Whiskey Beach.

He held a flashlight as he maneuvered in the dark. Some part of his mind thought, Power's off. The power's off again. He needed to kick-start the generator.

He walked by a wall of shelves filled with gleaming jars, all carefully labeled. Strawberry preserves, grape jam, peaches, green beans, stewed tomatoes.

Someone's been busy, he thought, circling around a mound of potatoes. A lot of mouths to feed in Bluff House. His family slept in their beds; Abra slept in his. A lot of mouths to feed, a lot of people to protect.

He'd made a promise to tend the house. Landons kept their promises.

He needed to get the power on again, restore the light, the warmth, the safety, and protect what was his, what was loved, what was vulnerable.

As he approached the generator, he heard the sound of the sea like a hum, a note that rose and fell, rose and fell, rose and fell.

And against the hum he heard the bright beat of metal against stone. A metronome keeping time.

Someone's in the house, striking at the house. Threatening what was his to protect. He felt the butt of a gun in his hand, looked down to see the glint of one of the dueling pistols in a light that had gone blue and eerie as the sea.

He moved through it while the hum built to a roar.

But when he stepped into the old section, he saw nothing but the trench scarring the floor.

He stepped to it, looked into it, and saw her.

Not Lindsay, not here. Abra lay in that deep scar, blood murderously red soaking her shirt, matting those wonderfully wild curls.

Wolfe stepped out of the shadows to stand in the blue light.

Help me. Help her. On the plea, Eli dropped to his knees to reach for her. Cold. Too cold. He remembered Lindsay as Abra's blood covered his hands.

Too late. No, he couldn't be too late. Not again. Not with Abra.

She's dead, like the other one. Wolfe raised his service weapon. You're responsible. Their blood's on your hands. This time you won't walk away.

The blast and echo of gunfire jolted Eli out of the dream, and into fresh panic. Gasping for breath, he pressed at the phantom pain in his chest, stared down, certain he'd see his own blood leaking through his fingers. Beneath his palm, his heart pounded, wild drumming against atavistic fear.

He groped for Abra, found the bed beside him cool and empty.

It was morning, he reassured himself. Only a dream, and now the sun streamed through the terrace doors and sprinkled white stars on the water. Everyone in Bluff House remained safe, secure. Abra had already gotten up, started the day.

Everything was fine.

He pushed up, saw the dog curled in her bed, one paw possessively over a toy bone. For some reason the sleeping dog settled him down another notch, reminded him reality could be just as simple as a good dog and a sunny Sunday morning.

He'd take the simple, as long as it lasted, over the complexities and miseries of dreams.

The minute Eli's feet hit the floor, Barbie's head came up and her tail swished.

"Everything's fine," he said out loud.

He pulled on jeans and sweatshirt, then went to look for Abra in her usual morning spot.

It didn't surprise him to find her in the gym, but it did to see his grandmother there with her. And it struck him as undeniably weird to see indomitable Hester Landon sitting cross-legged on a red mat wearing stretchy black pants that stopped just above the knee and a lavender top that left her arms and, with two deep scoops, much of her shoulders bare.

He saw the scar from her surgery running up her left arm at the elbow—deep trenches, he thought, as in the basement. Scars on what was his, what he loved, what he needed to protect.

"On an inhale, lean left. Don't overstretch, Hester."

"You've got me doing old-lady yoga."

The annoyance in Hester's voice made the whole scene marginally less weird.

"We're taking it slow. Breathe here. Inhale, both arms up, palms touch. Exhale. Inhale and lean right. Both arms up. Repeat that twice." As she spoke, Abra rose to kneel behind Hester and rub her shoulders.

"You've got a touch, girl."

"And you've got a lot of tension here. Relax. Shoulders down and back. We're just loosening up, that's all."

"God knows I need it. I wake up stiff, and stay that way. I'm losing my flexibility. I don't know if I can even touch my toes."

"You'll get it back. What did the doctors say? You weren't hurt worse—"

"Wasn't dead," Hester corrected, and with his view of her profile, Eli saw Abra squeeze her eyes shut.

"Because you have strong bones, a strong heart."

"A hard head."

"No argument. You've taken care of yourself and stayed active all your life. You're healing now, and need to be patient. You'll be doing Half Moons and Standing Straddles by summer."

"I often think it's a shame I didn't know those positions when my Eli was alive."

It took a moment for Eli to comprehend, then to be shocked and mortified. It took less for Abra's quick and wicked laugh.

"In loving memory of your Eli, exhale, navel to spine, and lean forward. Gently. Gently."

"I hope young Eli appreciates how limber you are."

"I can attest."

And the young Eli decided to beat a discreet retreat.

He'd make coffee, take a mug of it with

him and walk the dogs. By the time he'd finished that his grandmother should be dressed like his grandmother. And maybe her allusion to sex with his grandfather would have faded from his mind.

He caught the scent of coffee as he walked toward the kitchen, and found his sister, in pink pajamas, inhaling a cup.

Sadie stirred herself to stand from her sprawl on the kitchen floor so she and Barbie could sniff at each other.

"Where's the baby?"

"Right here." Tricia patted her anthill-size bump. "Big sister's upstairs having a Sunday snuggle with Daddy. I'm getting a window of quiet and the single stingy cup of coffee I'm allowed a day. You can have one, too, then help me hide eggs."

"I can do that, after I take the dogs for a walk."

"Deal." Tricia stooped to give Barbie a rub. "She's such a sweetheart, and nice company for Sadie. If she had a brother or sister, I'd snatch one up. She was wonderful with Sellie. So patient and gentle."

"Yeah." Some guard dog, Eli thought as he poured his coffee.

"I didn't have much time to talk to you, not alone. I wanted to say you look good. You look like Eli."

"Who'd I look like before?"

"Like Eli's gaunt, pasty-faced, slightly dull-witted uncle."

"Thanks."

"You asked. You're a little on the skinny side yet, but you look like Eli. For that I love Abra. A lot."

At his sidelong look, she angled her head. "Are you going to tell me she has nothing to do with it?"

"No. I'm going to say I don't know how I've lived with this family all my life without realizing the obsession with sex. I just overheard Gran make a sexual allusion to Abra about Granddad."

"Really?"

"Really. And now I have to burn it out of my memory. Come on, Barbie. Let's take Sadie for a walk."

But Sadie sprawled out again, yawned hugely.

"I'd say Sadie's taking a pass," Tricia observed.

"Fine. Just you and me, Barbie. We'll be back to play Easter Bunny in a few."

"Good enough. I wasn't just talking about sex," she called out.

He glanced back from the laundry room as he grabbed the leash. "I know."

He tried something different since he didn't have to keep to Sadie's dignified pace. And he had the beach to himself on an early Easter Sunday. Once he'd downed the coffee, he screwed the mug into the sand near the steps, then set off in a kind of half jog. When he asked his body how it felt about the idea, it wasn't altogether sure.

But the dog loved it. Loved it enough to increase the pace until Eli found himself in full jog. No question he'd pay for this one later, he decided. Good thing he had a massage therapist on hand.

He had a flash of her as she'd been in the dream, pale and bloody on the cold, stony dirt of the basement. The image sent his heart knocking harder than the run.

Eventually he managed to slow the dog to a walk again, pull in some of the moist air to soothe his dry throat.

So he was more anxious about the break-ins than he'd been willing to admit.

More concerned about his family, about Abra, than he'd wanted to admit in the cold light of day.

"We're going to have to do more about it than bark," he said to the dog, and turned her around to head home. "But we've got to get through today and to-morrow morning first."

He looked toward Bluff House, shocked to see how far they'd run. "Well, Jesus." Less than two months before he'd been prone, panting and covered in sweat at a half mile. Today, he'd breezed through twice that.

Maybe he really was himself again.

"Okay, Barbie, let's try for the circuit."

He ran back, the joyful dog beside him. When he looked up at Bluff House he saw Abra on the terrace, a hoodie over her yoga gear. She lifted her arm in a wave.

That was the picture he'd keep in his head, he promised himself. Abra with Bluff House at her back, and the breeze dancing through her hair.

He grabbed the mug. By the time he crested the beach steps, he was winded, but in a damn good way.

"A man and his dog," she said, greeting them both.

"A man, his dog and the theme from *Rocky. Adrian!*" He scooped her off her feet. Her laugh rang out as he gave her a spin.

"What was in that coffee, and is there any left?"

"It's going to be a good day."

"Is it?"

"Sure. Any day that starts out with chocolate bunnies and jelly beans for breakfast is a good day. We've got to hide eggs."

"Already done, Rocky. You missed out."

"Even better, now I get to hunt them. Give me some hints," he demanded. "You may not be aware, but Robert Edwin Landon, CEO of Landon Whiskey, chair or co-chair of countless worthy charitable boards and head of the renowned Landon family, would body-block his tiny little granddaughter to win the egg hunt."

"He would not."

"Okay, maybe he'd give the kid a break, but he'd sure as hell body-block his only son."

"Maybe true, but no hints from me.

Still, let's go inside and get your Easter basket before her father comes down and grabs them all."

It was a good day, though he ate enough candy that the idea of waffles for breakfast made him a little queasy. But he ate them anyway, and put everything aside to enjoy the moments.

His father in light-up bunny ears that made Selina belly-laugh. The pleasure on his grandmother's face when he gave her a pretty bowl filled with mixed spring bulbs in fragrant bloom.

Waging war with water pistols against his brother-in-law and accidentally (mostly) shooting his sister dead in the heart when she opened the terrace door.

Surprising Abra with a vivid green orchid because it reminded him of her.

They feasted on ham and roasted potatoes, tender asparagus and Abra's herbed bread, on eggs deviled out of their colorful shells—and more—in the formal dining room. Candles flickering, crystal winking, the sea singing its siren song against the rocky shore made the perfect backdrop for the very good day he'd predicted.

He couldn't remember the Easter before, with Lindsay's murder so fresh, with the hours he'd spent in interrogation, the living fear that the police would, again, knock on the door. And this time take him away in handcuffs. All that blurred now—the pale, strained faces of his family, the gradual and steady retreat of those he'd considered friends, the loss of his job, the accusations flung out at him if he ventured into public.

He'd gotten through it. Whatever hounded him now, he'd get through that.

He'd never give this up again, this feeling of home and of hope.

To Whiskey Beach, he thought, lifting his glass and catching Abra's eye, Abra's smile. He drank to it, and everything in it.

When he stood on Monday morning after helping load cars, the feeling of hope remained with him. He gave his grandmother a last good-bye hug.

"I'll remember," she whispered in his ear. "Stay safe until I do."

"I will."

"And tell Abra she won't be teaching

her morning yoga class without me much longer."

"I'll do that, too."

"Come on, Mom, let's get you in the car." Rob gave his son a one-armed man hug, a slap on the back. "We'll see you soon."

"Summer's coming," Eli said, helping his grandmother. "Make time, okay?"

"We will." His father walked around to the driver's seat. "It was good to have all the Landons in Bluff House again. Stay ready for us. We'll be back."

Eli waved them off, watched them until the road curved away. Beside him Barbie let out a quiet whine.

"You heard him. They'll be back." Turning, Eli studied Bluff House. "We have work to do before that. We're going to find out what that asshole was looking for. We're going to give Bluff House a clean sweep. Right?"

Barbie wagged her tail.

"I'll take that as a yes. Let's get started."

He started at the top. The third floor, the servants' domain back in the day, now served as storage for odd pieces of furniture, trunks that held vintage clothes or memorabilia previous Landons had been too sentimental to discard, and too practical to display.

After the search, the cops hadn't bothered to replace the dust sheets, so they lay in white piles like snowdrifts over the floor.

"If I were an obsessed treasure hunter, what would I be looking for up here?"

Not the treasure itself, Eli decided. "The Purloined Letter" aside, hiding in plain sight had its limits. No one could believe any of the previous occupants would have tucked a chest full of jewels away within the saggy divan or behind the spotty mirror.

He wandered around, poking into boxes and trunks, tossing dust covers back over chairs. The light streamed in so motes danced in beams, and the silence of the house accented the toss and suck of the surf.

He couldn't imagine living with the army of servants who'd once slept in the warren of rooms, or gathered in the larger space for meals or gossip. There'd never be true solitude, true silence, and forget genuine privacy.

A trade-off, he supposed. To maintain a house like this, and live and entertain as his ancestors did, required the army. His grandparents had preferred a less elaborate lifestyle.

In any case, the days of Gatsby were done, at least in Bluff House.

Still, it seemed a shame and a waste to have an entire floor occupied by shrouded furniture, boxes of books, trunks filled with dresses layered with tissue and sachets of lavender.

"It'd make a great artist's studio, wouldn't it?" he asked Barbie. "If I could paint. Gran can, but this is too much of a haul, and she likes using her sitting room for that, or painting on the terrace."

Taking a break, doing the shoulder rolls Abra had recommended, he prowled around the former servants' parlor.

"Still, the light's great. Little kitchen area over there. Update the sink, put in a microwave, update this bathroom," he added after taking a look at the old pull-chain toilet. "Or better, have these old fixtures rehabbed. Make use of some of the furniture that's just sitting here."

Frowning, he walked to the windows overlooking the beach. Generous windows, great view, a likely architectural decision rather than one done for the staff's benefit.

He moved off, into the gable, thinking of his first wandering through the day he'd arrived.

Yeah, he could work up here, he thought again. It wouldn't take much to fix it up a little. He didn't need much. Move a desk up, some files, shelves— and yeah, update this bathroom, too.

"What writer doesn't want a garret? Yeah, maybe. Maybe I'll do that once Gran's back home. I'll think about that."

Which wasn't addressing the purpose, Eli admitted, and did a second walk-through. He imagined housemaids climbing out of iron beds at dawn, bare toes curling against the cold floor. A butler putting on his starched white shirt, the head housekeeper checking off her list of duties for the day.

A whole world had existed here. One

the family had probably known little about. But what hadn't existed, as far as he could see, was anything worth the breaking and entering, or breaking the bones of an old woman.

He circled back into the wide hall, studied the old armoire against the—to him— unfortunate floral wallpaper. On close examination he saw no signs it had been moved in the past decade or more.

Curious, he attempted to do so now, putting his back into it. And didn't budge it more than an inch. He tried reaching into the narrow space behind it, then maneuvering his arm from underneath.

Not only would no mischievous little boy be able to shove it clear, but neither could a grown man. Not alone, Eli thought.

On impulse, he pulled out his phone and scrolled through the contacts Abra had keyed in. He hit Mike O'Malley's number.

"Hi, Mike, it's Eli Landon. . . . Yeah, good, thanks." He leaned back on the armoire, thought it as solid and intimidating as a redwood.

"Look, have you got a few minutes anytime today? . . . Really? If you've got the day off, I don't want to interrupt any plans. . . . In that case, I could use a hand with something. A little muscle?" He laughed at Mike's question about which muscle. "All of them . . . Appreciate it."

He hung up, looked at Barbie. "It's probably stupid, huh? But who can resist a secret panel?"

He trooped downstairs, detoured into his office for a minute to imagine moving his work space to the third floor. Not a completely crazy idea, he decided. More . . . eccentric.

The wallpaper would have to go, and there would probably be some issues with heat and AC, plumbing. Eventually he'd have to figure out what, if anything, to do with the rest of the space up there.

But it was good to think about it.

Barbie's head lifted. She let out a trio of barks seconds before the doorbell rang.

"Some ears you've got there," Eli told her, and headed downstairs in her wake.

"Hey. You were quick."

"You got me out of doing yard work— temporarily. Hey there." Mike gave Barbie a rub as she sniffed his pants. "I heard you got a dog. What's his name?"

"Her." Eli struggled with a wince. "Barbie."

"Dude." Pain and sympathy covered Mike's face. "Seriously?"

"She came with it."

"You can use that unless you get her a buddy and call him Ken. I haven't been in here for a while," Mike added as he wandered the foyer. "Hell of a place. Maureen said your family came up for Easter. How's Mrs. Landon doing?"

"Better. A lot better. I'm hoping she'll be back in Bluff House by the end of summer."

"It'll be great having her back. Not that we want to kick you out of Whiskey Beach."

"I'm staying."

"No shit?" Mike's grin stretched as he gave Eli a punch on the shoulder. "Man, glad to hear it. We could use some fresh meat in our monthly poker games. And we'd class it up holding it here when you're up."

"What's the buy in?"

"Fifty. We're small-time."

"Let me know next time you're setting up. The thing's upstairs," Eli said, gesturing and turning for the steps. "Third floor."

"Cool. I've never been up there."

"It hasn't been used since I was a kid. We would play up there in bad weather, and once or twice we got to bunk up there, tell ghost stories. Just storage now, really."

"So, we're hauling something down?"

"No. Just moving a piece. Big-ass armoire. Double armoire," he added as they topped the stairs. "In here."

"Nice space, bad wallpaper."

"Tell me."

Mike scanned the room, landed on the armoire. "Big mother." He crossed to it, ran his fingers over the carved front. "A beauty. Mahogany, right?"

"I think."

"I've got a cousin who brokers antiques. He'd piss his pants at a chance on this. Where are we moving it?"

"Just out a few feet." At Mike's blank look, Eli shrugged. "So . . . there's a panel behind it."

"A panel?"

"A passageway."

"Fucking A!" As he punched a fist in the air, Mike's face lit up. "Like a secret passage? Where does it go?"

"All the way down to the basement, from what I'm told. Just told. I had no idea. They were servants' passages," Eli explained. "They made my grandmother nervous, so she closed them up, but she just blocked off this one, and the one in the basement."

"This is very cool." Mike rubbed his hands together. "Let's move this sucker."

Easier said, they discovered. Since they couldn't lift it, and trying to shove it from either side proved impossible, they realigned, both on one end, then both on the other, walking it out a couple inches at a time.

"Next time we get a crane." Straightening, Mike rolled his aching shoulders.

"How the hell did they get it up here?"

"Ten men, and one woman telling them it might look better on the other wall. And if you tell Maureen I said that, I'll swear you're a dirty liar."

"You just helped me move a ten-ton

armoire. My loyalty is yours. See here? You can just see the edge of the panel. The ugly wallpaper mostly camouflages it, but when you know it's there . . ."

He felt around the chair rail, sliding his fingers over, under until they hit the release. When he heard the faint click, he looked at Mike.

"You game?"

"Are you kidding? Game is my middle name. Open her up."

Eli pressed on the panel, felt it give slightly, then open an inch in his direction. "Swings out," he murmured, and pulled it fully open.

He saw a narrow landing, then the drop of steep steps into the dark. Automatically, he felt the inside wall for a switch, and was surprised to find one.

But when he flipped it, nothing happened.

"Either there's no electricity in there, or no light. I'll get a couple of flashlights."

"And maybe a loaf of bread. For the crumbs," Mike explained. "And a big stick, in case of rats. Just the flashlights then," he said to Eli's stony stare.

"Be right back."

He grabbed a couple of beers while he was at it. The least he could do.

"Better than a loaf of bread." Mike took the beer and a flashlight, shone the light upward in the passage. "No lightbulb."

"I'll get some next time." Armed with the flashlight, Eli stepped into the passage. "Pretty narrow, but wider than I figured. I guess they'd need the space for carrying trays and whatever. The steps feel sound, but watch it."

"Snakes, very dangerous. You go first."

Snorting out a laugh, Eli started down. "I doubt we'll find a detested butler's skeletal remains or the dying words of a feckless housemaid carved into the wall."

"Maybe a ghost. It's spooky enough."

And dusty and dank. The steps creaked underfoot, but at least no rats gleamed out with red eyes.

Eli paused when his light played over another panel. "Let me think." And orient himself. "This should come out on the second-floor landing. See how it forks here? That one should come out in my grandmother's bedroom. That's always been the master, as far as I know. God, we'd have killed to have these open when we were kids. I could've snuck around, jumped out and scared the shit out of my sister."

"Which is exactly why your grandmother sealed up the doors."

"Yeah."

"Thinking of opening them again?"

"Yeah. No reason to, but yeah."

"Cool is its own reason."

They followed the passage, going down or taking a turn. From the blueprint in his head, Eli judged the panels had once opened in strategic places throughout the house, into parlors, the kitchen, a sitting room, a hallway and down to the depths of the basement.

"Hell. Should've moved the shelves barricading the other side first." But he found the lever, drew the door to him so he and Mike peered through old pots and rusted tools and into the basement.

"You've got to unseal this, man. Think of the Halloween parties."

But he was thinking of something else. "I could set him up," he murmured.

"Huh?"

"The asshole breaking in here, digging down here. I've got to think about this."

"Stake yourself out in here, lure him in. Classic ambush," Mike agreed. "Then what?"

"I'm thinking about it." He closed the door, vowing to move the shelves, formulate a plan.

"Let me know. I wouldn't mind being in on catching that guy. Maureen's still pretty freaked," Mike said as they started back up. "I don't know if she'll really relax until they catch the guy, especially when most of us figure he's the same one who plugged the PI. Stands to reason."

"Yeah, it does."

"And when she found out he planted that gun in Abra's place, she super freaked."

"Can't blame her for— What? What gun? What are you talking about?"

"The gun Abra found in her . . . Oh." After a pained wince, Mike stuffed his hands in his pockets. "Well, shit, she didn't tell you."

"No, she damn well didn't tell me. But you're going to."

"Get me another beer and my guts are spilled."

Promise

One sweetly solemn thought
Comes to me o'er and o'er;
I am nearer home to-day
Than I ever have been before.
—PHOEBE CARY

Twenty-one

At the end of a long day—two classes, a massive cleaning job and a pair of massages—Abra pulled up to her cottage.

And just sat.

She didn't want to go in. She hated knowing she didn't want to go inside her own home, tend to her own things, use her own shower.

She loved Laughing Gull, and had from the first instant she'd seen it. She wanted that feeling back, the pride, the comfort, the *rightness* of it, and all she felt was dread.

He'd spoiled it, whoever the hell he was, coming into her home, leaving his violence and death behind. A monster in the closet, in the form of a gun.

It left her two choices, she told herself. Let the monster win—give up, sit and brood. Or fight back and fix it.

Put that way, she decided, there wasn't a choice at all.

She shoved out of the car, muscled out her table, her bag, carted them both to the door. Inside, she leaned her table against the wall before carrying her bag into the living room.

Driving nearly twenty miles up the coast to buy the smudge stick had added onto her already crowded day, but when she took it out of her bag it felt like a positive action.

She'd burn the sage, cleanse her house. If she *felt* her house was cleansed, it *was* cleansed. And once she'd reclaimed her place, she'd get serious about adding a little greenhouse so she could grow her own herbs in bigger quantities. She'd make her own damn smudge sticks, and have fresh herbs year-round for cooking.

Maybe she'd sell them, too. Another enterprise. Create her own potpourri and sachets.

Something to think about.

But for now she did her best to clear her mind, to think only clean, positive thoughts as she lit the sage, held it over an abalone shell for safety and blew out the flame to encourage the smoke. Her home, she thought. The floors, the ceilings, the corners belonged to her.

The process, walking from room to room with the scent of white sage and lavender, calmed her, as did reminding herself what she'd made there, for herself, for others.

Faith, she thought, hope, and the symbols of them forged strength.

Once she'd finished the house, she stepped out onto her little patio, gently waving the smudge stick to send all that hope and faith into the air.

And saw Eli and the dog walking up the beach steps.

It made her feel a little foolish, standing there with her smoking sage as evening settled over the beach, as the man and the happy-faced dog climbed toward her.

To compensate, she stuck the smudge stick in the river rocks around her little Zen fountain where it would burn away naturally and safely.

"What a handsome couple." Smile in place, she walked over to greet them. "And a nice surprise. I just got home a few minutes ago."

"What're you doing?"

"Oh." She glanced as he did at the smudge stick. "Just a little homey ritual. Kind of a spring cleaning."

"Burning sage? That's a ward-off-evil-spirits kind of thing."

"I think of it as more a clearing out negativity. Did your family get off all right this morning?"

"Yeah."

"Sorry I couldn't stay to see them off. Busy day for me."

Something wrong, she thought, or something not quite right. All she wanted at that moment was quiet, peace and—a rarity for her—solitude. "I still have a lot to catch up on," she continued. "Why don't I stop by in the morning before my class, get your shopping list? I can pick up what you need before I come back to do the house."

"What I need is for you to tell me why I had to hear from Mike that someone put a gun in your house, that the police were here searching. That's what I need."

"I didn't want to bring it up with your family here. I called the police," she added.

"But not me. You didn't call me, or tell me."

"Eli, there wasn't anything you could do, and with a houseful of people—"

"That's bullshit."

Her hackles tingled. The comfort she'd found from the ritual struck against his anger, her own, flint against steel.

"It's not, and there was no point in me walking into Bluff House on Saturday announcing I'd just found a murder weapon in my incense box and had cops tromping all over my house."

"There was every point in telling me. Or there damn sure should have been."

"Well, I don't agree. And it was my problem, my decision."

"Your problem?" Insult punched through

temper. "That's how it is? You can come into my place with pots of soup, massage tables, Jesus, dogs. You can walk in, in the middle of the night, to close a fucking window and fight off an assault, but when somebody plants a gun on you, tries to implicate you in a murder, it's your problem? A murder most likely connected to me. But that's none of my business?"

"I didn't say that." Even to her own ears the defense sounded weak. "I didn't mean that."

"What do you mean?"

"I didn't want to dump all this on you and your family."

"You're in this because you're involved with me. And you pushed and wheedled your way in."

"Pushed and wheedled?" Her own insult bloomed so bright and hot, she whirled away to try to capture some of the smoke, and the calm, then immediately decided she'd have needed a smudge stick the size of Whiskey Beach Light to manage it. "Wheedled?"

"Damn right you did, from the minute I came back here. Now you're in, and you don't want to dump? You don't give any-body else a chance to dump. You're there with the shovel before the first clod hits the ground. But when it falls on you, you don't trust me enough to help."

"God. God! It isn't about trust. It's about timing."

"If that were true, you'd have found the time to tell me. You found it to tell Mau-reen."

"She was—"

"Instead of finding the time, you're up here lighting sage on fire and waving around a smoking stick."

"Don't make fun of my process."

"I don't care if you burn a field of sage or sacrifice a chicken. I care you didn't tell me you were in trouble."

"I'm not in trouble. The police know it wasn't my gun. I called Vinnie the minute I found it."

"But not me."

"No." She sighed, wondering how try-ing to do the right thing could go so hor-ribly wrong. "I didn't."

"My family left this morning, but you didn't tell me. You weren't going to tell me now."

"I needed to wave my smoking stick around and get comfortable in my house again. It's getting cold. I want to go in."

"Fine. Go in and pack a bag."

"Eli, I just want to be alone and quiet."

"You can be alone and quiet at Bluff House. It's a big place. You're not staying here by yourself until this whole goddamn mess is over."

"This is my house." Her eyes stung, and she wished she could blame it on the thinning, sluggish smoke. "I'm not letting some bastard drive me out of my house."

"Then we'll bunk here."

"I don't want you to bunk here."

"If you don't want us in, we'll stay out here, but we stay."

"Oh, for God's sake." She turned on her heel, strode back inside. She said nothing when he, with a slightly hesitant Barbie, followed her in.

Instead she went straight into the kitchen, poured herself a glass from an uncorked bottle of Shiraz.

"I know how to take care of myself."

"No question. You know how to take care of yourself and everybody else. You

don't know how, apparently, to let someone take care of you. That's conceit."

She slapped the glass on the counter.
"It's independence and capability."

"To a point, it is. Then it tips over into
conceit, and stubbornness. You've tipped.
This wasn't like you had a leaky pipe, so
you grabbed a wrench or called a plumber
instead of the guy you're sleeping with.
Add the guy you're sleeping with is involved with this whole clusterfuck. And
he's a lawyer."

"I called a lawyer," she said, then immediately wished she hadn't.

"Great. Good." Eli shoved his hands in
his pockets, paced a couple of circles.
"So you talked to the cops, a lawyer, your
neighbors. Anybody else other than me,
of course."

She shook her head. "I didn't want to
spoil your family's visit. It seemed point-
less for you, or any of you, to worry."

"You were worried."

"I needed to . . . Yes, all right. Yes, I've
been worried."

"I need you to tell me everything that
happened, in detail. I need you to tell me

what you said to the police, what they said to you. Everything you can remember."

"Because you're a lawyer."

The long, quiet look he sent her accomplished what words didn't. It made her feel foolish. It made her feel wrong.

"Because we're involved." His tone, quiet as the look, finished the job. "Because this started with me or with Bluff House, or both. And because I'm a lawyer."

"All right. I'll pack first." When he lifted his eyebrows, she shrugged. "It's too cold for you to sleep outside. And I know he's got no reason to come back here again. He has reasons to break into Bluff House again. Or it feels like it. So I'll pack some things and go with you."

Compromise? he wondered. Isn't this what his grandmother had spoken of? That give-and-take on both sides to find a balance.

"Good."

When she walked away, he picked up her unfinished wine. "We won that battle," he told Barbie. "But I don't think we've won the war. Yet."

He let her have quiet on the drive down, and stayed downstairs when she went up to unpack. If she put her things in another bedroom, he'd deal with it later. For now, it was enough to know she was with him, and safe.

In the kitchen, he poked in the fridge, the freezer. Leftover ham, he calculated, and plenty of sides. Even he should be able to put a decent enough meal together.

By the time she came down, he had the Monday night hodgepodge meal set up in the breakfast area.

"You can fill me in while we eat."

"All right." She sat, oddly comforted when Barbie elected to curl up by her feet instead of Eli's. "I'm sorry I made you feel I didn't trust you. That wasn't it."

"It's part of it, but we'll get into that later. Tell me exactly what happened. Step by step."

His response only dampened her already soggy mood. "I wanted to meditate," she began, and told him everything in as precise a manner as she could.

"You never touched the gun?"

"No. It fell when I dropped the box, and I left it there."

"As far as you know, they didn't find any prints that shouldn't have been there?"

"No, just the fibers."

"And the police haven't contacted you since?"

"Vinnie called me today, just to check in. He said they should have the ballistic results tomorrow or Wednesday, but more likely Wednesday."

"What about the gun itself? Was it registered?"

"He didn't tell me. I think he has to be careful what he says to me. But they know it wasn't mine. I've never owned a gun. I've never even held a gun. And if it was the gun used to kill Kirby Duncan, they know I was here, with you."

Handily covering each other, Eli thought. Just what would Wolfe make of that? "What did your lawyer say?"

"To call him if they wanted to question me again, and that he'd contact Detective Corbett directly. I'm not worried about being a murder suspect. Nobody thinks I killed Duncan."

"I could've planted the gun in your place."

"That would be stupid, which you're not."

"I could be using you for sex and patsy potential."

For the first time in what felt like hours, she smiled. "No more sex if you make me your patsy. And that's just not logical as it only turns the light back on, makes them look at you again. Which is exactly what whoever did plant it wanted, and why they suddenly made that anonymous call to Wolfe. The fact is, really, all this reeks of setup, and Corbett's not an idiot."

"No, I don't think he is. But there's another angle. It's possible you've had contact with the killer three times now. Here, in the bar and now with him planting the gun at your cottage. That's something to worry about, and you know it. You're not an idiot either."

"I can't do anything about that but be careful."

"You could leave, go visit your mother for a while. You won't," he added before she could speak. "And I don't blame you. But it's an option. Another option is to trust me."

Hearing him say it, knowing she'd given him cause to say it, made her absolutely miserable. "Eli, I do trust you."

"Not where it gets sticky, you don't. I don't know if I blame you for that, either. Men have let you down. Your father. It's one thing for it not to work out between him and your mother, but he's still your father. And he chose not to be one, not to be a real part of your life. He let you down."

"I don't dwell on it."

"That's healthy of you, but it's there."

When he let that hang in the air, she admitted defeat. "Yes, it's there. I don't really matter to him, and never have. I don't dwell on it, but it's there."

"You don't dwell because it's unproductive, and you like to produce."

"Interesting way to put it." Her lips curved again. "And true."

"And you don't dwell because you know it's his loss. Then there's the bastard who hurt you. That's letting you down big-time. You cared about him, trusted him, let him in, then he turned on you. He violated you."

"As bad as that was, if it hadn't happened, I might not be here."

"Positive attitude. Kudos. But it happened. You gave someone your trust and they broke it. Why wouldn't it happen again?"

"I don't think that way. I don't live that way."

"You lead an open, energetic, satisfying life that I often find amazing. The kind that takes spine and heart. It's admirable. You don't lean easily, and that's admirable, too, until it gets to the point where you could lean, where you should, and you won't."

"I would've told you if your family hadn't been here." Then she accepted, and told the whole truth. "I probably would've put it off for a while. I might've told myself you keep getting hammered, and there was no point adding to that until I knew more or it had been resolved in some way. I might have. But that's not about trust."

"Pity?"

"Concern. And my own confidence. I don't like the word 'conceit.' I needed to take care of myself, make decisions, handle problems and, yes, maybe take on other people's problems to build up the confidence Derrick shattered. I need to know I can take care of things when there's no one to depend on but myself."

"And when there is someone else to depend on?"

Maybe he was right again, and that was where it got sticky. And maybe it was time for a little self-evaluation.

"I don't know, Eli, I just don't know the answer because I haven't given myself that choice in a long time. And still, I leaned on you that night, after I was attacked. I leaned, and you didn't let me down."

"I can't get involved again with someone who won't give as much as she takes, take as much as she gives. I found out, the hard way, if you do you end up empty-handed and bitter. I guess we both have to decide how much we can give, how much we can take."

"I hurt you because I didn't reach out."

"Yeah, you did. And you pissed me off. And you made me think." He rose, picking up dishes. Neither of them had done justice to the meal. "I let Lindsay down."

"No, Eli."

"Yeah, I did. Our marriage might've been a mistake, but we were in it together. Neither of us got what we wanted or expected out of it. At the end, I couldn't stop what happened to her. I still don't know if she's dead because of some choice I made, choices we made together, or just some random piece of bad luck.

"I let my grandmother down, going longer and longer between times coming here, or seeing her at all. She didn't deserve that. We almost lost her, too. Would it have happened if I'd spent more time here, if I came here to stay with her after Lindsay's murder?"

"You're the center of the universe now? You want to talk conceit?"

"No, but I know, I *know* I'm somewhere in the center of this, and all of it's connected."

He turned to her, didn't go to her, didn't touch her, but stood with that space between them.

"I'm telling you, Abra, I'm not going to let you down. I'm going to do everything, whether you like it or not, whether you sleep with me or not, to make sure nothing happens to you. And when this is done, I guess we'll see where we are, and where we go from there."

Because she felt a little boxed in, she rose. "I'll do the dishes."

"I've got it."

"Balance, or as you said, give-and-take," she reminded him. "You fixed the meal, I clean up."

"Okay. I want a copy of your schedule."

She felt, literally, prickles of warning at the back of her neck. "Eli, it changes. That's the beauty of it."

"I want to know where you are when you're not here. I'm not a goddamn stalker. It's not about keeping tabs or trying to sew you in."

She put the plate she was holding on the counter, took a breath. "I want to say I didn't think that, or mean that. And I also realize something I didn't until today, until all this. I realize I brought more baggage with me from D.C. than I thought. I think— hope—it's down to a small hand tote. I hope I'll figure out how to toss that out."

"It takes time."

"I thought I'd finished the time, but apparently not quite. So . . ." She lifted the plate again, slid it into the dishwasher rack. "I'm here most of the day. I have my morning class, church basement, and I have a massage at four-thirty. Greta Parrish."

"Okay. Thanks."

She finished loading the dishwasher, began to wipe off the counters. "You haven't touched me, not once since you came up the steps to my cottage. Why is that? Because you're mad?"

"Maybe some, but mostly because I don't know how you feel about it."

Her eyes met his, held. "How do I know how I feel about you touching me if you don't?"

He brushed a hand down her arm first, then turned her toward him. Drew her in.

She dropped the rag on the counter, locked her arms around him.

"I'm sorry. I was holding things back, holding things in. But . . . Oh God, Eli, he was in my house. He went through my things. He touched my things. Derrick went through my things. He touched my things, broke things while he waited for me to come home."

"He won't hurt you." Eli pressed his lips to her temple. "I won't let him hurt you."

"I have to get past it. I have to."

"You will." But not alone. Not without him.

When she left the next morning, he told himself not to worry. Not only was the church less than two miles away, but he couldn't think of a single reason for anyone to harm her.

She'd be back by mid-morning, and once he knew she was safely in the house, he could work. With his mind too busy to slide into the story, he went down to the basement, spent nearly an hour unloading the shelves, walking them back.

It took more time to open the panel

from the basement side, and once he had, he decided to oil the hinges.

The creak added interesting atmosphere, but should he want to surprise anyone, silence served. Armed with a flashlight and a box of lightbulbs, he worked his way through the passage, testing each light, moving on, until he'd reached the third floor.

Once he'd oiled those hinges, he considered, then angled a chair in front of the panel, checked to make sure he could open and close it again, then backtracked.

He repositioned the shelves, again tested so he could easily move around them, in or out of the panel. Then he reloaded them.

Camouflage, he thought, should he want or need it.

Trap set, or nearly. All he needed was the hook and the bait.

Since working in the passages transferred dust, grime, he changed, washed up, then spent some time checking out video cameras and nanny cams on the Internet.

He was pouring himself his first Mountain Dew of the day when Abra came in with her market bags.

"Hi!" She dumped the bags, reached into one. "Look what I got you!" She turned to Barbie with a big rawhide bone. "This is for a good dog. Have you been a good dog?"

Barbie slapped her butt to the ground.

"I thought so. Have you been a good boy?" she asked Eli as she unsealed the bone.

"Do I have to sit on the floor?"

"I got makings for my lasagna, which is legendary, and for tiramisu."

"You can make tiramisu?"

"We're going to find out. I've decided to have a good feeling about today, and part—a good part—of the reason is balance. Or knowing we're working on finding a balance. Another?" Now she wrapped her arms around Eli for a squeeze. "I found out you don't hold grudges."

"I can hold grudges with the best of them," he countered. "But not against somebody I care about."

"Grudges are negative energy turned

inward, so I like knowing you can let go. And speaking of negative energy, I stopped by my cottage, and it felt better. Not all the way back, but it felt better."

"Due to a smelly smoking stick?"

She drilled a finger in his belly. "It worked for me."

"I'm glad, and sincerely hope you're not thinking we need a couple of cases of smelly smoking sticks to offset the negative energy in Bluff House."

"It couldn't hurt, but we can talk about that later."

Much, much later, he also sincerely hoped.

"Are you going to work now? I'll just strip the bed and grab the laundry, then I'll stay out of your way until you break."

"Fine. But I want to show you something first."

"Sure. What?"

"Up." He jerked a thumb at the ceiling before taking her hand. "You missed a spot."

"I did not." Automatically insulted, she picked up her pace as they went upstairs.

"A really big spot," he added. "Up."

"Third level? I only do that once a month. Just vacuum and dust. If you wanted it back in use, you should have—"

"Not that. Not exactly. I'm thinking about moving my office up there, though, into the south gable."

"Eli, that's a fabulous idea."

"Yeah, I'm playing with it. Great light, great view from there. Really quiet. Too bad I don't paint or sculpt because the old servants' hall would be a hell of a studio."

"I've thought the same. One of the beach-facing bedrooms would be a wonderful little library—like for your reference books, a kind of library/sitting room when you wanted to take a break but not actually stop work."

He hadn't thought that far, but . . . "Maybe."

"I could help you set it up if you decide to do it. Oh, these wonderful ceilings. So much potential, and I've always thought it was a shame not to use the whole house. Hester told me she used it years ago to paint, but found she worked better in her own sitting room, and best of all outside. It'd be hard on her to do two flights of stairs in any case."

"The whole house is exactly what I'm thinking of using again." He walked over, opened the panel.

"Oh! My God, this is fabulous. Just look at this." She dashed over to do just that. "This is so utterly cool."

"The lights work." He demonstrated. "Now. And it goes all the way to the basement. I moved the shelves out so the panel works down there."

"I would've played princess warrior in these as a kid."

"Really?" And he found he could picture it perfectly. "See, you missed a big spot."

"I'll get on that, if you make sure any spiders bigger than a housefly are dispatched first. You should open up all the panels."

"I'm thinking about it."

"To think of all the times I've cleaned in here and never realized this existed. It's . . . He doesn't know about this." Eyes alight, she looked at Eli. "He doesn't know."

"I don't think so. He sure as hell hasn't used it. It took Mike and I and a lot of sweat to move that armoire. And it took me over an hour working alone to move the shelves out far enough to get through."

"Laying an ambush. Eli—"

"I'm thinking about that, too."

"Proactive instead of defensive." Hands fisted on her hips, she strode around the room. "I knew this was going to be a good day. We can *do* something. We could catch him in the act."

"I'm thinking about it. It's not as simple as jumping out and saying *boo*. If the simplest explanation is also true, he's not just an intruder. He's a murderer. We don't just jump into this."

"We plan," she agreed. "I think creatively when I clean. So I'll get started, and we'll both think."

"And we wait to hear from the cops."

"Oh yeah." She deflated a little. "I guess we do. Maybe they'll trace the gun and this will all be done. It would be better that way. Not as exciting, but realistically better is better."

"Whatever happens, I won't let you down."

"Eli." She took his face in her hands. "Let's make a new pact, and promise not to let each other down."

"That's a deal."

Twenty-two

He had to work. He let plots and plans for proactive ambushes cook in the back of his brain, but he had to get the story out, get those words on paper.

He hadn't heard from his agent about what he'd sent her, but the holiday weekend bogged things down. And, he reminded himself, it wasn't as if he was her only client.

He wasn't even an important client.

Better to keep riding the wave of the story, and he'd have more to send in. If she had problems with what he'd already done, he'd deal with it.

He could go back, polish up another five chapters, send it off to give his agent a bigger part of the whole. But the story was running hot for him, and he didn't want to risk dousing it.

He didn't break until well into the afternoon when Barbie pulled him out of the zone by sitting at his knee, staring at him.

Her signal, he'd already learned, for: *Sorry to bother you, but I've gotta go!*

"Okay, okay, one second."

He backed up, saved, and realized he felt a little buzzed, as if he'd downed a couple of excellent glasses of wine in rapid succession. The minute he stood, Barbie scrambled out of the room. He heard her running down the steps at warp speed.

She'd sit, quivering, in the kitchen, he knew, waiting for him and the leash. He called out absently to Abra as he moved toward the kitchen, and found the dog exactly where he'd expected.

He also found an artful club sandwich under clear wrap, topped by a Post-it, on the counter.

Have some lunch after you walk Barbie.
XXOO Abra

"She never misses," he murmured.

He took the dog out, enjoyed the break nearly as much as Barbie, even when it began spitting chilly rain. With his hair damp, his dog soaked and his mind sliding back toward the book, he answered the phone in his pocket on his way up the beach steps.

"Mr. Landon, this is Sherrilyn Burke, Burke-Massey Investigations."

"Yeah." His guts tightened a little, anticipation and dread. "It's good to hear from you."

"I have a report for you. I could e-mail it, but I'd like to go over it with you in person. I can come out to you tomorrow, if that's convenient."

"Is there something I should worry about?"

"Worry? No. I like the face-to-face, Mr. Landon, where we can both ask and answer. I can be there about eleven."

Brisk, he thought, professional. And firm. "Okay. Why don't you send me the report in the meantime, then I'll be up-to-date when we ask and answer."

"Good enough."

"Do you know how to get to Whiskey Beach?"

"Had a nice weekend there several years ago. And if you've been to Whiskey Beach, you know Bluff House. I'll find you. Eleven o'clock."

"I'll be here."

Nothing to worry about, he thought, as he took Barbie inside. But of course, everything about Lindsay's murder, the police investigation, his own position worried him.

But he wanted those answers. Needed them.

He took his iPad and his lunch into the library. Abra would be running the vacuum or something upstairs, he assumed. And the rain made him want a fire. He lit one, then sat down with his tablet. He'd read the report while he ate.

Ignoring other e-mail for now, he downloaded the attachment from his investigator.

She'd personally reinterviewed friends, neighbors, coworkers—both his and Lindsay's. And reinterviewed Justin and Eden Suskind, as well as some of their neighbors, coworkers. She'd talked to Wolfe, and had cornered one of the assistant prosecutors.

She'd walked the crime scene, though it had long since been cleared and cleaned, and was even now staged for sale. She'd done her own reenactment of Lindsay's murder.

Thorough, he thought.

He read her summaries, which included impressions.

The Suskinds had recently separated. Not surprising, he mused, considering the strain a cheating spouse put on a marriage. Add murder and a barrage of media that had made their marriage fodder for the masses.

More surprising, he supposed, they'd stuck for nearly a year.

Two kids, though, he recalled. Too bad.

She'd spoken with desk clerks, bellmen, housekeeping at hotels and resorts that coincided with Lindsay's travel. And confirmed what he'd already known. Much of that travel had been in the company of Justin Suskind during the last ten or eleven months of her life.

How did he feel about that? he asked

himself. Not much, not anymore. The anger was done, finished. Even the sense of betrayal had dulled, like stone washed by water, those sharp edges had smoothed away.

He felt . . . sorry. Given the time, the process, he imagined the anger, the bitterness both he and Lindsay had felt would have burned itself out. They'd have gone their separate ways, they'd have moved on.

But neither of them had the chance. Whoever killed her had seen to that.

He owed it to them both to read the reports, meet the investigator, to do everything he could to find out why, who. Then put it away.

He read the report twice, thought it over as he sampled the smoothie he'd found in the fridge with its *Drink me* Post-it.

He decided to shift gears, got his notebook from the desk and yet another book on Esmeralda's Dowry from the shelves.

He spent the next hour winding along the author's speculative path. This one leaned heavily on the theory that the surviving seaman and the privileged daughter of the house, Violeta, had fallen in love. Her brother, Edwin, upon discovering them, had killed the lover. Violeta, reckless, wild, ran off to Boston, never to return. And Esmeralda's Dowry remained lost to the ages.

What Eli knew of family history confirmed Violeta had run off, been disowned and all but erased from any documents through the wealth, influence and fury of her family for the disgrace.

The matter-of-fact tone used to depict the events might not have been as entertaining as others he'd read in the last weeks, but seemed more based in sense.

Maybe it was time to hire a skilled genealogist to do whatever could be done to track down the reckless Violeta Landon.

Considering it, Eli pulled out his phone again when it signaled.

He saw his agent's name on the display, took one long, deep inhale.

Here we go, he thought, and answered.

He sat there with his notebook, his tablet, and his phone when Abra walked in.

"I'm done upstairs," she began. "You're

clear if you want to go back to work. I've got one more load of laundry in the dryer. I thought I'd get back into the passage-way. It's taking some time as I have to haul buckets in and out to get the steps really clean. And I thought if I did it naked it would be more fun."

"What?"

"Ah, as I thought, the naked got through the wall. Are you working here? Research-ing?" she asked, tipping her head to read the title of the book he'd set down: *Whis-key Beach: A Legacy of Mystery and Madness*. "Really?"

"It's mostly crap, but it has a few per-tinent details. It's got a section on the area, and the Landons during Prohibi-tion, that's pretty interesting. My great-great-grandmother helped run the product to local establishments, hiding the bottles under her skirt to elude au-thorities, who wouldn't ask her to lift them."

"Clever."

"I've heard that one before so it may be true. The theory on the dowry is the rescued seaman managed to hide it. Then he stole the fair and headstrong Violeta's heart and several pieces of her jewelry. That concluded in a wild chase on a stormy night where he went off the lighthouse cliff, courtesy of Edwin Landon, her dark-hearted brother. The dowry likely went with him, back into the unforgiving sea."

"Where it's secured in Davy Jones's locker?"

"According to this guy, the brigand and the treasure chest were dashed on the rocks, scattering the jewels like sparkling starfish. Or maybe it was jellyfish. Anyway."

"If that were true, I'd still think bits and pieces, at least, would've been recovered. You'd hear about that over the years."

"Not if people who snagged a shiny necklace or whatever kept their mouths shut, which he speculates, and seems very likely. Anyway," he said again.

Abra gave him a curious smile. "Anyway?"

"She liked it."

"Who? The headstrong Violeta?"

"Who? No. My agent. My book. The

chapters I sent her. She liked it. Or she's lying to spare my feelings."

"Would she? Lie?"

"No. She liked it."

Abra sat on the coffee table to face him. "Did you think she wouldn't?"

"I wasn't sure."

"Now you are."

"She thinks she can sell it on the five chapters."

"Eli, that's great."

"But she thinks she can make a bigger splash with the whole book."

"How close are you?"

"Nearly finished the first draft. Another couple of weeks there, maybe." Less, he thought, if it kept rolling as it had been. "Then I need to tighten it up. I don't know exactly."

"It's an important and very personal decision, but . . . Oh, Eli! You should go for the splash."

He had to grin at the way she bounced on the table. "Yeah, that's what she thinks."

"What about you?"

"The splash. I'd feel easier about having it done before she sends it out. She could be wrong and I'll rack up the new world record for rejections, but I'd have finished it."

She bumped her knee to his. "She could be right and you'll have sold your first novel. Don't make me get a smudge stick to banish negative thoughts and energy."

"Can we just have sex instead?" He grinned at her. "I'm always pretty positive about sex."

"I'll consider it. When are you going to let me read it?"

When he shrugged, she rolled her eyes. "Okay, let's go back to the previous request of some time ago. One scene. Just one scene."

"Yeah, maybe. One scene."

"Yay. You know, we should celebrate."

"Didn't I just suggest sex?"

Laughing, she slapped his leg. "There are other ways to celebrate."

"In that case, we can celebrate when I've finished it."

"Fair enough. I'm heading back to the dungeons."

"I can give you a hand."

"You could, or you could go back to work." She lifted her joined palms, arrowed them down like a diver toward the water. "Poised for the splash."

He smiled at her. "I should probably try for another couple hours. I'm going to lose time tomorrow. The investigator I hired is coming up to meet with me."

"News?" she asked, sitting again.

"I don't know. I read her report. Not much new, but she covered a lot of ground. The Suskinds separated."

"It's difficult to overcome infidelity, especially when it's so public. They have kids, don't they?"

"Yeah. Two."

"Even more difficult." She hesitated, shook her head. "And so I don't repeat a mistake, I need to tell you Vinnie got in touch a couple hours ago. The bullets they recovered from Duncan's body were fired by the gun I found in my cottage."

He put a hand over hers. "I would've been surprised if they didn't match."

"I know. The fact that I called Vinnie when I found it weighs on my side. And the anonymous tip to Wolfe from a disposable cell phone—that seems sticky.

But he wanted me to know that Wolfe's digging into my background, my movements, trying to put you and me together before Lindsay's murder."

"We weren't, so he can't."

"No, he can't."

"Relay all this to your lawyer."

"I did. He's on it. There's nothing, Eli, and I think Wolfe only cares about me as a conduit to you. If he somehow links us to Duncan's death, it's more feasible you were involved in Lindsay's."

"It goes both ways," he reminded her. "Since we're clear on Duncan, it adds weight to me being clear on Lindsay's."

"Then you agree with him on the basics. The two murders are connected somehow."

"I can't believe I'm this close to two murders, a near fatal accident, a series of break-ins and an assault without there being connections."

"I'm with you on that, but then everything's connected under it all." She rose again. "I'm going back to it so maybe we can figure out a way to be the hero and heroine of our own novel and help catch a bad guy."

"We should go out to dinner tonight."

Her eyebrows quirked. "We should?"

"Yeah. Barbie can guard the house. We should go out, have a nice dinner somewhere. You can wear something sexy."

"Are we having a date, Eli?"

"I've let that slide. Pick a place," he told her. "We'll go on a date."

"All right, I will." She came back to lean down, kiss him. "You'll have to wear one of your many ties."

"I can do that."

Good news, uneasy news, he thought when she left him. Questions to be asked and answered. But tonight, he was going out with a fascinating woman who made him think, who made him feel.

"I'm going back to work for a bit," he told Barbie. "Then you can help me pick out a tie."

He couldn't watch the house every hour of every day. But he continued to spot-check. He knew he could get back inside again, even if Landon had changed the code again. He'd prefer to continue his search with the house empty, but the way

Landon stuck to the place, he might have to risk going in when Landon was sleeping.

He'd begun to believe he'd gone in the wrong direction with the basement, at least that section of the mammoth space. But he had to finish to be sure. He'd spent so much time, so much sweat, so much money that he had to see it through.

He needed to get up to the third floor again. Somewhere in one of the trunks, under some cushion, behind some picture, he'd find a clue. A diary, a map, coordinates.

He'd been through the library in Bluff House while the old lady slept, but he'd found nothing of importance. He'd found nothing to match his own knowledge, his own meticulous and detailed research into Esmeralda's Dowry.

He knew the *truth*. Beyond the legend, beyond the adventure stories written about that storm-tossed night on Whiskey Beach, he *knew*.

The wind, the rocks, the raging sea, and only one man survived. One man, he thought, and a treasure beyond price.

Pirate booty, taken by might, by cour-

age, by blood. And his by right, his by
blood. The blood he shared with Nathanial Broome.

He was descended from Broome, who'd
claimed the treasure, and from Violeta
Landon, who'd given the pirate her heart,
her body and a son.

He had proof, written in Violeta's hand.
He often thought her message from the
grave had been written directly to him, to
give him the bits and pieces from letters,
from a single diary, all discovered after
the death of his great-uncle.

A stupid, *careless* man.

He was the heir now to that treasure.
Who had more right to the spoils than he?

Not Eli Landon.

He would have what was his. He'd kill
if need be.

He had killed. And now that he had, he
knew he could do so again. He knew, as
the days passed and his way to Bluff
House was barred, he knew he'd kill Eli
Landon before it was over, before it truly
could be over.

After he'd reclaimed what was his, he'd
kill Landon as Landon had killed Lindsay.

That was justice, he told himself. Rough

justice, and the kind the Landons deserved. The kind Nathanial Broome would have approved of.

His heart jumped when he saw them come out of the house. Landon in a suit, the woman in a short red dress. Holding hands, laughing into each other's faces.

Not a care in the world.

Had he been fucking her while he'd been with Lindsay? Self-righteous prick. He deserved to die. He wished he could do it, do both of them, right now.

But he had to be patient. He needed to regain his legacy, then he'd mete out justice.

He watched them get in the car, could see the woman lean over for a kiss before Landon drove out, away.

Two hours, he estimated. If he could have afforded to have them followed as before, he'd know more precisely. But he could risk two hours inside.

He'd paid a great deal for the alarm breaker, and money would become a serious issue soon. An investment, he reminded himself as he parked his car, lifted his bag out of the trunk.

He knew the police patrolled. He'd

watched them cruise by Bluff House, believed he had the basic timing. He thought he would've made a good pirate himself, and considered his aptitude further proof of his blood, his rights.

He knew how to evade, how to plan, how to take what he wanted.

The gloomy rain made good cover. He hurried through it, aiming for the side door—the easiest entry point, the most sheltered. He'd take time to make a wax impression of the woman's key. She wouldn't have taken that heavy ring she carried, not dressed for the evening. He'd find it, copy it.

And next time, he'd simply use a key to get in.

But now he took his jimmy out of his bag and hooked the alarm reader around his neck by the strap for easy access.

Even as he stepped to the door, the wild, warning barks erupted from inside.

He stumbled back, heart racing into his throat.

He'd seen Landon with a dog on the beach, but it had seemed friendly, playful. Harmless, the sort of dog you trusted with your kids.

He'd put a couple of dog biscuits in his bag, as a bribe.

The violence of the barking didn't speak of the easily bribed. It spoke of vicious teeth, snapping jaws.

Cursing, near to tears, he backed away. Next time, the next time he'd bring meat. Poisoned.

Nothing would keep him out of Bluff House and away from what was rightfully his.

He needed to calm down, and he needed to think. It infuriated him most of all that he needed to go back to work, at least for a few days. But that would give him time to think, and to plan. Maybe come up with a new idea to implicate Landon or the woman. To get one or both of them out of the house, into police custody for a time. Enough time.

Or maybe one of the Boston Landons would have an accident. That would draw the bastard out of the house. Clear the road.

Something to think about.

Now he needed to get back to Boston himself and regroup. Put in appearances, make sure he was seen where he was supposed to be seen, make sure he talked to those he was supposed to talk to.

Everyone would see an ordinary man going about his work, his day, his life. No one would see how extraordinary he was.

He'd rushed it, he thought now as he checked his speed, made sure he stayed within the posted limit. Knowing he was close had driven him too fast. He'd throttle back a bit, give everything and everyone time to settle.

When he came back to Whiskey Beach he'd be ready to move, ready to win. He'd claim his legacy. He'd dispense justice.

Then he'd live as he deserved to. Like a pirate king.

He drove carefully by the beach-front restaurant where Eli and Abra held hands across the table.

"I like dating," Abra commented. "I'd almost forgotten."

"Me, too."

"I like first dates." She picked up her wine, smiled over the glass. "Especially first dates where I don't have to decide if I'm going to let myself be talked into bed."

"I really like the last part of that."

"You're home. You're home in Whiskey Beach. It shows, and I know how it feels. Tell me your plans for Bluff House. You have them," she added, taking a finger off the stem of the glass to point at him. "You're a plan-maker."

"I used to be. For a while, for too long, just getting through the day was too much of a plan. But you're right, I've been thinking about plans for the house."

She edged forward, candlelight in her eyes, the roll of the sea through the wide glass beside them. "Tell me all."

"Practicalities first. Gran needs to come back. She'll stay in Boston and work on her therapy until she's ready, then she'll come home. I was thinking of an elevator. I know an architect who'd come out, take a look. There's going to be a time when she can't handle the stairs, so maybe an elevator's an option. If not, eventually we could see about turning the smaller parlor into a bedroom suite for her."

"I like the elevator. She loves her bedroom, and loves being able to go all over the house. It would help her have all that. I think it's years off, but it's good planning. What else?"

"Update that old generator, do something with the basement. I haven't figured that out yet. Not a priority. The third floor's more intriguing."

"New office space for the novelist."

He grinned, shook his head. "First on the list with the elevator—I want to have parties in Bluff House again."

"Parties?"

"I used to like them. Friends, family, good food, music. I want to see if I still like them."

The idea made her almost giddy. "Let's plan one, a big one, for when you sell your book."

"That's an if."

"I'm an optimist, so it's when."

He shifted when the waiter served their salads, waiting until they were alone again. Superstitious or not, he didn't want to plan a party around the book he'd yet to finish much less sell.

Compromise, he thought.

"Why don't we have a welcome-home party when Gran comes back."

"That's perfect." She gave his hand a squeeze before she picked up her fork. "She'd love it. I know a great swing band."

"Swing?"

"It'll be fun. A little retro. Women in pretty dresses, men in summer suits because I know she'll be back before the end of summer. Chinese lanterns on the terraces, champagne, martinis, flowers everywhere. Silver trays full of pretty food on white tables."

"You're hired."

She laughed. "I do some party planning here and there."

"Why am I not surprised?"

She tapped the air with her fork. "I know people who know people."

"I bet. What about you and plans? Your yoga studio."

"It's on the slate."

"I could back you."

She inched away, just a little. "I like backing myself."

"No investors allowed?"

"Not yet anyway. I'd like a good space, comfortable, serene. Good light. A mirrored wall, maybe a pretty little fountain. A good sound system the way the one at the church is absolutely not. Lighting I could dim. Color-coordinated yoga mats, blankets, blocks, that sort of thing. Eventually establish enough to take on a couple other instructors but nothing too big. And a little treatment room for massages. But for now I'm happy doing what I'm doing."

"Which is everything."

"Everything I like. Aren't we lucky?"

"I'm feeling pretty lucky at the moment."

"I meant that we're both doing what we like. We're sitting here on our first date, which I like, and talking about plans for doing other things we like. It makes having to do things you don't like no big deal."

"What don't you like?"

She smiled at him. "Right now, right here? I can't think of a thing."

Later, curled up warm and loose against him, slipping dreamily toward sleep, she realized she liked everything about being with him. And when she thought of to-morrow, she thought of him.

She understood as she drifted with the sea sighing outside, if she let herself slip just a little more, she would love.

She could only hope she was ready.

Twenty-three

From the name—Sherrilyn Burke—and the voice over the phone—brisk Yankee—Eli pictured a lanky blonde in a smart suit. He opened the door to a fortyish brunette in jeans, a black sweater and a battered leather jacket. She carried a briefcase and wore black Chucks.

"Mr. Landon."

"Ms. Burke."

She pushed a pair of Wayfarers on top of her short cap of hair, held out a hand to shake his. "Nice dog," she added, and held out a hand to Barbie.

Barbie politely shook.

"She's got a hell of a bark, but doesn't appear to have much bite."

"The bark does the job."

"I bet. Some house you've got here."

"It really is. Come on in. Can I get you some coffee?"

"I never turn it down. Black's good."

"Why don't you go in, sit down. I'll get it."

"Maybe we could save time, and I'll go to the kitchen with you. You answered the door, you're getting the coffee. That tells me it's the staff's day off."

"I don't have staff, which you already know."

"Part of the job. And, full disclosure," she added with a smile that showed off a crooked incisor, "I wouldn't mind a look around. I've seen some magazine spreads," she added. "But it's not like being in it."

"All right."

She studied the foyer as they walked on, then the main parlor, the music room with its double pocket doors that could open to the parlor for parties.

"It goes on and on, doesn't it? But in a livable way instead of a museum. I've wondered. You've kept the character, and that says something. Inside matches the out."

"Bluff House is important to my grand-mother."

"And to you?"

"Yeah, and to me."

"It's a big house for one person. Your grandmother lived here alone for the last several years."

"That's right. She'll come back when her doctors clear it. I'll stay with her."

"Family first. I know how it is. I've got two kids, a mother who drives me crazy and a father who drives *her* crazy since he retired. He put in his thirty."

"Your father was a cop?"

"Yeah, he was one of the Boys. But you knew that."

"Part of the job."

She smirked. Then turned into and around the kitchen. "This isn't part of the original, but it still manages to reflect the character. Do you cook?"

"Not really."

"Me either. This kitchen looks like one for serious cooking."

"My grandmother likes to bake." He

moved to the coffeemaker as she made herself at home on an island stool. "And the woman who takes care of the house is a pretty serious cook, I'd say."

"That would be Abra Walsh. She's . . . taking care of the house for you now."

"That's right. Is my personal life relevant, Ms. Burke?"

"Make it Sherrilyn. And everything's relevant. It's how I work. So I appreciate getting a sense of the house. I'm also an admirer of Ms. Walsh's mother. And from what I've learned, I got some for the daughter. She's making an interesting life for herself here, after some hard knocks. How about you?"

"Working on it."

"You were a decent lawyer, of your kind." She added that quick smile again. "Trying to be a writer now."

"That's right."

"Your name would make a splash. Old money, scandal, mystery."

Resentment curdled inside his belly like sour milk. "I'm not looking to make a splash off my family's money, or my wife's murder."

She shrugged. "It is what it is, Mr. Landon."

"Make it Eli if you're going to insult me."

"Just getting a gauge. You cooperated with the police more than I'd have expected after your wife's murder."

"More than I should have, in hindsight." He set her coffee in front of her. "I wasn't thinking like a lawyer. By the time I did start thinking, it was a little late."

"Did you love her?"

He'd asked for a woman, he reminded himself. Someone fresh and thorough. He'd gotten one, and an investigator nothing like the one he'd hired after Lindsay's death.

Now he'd have to deal with the result.

"Not when she died. It's hard not knowing if I ever did. But she mattered. She was my wife, and she mattered. I want to know who killed her. I want to know why. I spent too much of the last year defending myself and not enough really trying to find the answers."

"Being the prime suspect in a murder tends to keep you on the hot seat. She cheated on you. Here you're trying to have a fair and civilized divorce with a lot of money and family rep at stake. Even with the prenup, a lot of money and goods at stake, and you find out she's been playing you for a fool. You go into the house, one your money paid for as hers was still in trust when you purchased it. You confront her, lose your temper, pick up the poker and let her have it. Then, it's holy shit, look what I did. You call the cops, covering it with the old 'I came in and found her.'"

"That's the way they saw it."

"The police."

"The police, Lindsay's parents, the media."

"The parents don't matter, and the media, again, is what it is. And the cops couldn't, in the end, make the case."

"The police couldn't, not definitively, but that doesn't make me innocent to them, or anyone else. Lindsay's parents? They lost a daughter, so they do matter, and they believe I got away with it. The media may be what it is, but it's weight. They made a pretty good case in the court of public opinion, and my family suffered for that."

She studied him quietly as he spoke, and he realized now she'd gotten a sense of him just as she'd gotten one of Bluff House.

"Are you trying to piss me off?"

"Maybe. Polite people don't tell you much of anything. Lindsay Landon's case looked slam-dunk on the surface. Estranged husband, sex, betrayal, money, crime of passion. You're going to look at the husband first, and the person who discovers the body. You were both. No sign of break-in, of struggle. No sign of a burglary gone bad, the public fight with the victim earlier that day. A lot of weight."

"I'm aware of the weight."

"The problem is, that's all there is. Surface. You go below, and it falls apart. The timing's sticky—the time of death, the time you were seen by a number of witnesses leaving your office, the time you deactivated the alarm to come in. So you couldn't have gone in and out again, then back, as you were seen at your office, had appointments, conversations until after six p.m. And witnesses corroborate when the victim left the gallery where she worked. She entered the house, again verified, about two hours before you walked in the house that night."

"The cops figured the timing was tight, but it was possible for me to go in, argue, kill her, then try to cover it before calling nine-one-one."

"It didn't hold up well on reenactment, even the prosecutor's reenactment. Good coffee," she said in an aside, then continued. "Then there's forensics. No spatter on you, and you can't deliver blows like that without spatter. No spatter on your clothes, and witnesses verify the suit and tie you wore when you left the office. When did you have time, in an approximate twenty-minute window, to change your clothes, change back again? And where were the blood-spattered ones, or whatever you used to cover your suit?"

"You sound like my lawyer."

"He's a smart guy. Add no history of violence, no prior bad acts. And no matter how they came at you, you stuck to the story. They couldn't shake you off it."

"Because it was the truth."

"Added to it, the victim's own behavior weighed on your side. She was the one lying, the one cheating, the one planning

on a generous settlement while she carried on a secret affair. The media made
that case, too."

"It's easy to smear a dead woman, and
it's not what I wanted."

"But it helped, so did the phone calls
logged between her and Justin Suskind
after you confronted her that afternoon.
Shined the light on him awhile."

He couldn't face coffee, he realized,
and opened the refrigerator for water. "I
wanted it to be him."

"Problems there. One, motive. Unless
you subscribe to the theory she decided
to break it off or step back after her confrontation with you. The motive problem
deepens because she was good at keeping him a secret. Friends, coworkers,
neighbors—nobody knew about him.
Some suspected there was someone,
but she never talked about it. Too much
at stake. She didn't keep a diary, and the
e-mails between them were careful. They
both had a lot at stake. They met almost
exclusively in hotels or out-of-town restaurants, B-and-Bs. Nothing the cops
dug up pointed to any tension between
them."

"No." He wished that didn't continue to sting, even if the sting had gone dull. "I think she cared about him a great deal."

"Maybe she did, or maybe she just liked the adventure. You're probably never going to know for sure. But the biggest problem with Suskind as killer is he's alibied by his wife. His betrayed wife. She comes across as mortified, even devastated, by this affair, but she tells the police he was home that night. They had dinner together, alone as both kids were at a school function. Then the kids get home about eight-fifteen and confirm Mom and Dad are hanging out at home."

She opened her briefcase, took out a file. "As you know, the Suskinds recently separated. I figured she might change her tune now that the marriage is going under. I talked to her yesterday. She's bitter, she's tired, she's done with the husband and the marriage, but she doesn't change her story."

"Where does that leave us?"

"Well, if you cheat with one, maybe you cheat with others. Maybe another lover isn't happy about her and Suskind, or maybe another wife confronts her. I haven't found anybody yet, but that doesn't mean I won't. Mind?" Sherrilyn asked, and gestured to the coffeemaker.

"No, sure."

"I'd make it myself, but that machine looks like I'd need a training manual."

"No problem."

"Thanks. So you'll see—and I believe your previous investigator reported—she didn't always use a credit card for rooms. Sometimes she used cash, and that's hard to track.

"At this point we have witnesses who've identified Justin Suskind as her companion in several locations. Now we look for some that identify someone else."

He brought the fresh coffee back, sat again to skim through the files while Sherrilyn talked.

"She let her killer into the house. Turned her back on him. She knew who killed her, so we look at who she knew. BPD was thorough, but they liked you for it, and the lead investigator was dug in hard on that."

"Wolfe."

"He's a bulldog. You fit the bill for him.

I can see where he's coming from. And you're a criminal defense attorney. That's the enemy. He busts his ass to take bad guys off the street, you line your pockets getting them back out."

"Black and white."

"I was a cop for five years before I went private." Cupping the coffee in both hands, she leaned back to enjoy it. "I see plenty of gray, but it's a pisser when some hotshot suit gets an asshole a pass on some technicality or because he's got good style with some fancy tap dance. Wolfe looks at you, he sees rich, privileged, spoiled, conniving and guilty. He built a damn good circumstantial case, but he couldn't shoot it home. Now here you are in Whiskey Beach, and before you know it, there's another murder on your doorstep."

"Now you're not sounding like my lawyer. You sound like a cop."

"I have many voices," she said easily.

She took out another file, set it on the counter. "Kirby Duncan. He was basically a one-man operation, kept it low-key, and low-tech. He wasn't bargain basement, but you'd find him on the sale rack. Cops liked him. He'd been one of them and he played things pretty straight. Wolfe knew him, was friendly with him, and he's pissed off he can't pin this on you, then boomerang off it to circle your wife's death back on you."

"I got that, loud and clear," Eli agreed.

"But in this case, none of it fits. Duncan wasn't an idiot, and he wouldn't have met the guy he was shadowing alone, in a deserted area. Unless he got a wild hair to go to the lighthouse at night in the middle of a storm, he went to meet someone and most likely someone he knew. And someone killed him. You're alibied, and there's absolutely nothing to indicate you and Duncan ever met or spoke. Nothing to indicate you hauled your butt from Boston, where it's confirmed you were when Abra Walsh was assaulted here in this house, then arranged to meet Duncan, killed him, then hauled back to Boston to toss his office, his apartment, then hauled back here again. Nobody's buying that."

"Wolfe—"

Sherrilyn shook her head. "I'm not sure even Wolfe can swallow it, as hard as he

might try. Now if he can tie Walsh to it
somehow so you had help, or find you
contacted an accessory in Boston to do
that end, that would go down."

"Someone planted the murder weapon
in Abra's house."

"What?" She straightened up, her eyes
as sharp and annoyed as her tone. "Why
the hell didn't I know about this?"

"I'm sorry. I just found out myself Monday."

Mouth grim, she took a notebook and
pen out of her briefcase. "Give me the
rundown."

He told her what he knew, watched her
write her notes in what he thought of as
cop shorthand.

"Sloppy frame-up," she concluded.
"Whoever did it is impulsive, disorganized
and maybe a little stupid."

"He murdered a seasoned investigator,
and so far he's gotten away with it."

"Even stupid can be lucky. I'd like to
see this cottage before I go back to Boston."

"I'll ask Abra."

"And this trench in your basement. I'll
take a shot at the local boys, see how

much they'll share with me." She tapped
her pen on the page as she studied Eli.
"In our e-mail and phone conversations
you've indicated you think this may all be
connected."

"It's a lot of damn coincidence otherwise."

"Maybe. There's another one I dug up
I find interesting."

She took out yet another file. "About
five months ago, Justin Suskind purchased a property known as Sandcastle,
on the north point of Whiskey Beach."

"He . . . he bought property here?"

"That's right. It's deeded in the name
of Legacy Corp., a shell company he set
up. His wife isn't listed on the deed or
the mortgage. If and when they proceed
with a divorce, it should come out. It's
very possible, at this point, she's not
aware of it."

"Why the hell would he buy a house
here?"

"Well, it's a nice beach, and it's still a
buyer's market real-estate-wise." Her
smirk reappeared. "But the cynic in me
says he has other motives. We could
speculate he hopes to catch you in a mis-

take, and avenge his dead lover, but you weren't living here five months ago, and had no plans to."

"Bluff House was here. My grandmother . . ."

"None of this connects him in any way I can see with your wife's death, and that's why you hired me. But I love a puzzle or I wouldn't be in this business. Add nosy. He buys property here, reasonably close to your landmark family home, a place my information indicates you rarely visited after your marriage."

"Lindsay didn't like it here. She and my grandmother didn't get along."

"I'd imagine she might bring up the house, and all that goes with it, in pillow talk. So a few months after she dies, her lover buys the property. And you have a trench in the basement, a grandmother in the hospital, a PI shadowing you, then killed. And now the murder weapon planted in the home of the woman you're involved with. What's at the core of that, Eli? Not you. You weren't here when he took the first step. What's at the core?"

"Esmeralda's Dowry—something that probably doesn't exist, and if it does sure as hell isn't buried in the basement. He left my grandmother to die."

"Maybe. Can't prove it yet, but maybe. I wouldn't have given you all this information if my gauge didn't tell me you're not the type to fly off and do the stupid. Don't screw up my record on character judgment."

He shoved up because he did feel like flying off and doing the stupid. "He could've killed her. She lay there, God knows how long. A defenseless old woman, and he left her to die. He could've killed Lindsay."

He whirled back. "His wife could be lying, covering for him out of loyalty or fear. He's capable of killing. The odds are Duncan's on him, too. Who else? Who else would care what I was doing? I thought it was Lindsay's family, but this makes more sense."

"I did some digging there. Nosy," she repeated. "The Piedmonts had an excellent firm and two of their top investigators on this, in Boston. They let them go about three weeks ago."

"Let . . . They let it go?"

"My information is the investigators reported there was nothing left to find. I'm not saying they won't hire another firm, but I can say they didn't hire Kirby Duncan."

"If Suskind did, he'd know when I left the house, where I was, how much time he'd have to dig. He was in the house the night I was in Boston because Duncan told him I was in Boston. Then Abra came in. If she hadn't defended herself, he might've . . ."

Sherrilyn sat as he paced to the terrace doors and back. "You said Duncan was a straight shooter."

"That's his rep, yeah."

"Vinnie—Deputy Hanson—went to see him the night of the break-in here, to question him. He told Duncan about the break-in, about Abra. A straight shooter wouldn't like being used so a client could break the law, put hands on a woman. So Suskind killed him rather than risk exposure."

"It could make a tidy box, when and if it can be proved. Right now?" She tapped the files again. "All we can prove is he bought property. And his wife didn't strike me as loyal or afraid, not when I talked to her. Humiliated and bitter. I don't know why she'd lie for him."

"He's still the father of her children."

"True enough. I'll keep on it. Meanwhile, I'm going to take a look around here, see if I can find out what Suskind's been up to. Get a bead on him."

"I want you to give the cops what you have on him."

She winced. "That hurts. Listen, the cops will want to talk to him, ask questions, get their own gauge. It could scare him off, and we end up blowing our best angle. Give me a little time, say a week. Let me see what I can finesse."

"A week," Eli agreed.

"Why don't you show me the famous hole in your basement."

Downstairs she took a couple of shots with a little digital camera. "A lot of determination here," she commented. "I read up a little on this dowry, the ship and so on, but just to get a general overview. I'd like to have one of my people do some more in-depth research on it, if that's okay with you."

"It's fine. I've been doing some of my own. If there was anything, we'd have found it a long time ago. He's wasting his time."

"Probably. But it's a big house. Lots of hidey-holes, I imagine."

"Most of it was built years after the *Calypso*. Whiskey built it, generation by generation, along with the distilleries, the warehouses, the offices."

"You didn't go into the family business," she said as they started out.

"It's my sister's thing. She's good at it. I'll be the Landon in Bluff House. There's been one here," he explained, "always, since it was no more than a stone cottage on this bluff."

"Traditions."

"Matter."

"That's why you went back to the house in the Back Bay for your grandmother's ring."

"It wasn't marital property, even in the prenup that was clear. But at that point I didn't trust Lindsay."

"Why would you?" Sherrilyn commented.

"The ring belonged to the Landons. My

grandmother gave it to me to give to my wife as a symbol, that she was part of the family. Lindsay didn't honor that. And I was pissed," he added, closing the basement door behind them. "I wanted to take back something that was mine. The ring, the silver set—that had been in the family for two hundred years. The painting . . . That was stupid," he admitted. "I didn't want her to have something I'd bought out of sentiment, out of trust, when she'd betrayed that. Stupid, because after everything . . . I can't even look at it."

"That added more weight on your side. You went up, took the ring, just the ring. All that jewelry you'd bought your wife. You left it alone. You didn't take it, didn't throw it around the room, out the window. You exhibited no sign of violent behavior or disposition. You're not a violent man, Eli."

He thought of Suskind. Of Lindsay, of his grandmother, of Abra. "I could be."

She gave him a maternal pat on the arm. "Don't go changing. I booked a night at the B-and-B. I can have a chat with the owner about Duncan, about anyone who she saw him with. Sometimes people remember things over a blueberry muffin they don't when they're talking to cops. I want to see Abra's cottage, and sneak around Suskind's place. Maybe chat up any neighbors, some of the shopkeepers. He had to buy food, maybe a six-pack now and then."

"Yeah. Let me call Abra about the cottage."

He glanced at the list on the kitchen board as he took out his phone.

"Is that her schedule?"

"Today's."

"Busy woman."

Sherrilyn studied the schedule as Eli spoke with Abra. A woman with her hands in that many pies, she thought, knew a little about a lot of people. And that could be useful.

"She said you can get the key from her neighbor, the house to the right of the cottage. Maureen O'Malley."

"Great. I'm leaving those files for you. I have copies." She closed her briefcase, lifted it. "I'll keep you up-to-date."

"Thanks. You've given me a lot to process." As he walked her to the door, it struck him. "Six-pack. Beer. Bar."

"Make mine a draft."

"Abra, the second break-in. We were at the bar where she works on Fridays. She saw this guy, unfamiliar, unfriendly. He ordered another drink, but he left before she served it and as soon as I walked in."

"Can she describe him?"

"It's dark in there. She worked with a police artist, but the sketch isn't much. But . . ."

"If you showed her a picture of Suskind . . . Worth a shot, and there's one in the file. It only proves he was in the bar, which, seeing as he has a house here, isn't much. But it's more."

He wanted more still, Eli realized. It ground in his gut, the idea that the man his wife had betrayed him with might have killed her. Might have caused his grandmother's fall, and left her for dead. Might have assaulted Abra.

He'd invaded Bluff House. Everyone in Whiskey Beach knew of the Landons, so buying a house here was a deliberate act. One taken for proximity to Bluff House, he was certain of it.

He carried the files into the library, sat

at the old desk with them and his legal pad for his own notes.

And went to work.

When Abra came in shortly after five, he was still at it, and the dog who greeted her at the door stared at her with pleading eyes.

"Eli."

"Huh?" Blinking, he looked around, frowned. "You're back."

"Yes, I'm back, and actually a little late." She stepped up to the desk, scanned the piles of papers, the thick ream of notes, and picked up the two empty bottles. "A two–Mountain Dew session."

"I'll get those."

"Got them. Did you have lunch?"

"Ah . . ."

"Did you take the dog out?"

"Oh." He slid a glance down to the sad-eyed Barbie. "I got caught up."

"Two things. One, I'm not going to let you neglect yourself again, skipping meals, subsisting on nuclear-yellow soft drinks and coffee. And two, you're not allowed to neglect a dog who depends on you."

"You're right. I was busy. I'll take her out in a minute."

In answer, Abra simply turned and walked out, the dog at her heels.

"Shit." He looked at his papers, his progress, raked his hands through his hair.

He hadn't asked for the dog, had he? But he'd taken the dog, so that was that. Rising, he made his way to the kitchen, found it empty, with Abra's enormous bag on the counter. A glance out the window showed him she'd taken the dog out herself, and they were halfway down the beach steps.

"No need to be pissy about it," he muttered, and grabbed a jacket and Barbie's favored ball on the way out.

By the time he reached them, woman and dog were walking briskly along the shoreline.

"I got caught up," he repeated.

"Obviously."

"Look, I got a lot of new information from the investigator. It's important."

"So is the health and well-being of your dog, not to mention your own."

"I just forgot she was there. She's so

damn polite." Because it sounded like an accusation, he sent the dog a silent apology. "I'll make it up to her. She likes to chase the ball. See?" He unhooked the leash. "Go for it, Barbie!" And heaved the ball into the water.

The dog flew after it, on wings of joy.

"See? She forgives me."

"She's a dog. She'll forgive almost anything." Abra stepped nimbly out of range when the very wet Barbie returned to drop the ball on the sand.

Eli picked it up, threw it again.

"Would you have remembered to feed her? Her water dish was empty."

"Damn it." Okay, he sucked, right at the moment. "It won't happen again. I was—"

"Caught up," she finished. "So you forgot to water and walk your dog, forgot to eat. I imagine you didn't write. Instead, you spent all your time and energy on murders and treasure."

And damned if he'd apologize for that part. "I need answers, Abra. I thought you wanted them, too."

"I do." She searched for calm as he

thrilled the dog with another toss. "I do, Eli, but not at the expense of you, not if it costs you what you've rebuilt in yourself."

"That's not what this is. It's one afternoon, for Christ's sake. One where all kinds of doors opened up into areas I need to explore. Because rebuilding isn't enough if you don't know."

"I understand. I do. And maybe I'm overreacting, except about the dog, because there's just no excuse."

"How crappy do you want me to feel?"

She considered it, considered him. Considered Barbie. "Pretty crappy about the dog."

"Mission accomplished."

With a sigh, she slipped out of her shoes, rolled her pants to her knees to wade into the surf.

"I care about you. So much. It's a problem for me, Eli, caring so much for you."

"Why?"

"It's easier just to live my life. You've had experience there," she added, pushing her hair out of her face when the wind carried it. "It's easier just to live your life than to take that step again, that risk again. And it's scary when you can't seem to stop yourself from taking the step. I can't seem to stop myself."

The turn of conversation left him baffled, and a little uneasy. "You matter to me more than I thought anyone would, or could, again. It is a little scary."

"I'm not sure either of us would've felt this way if we'd met a few years ago. If we'd been the people we were then. You pulled yourself out of a pit, Eli."

"I had help."

"I don't think people take help unless they're ready for it, whether they know it or not. You were ready for it. It hurts my heart to remember how sad and tired and dark you were when you first came back to Whiskey Beach. It would break it to see you that way again."

"That's not happening."

"I want you to have your answers. I want them, too. I just don't want them to be something that sends you back into that pit, or that puts you on the other side of it, that changes you back into someone I don't know. It's selfish, but I want who you are now."

"Okay. Okay." He took a moment to

line up his thoughts. "This is who I am, and who I am forgets things, gets caught up and is learning to like having someone remind him not to. I'm not that different from who I was before all this happened. But what happened focused me. I don't want to be a problem for you, but I'm not going anywhere. I'm where I want to be. That's one answer I'm sure of."

She pushed at her hair again, angled her head. "Get rid of a tie."

"What?"

"Get rid of a tie. One tie, your choice. And let me read one scene of the book. One, again your choice. Symbolism. Throwing out something from before, offering me something from now."

"And that solves the problem?"

She wagged her hand back and forth. "We'll see. I guess I'll go figure out what's for dinner and make sure you eat." She gave him a poke in the belly. "You're still on the skinny side."

"Not a lot of meat on you either." To prove it, he plucked her up, made her laugh as her legs wrapped around his waist.

"Then we'll have a really big dinner."

She pressed her lips to his, hers still curved as he spun her around. And as she drew back, saw just where he was headed.

"Don't! Eli!"

She went into the surf with him, rolled and tumbled. Gasping, she managed to gain her feet, just as the next wave struck and sent her sprawling.

Laughing like a maniac, Eli pulled her up again. "I wanted to see what it was like."

"Wet. And cold." She shoved back her dripping hair as the excited dog swam around them. What did it say about her, she wondered, that his impulsive, silly act had wiped away her earlier annoyance and nerves? "Moron."

"Mermaid." He pulled her against him again. "That's what you look like, just as I thought."

"This mermaid has legs, currently freezing. And sand in very uncomfortable places."

"It sounds like a long, hot shower's on tap." Gripping her hand, he pulled her to shore. "I'll help you out with that sand."

He laughed again when the wind struck. "Christ! It's freezing. Come on, Barbie."

Caught up, that's what it said about her, she thought. She was just caught up. She managed to snag her shoes as they ran across the beach.

Twenty-four

The instant she dashed inside the mud-room, Abra peeled off her dripping hoodie, toed off her soggy shoes.

"Cold, cold, cold," she chanted, teeth chattering as she dragged off her wet top, wiggled out of her clinging pants.

The distraction of wet, naked, shivering Abra slowed Eli's progress. He was still struggling with his sodden jeans when she streaked away.

"Hold on a minute!" He fought off the jeans, his boxers, left the whole mess in a pile and a spreading pool of seawater and wet clumps of sand to race after her.

He heard her chanting still.

"Cold, cold, cold!"

He caught up just after the shower spray exploded along with her garbled cry of relief.

"Warm, warm, warm."

She let out a little shriek when he grabbed her from behind.

"No! You're still cold."

"Not for long."

He spun her around, plastering her against him, and grabbed a hank of her hair. And, covering her mouth with his, felt the heat rise.

He wanted to touch, everywhere, all that wet skin, those long lines, those subtle curves. He wanted to hear her throaty laugh, the catch of her sigh. When she shivered now, it was from arousal, anticipation, while the flood of hot water rained over them both.

Her hands glided over him, a light scrape of nails, an erotic dig of fingers. She turned with him under the spray, around and around through the pulsing waterfall, with her mouth a wet, hot demand against his.

He wanted her happy, wanted to erase

the trouble he'd seen in her eyes on the beach. He wanted to shield her from the trouble to come, as it surely would.

Trouble, he thought, that seemed to cling to him like skin.

At least here, here and now, there was only heat and pleasure and need. Here and now, he could give her all he had.

She held on to him, even when he turned her around to slide his hands over her, she hooked an arm back, around his neck to keep him close. And lifting her face as she might to the rain, opened.

Her body yearned toward more. Touch here, taste there—and patient, relentless, he stoked the yearning to a deep, glorious ache.

When she turned, mouth to mouth again, he braced her against the wet tiles, and filled her.

Slow now, slow, rising like the steam, falling like the water, floating on thick, wet clouds of pleasure. She looked through the mists, into his eyes. There were the answers, she thought. She had only to accept what she already knew, only to hold what her heart already wanted.

You, she thought, as she let herself go. I've been waiting for you.

When she pressed her face to his shoulder, shuddering with him on that final fall, she carried love.

Lost in her, he held her another moment, just held. Then he tipped her face back, touched his lips to hers. "About that sand."

Her laugh made the moment perfect.

In the kitchen, warm and dry, she plotted out dinner while he poured wine.

"We can just throw a sandwich together," he began.

"I don't think so."

"Are you trying to guilt me again, because I missed lunch?"

"No, I think I notched that belt." She set garlic, some plum tomatoes, a chunk of Parmesan on the counter. "I'm hungry, and you should be. Thanks." She took the wine, tapped her glass to his. "But since you brought it up, you should tell me what you were so caught up in."

"I met with the investigator today."

"You said she was coming." Intrigued, Abra turned from her hunt in the refrigerator. "You said before she had something new."

"You could say that." When a thought struck, he held up a finger. "Wait. I want to try something. It'll just take a couple minutes."

He went to the library for the files, slipped out the photograph of Justin Suskind. Taking it up to his office, he made a copy. He closed his eyes, tried to see the police artist sketch in his mind.

With a pencil he tried adding longer hair, shadowing the eyes. He couldn't claim to be Rembrandt, he thought—or even Hester H. Landon—but it was worth a shot.

He took the photo and copy back downstairs, detoured back to the library for the files and his notes.

When he got back to the kitchen she had two pots on the stove. A narrow tray of olives, marinated artichokes, cherry peppers sat on the island while she minced garlic.

"How do you do that?" he wondered, and popped an olive into his mouth.

"Kitchen magic. What's all that?"

"Files the investigator left, notes I've made. She went back to the beginning."

By the time he'd wound through it, pausing before telling her of Suskind's presence in Whiskey Beach, she'd tossed a bowl of campanelle, mixed with tomatoes, basil and garlic. He watched her grate Parmesan over it.

"You did that in like a half hour. Yeah, yeah, kitchen magic," he said before she could reply. He dug into the pasta, filled her bowl, then his.

Sliding onto the stool beside his, Abra sampled the dish. "Nice. It worked. So she thinks it's all connected, too?"

"Yeah, she— Nice?" he said after his own sample. "It's great. You should write this down."

"And spoil the spontaneity? She'll talk to Vinnie, right? And Detective Corbett."

"That's the plan, and she'll have a couple of fresh items to pass along."

"Such as?"

"Let's try this first." He turned over the doctored copy, set it on the counter between them. "Does this guy look familiar?"

"I . . . He looks like the man in the bar that night. A lot like the man in the bar." She lifted the photo, studied it carefully. "It looks more like him than I was able to translate to the police artist. Where did you get this?"

In answer, Eli turned over the original photo.

"Who is this?" she asked. "Shorter hair, and a cleaner, smoother look about him. How did she find the man I saw in the bar?"

"She didn't know she found him. This is Justin Suskind."

"Suskind, the man Lindsay was involved with? Of course." Annoyance flickered over her face as she tapped her fingers at her temple. "Damn it! I saw his picture in the paper last year, but I didn't remember or put it together. Didn't pay that much attention, I guess. What was he doing at the pub?"

"Staking things out. A few months ago he bought Sandcastle, a cottage on the north point."

"He bought a house in Whiskey Beach? I know that house." She jabbed a finger at Eli. "I know it. I do seasonal cleaning for one across from it. Eli, there's only one reason he would buy a house here."

"To gain access to this one."

"But it's crazy, it's crazy when you think about it. He was having an affair with your wife, and now he's . . . Did he have the affair so he could get information about the house, maybe hope to get more on the treasure? Or did he learn about all that during the affair?"

"Lindsay never had much interest in Bluff House."

"But she was a *connection*," Abra insisted. "She knew about the *Calypso*, the dowry, didn't she?"

"Sure. I told her about it the first time I brought her here. I showed her the cove where pirates used to moor. And about running whiskey during Prohibition. You know, impress the girl with local color and Landon lore."

"And was she? Impressed?"

"It's a good story. I remember her asking me to tell it at a couple of dinner parties back then, but that was more for laughs. She didn't think much of, or about, Whiskey Beach."

"Suskind obviously did, and does. Eli,

this is huge. He could be responsible for all of it. The break-ins, Hester's fall, Duncan's murder. Lindsay's—"

"He has an alibi for Lindsay."

"But wasn't that his wife? If she lied . . ."

"They're separated, and she's sticking by her original statement. A little reluctantly, Sherrilyn thinks, as she's not feeling very friendly toward Suskind these days."

"She could still be lying." Abra stabbed some pasta. "He's guilty of other crimes."

"Innocent until," Eli reminded her.

"Oh, don't go lawyer on me. Give me one good reason, other than bad behavior, he'd buy that house."

"I can give you a few. He likes the beach, he wanted an investment, his marriage is/was going south and he wanted a place to go, somewhere quiet so he could think it all through. He and Lindsay drove up here on a whim so she could show him Bluff House, so he bought the cottage here to remind him of that perfect day."

"Oh, that's all bullshit."

He shrugged a shoulder at the spike of annoyance. "Reasonable doubt. If I were representing him, I'd make a big deal over my client being questioned for simply buying a beach house."

"And if I were a prosecutor, *I'd* make a big deal over the series of coincidences and connections. A house on this particular beach, where your family owns a landmark home and which has since his purchase experienced a series of break-ins?"

She snorted, then fixed her face into serious lines. "Your Honor, I submit the defendant purchased said property and took residence in same for the sole purpose of illegally entering Bluff House to search for pirate treasure."

He smiled at her, leaned over to kiss her. "Objection. Speculative."

"I don't think I'd have liked Lawyer Landon."

"Maybe not, but with what's here, I'd've gotten Suskind off in a walk."

"Then flip it. How would Lawyer Landon build the case against?"

"By finding out he has knowledge of or interest in Esmeralda's Dowry, for one. Linking those fibers found at your place to him, that would be key. Tracing the gun to him. Tracing any of the tools in the basement to him, for that matter. If my grandmother could identify him as the intruder. And all the way back to breaking his wife's statement. Better yet, find a way to put him in the house when Lindsay was killed, and that's not going to happen. Dig up a witness or witnesses who would testify to some trouble between him and Lindsay. That would be a start."

Abra sipped her wine and considered. "I bet we'd find books and notes and all sorts of information on Bluff House and the dowry in his possession."

"Not without a search warrant, and you don't get those without probable cause."

"Don't interrupt with legalities." Abra dismissed them with a wave of her hand. "And they could do a CSI on the fibers and his clothes. The DNA from my pajamas."

"All requiring a warrant, which requires probable cause."

"And the gun—"

"Unregistered. That tells me he probably bought it on the street, for cash. Or from a shaky dealer, for cash. Not that hard to do in Boston."

"How do you trace something like that?"

"Show his picture around to known dealers in that kind of trade. Find the dealer, then get him to ID Suskind, then get him to agree to testify." Eli wove through the process and possibilities. "All of that takes the same kind of luck it does to win the Mega Millions lottery."

"Somebody has to win, eventually. Your investigator should do that, all of that. I think we need to let Hester remember on her own, if and when. And, honestly, the fact that it was dark? I don't think she really saw him. Just more a shadow, a shape."

"I'm with you there."

"The tools wouldn't be easy. He probably bought them months ago. Who remembers some guy buying a pickax or sledgehammer? But . . . I think you should go to Boston and talk to his wife."

"What? Eden Suskind? Why would she talk to me?"

"Well, hell, Eli, that shows what you

know about women. Especially angry, betrayed or sad women. You were both cheated on—her husband, your wife. That's a kind of bond. You shared a difficult experience."

"It's a pretty shaky bond if she thinks I killed Lindsay."

"There's only one way to find out. And while we're there, we could check out Kirby Duncan's office."

"We?"

"Of course, I'm going with you. A sympathetic female." Laying her hand on her heart, Abra shifted her expression into quiet sympathy.

"That's good. You're good at that."

"Well, I *do* feel sympathetic. She might feel safer if there's another woman. One who feels and can show that sympathy and understanding. And we definitely need to show Suskind's picture around Duncan's offices."

"That's what investigators are for."

"Sure, yeah, but aren't you curious? I can't do it this week, I'm already booked. Plus we should plan it a little more. I can probably juggle time next week. In the meantime, maybe your investigator will win the lottery, and we can keep an eye out for Suskind. And an eye on Sandcastle."

"We can't go lurking down there. If he spots us, we could scare him off. And you're not going near his place. Nonnegotiable," he said before she could respond. "That's a line, not in sand, in solid rock. We can't be sure he doesn't have another gun, but we can be reasonably sure if he does he'd use it. Duncan had one registered, and it wasn't found on his body, or—as far as I can find out—anywhere else."

"Speculative—but I mostly agree. We don't have to lurk. Come with me, I'll show you."

She led the way to the terrace, and the telescope. "According to Mike, the previous owners bought it as an investment property about five years ago right before the bubble burst. The economy bottomed out, people weren't spending as much on vacations, and so on," she continued as she turned the telescope south. "It was on the market for over a year, and they had to keep cutting the price. Then—"

She straightened up from her focus.

"Oh, for Christ's sake, I'm an idiot. You need to talk to Mike. He brokered the property."

"You're kidding."

"No, I wasn't thinking. He was the agent on that property. He might know something about something."

"I'll talk to him."

"For now, you can look." She tapped the scope. "Sandcastle."

Eli bent over, looked through the eye-piece. It stood near the north point, two-story clapboard, with a wide deck facing the beach. Windows and sliders shuttered with blinds, he noted. A short driveway and no car.

"Looks like nobody's home."

"So, it would be a perfect time to go down, take a closer look."

"No," he said, still studying the house.

"You know you want to."

Damn right he did, but he didn't want her with him.

"The only thing to see is a house, with the blinds closed."

"I bet we could pick the lock."

Now he did straighten. "Are you serious?"

She shrugged, had the grace to look sheepish. "I guess I sort of am. We might find some evidence that—"

"Would be completely inadmissible."

"Lawyer."

"Sane," he insisted. "We're not breaking into his—or anyone's—house. We're especially not breaking into the house of a man who may very well be a murderer."

"You'd do it if I weren't here."

"No, I wouldn't." At least he hoped to Christ he wouldn't.

She narrowed her eyes at his face, then sighed. "You wouldn't. At least tell me you'd *like* to."

"What I'd like is for him to be in there. I'd like to go down, kick in the door then beat the living crap out of him."

The cold rage in his voice got through, had her eyes widening. "Oh. Have you ever beaten the living crap out of anyone before?"

"No. He'd be my first. I'd enjoy it. Fuck speculative." He rammed his hands into his pockets as he paced the terrace. "Just fuck it. I don't know if he killed Lindsay, but odds are. And I know, I *know* he's responsible for what happened to Gran. I know he put his hands on you. He put a bullet in Duncan. He'll do it all again and more to get what he's after. And I can't do a goddamn thing about it."

"Yet."

He stopped, tried to shrug off some of the frustration. "Yet."

"What can you do at this point?"

"I can talk to Mike. I can think about talking to Eden Suskind, and the best way to approach her if I do. We can give the cops your ID of Justin Suskind, which gives them a reason to have a conversation with him—in a few days, to give Sherrilyn some time first. Not much is likely to come from that, but it should worry him when it happens. I can keep researching the dowry, and try to figure out why he thinks he'll find it here."

As he thought it through, he calmed. "I can trust the investigator to do her job. And as insurance? I can put together a plan to lure Suskind into the house so I can catch his sorry ass."

"We," she corrected.

"We can see his place, therefore he can sure as hell see Bluff House. So he's watching it, at least off and on. We'd have to make sure he was in there. Then we could make a show of leaving the house. Maybe we even take a couple of over-night bags."

"Like we were taking a quick trip."

"It would give him the perfect opening. We just park out of sight, circle back on foot and go in the south side. And into the passageway with a video camera. I've been looking at some online, and nanny cams."

"Excellent, proactive. And it could work. What about Barbie?"

"Crap. Yeah, he might not come in with her barking. We take her with us, leave her with Mike. Would they keep her for a few hours?"

"Absolutely."

"We'd need to refine it." And he'd want to walk it off, judge the timing. "It's a good backup. Hopefully, between Sherrilyn and the cops, they'll put together enough to pull him in and pressure him."

"I like the idea of huddling in a secret passage, with my lover." She wrapped her arms around him. "Preparing to am-bush a cold-blooded killer. It's like a scene from a romantic thriller."

"Just don't sneeze."

"As if. And speaking of scenes from a book . . ."

"Yeah, a deal's a deal. I'll pick one. Let me think about it."

"Fair enough. Now about that tie."

"You're serious about that?"

"Deadly. You can go pick one while I run those wet clothes I completely forgot about through the wash. Then I can look at those files while you do the dishes. Barbie will need her bedtime walk by then."

"You've got it all figured out."

"I do try." She kissed him, one cheek, then the other. "One tie," she repeated, and tugged him back inside.

More reluctant than he'd expected, he went upstairs, pulled his tie rack out of the closet.

He liked his ties. It wasn't as if he had an emotional attachment, but he liked having a variety. Choices.

Which still didn't explain why he'd brought them all to the beach, especially when he'd worn a tie a spare handful of times in the last six months.

Okay, maybe a slight emotional attachment. He'd won court cases in these ties, and lost a few. He'd selected one every day of his working life. Had loosened them during late nights at the office. Knotted and unknotted them countless times.

In another life, he admitted.

He reached for one—blue and gray stripes—changed his mind, lifted a maroon with a muted paisley pattern. Changed it yet again.

"Oh hell."

He shut his eyes, reached down and grabbed one blind.

It just had to be a freaking Hermès.

"Done."

It actually hurt to carry it away from the others. To offset the downer, he swung into his office.

She'd tell him it was good, he thought as he tried to decide what scene to give her. She'd lie.

He didn't want her to lie. He wanted it to be good.

Oddly, he realized that he knew just the scene for her to read—one where he could use her feedback.

He scrolled through his manuscript,

found the pages. Before he could change his mind, he printed them out.

"Don't be a pussy," he ordered himself, and took them and the tie downstairs.

She sat at the counter, one bare foot rubbing the flank of the dog that sprawled on the floor. And wore glasses with bold orange frames.

"You wear glasses."

She pulled them off like a dirty little secret. "Sometimes, for reading. Especially when the print's small. Some of this is really small."

"Put them back on."

"I'm vain. I can't help it."

He set the pages aside, took the glasses, slid them back on her nose. "You look cute."

"I thought going for punchy frames would make a difference, but I'm still vain, and still hate wearing them. Just for reading sometimes, and sometimes when I'm making jewelry."

"The things you learn. Really cute."

She rolled her eyes behind the lenses, then took the glasses off again when she spotted the tie. "Nice," she said, taking it from him. Then wiggled her eyebrows when she saw the label. "Hermès. *Very* nice. The ladies at the consignment shop are going to be very pleased."

"Consignment shop?"

"I can't just toss it. Somebody can use it."

He looked at it as she hopped up to tuck it into her bag. "Can I buy it back?"

With a laugh, she shook her head. "You won't miss it. Is that for me?" She gestured toward the printout.

"Yeah. One scene, it's just a couple of pages. I figured I'd get it all over with at once. Like ripping off a bandage."

"It's not going to hurt."

"It already does. I don't want you to lie to me."

"Why would I lie to you?"

He snatched up the pages as she reached for them. "You're a born nurturer, and you're sleeping with me. It goes against the grain for you to hurt anyone's feelings. You won't hurt my feelings. And that's a lie. But I need to know if it works, or if it doesn't, even if it hurts."

"I won't lie to you." She wiggled her

fingers for the pages. "Take your mind off what I'm doing and load the dishwasher."

She propped her feet on the second stool and, since they were right there, put on her glasses. After peering at him over the pages, giving him a shooing gesture, she picked up the half glass of wine she'd been nursing. And read.

She read it twice, saying nothing as dishes rattled and water ran in the sink.

Then she set the pages aside, took off her glasses so he could see her eyes clearly.

She smiled.

"I would've lied a little. The kind of thing I consider a soft lie, because it's like a cushion, it gives a soft landing to both parties."

"A soft lie."

"Yeah. I can usually manage those guilt-free. But I'm really glad I don't have to lie, even with a soft one. You gave me a love scene."

"Well, yeah. There was a reason. I haven't written many of them. Could be a weak spot."

"It's not. It's sexy and it's romantic, and

more, you showed me what they're feeling." She laid a hand on her heart. "I know he's bruised, here again," she said, tapping her hand. "She wants to reach him, and she so much wants him to reach her. I don't know all the reasons, but I know this moment mattered to both of them. It's not a weak spot."

"He didn't expect to find her. I didn't expect him to find her. She makes a difference, in him, in the book."

"Will he make a difference in her?"

"I hope so."

"He's not you."

"I don't want him to be, but there are pieces. She's not you, but . . . I'm pretty sure she's going to wear orange-framed reading glasses."

She laughed. "My gift to your literary oeuvre. I can't wait to read it, Eli, from start to finish."

"It'll be a little while yet. I couldn't have written that scene three months ago. I wouldn't have believed it, and I couldn't have felt it." He walked to her. "You've given me more than reading glasses."

She slid her arm around him, rested

her cheek on his chest. Hardly a wonder, she thought, once she'd taken that first risky step, the fall had followed so fast.

And she wouldn't regret it.

"Let's walk Barbie," she said.

At the words "walk" and "Barbie," the dog scrambled up and went into full-body wag.

"And I can tell you a couple of ideas I had for your new third-floor office."

"For my office."

Her lips curved as she drew back. "Just ideas. Including," she continued as she rose for the leash and one of his jackets, as hers was currently in spin dry, "a really wonderful painting at a shop in the village. One of Hester's, actually."

"Don't we have enough paintings in the house?"

"Not in your new office." She rolled up the sleeves of his jacket, zipped it. "Plus, your art in there should be inspiring, stimulating and personal."

"I know just what would inspire and stimulate and qualify as personal." He reached for another jacket. "A full-length photo of you, wearing just those glasses."

"Really?"

"Life size," he said as he hooked Barbie's leash.

"That's a definite possibility."

"What?" His head came up fast, but she was already walking out the door. "Wait. Seriously?"

Her laugh trailed back as he and the dog chased after her.

Twenty-five

Eli exchanged e-mails with his investigator, devoted an hour a day to researching Esmeralda's Dowry and dived into his book. He put Abra off on the trip to Boston as the book was running hot for him. He craved those hours inside it, and the possibility, tantalizingly close now, of truly redefining his life.

He also wanted time to prepare. If he seriously meant to meet Eden Suskind, to try to talk to her about very sensitive areas of their personal lives, he needed to do it right.

Not so different, to his mind, from questioning a witness at trial.

And he wouldn't mind another day or two testing out the video camera and nanny cam he'd bought.

In any case, he found himself reluctant to leave Whiskey Beach, even for a day. Periodically he wandered out to the terrace, took a look through the telescope.

Sherrilyn's brief daily reports told him Justin Suskind remained in Boston, going about his business, living in an apartment near his offices. He'd visited his home once, but only long enough to pick up his two children to take them to dinner.

Still, he could return anytime. Eli didn't want to miss him.

He tended to walk the dog north on the beach in the afternoon, and twice did his run with Barbie past Sandcastle, climbing up the north beach steps to return by the road route.

It gave him a closer look, a casual study of the doors, the windows.

The blinds on Sandcastle remained firmly shut.

He told himself he'd take a few more days, let everything settle, let it all simmer in his head.

And, if part of the simmering, the settling led to the remote possibility he'd run into Suskind on one of his walks, have the satisfaction of confronting him face-to-face.

Eli felt he'd earned it.

When he knocked off for the day, he let himself think of Abra. He went downstairs, put Barbie out on the terrace as they'd both learned she'd stay and enjoy a little sunshine before their walk.

Then he checked Abra's daily schedule. Five-o'clock class, he noted. Maybe he'd cook something.

On second thought, a much safer, more palatable thought, he'd get pizza delivered. They could eat outside in the dusky spring evening with the pansies and daffodils. He'd stick a couple of candles out there. She liked candles. He'd turn on the strings of glass balls he'd found in his search-and-rummage through storage and managed to repair and hung on the eaves over the main terrace.

Maybe he'd steal some of the flowers around the house and put them on the table. She'd appreciate that.

He'd have time to walk the dog, put in

an hour or so in the library, even set a nice outdoor table before she got home.

Got home, he thought. Technically, Laughing Gull was her home, but for all intents and purposes she lived in Bluff House, with him.

And how did he feel about that?

Comfortable, he realized. He felt comfortable about that. If anyone had asked him a few months before how he'd feel about being in any sort of relationship, he wouldn't have had an answer.

The question wouldn't have processed. There just hadn't been enough of *him* to form any part of any relationship.

He opened the refrigerator, thinking Mountain Dew or possibly Gatorade, and saw the bottle of water with its sticky note, one he'd ignored that morning.

Be good to yourself.
Drink me first.

"Okay, okay." He took out the water, peeled off the sticky note. It made him smile.

Did he say comfortable? True enough,

he decided, but more than comfortable, for the first time in a very long time, he was happy.

No, there hadn't been much of him at the start of things, but there'd been plenty of her. She filled the spaces. Now she made him want to do the same, even if it was only fumbling through a repair of a string of lights and hanging them because they'd made him think of her.

"Coming along," he murmured.

He'd walk the dog, drink the water, then shift to research mode.

At the knock on the door, he detoured to the front of the house.

"Hey, Mike." He stepped back—more progress, he thought. It pleased him to have a friend drop by.

"Eli. Sorry I didn't get back to you earlier. We've been slammed. Housing picking up, and rentals, too. The spring season's rocking it."

"That's good news." Still he frowned.

"What?"

"The tie."

"Oh, yeah, pretty cool, huh? I got it at the consignment shop. *Hermès*," he added with a tony accent. "Forty-five bucks, but it's good for impressing clients."

"Yeah." Eli had thought the same once. "Yeah, I bet."

"So I looked through my files on Sandcastle, refresh my memory, you know. I can give you what's public record, and some impressions. Some stuff, you know, falls into confidential."

"Got it. You want a drink?"

"Could use something cold. It's been a long one."

"Let's see what we've got." Eli led the way back to the kitchen. "Did you get the impression Suskind wanted it for a residence or an investment property?"

"Investment. The purchase was through his company, and there was some talk about company use. There wasn't a lot of talk," Mike added as they reached the kitchen. "Most of the deal was long-distance. E-mail, phone."

"Mmm-hmm. We've got beer, juice, Gatorade, water, Mountain Dew and Diet Pepsi."

"Mountain Dew? I haven't had that since I was in college."

"Super juice. You want one?"

"Why not?"

"Let's take this outside, keep Barbie company."

Mike spent a moment giving the delighted dog a rub before sitting down, stretching his legs out. "Now this is what I'm talking about. The flowers look good, man."

"Credit Abra. I'm on watering detail though, so that counts."

He liked doing it, liked watching the colors and shapes she'd crowded into pots grow, the shrubs along the edges of the stone flower. Occasionally he considered working out here, but realized he'd never get anything done. He'd just sit as he was now, listening to the wind chimes play their tune along with the whoosh of the sea while he looked out at the water, with his dog sitting beside him.

"Have you seen any scantily clads yet through that thing?"

Eli glanced at the telescope. "Oh, one or two."

"I should get me one."

"Sad to say I've spent more time looking north. I've got a good view of Sandcastle from here."

"I was down that way today. It looks closed up."

"Yeah. He hasn't been there for a while."

"Damn shame to see it sit empty. I could rent it in a heartbeat—by the week, a long weekend."

Interested, Eli shifted. "I bet you could. Maybe you should give him a call, see if he's interested."

After another swing of Dew, Mike nodded. "I can do that. Do you really think this guy's been breaking in here, that he killed that PI?"

"I've been going at it from every angle, circling around. That's where I keep coming back."

"Then he'd be the one who hurt Mrs. Landon."

"I can't prove it, but yeah. If the rest fits, that fits."

"Son of a fucker," Mike muttered, and opened his briefcase. "I've got his cell number in the file. Let's see what he has to say."

After opening the file, Mike punched the number into his phone. "Hey, hi there, Justin. It's Mike O'Malley, O'Malley and

Dodd Properties up in Whiskey Beach. How are you doing today?"

Eli sat back, listened to Mike do his chatty salesman patter. And, he thought, the man he believed was responsible for death, for pain, for fear was speaking on the other end. The man who'd taken lives, and broken his own to bits.

And he couldn't reach him, not yet. Couldn't touch him, couldn't stop him. But he would.

"You've got my number if you change your mind. And if there's anything I can do for you down here, you just give me a call. We're having some beautiful weather this spring, and it promises to be a terrific summer. You ought to come up, take advantage of us. . . . Oh, I know how that goes. All right, then. Bye."

Mike clicked off the phone. "Just as stiff and unfriendly as I remember. They're not interested in renting the property at this time. Some noise about possible company or family use coming up. He's a busy man."

"How'd he find the property?"

"The Internet, bless it. He hit our webpage. He had three places earmarked to start. One's a block back so you lose the oceanfront, but it's a nice quiet street, and an easy walk to the beach. The other's just south, closer to our place, but the owners decided to pull it off the market, let it ride for another season. Good move, because we've booked it solid this summer."

Mike took a long pull of Mountain Dew. "Man, this takes me back. Anyway, we made an appointment. He wanted either me or Tony—Tony Dodd, my associate—to show the properties. Insisted it had to be one of us. I got a note right here in the file because I got attitude right off the get-go from him. No problem, a sale's a sale."

"He doesn't have time to waste on underlings. He's too important. I get him."

"Yeah, he made that clear," Mike agreed. "So, he comes in later that week. Expensive suit, two-hundred-dollar haircut. He's got that entitled, prep-school superiority all over him. No offense, you probably went to one."

"I did, and none taken. I know the type."

"Okay. He doesn't want coffee or small

talk. He's on a schedule. But when I'm driving him down to look at the two properties, he asks about Bluff House. Everybody does, so I didn't think anything of it. I remember we had one of those smoky skies that day, cold, gloomy, and the house looked like something right out of a movie. Some old gothic film, you know, the way it sits up here. I give him the spiel, the history, the pirate deal because it always grabs a client's interest. And Christ, Eli, I hope to God I didn't say anything to bring this on."

"He already knew. He was here because he knew."

"I didn't like him, but I didn't jump to homicidal maniac or anything. Just tight-assed rich prick. I showed him the place a block back first. Sandcastle's newer, bigger and a bigger commission. Plus I tagged him as going for the bigger. But I took him through the other. He asked what most people ask, did the wandering through, and out on the top deck. You can see the ocean from the deck."

"And Bluff House."

"Yeah. He wasn't too happy about the proximity of the other houses, wanted to

know which ones had permanent resi-
dents, which were rentals. But that's not
an unusual question. I took him down to
Sandcastle. It's got some nice features,
and the other houses aren't as close in.
He spent a lot of time outside again, and
yeah, you can see Bluff House from there.

"He met the asking price on the spot,
which isn't usual. In fact, actually pretty
damn stupid in this market, since the sell-
ers were prepared to go lower. But I just
figured he thought dickering was beneath
him. I said how I'd take him to lunch, and
we could deal with the paperwork, and I
could contact the owners. Not interested."

With a sour look, Mike tapped the face
of his own watch. "Tick, tick, tock, you
know? I had to put the contract together
quick and fast. He wrote a check for the
earnest money, gave me his contact information. And took off. It's tough to
complain about an easy sale, but he irri-
tated me."

"And the rest? Did it go as fast and
smooth?"

"Settled in thirty days. He came in,
signed the papers, took the keys. He

barely said anything more than yes or no. We do a nice welcome basket for new owners—a bottle of wine, some fancy cheese and bread, a potted plant, some coupons for local shops and restaurants. He left it sitting on the table. Couldn't be bothered to take it."

"He had what he wanted."

"I haven't seen him since. I wish I knew more, but if you figure out how to catch the bastard, you let me know. I'm all about being in that."

"I appreciate it."

"I'm going to get going. Look, why don't I throw some burgers on the grill tomorrow night. You and Abra come on over."

"It sounds good to me."

"I'll see you then. Thanks for the Dew."

After Mike left, Eli laid a hand on Barbie's head, scratched gently behind her ears. He thought about the man Mike had just described.

"What did she see in him?" he wondered. Then he sighed. "I guess you never know who's going to pull at you, or why." He shoved to his feet. "Let's go for a walk."

He gave it a few more days, just a few more days. The routine lulled him. Morning runs on the beach with the dog, or yoga if Abra charmed him into it. Solid blocks of writing time, with the windows open, the balm of sea air now that May blew sweetly through.

Reading out on the terrace with a dog sprawled at his feet, he learned more about the history of the house and the village whiskey built than he'd ever expected to.

He'd known the original distillery had expanded in the late 1700s after the war. He hadn't realized, or retained, in any case, that the extensive expansions on the once modest house had begun shortly after. They'd added a bathhouse at considerable expense, according to his source, the first in Whiskey Beach.

Within twenty years, Landon Whiskey, and Bluff House, expanded again. Landon Whiskey built a school, and one of his ancestors caused a scandal by running off with the schoolmistress.

Before the days of the Civil War, the house stood three elegant stories tall, tended by a small army of servants.

They'd continued their firsts. The first house with indoor plumbing, the first with gaslight, then with electricity.

They'd weathered Prohibition, cagily running whiskey, supplying speakeasies and private customers.

The Robert Landon his father had been named for bought and sold a hotel—and then a second in England—and married a daughter to an earl.

But no one spoke, unless in joking terms, from what he'd found, of pirate treasure.

"Finally!" Abra swung her purse over her arm as they walked out of the house. She'd dressed conservatively—to her mind—for their trip into Boston in black pants, strappy wedges, a poppy-colored floral blouse with some flounce. Long, multi-stone earrings danced as she tugged at Eli's hand.

To Eli she looked like an updated and sexy flower child, which, he supposed, wasn't far off the mark.

When they reached the car, he glanced

back and saw Barbie staring at him from the front window.

"I just hate leaving her."

"Barbie's fine, Eli."

Then why was she giving him the sad-dog look?

"She's used to having somebody around."

"Maureen promised to come down and walk her this afternoon, and the boys will come down, take her to the beach and play with her."

"Yeah." He jiggled his keys in his hand.

"You have separation anxiety."

"I do . . . maybe."

"And it's incredibly sweet." She kissed his cheek. "But this is a good thing to do. It's a step, and steps have to be taken." She slid into the car, waited for him to get in beside her. "Plus I haven't been in the city for over three months. And never with you."

He shot one last glance back at the window, and the dog framed in it.

"We're going to try to shoehorn our way into a conversation with the wife of the man we think committed murder in addition to breaking and entering. Oh, and adultery. Let's not leave that one out. It's not exactly a pleasure trip."

"That doesn't mean it can't be pleasant. You've thought for days about how you're going to approach Eden Suskind. You've worked out approaches depending on if she's at work or at home. You're not the enemy, Eli. She can't possibly see you as the enemy."

He drove along the coast road, wound through the village. "People treat you differently, even people you know, after you've been accused of a crime. Of killing. They're nervous around you. They avoid you, and if they can't avoid you, you can see on their faces they wish they had."

"That's done."

"It's not. It's not done until the person who killed Lindsay is caught, arrested and tried."

"Then this is a step toward that. He's going to come back to Whiskey Beach. When he does, Corbett's going to talk to him. I wish we didn't have to wait for that."

"It's tricky for Corbett to go into Boston on this. And he doesn't want to pass it to Wolfe. I'm grateful for that."

"We've got Suskind's address now, his office and his apartment. We could cruise by, watch him for a change."

"For what?"

"Curiosity. We'll just put that on the back burner." Switch gears, Abra decided. She could all but see the tension twisting up the muscles in the back of his neck. "You were up late with all your books last night. Anything interesting?"

"Yeah, actually. I found a couple that go pretty deep into the history of the house, the family, the village, the business. How they're all connected. Symbiotic."

"Such a nice word."

"I like it. Landon Whiskey got a boost during the Revolutionary War. With the blockades, the colonists couldn't get sugar, molasses, so no rum. Whiskey became the choice for the colonial army, and the Landons had their distillery."

"So George Washington drank your whiskey."

"Bet your ass. And after the war, they expanded both the business and the

house. A big deal on the house, too, because Roger Landon, headstrong Violeta's and possibly murderous Edwin's
father, who was in charge then, had a rep
for being a cheapskate."

"A good, frugal Yankee."

"A notorious skinflint, but he put what
was pretty serious money into the house,
furnishings, and into the business. When
he died, his son took over, and since
good old Rog didn't give it up until he
was near eighty, Edwin Landon had
waited a good long time to take the reins.
He expanded again, everything. He and
his wife, the French émigré—"

"Ooh-la-la."

"You bet. They were the first to start
holding big, elaborate parties. And one of
their sons, Eli—"

"I like him."

"You should. He built—had built—the
first village school. His youngest brother
fell for the schoolteacher, and they ran off
together."

"Romance."

"Not so much. They were killed heading west to make their own fortune."

"That's very sad."

"In any case Eli continued the tradition of expanding the house, the business, and the parties continued—with some scandals and tragedies thrown in—up to Prohibition. If things got lean, you wouldn't know it by the way they lived. The twenties roared into the thirties, and the government realized they had screwed up and banning whiskey was costing them one hell of a lot. People bellied back up to the bar, in the open, and we opened another distillery."

"The whiskey empire."

"Through it, we've had art connoisseurs—and those reputed to have had affairs with artists—suicides, two who spied for the Allies, and plenty who died in various wars, a dancer who soared to fame in Paris, and another who ran away with the circus."

"I like that one especially."

"A duchess through marriage, a cardsharp, a cavalry officer who died with Custer, heroes, villains, a nun, two senators, doctors, lawyers. You name it, they're probably in there."

"It's a long line. Most people don't—or can't—trace their family back that far, or have a place that's been in that family for so many generations."

"True enough. But do you know what's missing?"

"A suffragette, a Playboy bunny, a rock star?"

He laughed. "We had some of the first. I didn't come across any of the other two. What's missing is Esmeralda's Dowry. It's mentioned along with the *Calypso*, the wreck, some speculation on Broome— did he survive or was the survivor a simple seaman? Speculation again on the dowry: Did *it* survive? But in these two most in-depth and sensible histories I've come across, the weight's on no."

"That doesn't mean they're right. I prefer believing it survived, just like in my version, the young brother and schoolteacher made their way west and plowed fields and made babies."

"They drowned when their wagon tipped over crossing a river."

"They planted corn and had eight children. I'm firm on that."

"Okay." Either way, he thought, they'd been dead a very long time. "On the dowry, it makes me wonder, again, what information Suskind has that I don't. What makes him so sure that he'd risk so much, that he'd kill? Or is it all just bullshit?"

"What do you mean?"

"What if it has nothing to do with the long-lost treasure? I just jumped there, automatically. Somebody digging in the basement. What else?"

"Exactly, Eli." Puzzled, she turned to study his profile. "What else?"

"I don't know. Nothing I've found takes me anywhere else. But nothing I've found, realistically, takes me there either." He glanced at her. "I think he's just fucking batshit."

"That worries you."

"Damn right it does. You can't reason with crazy. You can't predict it. You can't really plan for it."

"I'm going to disagree."

"Okay. And?"

"I'm not saying he isn't twisted. I think anyone who takes a life, unless it's in defense of self or another, is twisted. But you know, it's verified that he and Lindsay were involved."

"Yeah. Yeah," he repeated. "And she

wouldn't go for crazy. Not overtly crazy. But people can hide their nature."

"Do you think so? I just don't, at least not for long. I think what we are shows. Not just in our actions, but in our face, our eyes. He's worked on this for more than a year and a half—closer to two years now—as far as we know. Getting close to Lindsay, talking her into driving to Whiskey Beach when she didn't like it. So there's probably some charm in there. He's also juggling a wife, children, a job. Twisted, I think, yes, but not batshit. Batshit's out of control. He's still maintaining."

"Twisted's bad enough."

When they fought their way into Boston traffic, he turned to her again. "You're sure about this?"

"I'm not sitting in the car, Eli. Forget that. I think we should drive by her house first. If there's no car, we can check her work. She's part-time, so it's a toss-up. So much energy in the city! I love it for a day or two, then, boy, I want out."

"I used to think I needed it. Not anymore."

"Whiskey Beach is good for a writer."

"It's good for me." He laid a hand over hers. "So are you."

She brought his hand to her cheek. "The perfect thing to say."

He followed the GPS, though he thought he could have found the house. He knew the area, actually had friends— or former friends—who lived there.

He found the pretty Victorian, painted pale yellow, with a bay window on the side where stairs led down from a deck.

A BMW sedan sat in the drive, and a woman in a wide-brimmed hat was watering pots of flowers on the side deck.

"Looks like she's home."

"Yeah. Let's do this."

The woman set down her watering can as they pulled in behind the BMW, and came to the edge of the deck.

"Hello. Can I help you?"

"Mrs. Suskind?"

"That's right."

Eli walked to the base of the steps. "I wonder if you have a few minutes to talk to me. I'm Eli Landon."

Her lips parted, but she didn't step back. "I thought I recognized you." Her gaze, calm and brown, slid to Abra.

"This is Abra Walsh. I realize this is an intrusion, Mrs. Suskind."

She let out a long sigh, and sadness moved in and out of her eyes. "Your wife, my husband. That should put us on a first-name basis. It's Eden. Come on up."

"Thank you."

"There was an investigator here last week. And now you." She pulled off her hat, ran her hand over a sunny swing of hair. "Don't you want to put it behind you?"

"Yes. Very much. I can't. I didn't kill Lindsay."

"I don't care. That sounds horrible. It is horrible, but I can't care. You should sit down. I've got some iced tea."

"Can I help you with it?" Abra asked her.

"No, that's fine."

"Then would you mind if I used your bathroom? We drove down from Whiskey Beach."

"Oh, you have a home there, don't you?" she said to Eli, then gestured to Abra. "I'll show you."

It gave Eli a chance to gauge the

ground. An attractive woman, he thought, an attractive house in an upscale neighborhood with well-tended gardens, a thick green lawn.

About fifteen years of marriage, he recalled, and two attractive kids.

But Suskind had tossed it all aside. For Lindsay? he wondered. Or for an obsessive treasure hunt?

A few moments later, both Eden and Abra came out again with a tray holding a pitcher and a trio of tall, square glasses.

"Thanks," Eli began. "I know this has been hard for you."

"You would know. It's terrible to realize the person you trust, the person you've built a life with, a home with, a family with, has betrayed you, has lied. That the person you love betrayed that love and made a fool of you."

She sat at the round teak table under the shade of a deep blue umbrella. Gestured them to join her.

"And Lindsay," Eden continued. "I considered her a friend. I saw her almost every day, often worked with her, had drinks with her, talked about husbands with her. And all the time she was sleeping with mine. It was like being stabbed in the heart. For you, too, I guess."

"We weren't together when I found out. It was more a kick in the gut."

"So much came out after . . . It had gone on nearly a year. Months of lying to me, of coming home from her to me. It makes you feel so stupid."

She addressed the last directly to Abra, and Eli saw Abra had been right. Another woman, a sympathetic one, made it all easier.

"But you weren't," Abra said. "You trusted your husband, and your friend. That's not stupid."

"I tell myself that, but it makes you question yourself, what do you lack, what don't you have, didn't you do? Why weren't you good enough?"

Abra put a hand over hers. "It shouldn't, but I know."

"We have two kids. They're great kids, and this was devastating for them. People talk, we couldn't shield them from it. That was the worst." She sipped at her tea, fought visibly to conquer tears. "We tried. Justin and I tried to hold it together, to make it work. We went to counseling, took a trip together." She shook her head. "But we just couldn't put it back together. I tried to forgive him, and maybe I would have, but I couldn't trust him. Then it started again."

"I'm sorry." Now Abra squeezed her hand.

"Fool me once," Eden continued, blinking her eyes clear. "Late nights at the office, business trips. Only this time, he wasn't dealing with someone ready to be stupid or trusting. I'd check on him, and I knew he wasn't where he said he'd be. I don't know who she is, or if there's more than one. I don't care. I just don't care anymore. I have my life, my kids—and finally a little pride. And I'm not ashamed to say when I divorce him, I'm going to gut him like a fish."

She let out a breath, a half laugh. "I'm still pretty mad, obviously. I took him back, after what he'd done, and he threw it in my face. So."

"I didn't have time to make that choice." Eli waited until Eden looked back up and over at him. "I didn't have much time to be mad. Someone killed Lindsay the same day I found out what she'd done, what she'd been doing even when I thought we were trying to make our marriage work."

Sympathy covered Eden's face as she nodded. "I can't imagine what that's like. When I was at my lowest, when the news seemed to be round-the-clock about her death, the investigation, I tried to imagine what it would be like if Justin had been the one murdered."

She pressed her fingers to her lips. "That's terrible."

"I don't think so," Abra said quietly.

"But even at my lowest, I couldn't imagine it. I couldn't imagine how I'd feel in your place, Eli." She paused a moment, sipped her tea. "You want me to tell you I lied to protect him. That he wasn't with me that night. I wish I could. God, I wish I could." She closed her eyes. "I shouldn't think that way about him. We made two beautiful children together. But right now I wish I could tell you what you want to hear. The truth is, Justin came home that night, about five-thirty, no more than a few minutes after that. It all seemed so normal. He even kept his phone out, as he'd started to do the last several months. He said he was expecting an important e-mail from work, and might have to grab his overnight bag and head out. But it wouldn't be for a couple hours anyway, if that."

Eden shook her head. "I realized later, of course, he was waiting for a message from Lindsay, that they'd made plans to go away for a day or two. But that night, I thought it was just the usual. The kids were both at school—a rehearsal for a play they were both in, and pizza after. It was nice, just the two of us, and the rain. I made dinner—chicken fajitas, and he made margaritas. We just had an easy evening, nothing special. Just enjoying ourselves as a couple before the kids came home, and the noise came back.

"We were doing just that when the phone rang. It was Carlie from the gallery. She'd seen a bulletin on TV. She told me Lindsay was dead, that they said it might be foul play."

A calico cat padded up the steps, leaped into her lap. Eden stroked it as she finished. "I should've known then, right then. He was so shaken. He went white. But I was so shocked, too. And I was thinking about Lindsay, so I never thought . . . I never would have believed they'd been involved. When the police came, when they told me, I didn't believe it. Then . . . I couldn't not believe it. I'm sorry, Eli, I'm so very sorry I can't help you."

"I appreciate you talking to me. It can't be easy."

"I'm putting it behind me. All of it, though it takes some doing. You should do the same."

When they were back in the car, Abra rubbed a hand over his. "I'm sorry, too."

"Now we know." And still something troubled him.

Twenty-six

Kirby Duncan's office took up a square of miserly space in a scarred brick building that had bypassed any attempt at urban revitalization. It bumped against the cracked sidewalk with its first-floor display windows touting psychic readings on one side, an adult toy shop on the other.

"Almost one-stop shopping," Abra considered. "You can go to Madam Carlotta and find out if you're going to get lucky enough to consider dropping a few bucks in The Red Room."

"If you have to ask a psychic, you're probably not going to get lucky."

"I read tarot," she reminded him. "It's an ancient and interesting form of seeking knowledge and self-awareness."

"It's cards." He opened the center door and stepped into a skinny lobby and steps leading up.

"I'm definitely doing a reading for you. Your mind's too closed off to possibilities, especially for a writer."

"As a lawyer, I defended an alleged psychic a few years back for bilking clients out of a considerable amount of money."

"People who bilk other people don't have a real gift or calling. Did you win?"

"Yeah, only because her clients were wide open to possibilities, and deeply stupid."

She gave him a light elbow jab, but she laughed.

On the second level, frosted glass doors advertised BAXTER TREMAINE, ATTORNEY AT LAW, something called QUIKEE LOANS, another outfit called ALLIED ANSWERING SERVICE, and KIRBY DUNCAN, PRIVATE INVESTIGATION.

Police tape crossed over Duncan's frosted glass.

"I'd hoped we could go in, look around."

"Open murder case." Eli shrugged. "They want to keep the scene of the break-in secure. Wolfe would be part of this. He doesn't let go easily."

"We can go down and talk to the psychic, see if Madam Carlotta has any insight."

He spared her a glance then walked to the lawyer's door.

In the broom-closet space of reception a woman on the slippery end of forty pecked industriously at a keyboard.

She paused, pulled the gold cheaters from her face so they dangled by the braided chain around her neck.

"Good morning. Can I help you?"

"We're looking for information on Kirby Duncan."

Though her law office smile stayed in place, she eyed both of them through cynical eyes. "You're not cops."

"No, ma'am. We'd hoped to consult with Mr. Duncan on a . . . personal matter while we're in Boston. We just came by hoping he could squeeze us in, then saw the police tape over his door. Was there a break-in?"

Her eyes remained cynical, but she swiveled her chair around to face them more directly. "Yes. The police haven't cleared the scene yet."

"That's too bad."

"And another reason not to live in the city," Abra put in with the faintest of southern drawls. Eli merely patted her arm.

"Is Mr. Duncan working out of another office? I should've called him, but I couldn't find his card. I remembered where the office was. Maybe you could direct us to where he's working now, or maybe you have his number so we can call him?"

"It won't do you any good. Mr. Duncan was shot and killed a few weeks ago."

"Oh my God!" Abra gripped Eli's arm. "I want to go. I really just want to go home."

"Not here," the receptionist qualified, and added with a thin smile, "And not in the city. He was working up north, a place called Whiskey Beach."

"This is terrible. Just terrible. Mr. Duncan helped me with a . . ."

"Personal problem," the receptionist supplied.

"Yes, a couple of years ago. He was a nice guy. I'm really sorry. I guess you knew him."

"Sure. Kirby did some work for my boss from time to time, and for the loan company across the hall."

"I'm really sorry," Eli repeated. "Thanks for your help." He took a step back, stopped. "But . . . you said he was up north, but there was a break-in here. I don't understand."

"The cops are working on that. It looks like whoever killed him came looking for something here. All I know is he told the boss he'd be in the field for a few days. The next thing I know there's police tape on the door, and the cops are asking if I saw anything or anyone suspicious. I didn't, though you can get some of that here with people looking for help with personal problems."

"I guess."

"The way I hear it, it happened the same night he was killed, or most likely. So there wouldn't have been anyone around to see anything. So . . . I can give you a referral to another investigator."

"I just want to go." Abra tugged at Eli's hand. "Can we just go home, deal with this there?"

"Yeah. All right. Thanks anyway. It's a real shame."

When they stepped out Eli considered trying one of the other two offices, but he didn't see the point. Abra stayed quiet until they headed down the stairs.

"You're really good at that."

"At what?"

"Lying."

"Prevaricating."

"Is that what lawyers call it?"

"No, we call it lying."

She laughed, bumped shoulders with him. "I don't know what I expected to find out coming here. The break-in happened either really late at night or early in the morning. No one would've seen any-thing."

"I got something out of it."

"Share," she insisted as they got back in the car.

"If we go with the theory Suskind hired Duncan, you've got an upper-middle-class type. A suit type, family-in-a-big-house-in-the-pretty-burbs type. Status is important to him. But when he hires an investigator he goes down-market."

"Maybe someone recommended him."

"I doubt it. I think he didn't want high-end with high rates for two reasons. One, he didn't want anyone who might have done work for anyone in his own circle. Two, and I think more telling, he'd be hit with a lot of expenses."

"He bought a beach house," Abra began.

"An investment toward the jackpot. And he attempts, at least, to hide his ownership."

"Because he knows he's headed for a divorce. The man's a worm," Abra stated. "On the karma wheel, he'll come back as a slug next."

"I'm open to that possibility," Eli decided. "In his current slot on the karma wheel, he's going to have legal fees—and he'll go high-end there—child support, marital settlement. I'm thinking he paid Duncan in cash, to keep it off the books. No record of the outlay when he has to show his finances to the lawyers."

"He still had to break in, search, because an investigator's going to keep records of clients, even cash transactions."

"Files, electronic or paper, copies of cash receipts, a logbook, client list," Eli agreed. "He wouldn't want to be connected as a client of an investigator hired to shadow me, who'd ended up dead. Very sticky."

"Very." She considered. "He probably never came here, did he, to the office?"

"Probably not. He'd want to meet somewhere like a coffee shop or bar. Not in his area or Duncan's." Eli pulled up at another building—steel and block.

"This is where he lived?"

"Second floor. Dicey area."

"What does that tell you?"

"That Duncan felt he could handle himself, wasn't worried about his car getting stripped, his neighbors screwing with him. Tough guy maybe, or just one who figured he knew the score and how to play the game. Someone like that wouldn't think twice about meeting a client alone."

"Do you want to go in, talk to some of the neighbors?"

"No point. The cops would have already. Suskind wouldn't have come here other than to go through the apartment. Not only because he wouldn't have a reason to meet Duncan here, but because this area would scare him. South Boston's not his turf."

"It's not yours either, whiskey baron."

"That's my father, or my sister the baroness. Anyway, I've done some pro bono work out of Southie. Not my turf, no, but not uncharted territory. Well, I guess we hit the highlights, or more like the lowlights."

"He was just doing his job," Abra said. "I didn't like him, or didn't like the way he was doing his job the time he talked to me, but he didn't deserve to die for doing his job."

"No, he didn't. But you could consider he's getting another spin on the karma wheel."

"I know pandering when I hear it, but well done. And I'll do just that."

"There you go. Let's go see how Gran's doing before we head back."

"Would you drive me by the house where you lived with Lindsay?"

"Why?"

"So I can get a sense of who you were."

He hesitated, then thought, Why not? Why not do the full circle? "Okay."

It felt odd to travel those roads, to head in that direction. He hadn't been by the house in the Back Bay since he'd been allowed to clear out what he wanted. Once he had, he'd hired a company to sell the rest, then he'd put the house on the market.

He'd thought cutting those ties would help, but he couldn't say it had. He passed shops and restaurants that had once been part of his routine. The bar where he'd often had drinks with friends, the day spa Lindsay had favored, the Chinese place with its incredible kung pao chicken and grinning delivery boy. The pretty trees and trim yards of what had once been his neighborhood.

When he pulled up in front of the house, he said nothing.

The new owners had added an ornamental tree to the front, something with weeping branches just starting to bloom in delicate pink. He saw a tricycle on the front walk, bright red and cheerful.

The rest looked the same, didn't it? The same peaks and angles, the same glinting windows and wide front door.

So why did it seem so foreign?

"It doesn't look like you," Abra said beside him.

"It doesn't?"

"No, it doesn't. It's too ordinary. It's big, and beautiful in its way. Beautiful like a stylish coat, but the coat doesn't fit you, at least it doesn't fit you now. Maybe it fit the you with the Hermès tie and Italian suit and lawyerly briefcase who stopped in the local coffee shop for an overpriced specialty coffee while he answered texts on his phone. But that's not you."

She turned to him. "Was it?"

"I guess it was. Or that was the road I was on, whether or not the coat fit."

"How about now?"

"I don't want the coat back." He studied her. "When the house finally sold a few months ago, it was a relief. Like shedding a layer of skin that had gotten too tight. Is that why you wanted to come by here? So I'd admit that, or see that?"

"It's a nice side benefit, but primarily, I

was nosy. I had a coat not that different once. It felt good to give it to someone it suited more. Let's go see Hester."

Another familiar route, from one home to another. As the distance increased from the Back Bay, the tension in his shoulders eased. Automatically he stopped at the florist near his family home.

"I like to get her something."

"The good grandson." Pleased, she got out with him. "If I'd been thinking, we could've gotten something in Whiskey Beach. She'd have gotten a kick out of that."

"Next time."

Abra smiled as they went in. "Next time."

Abra wandered, leaving the selection to him. She wanted to see what he'd choose, and how he'd go about it. She hoped he didn't go for the roses, however beautiful. Too expected, too usual.

It pleased her when he went for the blue iris and mated them with some pink Asiatic lilies.

"That's perfect. It says spring, and boldly. Very, very Hester."

"I want her home before the end of summer."

Abra leaned her head against his shoulder while the florist wrapped and rang. "So do I."

"It's good to see you, Mr. Landon." The florist offered Eli a pen to sign the receipt. "Give our best to your family."

"Thanks. I will."

"Why do you look so surprised?" Abra asked as they started out.

"I got used to people I knew in my other life . . . we'll say, either pretending not to know me or just walking away."

She rose on her toes to kiss his cheek. "Not everyone's an asshole," she said.

And they walked out to where Wolfe stood by Eli's car. For a moment, past and present overlapped.

"Nice flowers."

"And legal," Abra said cheerfully. "They have more nice ones inside if you're in the mood."

"You've got business in Boston?" he asked, keeping his eyes on Eli.

"As a matter of fact." He started to step around Wolfe to open the car door for Abra.

"Why don't you explain what business you had in Duncan's office building, asking questions?"

"That's legal, too." Eli handed the flowers to Abra to free his hands.

"Some people can't resist going back to the scene of the crime."

"And some can't resist beating a dead horse. Is there anything else, Detective?"

"Just that I'm going to keep on digging. The horse isn't buried yet."

"Oh, that's just enough!" Incensed, Abra shoved the flowers back at Eli, then dug into her bag. "Here, take a look. *This* is the man who's been breaking into Bluff House."

"Abra—"

"No." She rounded on Eli. "Enough. This is the man I saw in the bar that night, and the man who most likely grabbed me when I was in Bluff House. This is the man who almost certainly killed Duncan Kirby—someone you knew—and then planted the gun in my house before making that anonymous call to you. And if you'd stop being ridiculous you'd ask yourself why Justin Suskind bought a house in Whiskey Beach, why he hired

Duncan, why he killed him. Maybe he didn't kill Lindsay, but maybe he did. Maybe he knows *something* because he's a criminal. So be a cop and do something about it."

She grabbed the flowers back, wrenched open the door herself. "Enough," she repeated, and slammed it shut.

"Your girlfriend's got a temper."

"You push buttons, Detective. I'm going to visit my grandmother, then I'm going back to Whiskey Beach. I'm going to live my life. You do whatever you have to do."

He got in the car, yanked on his seat belt and drove away.

"I'm sorry." Leaning her head back, Abra closed her eyes a moment, tried to find her center again. "I'm sorry, I probably made it worse."

"No, you didn't. You surprised him. And the sketch of Suskind surprised him. I don't know what he'll do about it, but you caught him off guard."

"Small consolation. I don't like him, and nothing he does or doesn't do is going to change that. Now . . ." She let out a couple of long, deep breaths. "Clear the air, settle the mind. I don't want Hester to see I'm upset."

"I thought it was mad."

"Not that different."

"It is when you do it."

She thought that over as he turned the last corner to the Beacon Hill house.

And this, she decided, was more Eli. Maybe because the house exuded, to her, the sense of history and generational family. She liked the feel of it, the lines, the landscape so long established, colored now with early spring bloomers.

She put the flowers back in his hand as they walked to the door. "The good grandson."

And they went in to see Hester.

They found her in her sitting room with a sketchbook, a glass of cold tea and a small plate of cookies. Setting the sketchbook and her pencil aside, she held out both hands.

"Just what I needed to cheer up my day."

"You look tired," Eli said immediately.

"I have good reason. I just finished my daily physical therapy. You just missed meeting the Marquis de Sade."

"If it's too hard on you, we should—"

"Oh, stop." She waved that away with one impatient flick of the wrist. "Jim's wonderful, and has a nice sharp humor that keeps me on my toes. He knows what I can handle, and how hard to push. But after a session, I'm tired out. Now I'm reviving seeing both of you, and those gorgeous flowers."

"I thought I might have to step in, point Eli in the right direction, but it turns out he has excellent taste. Why don't I take them down to Carmel, so we can put them in a vase for you?"

"Thank you. Have you had lunch? We can all go down. Eli, give me a hand."

"Why don't you just sit for a while first." To close that deal, he sat himself. "We'll go down after you recover from de Sade." He gave Abra a nod, then turned to Hester when she took the flowers out. "You don't have to push so hard."

"You forget who you're talking to. Pushing hard is what gets things done. I'm glad you came, glad you brought Abra."

"It's not as hard to come into Boston now."

"We're working on healing, both of us."

"I didn't push very hard in the early days of it."

"Neither did I. We had to get some traction first."

He smiled. "I love you, Gran."

"You'd better. Your mother should be home in about two hours, though your father won't until after six. Are you going to stay to see your mother at least?"

"That's the plan, then we'll head back. I have a house and a dog to look after."

"Looking after things is good for you. We've come a long way, both of us, in the last few months."

"I thought I'd lost you. We all did. I guess I thought I'd lost myself."

"Yet here we are. Tell me how the book's coming."

"I think it's coming okay. Some days are better than others, and sometimes I think it's just crap. But either way being able to write makes me wonder why I haven't done it all along."

"You had a talent for the law, Eli. It's a pity you couldn't make that your hobby, or we could say a sideline, and writing your vocation. You could do that now."

"Maybe I could. I think we all know I'd have been lousy in the family business. Tricia was always the one to follow in those footsteps."

"And damn good at it."

"She is, but even though it wasn't for me, I've been learning more about it, or its history. Paying more attention to all its roots and beginnings."

Her eyes lit with approval. "You've been spending time in the library at Bluff House."

"Yeah, I have. Your grandmother-in-law ran whiskey."

"She did. I wish I'd known her better. What I do remember is a feisty, hard-headed Irishwoman. She intimidated me some."

"She must have been formidable to do that."

"She was. Your grandfather adored her."

"I've seen photos—quite the looker—and found more poking around Bluff House. But the roots of Landon Whiskey go back a lot further, to the Revolution."

"Innovation, the heart of gamblers, the head of businessmen, risk and reward.

And the understanding people enjoy a good stiff drink. Of course, the war helped, as cold-blooded as that is. Fighting men needed whiskey, wounded men needed it. In a very true way, Landon Whiskey was forged in a fight against tyranny and a quest for liberty."

"Spoken like a true Yankee."

Abra came back with a vase of artfully arranged flowers. "They're absolutely beautiful."

"They really are. Should I put them in here, or in your bedroom?"

"In here. I'm spending more time sitting than lying down these days, thank God. Now that Abra's back, why don't we talk about what you really want to know."

"You think you're smart," Eli said.

"I *know* I am."

He grinned, nodded. "We're winding around what I really want to know. My way of thinking is the history of the house, of the business, might have some part in the whole. I just haven't figured it all out. But we can jump forward a couple of centuries."

"I can't see his face." Hester fisted a hand in her lap. The emerald she often wore on her right hand fired at the gesture. "I've tried everything I can think of, even meditation—which, you know, Abra, I don't do particularly well. All I see, or remember, is shadows, movement, the impression of a man—that shape. I remember waking up, thinking I heard noises, then convincing myself I hadn't. I know I was wrong about that now. I remember getting up, going to the stairs, then the movement, the shape, the impression, and the instinct to get downstairs and away. That's all. I'm sorry."

"Don't be sorry," Eli told her. "It was dark. You may not remember a face because you didn't see it, or not distinctly enough. Tell me about the sounds you heard."

"I remember them better, or think I do. I thought I'd been dreaming, and may very well have been. I thought, Squirrels in the chimney. We had them once, long ago, but we put in guards, of course, since then. Then there was creaking, and half asleep I thought, Who's upstairs?

Then I woke up fully, decided I'd imagined it and, restless, finally decided to go downstairs for some tea."

"What about scents?" Abra asked.

"Dust. Sweat. Yes." Eyes closed, Hester focused. "Odd, I didn't realize that until now, until you asked."

"If he came down from the third floor, is there anything up there, anything you can think of he would've been after?"

She shook her head at Eli. "Most of what's up there is sentiment and history, and what no longer fits in the practical living space. There are some wonderful things—clothes, keepsakes, journals, old household ledgers, photos."

"I've been through a lot of it."

"It's on my long-range plan to have a couple of experts in, catalog for, eventually, a Whiskey Beach museum."

"What a wonderful idea." It made Abra beam. "You never told me."

"It's still in the planning-to-plan stages."

"Household ledgers," Eli thought aloud.

"Yes, and account books, guest lists, copies of invitations. I haven't been through everything for a long time, and honestly really never through it all. Things change, times change. Your grandfather and I didn't need a big staff after the children left, so we started using the third floor for storage. I tried painting up there for a year or two. There was only Bertie and Edna by the time Eli died. You must remember them, young Eli."

"Yeah, I do."

"When they retired, I didn't have the heart to have any live-ins. I only had the house and myself to look after. I can only think this person was up there out of curiosity or hoped to find something."

"Is there anything up there that goes back to the Landons from the time of the *Calypso* wreck?"

"There must be. The Landons have always been ones for preserving. The more valuable items from that time, and others, are displayed throughout the house, but there would be some flotsam and jetsam on the third floor."

Her eyebrows drew together as she tried to think. "I neglected that area, I suppose. Just stopped seeing it, and told myself I'd get around to hiring those experts one day. He might have thought there'd be maps, which is foolish. If we'd known X marked the spot, we'd have dug up the dowry ourselves long before this. Or he assumed there'd be a journal, one of Violeta Landon's perhaps. But the story goes that after her brother killed her lover, she destroyed her journals, their love letters and all of it. If indeed they existed. If they did and survived, I should have heard of them, or come across them at some point."

"Okay. Do you remember getting any calls, inquiries, having anyone come by asking about brokering some of the mementos, the antiques, anyone asking for access because they were writing a story, a book?"

"Lord, Eli, I can't count the times. The only thing that's tempted me to hire anyone but Abra was the idea of having someone deal with the inquiries."

"Nothing that really stands out?"

"No, nothing that comes to mind."

"Let me know if you think of anything." And she'd had enough, Eli judged, and looked a little pale again. "What's for lunch?"

"We should go down and find out."

He helped her up, but when he started

to lift her, she brushed him back. "I don't need to be carried. I manage well enough with the cane."

"Maybe, but I like playing Rhett Butler."

"He wasn't carrying his grandmother downstairs to lunch," she said when Eli scooped her into his arms.

"But he would have."

Abra retrieved the cane, and as she watched Eli carry Hester downstairs, understood completely why she'd fallen in love.

Twenty-seven

A good day, Abra thought when they said good-bye to Hester. She reached for Eli's hand to say exactly that as they walked to the car. Then spotted Wolfe leaning against his across the street.

"What is he doing?" she demanded. "Why? Does he think you're going to suddenly walk over there and confess all?"

"He's letting me know he's there." Eli got behind the wheel, calmly started the engine. "A little psychological warfare, and surprisingly effective. It got to the point last winter where I rarely left the house because if I went for a damn haircut, I couldn't be sure he wouldn't walk in and take the chair next to me."

"That's harassment."

"Technically, and yeah, we could've filed charges, but at that point he'd have gotten a slap. Wouldn't really change anything, and the truth is I was too damn tired to bother. It got easier to just stay put."

"You put yourself under house arrest."

He hadn't thought of it that way, not at the time. But she wasn't wrong. Just as he'd thought, in some corner of his mind, of his move to Whiskey Beach as a self-imposed exile.

Those days were finished.

"I didn't have anywhere to go," he told her. "Friends eased away or just vanished. My law firm let me go."

"What about that 'innocent until proven guilty' tack?"

"That's the law, but it doesn't hold much weight with important clients, reputations and billable hours."

"They should've stuck by you, Eli, even if only out of principle."

"They had other associates, partners, clients, staff to consider. Initially they called it a leave of absence, but I was done, and we all knew it. Anyway, it gave me the time and the reason to write, to try to focus on that."

"Don't turn it into them doing you a favor." Her voice snipped, sharp as scissors. "You did yourself the favor. You did the positive."

"I grabbed a lifeline with writing, and it's more positive than letting go. When they didn't come to arrest me, and believe me that was something I waited for every day, it gave me the chance to go to Bluff House."

A kind of purging, Abra thought. A hulling out that had left him tired and tense and, to her mind, entirely too willing to accept the hand dealt him.

"And now?" she asked.

"Now, the lifeline's not enough. I can't just hold in place, wait for the fall. I'm going to fight back. I'm going to find the answers. When I have them, I'm going to stuff them down Wolfe's throat."

"I love you."

He glanced at her with a smile, but it faded into a look of wary surprise when he saw her eyes. "Abra—"

"Uh-uh, better watch the road." At her gesture, he tapped the brakes before he rear-ended a hatchback.

"Terrible timing," she continued. "Not romantic, not convenient, but I believe in expressing feelings, especially the positive ones. Love's the most positive feeling there is. I like feeling it, and I wasn't sure I would. We've got such crap behind us, Eli, and we can't help that some of it's still sticking to the bottom of our shoes. Maybe it helps make us who we are. But the bad thing is it makes us hesitate to trust again, reach out again, take those risks again."

Amazing, she thought, just amazing that saying the words out loud made her feel stronger, freer. "I don't expect you to take those risks just because I did, but you should feel good, and you should feel lucky that a smart, self-aware, interesting woman loves you."

He navigated the tricky traffic to squeeze his way onto 95 North. "I do feel lucky," he told her. And panicked.

"Then that's enough. We need better tunes," she decided, and began to search and scan his satellite radio.

That's it? he thought. I love you, let's change the channel? How the hell was a man supposed to keep up with a woman like that? She was a lot harder to negotiate than Boston traffic, and even more unpredictable.

As the miles passed, he tried to think of something else, but his thoughts kept circling back to it like fingers seeking out a nagging itch. Eventually he'd have to respond, somehow. They'd have to deal with the . . . issue. And how the hell was he supposed to think clearly, rationally, about love and all it implied when he had so much else to deal with, to work through, to resolve?

"We need a plan," Abra said, and tossed him straight back into panic mode. "God, your face." She couldn't stop the laugh. "It's a study of barely restrained male terror. I don't mean an Abra-loves-Eli plan, so relax. I mean a Justin-Suskind-risked-sneaking-up-to-the-third-floor-of-Bluff-House-and-why plan. We need to systematically go through what's up there."

"I've started doing that a couple hours

a day, every day, and I've barely made a dent. Have you seen how much is up there?"

"That's why I said systematically. We stick with the stance he's after the dowry. We expand that by the reasonable assumption he has information, right or wrong, that caused him to dig in that area of the basement. And we can further expand that by logical speculation. He was looking for more information, another lead, something that confirms—to his mind—the location."

Eli imagined there were a lot of invisible or missing dots, but all in all it wasn't a bad way to connect what they had.

"For all we know he found what he was after."

"Maybe, but he's come back to the house since then. He still thinks the house is the key."

"Things weren't jumbled up." Eli thought it through. "I don't know what kind of order things had in the trunks, the chests and storage boxes, the drawers in all that furniture up there, so they could have been searched through prior to the police. But if he did, he was careful about it. Then the cops went through it, and now it's pretty jumbled up."

"How could he know someone wouldn't go up there, and before he found what he wanted. He didn't want anyone to know he had access to the house. We wouldn't have known if we hadn't been wandering around the basement in the dark."

"We were wandering around the basement because he cut the power. That's a big clue to a B-and-E."

"Okay, that's a good point. But would you have searched down there? If you'd come home, called the police, it's really unlikely you'd have gone down to the basement, looking for signs the intruder had been down there. Or if you did, it's not likely you'd have gone beyond the wine cellar."

"Okay. He took a calculated risk."

"Because he wants and needs the access, and maybe, if we do that systematic search, we'll find out more about why. We have to wait for him to come back before we can try the ambush agenda," she reminded him. "We might as well do something active until. More active," she amended. "I know you've been researching and cross-referencing, and plotting out theories and connections, and the trip today gave us new information to process. But I like the idea of actually getting my hands into things."

"We can take a deeper look."

"And spending some time up there might give you more ideas about how to use that space. I'm going to pick you up a paint fan."

"You are?"

"Colors inspire."

"No," he said after a moment, "I can't keep up."

"With what?"

"You." Relief when he finally cruised through the village tempered with frustration. Love to radio stations, systematic searches to ambushes to paint fans. "How many directions can you go in at one time?"

"I can think in a lot of directions, especially if I consider them important, relevant or interesting. Love's important, and certainly on a different level I think music on a drive's important. Searching on the third floor and refining any plan to, hopefully, catch Suskind inside the house are absolutely relevant, and paint colors are interesting—and eventually both important and relevant."

"I surrender," he said as he pulled up and parked at Bluff House.

"Good choice." Abra got out of the car, spread her arms, turned a circle. "I love the way it smells here, the way the air feels. I want to take a run on the beach and just *fill* myself with it."

He couldn't take his eyes off her, couldn't block the lure of her. "You matter to me, Abra."

"I know it."

"You matter more than anyone has."

She lowered her arms. "I hope so."

"But—"

"Stop." She hauled her bag out of the car, shook back her hair. "You don't have to qualify it. I'm not looking for you to balance the scales. Take the gift, Eli. If I gave it too soon or wrapped it the wrong way, it can't be helped. It's still a gift." She started for the door, and from inside, Barbie sent out a fury of barks.

"Your alarm's going off. I'll change and take her with me for that run."

He got out his keys. "I could use a run, too."

"Perfect."

She said no more about it, and instead plowed straight on with the new agenda. They unpacked trunks, with Abra diligently inventorying the contents on a laptop.

They weren't experts, she'd stated, but an organized itemization might help with Hester's hope for a museum. So they separated, studied, cataloged and replaced with Eli culling out the household ledgers, account books and journals.

He paged through them, making his own notes, outlining his own theory.

She had to work, and so did he, but he adjusted his own schedule to include what he thought of as mining-the-past time. He added to his stack of household ledgers with meticulous recordings of purchases of fowl, beef, eggs, butter and various vegetables from a local farmer named Henry Tribbet.

Eli decided Farmer Tribbet was an ancestor of his drinking pal Stoney. He amused himself imagining Stoney wearing a farmer's straw hat and overalls when Barbie let out a warning woof, then dashed out, barking.

He rose from the temporary work space of card table and folding chair, started out. A moment after the barking stopped, Abra called up.

"It's just me. Don't come down if you're busy."

"I'm on three," he called back.

"Oh. I've got a few things to put away, then I'll be up."

It sounded good, he admitted. To hear her voice break through the silence of the house, to know she'd come upstairs to join him, work with him, bring up bits and pieces of her day and the people in it.

Whenever he tried to imagine his days without her in them he remembered the dark cloud of time, his self-imposed house arrest where everything had been dull, colorless, heavy.

He'd never go back there, he'd pushed too far into the light to ever go back. But he often thought the brightest light was now Abra.

A short time later, he heard her coming up at a jog. He watched for her.

She wore knee-length jeans and a red T-shirt that claimed: *Yoga Girls Are Twisted.*

"Hi, I had a massage cancel, so—" She stopped on her way to the table where he sat, anticipating her hello kiss. "Oh my God!"

"What?" He sprang up, ready to defend against anything from a spider to a homicidal phantom.

"That dress!" She all but leaped on the dress he'd left draped over the trunk he was cataloging.

She snatched it up as his heart gratefully descended from his throat, and rushed to the mirror she'd already undraped. As he'd seen her do with ball gowns, cocktail dresses, suits and whatever else caught her fancy, she held up the boldly coral twenties-style dress with its low waist and knee-length fringed skirt.

She turned right and left so the fringes lifted and twirled.

"Long, long pearls, masses of them, a

matching cloche hat and a mile-long silver cigarette holder." Still holding it, she spun around. "Imagine where this dress has been! Dancing the Charleston at some fabulous party or some wild speakeasy. Riding in a Model T, drinking bathtub gin and bootleg whiskey."

She spun again. "The woman who wore this, she was daring, even a little reckless, and absolutely sure of herself."

"It suits you."

"Thanks, because it's fabulous. You know with what we've found and cataloged already, you could have a fashion museum right up here."

"I'll take the option of a poke in the eye with a sharp stick."

Men would be men, she supposed, and she had no desire to change that status.

"Okay, not here, but you definitely have enough for a fantastic display in Hester's museum. One day."

Unlike Eli, she carefully folded the dress with tissue. "I checked the telescope before I came up. He's still a no-show."

"He'll be back."

"I know it, but I hate waiting." Belatedly, she walked over to kiss him. "Why aren't you writing? It's early for you to stop for the day."

"I finished the first draft, so I'm taking a break, letting it cook a little."

"You finished it." She threw her arms around his neck, shook her hips. "That's fantastic! Why aren't we celebrating?"

"A first draft isn't a book."

"Of course it is, it's just a book waiting for refinement. How do you feel about it?"

"Like it needs refinement, but pretty good. The end went quicker than I'd expected. Once I really saw it, it moved."

"We're absolutely celebrating. I'm going to make something amazing for dinner, and put a bottle of champagne from the butler's pantry on ice."

Thrilled for him, she dropped onto his lap. "I'm so proud of you."

"You haven't read it yet. Just one scene."

"It doesn't matter. You finished it. How many pages?"

"Right now? Five hundred and forty-three."

"You wrote five hundred and forty-three

pages, and you did that through a personal nightmare, you did that during a major transition in your life, through continuing conflict and stress and upheaval. If you're not proud of yourself you're either annoyingly modest or stupid. Which is it?"

She lifted him, he realized. She just lifted him.

"I guess I'd better say I'm proud of myself."

"Much better." She kissed him noisily, then wrapped her arms around his neck again. "By this time next year, your book will be published or on its way to publication. Your name's going to be cleared, and you'll have all the answers to all the questions hanging over you and Bluff House."

"I like your optimism."

"Not optimism alone. I did a tarot reading."

"Oh, well then. Let's spend my staggering advance on a trip to Belize."

"I'll take it." She leaned back. "Optimism and a tarot reading equal a very powerful force, Mr. Mired in Reality, especially when you add effort and sweat. Why Belize?"

"No clue. It was the first thing to pop into my mind."

"Often the first things are the best things. Anything interesting today?"

"Nothing that pertains to the dowry."

"Well, we still have plenty to go through. I'll start on another trunk."

She worked alongside him, then decided to change gears, abandon the trunk and work her way through an old chest of drawers.

It was amazing what people kept, she thought. Old table runners, faded pieces of embroidery or needlepoint, children's drawings on paper so dry she feared it would break and crumble in her hands. She found a collection of records she thought might be from the same era as the gorgeous coral dress. Amused, she uncovered a gramophone, wound it up, and set the record to play.

She grinned over at Eli as the scratchy, tinny music filled the room. She did some jazz hands, a quick shimmy, and had him grinning back.

"You ought to put the dress on."

She winked at him. "Maybe later."

She danced back to the chest of drawers, opened the next drawer.

She made piles. So much unused or partially used fabric, she noted, arranging them in neat piles. Someone had used the chest of drawers for sewing at one time, she thought, storing silks and brocades, fine wools and satins. Surely some lovely dresses had come from this, and others simply planned and never realized.

When she reached the bottom drawer, it stuck halfway open. After a couple of tugs, she lifted out scraps of fabric, and an envelope of pins, an old pincushion fashioned to resemble a ripe, red tomato, a tin box of various threads.

"Oh, patterns! From the thirties and forties." Carefully, she lifted them out. "Shirtwaists and evening gowns. Oh God, just *look* at this sundress!"

"You go ahead."

She barely spared him a glance. "They're wonderful. This whole project has made me wonder why I never tried vintage clothing before. I wonder if I can make this sundress."

"Make a dress?" He flicked her a glance. "I thought that's what stores were for."

"In that yellow silk with the little violets, maybe. I've never sewn a dress, but I'd love to try it."

"Be my guest."

"I could even try on that old sewing machine we found up here. Just to keep it all vintage." Imagining it, she stacked the patterns, turned back to the empty drawer.

"It's stuck," she muttered. "Maybe something's caught . . ."

Angling herself, she reached in, searched the bottom of the drawer above for a blockage, then the sides, then the back. "I guess it's just jammed or warped or . . ."

Then her fingers trailed over what felt like a curve of metal.

"Something's back here in the corner," she told Eli. "In both corners," she discovered.

"I'll look in a minute."

"I can't see why it's hanging up the drawer. It's just—"

Impatient, she pushed at the corners, and the drawer slid out, nearly into her lap.

Eli glanced up again at her surprised "Oh!"

"Are you okay?"

"Yes, just bumped my knees a little. It's like a compartment, Eli. A secret compartment in the back of this drawer."

"Yeah, I've found a few of those in desks, and one in an old buffet."

"But did you find anything in them like this?"

She held up a wooden box, deeply carved with a stylized, looping *L*.

"Not so far." Intrigued now, he stopped his inventory when she brought the box to the table. "It's locked."

"Maybe the key's in the collection we've been compiling, more of which I found in the hidden drawer in the old buffet."

She glanced over at the jar they were using to store keys found during the third-floor rummage. Then just pulled a pin out of her hair.

"Let's try this first."

He had to laugh. "Seriously? You're going to pick the lock with a hairpin?"

"It's the classic way, isn't it? And how complicated can it be?" She bent the pin, slid it in, turned, wiggled, turned. Since she seemed determined to open the box, Eli started to get up for the jar. Then heard the quiet click.

"You've done this before?"

"Not since I was thirteen and lost the key to my diary. But some skills stay with you."

She lifted the lid, found a cache of letters.

They'd come across letters before, most of them as long and winding as the distance between Whiskey Beach and Boston, or New York. Some from soldiers gone to war, she thought, or daughters married and settled far away.

She hoped for love letters as she'd yet to find any.

"The paper looks old," she said as she carefully took them out. "Written with a quill, I think, and— Yes, here's a date. June 5, 1821. Written to Edwin Landon."

"That would have been Violeta's brother." Eli pushed his own work aside, shifted to look. "He'd have been in his sixties. He died in . . ." He scoured his mind for the family history he'd pored over. "I think 1830 something, early in that decade anyway. Who's it from?"

"James J. Fitzgerald, of Cambridge."

Eli noted it down. "Can you read it?"

"I think so. 'Sir, I regret the unfortunate circumstances and tenor of our meeting last winter. It was not my intention to intrude upon your privacy or your goodwill. While you made your opinions and decision most . . . most abundantly clear at that time, I feel it imperative I write to you now on behalf'—no— 'behest of my mother and your sister, Violeta Landon Fitzgerald.'"

Abra stopped, eyes huge as they met Eli's.

"Eli!"

"Keep reading." He rose to go study the letter over her shoulder. "There's no record in the family history of her marrying or having children. Keep reading," he repeated.

"'As I communicated to you in January, your sister is most grievously ill. Our situation continues to be difficult with the debts incurred at my father's death two years past. My employment as a clerk for Andrew Grandon, Esquire, brings me an honest wage, and with it I have well supported my wife and family. I am now, of course, seeing to my mother's needs in addition to attempting to reconcile the debts.

" 'I do not and would not presume to approach you for financial aid on my own behalf, but must again do so in your sister's name. As her health continues grave, the doctors urge us to remove her from the city and to the shore, where they believe the sea air would be most beneficial. I fear she will not live to see another winter should the current situation continue.

" 'It is your sister's most heartfelt wish to return to Whiskey Beach, to return to the home where she was born and which holds so many memories for her.

" 'I appeal to you, sir, not as an uncle. You have my word I will never ask for consideration for myself due to that familial connection. I appeal to you as a brother whose only sister's wish is to come home.' "

Mindful of its fragility, Abra set the letter aside. "Oh, Eli."

"She left. Wait, let me think." He straightened, began to wander the room. "There's no record of her marriage, any children, of her death—not in family records, anyway—and I've never heard of this Fitzgerald connection."

"Her father had records destroyed, didn't he?"

"That's what's been passed down, yeah. She ran off, and he not only cut her off, he basically eliminated all records."

"He must have been a small, ugly man."

"Tall, dark and handsome in his portraits," Eli corrected, "but you mean inside. And you're probably right. So Violeta left here, estranged from the family, and went to Boston or Cambridge and they disowned her. At some point she married, had children—at least this son. Was Fitzgerald the survivor of the *Calypso*? An Irish name, not a Spanish one."

"He could've been impressed. Is that the term? Or just as likely she met and married him after she left home. Was

there really never any attempt to reconcile, until this? Until she was dying?"

"I don't know. Some of the stories
speculate she ran away with a lover, most
just speculate she ran off after her lover
was killed by her brother. During this research, I've come across a couple of
speculations she was shipped off because she was pregnant, and then disowned because she wouldn't fall in line.
Basically, they erased her, so there are no
family records or mentions of her after
the late 1770s. Now that we have this, we
can do a search for James J. Fitzgerald,
Cambridge, and work back from there."

"Eli, the next letter, it's written in Sep-
tember of the same year. Another plea.
She's worse, and the debts are mounting
up. He says his mother's too weak to hold
a pen and write herself. He writes her
words for her. Oh, it breaks my heart.
'Brother, let there be forgiveness. I do not
wish to meet God with this enmity between us. I beseech you, with the love we
once shared so joyfully, to allow me to
come home to die. To allow my son to
know my brother, the brother I cherished,

and who cherished me before that horrible day. I have asked God to forgive me for my sins and for yours. Can you not forgive me, Edwin, as I forgive you? Forgive me and bring me home.'"

She wiped tears from her cheeks. "But he didn't, did he? The third letter, the last. It's dated January sixth. 'Violeta Landon Fitzgerald departed this world on this day at the hour of six. She suffered greatly in the last months of her time on this earth. This suffering, sir, is on your hands. May God forgive you for I shall not.

" 'On her deathbed, she related to me all that occurred in those last days of August in the year 1774. She confessed her sins to me, the sins of a young girl, and yours, sir. She suffered and died wishing for the home of her birth and her blood, and for the embrace of family refused her. I will not forget nor will any of my blood. You have your riches and hold them dearer than her life. You will not see her again, nor meet with her in Heaven. For your actions you are damned, as are all the Landons who spring from you.'"

She set the last letter with the others. "I agree with him."

"By all accounts Edwin Landon and his father were hard men, uncompromising."

"I'd say these letters bear that out."

"And more. We don't know if Edwin responded, or what he wrote if he did, but it's clear both he and Violeta 'sinned' in August of 1774. Five months after the *Calypso* wrecked on Whiskey Beach. We need to search for information on James Fitzgerald. We need a date of birth."

"You think she was pregnant when she left, or was disowned."

"I think that's the kind of sin men like Roger and Edwin Landon would condemn. And I think, given the times, their rise in society, in status, in business, a daughter pregnant with the child of someone less, someone outside the law? Untenable."

He walked back to her, studied the letter again, the signature. "James would have been a common name, a popular one. Sons are often named for fathers."

"You think her lover, the seaman from the *Calypso*, was James Fitzgerald?"

"No. I think her lover was Nathanial James Broome, and he survived the wreck of his ship, along with Esmeralda's Dowry."

"Broome's middle name was James?"

"Yeah. Whoever Fitzgerald was, I'm betting she was pregnant when she married him."

"Broome might have run off with her, changed his name."

Eli ran a hand down her hair absently, remembering how she'd given the doomed schoolteacher and long-ago Landon a happy ending.

"I don't think so. The man was a pirate, fairly notorious. I don't see him settling down quietly in Cambridge, raising a son who becomes a clerk. And he'd never have let the Landons have the dowry. Edwin killed him, that's how I see it. Killed him, took the dowry, tossed his sister out."

"For money? At the bottom of it, they cast her out, *erased* her, for money?"

"She took for a lover a known brigand. A killer, a thief, a man who would certainly have been hanged if caught. The Landons are accumulating wealth, social prestige and some political power. Now their daughter, whom they'd have married to the son of another wealthy family, is ruined. They may be ruined as well if it becomes known that they harbored or had knowledge of a wanted man being harbored. She, the situation, her condition needed to be dealt with."

"Dealt with? *Dealt* with?"

"I'm not agreeing with what was done, I'm outlining their position and probable actions."

"Lawyer Landon. No, he wouldn't be one of my favorite people."

"Lawyer Landon's just stating their case, the case of men of that era, that mind-set. Daughters were property, Abra. It wasn't right, but it's history. Now instead of being an asset, she was a liability."

"I don't think I can listen to this."

"Get a grip on yourself," he suggested when she pushed to her feet. "I'm talking about the late eighteenth century."

"You sound like you're okay with it."

"It's history, and the only way I can try to get a clear picture is to think logically and not emotionally."

"I like emotion better."

"You're good at it." So, they'd use that,

too, he decided. Both emotion and logic. "Okay, what does your emotion tell you happened?"

"That Roger Landon was a selfish, un-feeling bastard, and his son, Edwin, a heartless son of a bitch. They had no right to throw away a life the way they threw away Violeta's. And it's not just *history*. It's people."

"Abra, you realize we're arguing about someone who died nearly two hundred years ago?"

"And your point?"

He rubbed his hands over his face. "Why don't we say this? We've reached the same basic conclusion. Part of that conclusion is Roger and Edwin Landon were coldhearted, hard-minded, oppor-tunistic bastards."

"That's a little better." Her eyes nar-rowed. "Opportunistic. You really believe, not only the dowry existed, not only that it came ashore with Broome, but that Edwin killed Broome and stole the dowry."

"Well, it was already stolen property, but yeah. I think he found it, took it."

"Then where the hell is it?"

"Working on that. But all this is moot if the basic premise is wrong. I need to start tracing Violeta's son."

"How?"

"I can do it myself, which would take time because it's not my field, but there are plenty of tools, some good genealogy sites. Or I can save time and contact someone whose field it is. I know a guy. We were friendly once."

She understood—someone who'd turned his back on Eli. And, she realized, however logical his argument, he understood what Violeta had gone through. He knew what it was to be cast aside, condemned, ignored.

"Are you sure you want to do that?"

"I thought about doing it weeks ago, but I put it off. Because— No, I don't really want to do it. But I'll try to take a page out of Violeta's book. When the chips are down, it's better to forgive."

She moved to him, took his face in her hands. "You're going to get that celebration after all. In fact, I'm going to go down and start on that. We should put those letters somewhere safe."

"I'll take care of it."

"Eli, why do you think Edwin kept the letters?"

"I don't know, except Landons tend to keep things. The chest of drawers may have been his, and putting them in that hidden niche might have been his way of keeping them but not seeing them."

"Out of sight, out of mind, like Violeta." Abra nodded. "What a sad man he must have been."

Sad? Eli thought when she left. He doubted it. He thought Edwin Landon would have been a self-satisfied son of a bitch. No family tree grew without a few bent branches, he supposed.

He used his laptop to search for the contact number for an old friend, then took out his phone. Forgiveness, he discovered, didn't come easy. But expediency did. Maybe forgiveness would follow, and if not, he'd still have answers.

Twenty-eight

With her hair bundled up, her sleeves hiked to her elbows, Abra looked up from layering slices of potato in a casserole dish when Eli came into the kitchen.

"How'd that go?"

"Awkward."

"I'm sorry, Eli."

He only shrugged. "More awkward for him than for me, I think. Actually, I knew his wife better. She's a paralegal at my old firm. He teaches history at Harvard and sidelines in genealogy. We played basketball a couple times a month, downed a few beers here and there. That's all."

That was enough, to Abra's mind, to deserve a little loyalty and compassion.

"Anyway, after the initial stumbling around and that strained and overenthusiastic 'Good to hear from you, Eli,' he agreed to do it. In fact, I think he feels guilty enough to make it a priority."

"Good. It helps balance the scales."

"Then why do I want to punch something?"

She considered the potato she'd just sliced in several vicious whacks. She knew exactly how he felt.

"Why don't you go pump some iron instead? Work up an appetite for stuffed pork chops, scalloped potatoes and green beans amandine. A manly celebration meal."

"Maybe I will. I should feed the dog."

"Already done. She's now stretched out on the terrace watching people play in what she considers her yard."

"I should give you a hand."

"Do I look like I need one?"

He had to smile. "No, you don't."

"Go, pump it up. I like my men ripped."

"In that case, I might be a while."

He sweated out the frustration and the depression that wanted to walk hand in hand. And once he'd showered off the dregs, he found he could let it go.

He had what he needed, an expert to solve a problem. If guilt helped solve the problem, it didn't and shouldn't matter.

On impulse, he took Barbie for a walk into the village. It struck him that people spoke to him, called him by name, asked how he was doing without any of the wariness, the awkwardness he'd become so accustomed to.

He bought a bouquet of tulips the color of eggplant. On the way back, he waved to Stoney Tribbet as the old man strolled toward the Village Pub.

"Buy you a beer, boy?"

"Not tonight," Eli called back. "I've got dinner waiting, but keep a stool open for me Friday night."

"You got it."

And that, Eli realized, made Whiskey Beach home. A stool at the bar on Friday night, a casual wave, dinner on the stove and knowing the woman you cared for would smile when you gave her purple tulips.

And she did.

The tulips stood along with candles on the terrace table with the surf crashing, the stars winking on. Champagne bubbled, and right there, right then, Eli felt all was right with his world.

He'd come back, he thought. Shed the too-tight skin, turned the corner, rounded the circle—whatever analogy worked. He was where he wanted to be, with the woman he wanted to be with and doing what made him feel whole, and real.

He had colored lights and wind chimes on the terrace, pots of flowers and a dog napping at the top of the beach steps.

"This is . . ."

Abra lifted her eyebrows. "What?"

"Just right. Just exactly right."

And when she smiled at him again, it was. Just exactly right.

Later, when the house lay quiet and his body still thrummed from hers, he couldn't say why sleep eluded him. He listened to the rhythm of Abra's breathing, and the muffled yips from Barbie as she dreamed, he imagined, of chasing a bright red ball into the water.

He listened to Bluff House settle, and imagined his grandmother wakened late at night by noises that didn't fit the pattern.

Restless, he rose, thought to go down for a book. Instead he climbed up to the third floor to the stack of ledgers. He sat at the card table with his legal pad, his laptop.

For the next two hours he read, calculated, checked dates, cross-referenced from household accounting to business accounting.

When his head throbbed, he rubbed his eyes and kept going. He'd studied law, he reminded himself. Criminal law, not business law, not accounting or management.

He should pass this to his father, to his sister. But he couldn't let go of it.

At three in the morning he pushed away. His eyes felt as though he'd scrubbed his corneas with sandpaper, and a toothy vise clamped over his temples and the back of his neck.

But he thought he knew. He thought he understood.

Wanting time to process, he went downstairs, dug aspirin out of the kitchen cabinet. He downed them with water he drank like a man dying of thirst before walking out onto the terrace.

The air glided over him like a balm and smelled of sea and flowers. Starlight showered and the moon, waxing toward full, pulsed against the night sky.

And on the cliff, above the rocks where men had died, Whiskey Beach Light circled its hopeful beam.

"Eli?" In a robe as white as the moon, Abra stepped out. "Can't sleep?"

"No."

The air rippled her robe, danced through her hair, and the moonlight glowed in her eyes.

When, he wondered, had she become so beautiful?

"I have some tea that might help." She came to him, automatically reached up to rub at his shoulders, seek out tension. When her eyes met his, her look of concern turned to one of curiosity. "What is it?"

"A lot of things. A lot of big, unexpected things in one even more unexpected bunch."

"Why don't you sit down? I'll work on these shoulders and you can tell me."

"No." He took her hands, held them between his. "I'll just tell you. I love you, too."

"Oh, Eli." She gripped his fingers with hers. "I know."

Not the reaction he'd expected. In fact, he thought, it was a little irritating. "Really?"

"Yes. But God." Her breath caught as she wrapped her arms around him, held tight with her face pressed to his shoulder. "God, it's so wonderful to hear you say it. I told myself it would be okay if you didn't say it. But I didn't know it would feel like this to hear it. How could I know? If I had, I'd have hounded you like a wolf to drag those words out of you."

"If I didn't say it, how do you know?"

"When you touch me, when you look at me, when you hold me, I feel it." She looked up at him, eyes drenched. "And I couldn't love you this much without you loving me back. I couldn't know how right it is to be with you if I didn't know you loved me."

He brushed at her hair, all those tumbled curls, and wondered how he'd ever gotten through a single day without her. "So, you were just waiting for me to catch up?"

"I was just waiting for you, Eli. I think I've been waiting for you ever since I came to Whiskey Beach because you're all that was missing."

"You're what's right." He laid his lips on hers. "What's just right. It scared the hell out of me at first."

"I know, me too. But now?" Tears spilled out of mermaid eyes and sparkled in the moonlight. "I feel absolutely courageous. What about you?"

"I feel happy." Struck with tenderness, he kissed the tears away. "I want to make you as happy as I am."

"You do. It's a good night. Or day, I guess. Another really good day." She pressed her lips to his again. "Let's give each other lots more good days."

"That's a promise."

And Landons keep their promises, she

thought. Overwhelmed, she wrapped around him again. "We found each other, Eli. Just when, just where we were supposed to."

"Is that a karma thing?"

She drew back to laugh up at him. "You're damn right it is. Is this why you couldn't sleep? Because you suddenly accepted your karmic path and wanted to tell me?"

"No. Actually, I didn't know I was going to say it until you walked out here. One look at you, and it blew through me, all of it."

"We should go back to bed." Her smile was full of promise. "I bet I can help you sleep."

"There's another reason I love you. You always have really good ideas." But as he took her hand, he remembered. "Jesus, I got caught up."

"A habit of yours."

"No, I mean I forgot why I came out here in the first place, *why* I couldn't sleep. I went up and started working on the books—the ledgers, the accounts."

"All those numbers and columns?" Instinctively she reached up to rub at temples she imagined ached. "You should have nodded off inside five minutes."

"I found it, Abra. I found Esmeralda's Dowry."

"What? How? My God, Eli! You're a genius." She grabbed him, circled and swayed. "Where?"

"It's here."

"But here where? And do I need a shovel? Oh, oh! We have to take it to Hester, to your family. It needs to be protected, and . . . There must be a way to trace Esmeralda's descendants, make them a part of the discovery. Hester's museum. Can you imagine what this means to Whiskey Beach?"

"Talk about running with it," he commented.

"Well, Eli, *think* of it. Treasure unearthed after more than two centuries. You could write another book about it. And just think of all the people who'll be able to see it now. Your family could lend pieces to the Smithsonian, the Met, the Louvre."

"That's what you'd do? Donate, lend, display?"

"Well, yes. It belongs to the ages, doesn't it?"

"One way or the other." Fascinated by her, he studied her glowing face. "Don't you want it? Even a piece of it?"

"Oh, well . . . Now that you mention it, I wouldn't say no to one tasteful piece." She laughed, spun in a circle. "Oh, just think of the history, the mystery solved, the magic uncorked."

She stopped, laughed again. "Where the hell is it? And how fast can we get it and secure it?"

He turned her, gestured. "We've already got it. It's already secured. Abra, it's Bluff House."

"What? I don't understand."

"My ancestors weren't as altruistic or philanthropic as you. They not only kept it, they spent it." He gestured toward the house. "Built not just on whiskey, but pirate booty. The expansion of the distillery—the timing of it—the expansion of the house, those first innovations, the lumber, the stone, the labor."

"You're saying they sold the dowry to expand the business, to build the house?"

"In pieces, I think, if I'm reading all the accounting right. Over a generation or two, starting with the coldhearted Roger and Edwin."

"Oh. I have to adjust." She pushed at her hair and, he imagined, pushed back her excited thoughts of museums, and sharing. "Bluff House *is* Esmeralda's Dowry."

"Essentially. It doesn't add up otherwise, not if you really dig into the expenditures, the revenue. Family lore says gambling—they liked to gamble and they were lucky. And they were smart businessmen. Then the war, the buildup of the country. All of that, yeah, but gamblers need a stake."

"You're sure it was the dowry."

"It's logical. I want Tricia to take a look, to analyze, and I want to hear back on James Fitzgerald. It adds up, Abra. It's in the walls, the stone, the glass, the gables. They accounted for it, in their own way, Roger and Edwin, because they considered it theirs."

"Yes." She nodded at that. "Men who could cut a daughter, a sister, so completely out of their lives would consider it theirs. I see that."

"Broome came with it to Whiskey Beach, and Whiskey Beach was theirs. They gave him shelter, and he disgraced their daughter, their sister. So they took what he stole and built what they wanted."

"Ruthless," she murmured. "Ruthless and wrong, but . . . it's poetic, too, isn't it?" She leaned her head on his shoulder. "And, in a way, a happy ending. How do you feel about it?"

"Maybe a lot of it was built on blood and betrayal. You can't change history, so you live with it. The house weathered it. So did the family."

"It's a good house. It's a good family. I think both more than weathered history."

"Ruthless and wrong," he repeated, "and I can be sorry for that. Lindsay's murder was ruthless and wrong. All I can do about any of it is try to find out the truth. Maybe that's justice."

"That's why I love you," she said quietly. "Just that. It's too early to call Tricia, and I don't think either of us is going to get any more sleep. I'm going to make us some eggs."

"That's why I love you." On a laugh, he

turned to her, pulled her in. And as his gaze drifted over her head, he went still.

He saw, down at the point, a shimmer of light. "Wait."

He moved quickly to the telescope, peered through. Straightening, he looked at Abra.

"He's back."

With a hand gripped on his arm, she looked for herself. "I kept wishing for this, so it could be done and over, but now that it is . . ." She took a moment to evaluate. "I feel the same way. Now, we *do* something." She sent him a cool, fierce smile. "Let's break some eggs."

While she did so literally, and Eli made coffee, it struck him it might have been any morning, even if it started at barely five a.m. Two people in love—and that was new and fresh and *energizing*—fixing breakfast.

All you had to do was leave out the murderer.

"We could call Corbett," Abra said, rinsing berries in the sink. "He could have that conversation."

"Yeah, we could."

"And that wouldn't accomplish much. A conversation over a man I saw in a bar."

"A man Lindsay cheated with, who bought property in Whiskey Beach."

"Which Lawyer Landon tells me won't hold up in court."

Eli studied her, set her coffee on the counter. "It's a step."

"A small one on a very slow walk, and one that lets Suskind know *you* know. Doesn't that forearm him?"

"A step that may spook him, even might influence him to leave Whiskey Beach. The threat here's eliminated while the investigation into Duncan's death continues, and we take the next steps to verifying the facts regarding the dowry, Edwin Landon, James Fitzgerald and so on."

" 'Verifying the facts regarding' is edging toward more lawyer talk."

"Even when I practiced law, lawyer snark didn't bother me."

She sliced some butter into a heated skillet, smiled at him while it sizzled. "Such a fine line between truth and snark. In any case, action's more satisfying than snark. We've got a shot, Eli, at proving he's the one breaking into Bluff House. Prove that and it not only leads to hanging him for Hester's fall, and that's huge, I think, for both of us, but it adds weight to his association with Duncan. Link them together, and it's a short slide to incriminating him for murder."

"A lot of soft spots on that path."

She poured beaten eggs into the skillet. "They hounded you for a year over Lindsay's death, with less cause, with no evidence. I say we give karma a hand and let the man who, at the least, played a part in that experience the same."

"Is 'karma' another word for 'payback' in this case?"

"You say potato."

She plated eggs, fruit, slices of whole wheat bread she'd toasted. "Why don't we eat in the morning room? We can watch the sun come up."

"Before that, is it sexist for me to say I love watching you cook breakfast, especially in that robe?"

"It would be sexist if you expected or demanded it." Slowly, she trailed her fingers down the side of the robe. "Enjoying it just shows you have good taste."

"That's what I thought."

They carried the plates, the coffee into the morning room, sat in front of the wide bow of glass. Abra scooped up a bite of eggs.

"To continue that thought," she added, "it would be sexist for you to think you need to get me safely out of the way before you follow through on the plan to lure Suskind into the house."

"I didn't say anything about that."

"A woman in love is a mind reader."

God, he hoped not, though she'd already showed that aptitude too often for comfort. "If we tried the lure, and if it worked, there's no need for both of us to be here."

"Fine. Where will you be while I video him from the passage?" Expression placid, she popped a berry into her mouth. "I'd need to be able to contact you as soon as it's done."

"Being a smart-ass before dawn's annoying."

"So is any attempt to protect the little

woman. I'm not little, and I think I've already demonstrated I can handle myself."

"I didn't know I loved you when I first started talking about doing this. I hadn't—wasn't able—to open up to everything I feel for you. And it changes everything." He laid a hand over hers. "Everything. I want the answers. I want the truth about what happened to Lindsay, to Gran, about everything that's happened since I came back to Whiskey Beach. I want them on what happened two hundred years ago. But I could let it go, every bit of it, if I thought finding those answers could hurt you."

"I know you mean that, and it just . . ." She turned her hand under his so their fingers linked. "It just fills me. But I need the answers, too, Eli. For us. So let's trust each other to take care of each other, and find them together."

"If you stayed at Maureen's, I could signal you when and if he comes in. Then you could call the cops. They'd move in while he was here. Caught in the act."

"And if I'm with you, I can contact the police from right here, while you run your famous video camera."

"You just want to play in the secret passage."

"Well, who wouldn't? He hurt you, Eli. He hurt my friend. He would have hurt me. I'm not going to sit at Maureen's. Together, or not at all."

"That sounds like an ultimatum."

"Because it is." She lifted her shoulders, let them fall in the most casual gesture. "We can fight about it. You can get mad, I can be insulted. I just don't see the point, especially on such a gorgeous morning when we're in love. The point I see, Eli, is I've got your back. And I know you've got mine."

What the hell was he supposed to do with that? "It might not work."

"Negative thinking's unproductive. Plus, past history and pattern say it will work. This could be over, Eli, or at the very least he could be in police custody, charged with breaking and entering, maybe destruction of property, by tonight. And he'd be questioned on all the rest."

She leaned forward. "When that happens, Wolfe's going to have his first taste of crow."

"You had that ace up your sleeve," Eli replied.

"It's karma time, Eli."

"All right. But we're going to work this out, account for every contingency."

She poured them both a second cup of coffee. "Let's strategize."

While they talked, the sun broke over the horizon, splashing gold over the night-dark sea.

Just another day, Eli thought when Abra dashed out for her morning class. Or it would seem so to anyone watching the movements, the comings, the goings, of Bluff House.

He walked the dog, crossing the beach at a light jog and in full view of Sandcastle. To please Barbie as much as to form a picture, he spent a little time throwing the ball for her, letting her splash into the water, swim out again.

Back home, she sprawled on the sunny terrace, and Eli went in to call his sister.

"Boydon Madhouse, and how are you, Eli?"

"Pretty good." He held the phone an

inch from his ear as shrill shrieks threatened to break his eardrum. "What the hell
is that?"

"Selina strongly objects to being in
time-out." Tricia raised her own voice,
and Eli made it two inches. "And the longer Sellie screams and misbehaves, the
longer she'll be in time-out."

"What did she do?"

"Decided she didn't want her strawberries at breakfast."

"Oh, well, that doesn't seem—"

"So she threw them at me, which is
why she's in time-out. I have to change
my shirt, which further means she'll be
late for day care and I'll be late for the office."

"Okay. This is a bad time. I'll call you
later."

"We're going to be late anyway, and I
have to cool off so I don't give my beloved
child a strawberry facial. What's up?"

"I dug up some old household and
business ledgers. Really old, going back
to the late 1700s, into the early 1800s.
I've been going through them, pretty
carefully, and I've come to some interesting conclusions."

"Such as?"

"I'm hoping you have time to look them over yourself, and we'll see if your conclusions jibe with mine."

"You don't want to give me a clue?"

Boy, he really wanted to. But . . . "I don't want to influence you. Maybe I went off some shaky ledge."

"You've got my attention. I'd love to play with them."

"How about I scan you a few pages, just to give you a start? I should be able to come in, maybe the end of the week, bring the ledgers to you."

"You could. Or Max, the currently time-outed Sellie and I could come up Friday evening, have a weekend at the beach and I can play with them."

"Even better. But there'll be no strawberries if they cause this reaction."

"Usually she loves them, but girls do have their moods. I've got to go unshackle her, get us out of here. Send me what you can, and I'll take a look."

"Thanks. And . . . good luck."

Following his morning agenda, he went up for his laptop. He sat out on the terrace, in view of Sandcastle, his trusty

Mountain Dew on the table, as he scanned through his e-mails.

He opened one from Sherrilyn Burke first, began to read her updated report on Justin Suskind.

The man hadn't spent much time at work since the last report, Eli noted. A day here and there, a handful of out-of-office meetings. The most interesting, Eli found, had been to a law firm where he met with an estate specialist. And stormed out, obviously angry.

"Didn't get the answers you wanted," Eli sympathized. "I know just how you feel."

Through the report, he followed Suskind as he picked up his kids from school, took them to the park, to dinner, then home. His brief visit with his wife hadn't gone any better than his meeting with the lawyer, as he'd left in visible temper to speed away.

At ten-fifteen the night before, he'd left his apartment with a suitcase, a briefcase and a storage box. He'd driven north out of Boston, stopping at an all-night supermarket for a pound of ground beef.

He'd made a second stop an hour later,

veering off the highway to a twenty-four-hour box store where he'd purchased a box of rat poison.

Ground beef. Poison.

Without reading further, Eli surged to his feet.

"Barbie!"

He had a moment of sheer panic when he didn't see her on the terrace. Even as he raced forward, she scrambled to her feet from where she sat at the top of the beach steps. Tail happily wagging, she trotted to him.

Eli simply went down to his knees, wrapped his arms around her. Love, he realized, could sometimes come fast, but it didn't make it any less real.

"Fucker. The *fucker*." Leaning back, Eli accepted the adoring licks. "He's not going to hurt you. I'm not going to let him hurt you. You stick with me, girl."

He led her back to the table. "You stay right here with me."

In response she laid her head in his lap, sighed in contentment.

He read the rest of the report, then e-mailed back his own, which started with:

The bastard plans to poison my dog. If you're in Whiskey Beach, don't come here. I don't want him wondering who you are. I'm done waiting around for him to make the next move.

He gave her an overview of what his research had unearthed, and the basics of what he'd done, and planned to do.

Planned to do rather than what he wanted to do right that minute—go straight to Suskind and kick the living shit out of him.

Temper still raw and ripe, Eli took his work and his dog back inside.

"No more going out by yourself until this bastard's behind bars."

He pulled out his phone when it rang, unsurprised to see Sherrilyn's name on the display.

"This is Eli."

"Eli, Sherrilyn. Let's talk about this idea of yours."

He heard the unsaid "stupid," shrugged. "Sure. Let's talk."

He wandered the house as they spoke because it served to remind him what he was fighting for. And it had come down to a fight for him, even if he was denied the satisfaction of physical blows.

He walked to the third floor, and the curved glass of the gable where he imagined writing one day, once the fight was done and won, once he'd secured safety for all he loved, and his own self-respect.

"You've got some valid points," he said at length.

"And you're not going to listen to them."

"I did listen to them, and you're not wrong. The thing is, if I step back from this, let the police handle it all, or even let you, I'm back where I was a year ago. Just letting it all happen, letting the situation carry me instead of me carrying it. I can't go back to that. I need to do this for myself, for my family. And in the end, I want him to know that. I need that when I think of Lindsay, my grandmother, this house."

"You didn't believe his wife."

"No."

"What did I miss?"

He lowered his hand to Barbie's head

when she leaned against him. "You said you had kids. You're married."

"That's right."

"How many times?"

She let out a laugh. "Just the one. It's worked out pretty well."

"That might be it. You haven't gone through the dark side. Maybe I'm wrong and that's what's coloring it. But I don't think so. The only way to be sure is to box him in. That's what I'm going to do, here, on my turf. In my place."

She let out a sigh. "I can help."

"Yeah, I think you can."

When he'd finished talking to her, he felt lighter somehow. "You know what?" he said to the dog. "I'm going to work for a couple hours, remind myself what my life's supposed to be about. You can hang with me."

He left the past, and what would come behind it, and went down to surround himself with the now.

Twenty-nine

Abra swung into the market, list in hand. She'd finished back-to-back classes, and a sports massage on a client prepping for a 5K, and polished it off with a last-minute cleaning in a rental cottage. Now she just wanted to grab what she needed and get back to Eli.

Honestly, she thought, that's what she'd like to do for the rest of her life. Get back to Eli.

But tonight could prove to be the turning point for him. For them. The point where they could begin to leave the questions and the pain of the past *in* the past, and start working toward tomorrow.

Whatever tomorrow brought, she'd be happy because he'd brought love back into her life. The kind of love that accepted, understood and—even better—enjoyed who and what she was.

Could there be anything more magical and marvelous than that?

She visualized lifting the little hand tote of baggage she still carried, then flinging it into the sea.

Done and gone.

But now wasn't the time for dreaming, she reminded herself. Now was the time for doing. For righting wrong. And if there was some adventure mixed in, so much the better.

She reached up for her preferred counter spray—biodegradable, no animal testing—dropped it in her basket and turned.

She all but bumped into Justin Suskind.

She couldn't stop the quick gasp, but tried to turn it quickly into a flustered apology even as her heart kicked like a startled mule.

"I'm so sorry. I wasn't paying attention." Praying she didn't tremble, she
tried an easy smile she felt quiver at the
edges.

He'd cut his hair, short, lightened it to
a sun-streaked blond. Unless he'd spent
the last two weeks catching rays, he'd
made use of a self-tanner.

And she was reasonably sure he'd had
his eyebrows waxed.

He gave her one hard stare, started to
move on.

On impulse she shifted, used her elbow
and knocked a few items from the shelf
to the floor.

"God! I'm such a klutz today." Crouching to retrieve them, she blocked his path.
"Isn't it always the way when you're running behind schedule? I need to get
home. My boyfriend's taking me into
Boston for dinner and a suite at The
Charles, and I haven't even decided what
to wear."

She rose with an armload of cleaning
products, sent him an apologetic smile.
"And I'm *still* in your way. Sorry."

She stepped aside, began to shelve

what she'd dropped, and resisted looking after him as she heard him walk away.

Now you know, she thought. Or you
think you know. You won't miss your *opportunity* any more than I could miss
mine.

She ordered herself to complete her
list, in case he was watching her. Even
stopped to chat with one of her yoga students for a moment. Everything's normal,
she told herself. Just a quick stop at the
market before your big night in Boston.

And because she was watching, she
caught a glimpse of him sitting in a dark
SUV in the lot as she put her market bags
in the car. Deliberately she turned the
radio up, checked her hair, dabbed on
some lip gloss, then pulled out to drive
home just a few miles over the speed
limit.

As she turned into Bluff House, she
watched in her rearview as Suskind continued on. Grabbing her bags, she dashed
into the house.

"Eli!" After dumping the bags, she
made the next dash up the stairs and
veered toward his office.

As her shout had him up and out, they nearly ran into each other. "What? Are you all right?"

"I'm fine, I'm good. I also just earned the think-fast-and-act-your-ass-off award. I literally bumped into Suskind at the market."

"Did he touch you?" Instinctively, Eli grabbed her arms, searched for injuries.

"No, no. He knew who I was, but I played dumb, or rather really smart. I knocked some things off the shelf so he couldn't get by me, then babbled about being clumsy and being in a hurry because my guy was taking me to Boston for dinner and a night of whoopee at The Charles."

"You talked to him? Jesus, Abra."

"*At* him. He didn't say a word, but he did wait for me to check out. He sat in his car in the lot, then followed me back. Eli, he thinks we're going to be out of the house overnight. It's his big chance. We don't have to count on him watching and seeing us leave. He's planning it all right now. It fell in our lap, Eli. It's on tonight. This is it."

"Was he following you? I mean before you left the store?"

"I . . . No, no, I don't think so. He had a basket. He had things in a basket, and I don't think he'd have gotten so close if he'd been watching me. It was fate, Eli. And fate's on our side."

He'd have called it chance, or maybe luck, but he wouldn't argue. "I got a report from Sherrilyn. He stopped at two different markets, miles apart, on the way to Whiskey Beach."

"Maybe he has a grocery store fetish."

"No, he's being careful, not buying his personal items from the same places he bought a pound of ground beef and a box of rat poison."

"Rat poison? I've never heard of anyone seeing rats at . . . Oh God." Shock hit first, then fury. "That—that son of a bitch. He plans to poison Barbie? That miserable excuse for a human being. It's a good thing I didn't know. I'd've given him another shot to the balls."

"Easy, tiger. What time's our reservation?"

"Our what?"

"For dinner."

"Oh. I didn't get that detailed."

Eli checked his watch. "Okay, we should leave about six. You worked it out with Maureen?"

"Yes, they'll keep Barbie. So we'll just go as we planned. Leave here with the dog, drop her off at Maureen's, then circle back on foot to the south side, then— Crap."

She put her hands to her head, did a little dance in place. "Dinner date. I have to wear heels to make it look real. Okay, okay, I'll stuff some sneakers in my bag, change shoes for the jog back. And don't give me that look. Footwear's important."

"We need to talk it all through again, and I need to fill you in on how Sherrilyn's playing into it."

"Then let's do it downstairs. I need to put away what I got at the market before my encounter. Then I need to figure out what to wear for our fake romantic evening-slash-ambush."

He went over every angle, then went over them again from a different direction. He spent time in the passage, then behind the shelves, checking the scope of the video camera, testing it. Just a backup now, he thought.

If things went wrong, he had a secondary backup.

"You're questioning yourself," Abra said as she checked the lines and fit of the dress she'd put on over a black tank and yoga shorts.

"I used to believe in the system, absolutely. I was part of the system. Now I'm going around it."

"No, you're working through it, just in a different way. And even that's a testament, Eli, when the system failed you. You have a right to defend your home, and a right to do whatever you can to clear your name."

She added earrings not only to complete the look, but because they boosted her confidence. "You even have a right to enjoy it."

"You think so?"

"Yes, I do."

"Good because I am. And I'm going to. You look great. I'm definitely taking you to dinner in Boston and a night of whoopee when this is over."

"I'd like that, but I have an even better idea. When this is over, you need to have the first of those parties you talked about. You need to have a blowout."

"That is a better idea, but I'll need help with it."

"Fortunately I find myself not only free, but willing and able to help with it."

He took her hand. "I think there's a lot we need to talk about. After."

"We have a long and I predict happy summer to talk about everything, anything." She turned his wrist to check his watch. "It's six on the dot."

"Then we'd better get started."

He carried down the overnights while Abra gathered what they'd packed for the dog. Downstairs, Eli contacted Sherrilyn.

"We're leaving the house now."

"You're sure about this, Eli?"

"This is how I want to handle it. I'll call again when we're back in."

"All right. I'll move into position. Good luck."

He switched the phone to vibrate, slipped it back into his pocket. "Here we go."

Abra used two fingers to push up the corners of Eli's mouth. "Happy face. Remember, you're going out to dinner and a fancy hotel with a very hot woman, and odds are you're going to get lucky several times."

"Since we're spending at least part of the evening in a dark passageway in a dark basement, and potentially the rest of it dealing with cops, will I still get lucky?"

"Guaranteed."

"See my happy face?"

They walked outside.

"Do you know what I just love?" she asked him as she opened the back of the car for the dog, for the overnights. "I love that he's watching us right now thinking *he's* the one who's getting lucky."

Eli closed the door, pulled her into his arms. "Let's give him a little show."

"Happy to." With enthusiasm, Abra wrapped around Eli, lifted her face for the kiss. "Teamwork," she murmured against his mouth. "That's how we do things in Whiskey Beach."

He opened the passenger door. "Remember, once we get to Maureen's we need to move fast. We don't know how long he might wait."

"Fast is my best speed."

When they pulled up at Maureen's, Eli grabbed the bag holding his change of clothes, Abra's shoes.

Maureen had the door of the cottage open before they got to it. "Look, both of you, Mike and I have been talking, and—"

"Too late." The instant she was inside, Abra yanked down the zipper of her dress. As she wiggled out of it, Eli pulled off his suit jacket, loosened his tie.

"If we just waited, watched, then called the police—"

"Something could spook him," Eli said on his way to their powder room with jeans and a black T-shirt. "He could leave before they got there."

"It's more that"—Abra stepped out of her heels as Eli closed the door—"he needs to have a part in this. I need to help him. We've been over this."

"I know that, but if he really killed some-one—"

"He did." To keep it simple, Abra sat on the floor to pull on sneakers. "It's likely he killed two people. And tonight, we're starting the chain holding the anchor that's going to take him down for it."

"You're not crime fighters," Mike began.

"We are tonight." Abra hopped up as Eli stepped out. "We even look the part. Where are the kids?"

"Upstairs playing. They don't know anything about this, and we didn't want them to hear us talking you out of what they don't know anything about."

"They'll have fun with Barbie." She kissed Maureen, then Mike. "I'll call you as soon as we're done. Fast?" she said to Eli. "Out the back."

"I'm right behind you." He took one extra moment. "I won't let anything happen to her. If there's any chance of it, I'll call it off."

"Don't let anything happen to either of you." Hurrying after them, Maureen watched them cross the back of her cottage to the back of Abra's. "Mike." She reached back for his hand. "What should we do?"

"Get the kids, take the dog for a walk."

"A *walk*?"

"On the beach, honey. We can see

Bluff House, maybe keep an eye on things."

Her hand squeezed his. "Good thinking."

Eli unlocked the side door of Bluff House, quickly reset the alarm before turning to Abra. "Be sure."

"Stop it." With that, she led the way to the basement. "It's barely ten after six. We were fast."

Once the door shut behind them, Eli switched on his flashlight to lead the way down and through the passage. It could take minutes, he thought, or hours. But he went with the odds. "He'll probably wait until dusk, maybe even dark, figuring he has all night."

"Whatever it takes." She edged behind the shelves with him and into the passage.

For now they used the overhead light. Abra took her position on the steps to check the laptop monitor and the nanny cam they'd set up on the third floor. Eli checked the video camera once again as he contacted Sherrilyn.

"We're inside the passage."

"No movement from Suskind yet. I'll let you know when and if."

"It'll be when."

"Positive thinking," Abra approved when Eli put the phone away.

"He sure as hell didn't come back here to surf or sunbathe. This is his goal, this is his chance to try for it again. Once he leaves Sandcastle, we go to dark."

"And all quiet, like a submarine. I've got it, Eli. If he goes to the third floor, the nanny cam will record him. If he comes down here, and that's most likely, we do. The sun sets in less than two hours, if he waits that long. We've probably got some time to pass."

And now they were closed in, without even enough room to pace off the tension.

"Should've brought a deck of cards," he commented. "Since we didn't, why don't you tell me how you'd do a yoga studio if you had one."

"Oh, hopes and dreams? I can pass lots of time that way."

She passed less than an hour before she stopped, angled her head. "Is that the phone? The house phone?"

"Yeah. It could be anyone."

"Or it could be him, just making sure

nobody's here." She shook her head when the faint ringing stopped. "We can't hear from down here if the caller's leaving a message."

Moments later, the phone vibrated in Eli's pocket.

"He's on the move," Sherrilyn told him. "Carrying a large duffel. He's going to use his car. Just stay on the line a minute, let me see how he plays it."

Eli repeated the statement in a whisper to Abra, and watching her eyes, saw them light with anticipation.

No fear, he thought. Just none.

"He's using the drive of a rental cottage about an eighth of a mile from Bluff House. He's out and heading toward you on foot."

"We're ready for him. Give him that fifteen after he's in before you make the call."

"You got it. You were right about this part of it, Eli. I hope you're right about the rest. I'll be seeing you."

He turned his phone off, tucked it away. "You stay in here, as agreed."

"All right, but—"

"No buts. We don't have time to change

the plan. Stay here, stay quiet and turn the light off." He took a moment to lean down and kiss her.

"You just remember I have your back."

"I'm counting on it." And on her staying closed in and safe.

He slipped out, easing the panel closed behind him. He took his position behind the shelves, letting his eyes adjust to the dark.

He could just switch the camera to record, stay inside with Abra. But he needed to see, to hear, needed to have his hand all the way in and be right there to make any change if necessary.

He didn't hear the back door open. He wasn't sure if he heard footsteps or imagined them. But he heard the creak of the basement door, and the heavy footfalls on the narrow stairs.

Showtime, he thought, and switched the camera on.

He came in slowly, leading with the flashlight. Eli watched the wide beam sweep, sending its backwash from the generator room into the area beyond. Then the leading edge of it, into the old section, the man holding it no more than a shadow as the light painted over the walls, the floor, then lit over the shelves.

In the beats the beam crept over the shelves, the wall, Eli's heart kicked. He braced, ready—maybe eager—to pursue, to fight.

But the beam passed on.

Secure now, Eli thought, as the work light flashed on. He saw Suskind clearly for the first time.

Dressed in black as he himself was, his hair clipped short now and streaked with blond. A new look, Eli decided, another way to blend into the vacation crowd.

He checked the viewfinder on the camera, adjusted it minutely as Suskind picked up the pickax. Those first hard thuds of blade striking ground rang satisfying to Eli.

Now you're done, he thought. Now we've got you.

He had to strap down the part of him that wanted to step out, to confront. Not yet, he ordered himself. Not quite yet.

Because his ears were tuned for it, he heard the sirens—dim against the thick walls—and watched Suskind continue to hack and dig at the ground, watched the sweat of the effort bead and roll on his face despite the cool air.

When the sirens silenced, Eli counted it off, and watched Suskind freeze when footsteps sounded overhead.

Suskind gripped the pick like a weapon now, eased over—very slowly, eyes wheeling left, right—to switch off the work light.

Eli gave him ten seconds in the dark, gauged his location by the labored breathing. As he slipped out from behind the shelves, he aimed his own flashlight, switched it on.

Suskind flung up an arm to shield his eyes from the glare.

"You're going to want to drop the pick, and switch the light back on."

Suskind squinted, took a two-handed grip on the pick. Eli waited as Suskind rolled to the balls of his feet.

"Try it and I'll shoot you. I've got the Colt .45, the Peacemaker, from the third-floor gun collection, aimed at you, center mass. You may not be familiar with it, but it's loaded and it still works."

"You're bluffing."

"Try me. Please. And do it before the cops make it down here. You owe me blood for my grandmother, and I'm happy to take it."

Feet pounded down the stairs; Suskind's fingers whitened on the handle of the pick. "I'm entitled! This house is as much mine as yours. Everything in it's as much mine. The dowry's *more* mine."

"You think?" Eli said easily, then called out, "Back here. Hit some lights. Suskind's holding a pickax in a threatening manner."

"I should have killed you," Suskind said between his teeth. "I should have killed you after you murdered Lindsay."

"You're a fool. And that's really the least of it."

He stepped back, just a little, when the first light spilled into the far edge of the area, and shifted his gaze—again just a little—to meet Abra's eyes.

He'd heard her slip out behind him, out of safety.

Corbett, Vinnie and another uniformed deputy stepped in, fanned out, weapons drawn.

"Drop it," Corbett ordered. "Drop it now. There's no way out, Suskind."

"I have every right to be here!"

"Drop it. Put your hands up, and do it *now*."

"Every right!" Suskind tossed the pick aside. "He's the thief. He's the murderer."

"Just one thing," Eli said easily as he stepped forward, and between the police and Suskind.

"I want you to step back, Mr. Landon," Corbett ordered.

"Yeah, I got it." But first. He waited until Suskind met his eyes, until he was certain they *saw* each other. Then he punched his fist into Suskind's face with all the rage, all the pain, all the misery of the last year behind it.

When Suskind fell against the wall, Eli stepped back, lifted his hands to show he was done. "You owed me blood," he said, lowering one hand to show the smear of it over his knuckles.

"You'll pay for that. You'll pay for it all."

He didn't think as Suskind reached behind his back, just acted. The second blow knocked Suskind to the ground, had the gun he'd pulled clattering to the floor.

"I'm done paying."

"Hands where I can see them," Corbett snapped when Suskind moved. "You put your hands in the air, now! Stay back, Mr. Landon," Corbett warned him, using his foot to kick the gun out of reach. He nodded at Vinnie. "Deputy."

"Yes, sir." Vinnie pulled Suskind to his feet, pushed him to face the wall to check for other weapons. He removed the holster secured at the small of Suskind's back, passed it to the other deputy. "You're under arrest for breaking and entering, trespassing, destruction of private property," he began as he cuffed Suskind's wrists. "Additional charges include two counts of assault. Looks like we get to add concealing a dangerous weapon and intent to injure onto that."

"Read him his rights," Corbett ordered. "Take him in."

"You got that." Vinnie gave Eli a subtle thumbs-up before he and the other deputy gripped Suskind's arms and pulled him out of the room.

Corbett holstered his weapon. "That was a stupid move. You could've gotten yourself shot."

"I didn't." Once again, Eli looked at his blood-smeared hand. "He owed me."

"Yeah, I guess he did. You set this up. You set him up."

"Did I?"

"I get a call from your investigator saying she just observed Justin Suskind breaking into Bluff House, and believes he might be armed. She's concerned for your safety."

"That sounds reasonable, and responsible, especially since he did break in, and he was armed."

"And the two of you just happened to be down here, on the spot?"

"We were . . . exploring the passages." Abra tucked her arm through Eli's, added a wicked smile. "You know, a little Pirate and Wench. We heard the noises in here. I didn't want Eli to come out, but he felt he had to. I was going to go up, call the police, but we heard you coming."

"Handy. Where's the dog?"

"Having a sleepover at a friend's," Eli said equably.

"Setup." Corbett shook his head. "You could've trusted me."

"I did. I do. My house, my grandmother, my life. My woman. But I trust you, and that's why I'd like to tell you a story before you interview Suskind. Some of the story plays into more recent events. I know who killed Lindsay, or I'm damn near close to knowing."

"You've got my attention."

"I'll tell you, but I want to observe the interview. I want to be there."

"If you have information or evidence regarding a homicide, you don't bargain."

"I have a story, and I have a theory. I think you'll like both. I think even Detective Wolfe will be interested. I want to observe, Detective. It's a good bargain for both of us."

"You can ride in with me, we'll talk about it."

"We'll get ourselves there."

Corbett hissed out a breath. "Get your investigator there, too."

"No problem."

"Setup," Corbett repeated under his breath, and headed back through the passage to the stairs.

"You didn't stay inside," Eli said to Abra.

"Please, if you thought I would, you may love me but you don't know me."

He took a handful of her hair, tugged it.

"Actually, it played out pretty much the way I figured."

"Let me see that hand." She lifted it, gently kissed his bruised knuckles. "This must hurt."

"Yeah, it does." He laughed a little, winced a little as he flexed his fingers. "But in a good, satisfying way."

"I'm strongly nonviolent, except in the case of defending self or others. But you were right. He owed you that." She kissed his hand again. "And, I confess, I liked watching you punch the bastard."

"That doesn't sound nonviolent."

"I know. Shame on me. What I'd like to mention, now that we're alone? You had a gun. That wasn't part of the plan we discussed."

"It was a kind of amendment."

"Where is it? I turned off the camera," she added, "as soon as the cops came in."

Saying nothing, Eli walked over, took the gun he'd put back on the shelf. "Because I think I do know you, and I figured you wouldn't stay back, I wasn't going to take any chances. Not with you."

"Big cowboy gun," she added. "Would you have used it?"

He'd asked himself the same question when he took it from the locked case, when he loaded it. He looked at her now, into what she was, what she meant to him.

"Yeah. If I had to, if I thought he'd get past me to you. But as I said, it played out the way I thought it would."

"You think you're smart."

"Except for a relatively short span of time when I shut down, I've always been smart." He hooked an arm around her, drew her in to press his lips to the top of her head.

I've got you, don't I? he thought. That makes me pretty damn smart.

"I need to contact Sherrilyn, have her meet us at the station. And I need to put this back where it belongs."

"Then I'll get the camera and call Maureen, let them know it's all clear. Teamwork."

"I like the sound of it."

Corbett sat across from Suskind, took a good, long study. He hadn't asked for a lawyer—yet—which Corbett deemed stupid. But stupid often made his job easier so he wouldn't argue about it. He had Vinnie standing inside the door. He liked the deputy's rhythm, and felt he'd be an asset in the room.

But he concentrated on Suskind, on the nervous tics—the way the man's fingers flexed and unflexed on the table, the jerk of a muscle in his jaw—his bruised and swollen jaw. And on the hard, stubborn line of his mouth, which sported a split lip.

Nervous, yes, Corbett decided, but absolutely dug in on his own sense of right.

"So . . . that's a pretty big hole in the basement at Bluff House," Corbett began. "A lot of work, a lot of time involved. Did you have some help?"

Suskind stared back, said nothing.

"I figure not. It strikes me like this was your job, your mission, not something to share. Your . . . you said 'right,' didn't you?"

"It is my right."

Shaking his head, Corbett tipped back in his chair. "You're going to have to explain that one. All I see is the guy who got caught sleeping with Landon's wife breaking into Landon's house to dig a big hole in his basement."

"It's as much my house as his."

"How do you figure?"

"I'm a direct descendant of Violeta Landon."

"Sorry, I'm not real familiar with the Landon family tree." He glanced at Vinnie now. "Are you more up on that, Deputy?"

"Sure. She's the one who supposedly rescued the seaman who survived the wreck of the *Calypso* way back when. Nursed him back to health. Some versions have them bumping hips, and getting caught at it."

"It wasn't a seaman, but the captain. Captain Nathanial Broome." Suskind tapped his fist on the table now. "He didn't just survive, he survived with Esmeralda's Dowry."

"Well, there's a lot of theories and stories about that," Vinnie began.

Suskind smashed his fist on the table. "I know the truth. Edwin Landon killed Nathanial Broome because he wanted the dowry, then he put his own sister out of the house, convinced his father to disown her. She was carrying Broome's child, his son."

"That sounds like bad luck for her," Corbett commented. "But it was a long time ago."

"She was pregnant with Broome's child!" Suskind repeated. "And when she was dying, suffering in poverty, and that child, then a grown man, pleaded with Landon to help his sister, to let her come home, he did *nothing*. That's who the Landons are, and I have every right to take what's mine, what was hers, what was Broome's."

"How'd you come by all this?" Vinnie asked casually. "A lot of stories go around about that treasure."

"They're stories. This is *fact*. It's taken me nearly two years to put it all together, a piece at a time. I've got letters, and they cost me, written by James Fitzgerald, Violeta Landon's son by Nathanial Broome. They detail what she told him happened that night on Whiskey Beach. He walked away from it, from his rights, Fitzgerald— her son. I won't!"

"Sounds to me like you should've been talking to a lawyer," Corbett put in, "not hacking holes in basements with a pickax."

"You think I didn't *try*?" Suskind jerked forward, face washed angry red. "Nothing but a runaround, nothing but excuses. It was too long ago, she wouldn't have legally inherited in any case. No legal claim. What about my blood claim, my moral claim? The dowry was booty belonging to *my* ancestor, not Landon's. It's mine."

"So, with this moral, blood claim behind you, you broke into Bluff House on numerous occasions and— Why the basement, specifically?"

"Violeta told her son Broome instructed her to hide it there to keep it safe."

"Okay, and you don't think in a couple hundred years somebody found it, maybe spent it?"

"She hid it. It's there, and it's mine by right."

"And you figure that right equals breaking in, damaging property and pushing an old woman down the stairs?"

"I didn't push her. I never laid a hand on her. It was an accident."

Corbett hiked up his eyebrows. "Accidents happen. How did this one?"

"I needed to look around on the third floor. The Landons have a lot of things stored up there. I needed to see if I could find something to give me more specifics on the dowry. The old woman got up, she saw me, she ran and she fell. That's it. I never touched her."

"You saw her fall?"

"Of course I saw her fall. I was *there*, wasn't I? It wasn't my fault."

"Okay, let's be clear. You broke into Bluff House on the night of January twentieth of this year. Ms. Hester Landon was in the house, and she saw you, tried to run from you and fell down the stairs. Is that accurate?"

"That's right. I never touched her."

"But you did touch Abra Walsh on the night she entered Bluff House, after you'd cut the power, broken in."

"I didn't hurt her. I just needed to . . . restrain her until I could get out. She attacked me. Just like Landon attacked me tonight. You *saw* that."

"I saw you reach for a weapon you had concealed." Corbett glanced at Vinnie.

"Yes, sir. I witnessed same, and we have the weapon in evidence."

"You're lucky you only took a couple punches. Now, let's go back to the night you and Abra Walsh tangled in Bluff House."

"I just told you. She attacked me."

"That's an interesting take on it. And did Kirby Duncan attack you, too, before you shot him and pushed his body off the lighthouse cliff?"

The muscle in Suskind's jaw twitched again, his gaze shifted. "I don't know what you're talking about, or who Kirby Duncan is."

"Was. I'll refresh you. He's the private investigator out of Boston you hired to watch Eli Landon." Corbett held up a hand before Suskind could speak. "Let me save us some time here. People always think they're covering their tracks. Like breaking into Duncan's office, his apartment, getting rid of his records. But when people are in that push of the moment, they forget little things. Like backup files. And what they keep themselves, which will turn up as we've got a team searching your house here, and another in Boston going through your apartment."

He let that sink in.

"Then the weapon you pulled, which we've confirmed was registered to Kirby Duncan. How did you gain possession of Duncan's weapon?"

"I . . . found it."

"Just a lucky break?" Now Corbett smiled at him. "Where did you find it? When? How?" Corbett shoved into Suskind's space. "No answer for that. Take some time to think about it, and while you are, add this in. A lot of people figure wearing gloves or wiping a gun covers their ass. But they just don't think of wearing gloves when they load one. You planted the gun in Abra Walsh's house, Suskind, but it wasn't her prints on the bullets the ME dug out of Duncan. Guess whose?"

"It was self-defense."

"Reasonable. Tell me about that."

"He came at me. I defended myself. He . . . attacked me."

"Like Abra Walsh attacked you?"

"I didn't have any choice. He came at me."

"You shot Kirby Duncan, pushed his body off the lighthouse cliffs?"

"Yes, in self-defense—and I took his

gun. He rushed me, he was armed, we struggled. It was an accident."

Corbett scratched the side of his neck. "You're pretty accident-prone. But the thing is, we're good at our jobs around here. Kirby Duncan wasn't shot at close range during a struggle. Forensics doesn't back that story up."

"That's what happened." Suskind folded his arms now. "It was self-defense. I have a right to defend myself."

"You have a right to break into private property, to dig around in it, to walk away from an injured woman who fell because you'd broken into her home while she was sleeping, to assault another and to kill a man? You're going to find out the law doesn't give you a single one of those rights, Suskind, and you'll have a long time to think about that in prison when you're serving a life sentence for first-degree murder."

"It was self-defense."

"Is that going to be your story for why you killed Lindsay Landon? Did she attack you, threaten you, so you had to bash in the back of her skull to defend yourself?"

"I didn't kill Lindsay! Landon killed her, and you cops let him get away with it. Money, family name, that's why she's dead and he's free, and he's lording it in a house that's rightfully mine."

Corbett glanced toward the two-way mirror, gave the faintest nod. Nearly sighed. He hoped he wasn't making a mistake, but a deal was a deal.

"How do you know Landon killed her?"

"Because he did. She was afraid of him."

"She told you she was afraid of her husband?"

"She was a wreck after he went at her in public that day. She said she didn't know what he might do. He'd threatened her, told her he'd make her sorry, make her pay. It's on record! I promised her I'd take care of her, take care of everything. She loved me. I loved her. Landon was already done with her, but when he found out about us, he couldn't stand that she was happy. He went over there, and he killed her, then he bought off the cops and walked."

"So Wolfe was paid off?"

"Damn right he was."

Corbett glanced around, nodded again when Eli walked in. "Eli Landon entering interview. Mr. Suskind, I think, again, we can save some time, get this all straightened out, if Mr. Landon's a part of this process. If you object to having him here, just say so and he's out."

"I've got plenty to say to him, here and now. You murdering bastard."

"That was going to be my line. But let's talk." Eli took a seat at the table.

Thirty

"You didn't want her."

"No," Eli agreed, "I didn't, and I wanted her less when I found out she'd lied to me, cheated on me, used me. Did she know why you started the affair? Did she know you were using her to get information on me, on Bluff House, the family, the dowry?"

"I loved her."

"Maybe you did, but you didn't start sleeping with her out of love. You did it to screw with me, and to pump her for anything I might have told her about the dowry."

"I *knew* her. I understood her. You didn't even know who she was."

"God, you're right about that. No argument. I didn't know her, I didn't want her, I didn't love her. I didn't kill her."

"You went in that house, and when she told you to go to hell, to get out, that she and I were going to be together, to get married, start our lives, you killed her."

"Tough marrying her when you already have a wife."

"I'd already told Eden I wanted a divorce, and when Lindsay told you we were both getting free, you couldn't stand it. You didn't want her, but you didn't want anyone else to have her."

"I thought your wife didn't know about you and Lindsay until after Lindsay's murder."

Suskind's hands balled on the table. "She didn't know about Lindsay."

"You just told your wife, the mother of your two kids, you wanted a divorce, and she didn't ask any questions?"

"It's none of your business what's between me and Eden."

"It's funny though. Lindsay and I sure weren't so civilized and reasonable when we were heading toward divorce. A lot of arguing, a lot of accusations and blame. I guess your wife's a better person, one who'd just step away, let you have what you wanted. Where were you going the night Lindsay died? Come on, Justin, she was packing, we'd had an ugly public fight, and she was upset. You were in love with her, and you'd already asked your wife for a divorce. Lindsay wasn't going out of town without you."

"It's none of your business where we were going."

"But when you went by to pick her up . . ."

"It was too late! You'd killed her. The police were already there."

When he lunged up, Vinnie simply stepped over, put a hand on Suskind's shoulder and shoved him down again. "Keep your seat."

"Keep your hands off me! You're as guilty as he is. Every one of you. I couldn't even stop that night, couldn't even see her. I could only ask one of the neighbors standing out in the rain what was going on. And he told me there must've been some sort of a break-in and the woman who lived in the house was dead. She was dead, and you'd already started sliding out of it."

Saying nothing, Eli glanced at Corbett and tacitly passed the ball.

"What you're saying now doesn't jibe with your previous statements to the police in the matter of Lindsay Landon's murder."

"I know how it works. Do you think I'm stupid? If I admitted to being anywhere near the house, the cops would've pinned it on me. He killed her." Suskind jabbed a finger toward Eli. "You *know* it, and you've got me in here for doing what I had a right to do. Do your job. Arrest him."

"If I'm going to do my job, I have to have it all straight. I need the facts. What time did you drive by the Landon house in the Back Bay?"

"About seven-fifteen."

"And after that?"

"I went straight home. I was half crazy, I couldn't think. Eden was making dinner, and she told me she'd just heard a bulletin that Lindsay had been killed. I broke down. What do you expect? I loved her. I was out of my mind, and Eden helped me calm down, helped me think it through. She was worried about me, about our kids, so she said she'd tell the police I'd been there, with her, since five-thirty, that we shouldn't have to go through the scandal and the pressure because of what Landon had done."

"She lied."

"She protected me and our family. I'd let her down, but she stood up for me. She knew I didn't kill Lindsay."

"Yes, she did," Eli agreed. "She knew you didn't kill Lindsay. And she knew I didn't kill Lindsay. She gave you an alibi, Justin, one the cops believed. And you gave her one that put her at home, with you, being the good wife, sharing some margaritas, cooking dinner for the two of you when she'd gone over to confront Lindsay, and Lindsay had let her in."

"That's a lie. A ridiculous, self-serving lie."

"And Lindsay probably said to her something along the lines of what she said to me the last time we spoke. That she was sorry, but that's the way it was. She loved you, and you were both entitled to be happy. So Eden grabbed the poker in a rage and killed her."

"She couldn't do that."

"You know better. She lashed out because the woman she thought was her friend had made a fool out of her. The woman she'd thought was her friend threatened everything she held close. The husband she'd lived with, trusted, believed in had betrayed her, and would destroy their marriage for someone else's wife."

"She didn't just say you can have a divorce," Corbett put in. "You fought, she demanded, and you told her you were in love with someone else. Then you told her who."

"That doesn't matter."

"When? When did you tell her about Lindsay?"

"The night before the murder. It doesn't matter. Eden protected me, and all she asked in return was for me to give our marriage another try, another few months. She did it for me."

"She did it for herself." Eli pushed to his feet. "Both of you, all for yourselves, and the hell with anyone else. You could've had her, Justin. All I wanted was my grandmother's ring, but Eden wanted more than that, and she used you to get it. It's hard to blame her."

He walked out, and straight to Abra. She pushed off the bench where she'd waited, held tight when his arms came around her, when his forehead dropped to hers.

"It was hard," she said quietly.

"More than I thought it would be."

"Tell me."

"I will. All of it. Let's go home, okay? Let's get the hell out of this and go home."

"Eli." Vinnie walked quickly out of the interview room. "Hold up just a second." He paused, taking a scan of Eli's face. "How are you doing?"

"All in all? Good. It's good to have it out, to start thinking it can be over."

"I'm glad to hear it. Corbett wanted me to tell you, when he's finished with Suskind, he'll contact Wolfe directly. They'll pick up Eden Suskind and talk to her. Corbett, if you want my opinion, is going to go into Boston to be in on that."

"That's for them. I'm out of it. None of

it's part of my life anymore. Thanks for your help, Vinnie."

"Part of the job, but you could buy me a beer sometime."

"As many as you want."

Abra stepped around, took Vinnie's face in her hands, laid her lips softly on his. "He'll buy the beer, but that's from me."

"Might be better than beer."

"Let's go home," Eli repeated. "This is done."

But it wasn't, not for him. Not quite.

The next morning, with Abra by his side, Eli sat across from Eden Suskind.

Though pale, she kept her gaze steady, her voice absolutely calm.

"I appreciate both of you coming into Boston this way. I know it's an inconvenience."

"You had something you wanted to say to me, to us," Eli corrected.

"Yes. I could see when you came to my home the two of you had something strong between you. I've always believed in that, that bond, that connection, and

the promises that come out of it. I built
my adult life on that, only to have it broken. So I wanted to talk to both of you.
I've been speaking with the police for
some time now since last night, in the
presence of my lawyer, of course."

"That's wise."

"Justin hasn't been, but then he's always been impulsive, a little rash. I balanced that out, as I tend to think things
through, weigh options. We were a good
team for a long time. You understand
what I mean about balance," she said to
Abra.

"Yes, I do."

"I thought you would. Now that Justin
has confessed to, well, so much, now
that I know what he's done, I can, and I
want to, move on. I can't protect him,
balance him, hope that he'll come to his
senses again and put our family first. It's
never going to happen. The police believe he killed a man in cold blood."

"Yes."

"And he caused your grandmother serious injury."

"Yes."

"It's his obsession. That's not an excuse, but it's simple fact. About three years ago his great-uncle died, and Justin found letters, a journal, all these things that connected his family to yours, and to that dowry."

"Information about Violeta Landon, Nathanial Broome?"

"Yes. I don't know much as he started hoarding it all, keeping it from me. Everything began to change from that point. He kept pushing, digging, paying heavy fees. I won't bore you with problems Justin had in the past, his ability and need to blame others for failures or mistakes or shortcomings. But I'll tell you that the more he learned about this part of his ancestry, the more he felt you and your family were to blame for everything he didn't have that he wanted. More, when he learned I actually knew your wife, and worked with her from time to time, he saw it as a sign. Who knows? Maybe it was."

"He pursued her."

"Yes. I didn't know to what extent. He deceived me there, and I think, honestly?

He began to want her, to convince himself he loved her because she was yours. He wanted what was yours, and saw it as his right. I didn't know about the property in Whiskey Beach, or the investigator, or the break-ins. I only knew, in those months before Lindsay's death, my husband was slipping away from me, lying to me. I think we know, don't we?" she said to Abra.

"Yes, we probably do."

"I tried everything, and finally stopped arguing with him about the time, the money, and convinced myself to simply wait it out. He'd had obsessions before, pulled away a bit before, but he always settled back again."

She paused a moment, tucked the swing of her hair behind her ear. "This time, it was different. He told me he was filing for divorce. Just like that, as if it was nothing but a formality. He didn't want our life any longer, couldn't pretend to love me any longer. Again, I won't bore you, but he shattered me. We fought, and said terrible things, as people do, and he told me he'd been involved with Lindsay, that she was his soul mate—those hack-neyed words—and that they intended to be together."

"That must've been terribly hurtful," Abra said when Eden fell silent.

"It was horrible. The worst moment of my life. Everything I loved and believed in was slipping through my fingers. He said we'd tell the children over the weekend so we'd have plenty of time with them to ease the blow, and in the meantime, he'd sleep in the guest room, and we'd main-tain a civilized front. I swear to you, I could hear Lindsay's words coming out of his mouth, her way, her tone. You un-derstand me?" she asked Eli.

"Yeah, I do."

Her shoulders very straight, she nod-ded. "What I say next is without my law-yer or the police present, without the record, but I feel you deserve to hear it, and for me to say it to you."

"I know you killed her."

"Aren't you interested in knowing what happened that night? In knowing why and how?"

Before Eli could speak, Abra laid a hand over his. "I am. I'd like to know."

"There's that balance at work. You'd walk away because you're so angry, and she'll help you stay because knowing will help you close the door on this, as much as you ever will."

"You had to confront her," Abra began.

"Wouldn't you? He called to tell me he'd changed his mind and we'd have to put off telling the children together for a few days. Lindsay was upset because she'd fought with you, Eli, and she needed to get away for a few days. He needed to be with her. She needed, he needed. Nothing his family needed. I think they brought out the worst in each other," Eden said. "Their most selfish selves."

"You may be right." Eli turned his hand to hold Abra's, and thought how lucky he was.

"So, yes, I went to confront her, to try to reason with her, even to plead with her. She was angry, very angry still over your confrontation, what you'd said to her. And, I think, looking back, maybe a little guilty. But not enough. She let me in, took me into the library because she wanted to finish it, clear the slate, so she and Justin could move on. Nothing I said made any difference to her. Our own friendship meant nothing, my children meant nothing, my marriage, or the hurt they were causing. I begged her not to take my husband, not to take the father of my children, and she told me to grow up. This was how things were, how things worked. She said horrible things to me, cruel things, vicious things, and she turned her back on me. She dismissed me and my pain as nothing."

After a pause, Eden folded her hands on the table. "The rest blurs. It was like watching someone else, someone else who grabbed the poker and struck out. I lost my mind."

"That might work," Eli said evenly, "if your lawyer's as good as you are."

"He's very good, but regardless, I never went into that house intending to harm her, but to plead with her. And when I regained my senses, when it was too late, I thought of my family, my children, and what this would mean. I couldn't change what I'd done in that moment of insanity, and I could only try to protect my family. So I went home. I took the clothes I'd worn there and cut them up. I bagged the pieces, weighed them down and drove out to throw them in the river. Then I came back home, and I started dinner. When Justin came home, he was hysterical, so I realized we could protect each other, as it should be, as it's meant to be, and we'd try to put it behind us and rebuild our marriage. I felt he needed me. Lindsay would have ruined him. In fact, she did. And what she left me was a man I couldn't fix, couldn't save. I let him go, and did what I had to do to protect myself."

"But you stood by and let what you'd done ruin Eli's life."

"I couldn't stop it, or change it, though I was sorry, sincerely, that someone who'd been betrayed as I had would lose so much more. But in the end, I didn't ruin his life. Lindsay did. She ruined his, mine, Justin's. Even dead, she ruined us all. Now my children will be scarred."

Her voice wavered a little, then strengthened again. "Even when my lawyer makes a deal with the prosecutor I have every confidence he'll make, they'll be scarred. You'll have your balance, your chance for a future. I'll have two children who'll be shattered by what their father's done out of selfishness, and what their mother did out of desperation. You're free, and though I may not be punished to the extent you feel just, I'll never be free."

Eli leaned across the table. "Whatever she did, or planned to do, she didn't deserve to die for it."

"You're kinder than I. But we can take it back to its roots. Your ancestor committed murder out of greed, cast off his own sister, for the same reasons. Without that, we wouldn't be here. I'm really just a piece of all of it."

"Believing that may help you get through the next few weeks." Eli got to his feet.

Once more, Abra put a hand over his as she rose. "For the sake of your children, I hope your lawyer is as good as you believe."

"Thank you. I really wish both of you all the best."

He had to walk out, get out. "Jesus Christ" was all he could say when Abra gripped his hands.

"Some people are twisted, in ways that don't show. In ways they themselves don't see or understand. It may be circumstances that twisted her, Eli, but she'll never really see it."

"I could get her off," he stated. "I could get her off with five years, and she'd only do two."

"Then I'm glad you're not a defense attorney anymore."

"So am I." His hand tightened on hers as Wolfe walked down the hall.

"Landon."

"Detective."

"I was wrong, but you looked good for it."

As Wolfe kept walking, Eli turned. "And that's it? That's it from you?"

Wolfe glanced back. "Yeah, that's it."

"He's embarrassed," Abra commented, and only smiled when Eli sent her a baffled stare. "He's an asshole, but he's also embarrassed. Forget him, and remember karma comes around."

"I don't know about karma, but I'll start working on forgetting him."

"Good. Let's buy some flowers for

Hester and go tell your family this most excellent news. Then we'll go home, and see what happens next."

He had some ideas about that.

He waited a few days, letting it all sink in for both of them. He had his life back, and didn't need the media reports about Eden Suskind's arrest for Lindsay's murder, or Justin Suskind's for Duncan's, to tell him just that.

He had his life back, but not the life he'd had once, and he was glad of it.

He made plans, some with Abra—they'd throw Bluff House open for a major party for the Fourth of July. He showed her the very preliminary plans for installing an elevator so his grandmother could come home and live comfortably.

And some plans he didn't share with her—yet.

So he waited, walked his dog, wrote, spent time with the woman he loved and began to look at Bluff House in a whole new light.

He chose an evening with soft breezes,

and the promise of sunset, the anticipation of a full moon.

Doing his part, he dealt with the dinner dishes while she sat at the island working on her schedule for the upcoming week.

"I think, if I fiddle a little, I could add Zumba in the fall. It's popular for a reason, and I can get certified."

"I bet you could."

"Yoga's always going to be my core, but I like adding in some other choices, keeping it fresh." Rising, she pinned her new schedule to the board.

"Speaking of keeping it fresh, I want to show you something on the third floor."

"In the passage? Are you thinking about trying out Pirate and Wench?"

"Maybe, but there's something else first."

"You know it's too bad we can't throw that floor open for our big bash in July," she said as she walked with him. "It's too complicated, and too full of things right now, but boy, we could rock it."

"Maybe someday."

"I always like somedays."

"Funny, I've realized I do, too. It's taken a while."

He guided her into the old servants' quarters where a bucket held a bottle of champagne.

"Are we celebrating?"

"I sure as hell hope so."

"I'm also fond of celebrations. You have blueprints up here." She moved to the table he'd uncovered, studied them. "Eli! You've started on plans for your office. Oh, this is great. It's going to be fabulous for you. You're adding an outside entrance to the terrace? It's a great idea. You can go in and out, from right in there, sit out and contemplate. You didn't tell me!"

She spun around.

"They're just preliminary. I wanted some of it down, and to find out what could be done before I showed you."

"Well, preliminary or not, it's a good reason to pop a cork."

"That's not why."

"You have more."

"Yeah, it's a lot more. See, the architect left this space here unnamed. This area we're standing in, the bath over there. I asked him to just draw it up, basi-cally, and leave it blank."

"More plans." She turned a circle, then another. "There's so much you could do with it."

"No, not really, but you could."

"I could?"

"You could have your studio."

"My— Oh, Eli, that's so good of you, so sweet, but—"

"Hear me out. Your clients or students—whatever—would have the entrance here, off the terrace. It's three floors up, but hell, if they're coming to exercise, the climb's part of it. If you're doing the se-nior yoga deal or whatever, there's the el-evator. And there's this area here. You could have your massage therapy room. I'm working here, north wing, private, so none of this interferes with me. I asked Gran what she thought, and she thought it was great, so you've got the go-ahead there."

"You've been doing a lot of thinking."

"I have, and it's all been about you. About us. About Bluff House. About, well, somedays. What do you think?"

"Eli." Overwhelmed, she wandered the

space, could see it, just see it. "You're handing me one of my dreams, but—"

"You could reciprocate, and give me mine."

He dug in his pocket, pulled out a ring.

"It's not the one I gave Lindsay. I didn't want to give you that ring, so I asked Gran if I could have another. It's old, and one she especially loves, and wanted it to go to you, someone she especially loves. I could have bought you one, but I wanted you to have something that's been handed down. Symbolic. You're big on symbols."

"Oh God. Oh my God." She could only stare at the perfect square-cut emerald.

"I didn't want to give you a diamond. Too conventional. And this, anyway, this reminded me of you. Your eyes."

"Eli." She rubbed the heel of her hand between her breasts as if to keep her heart beating. "I just . . . I haven't gone here. I haven't thought of this."

"So think of it now."

"I thought we'd talk about me moving in, officially living together. Taking that next step."

"We can do that. If that's all I can get

for now, we can do that. I know it's fast, and I know we've got big mistakes be-hind us. But they're behind us. I want to marry you, Abra. I want to start a real life with you, a family with you, to share a home with you."

He swore he could all but feel the ring burn in his hand like a flame, like life. "I look at you, and I see all the somedays, all the possibilities of them. I don't want to wait to start, but I will. I'll wait, but you have to know you not only helped me come back, to really see the life I wanted and could have, but you're the life I want."

Her heart didn't stop beating, but it filled. She stared at him as the windows behind him washed pink and gold with the setting sun. And she thought, There's love. There it is. Take the gift.

"I love you, Eli. I trust my own heart, I learned to do that. I think love is the most powerful and most important thing in the universe, and you have mine. I want yours. We can make the life we both want. I believe that. We can make that life together."

"But you want to wait."

"Hell no." She laughed, all but flew to

him. "Oh God! Here you are. The love of my life."

With her arms tight around him, she found his mouth with hers, sank and sank and sank into the first kiss of the new promise.

He swayed with her, holding on. "It would've killed me to wait."

"Some happy you just have to grab." She held out her hand. "Make it official." When he slid the ring on her finger, she put her arms around him again, held her left hand up to the sunset light. "It's beautiful and warm."

"Like you."

"I love that it's old, that it's been passed down through your family. I love that I'm your family. When did you ask Hester for this?"

"When we took her flowers, after going in to see Eden Suskind. I couldn't ask you, didn't want to ask you, until that was over. It's new now, for both of us. Take the space, Abra, take me, let's just take it all."

"All is exactly what we'll take." She pressed her lips to his, soft, long, loving. "And then we'll make more."

The ring on her hand caught the last rays of the sun, flashed, as it had for Landon women for generations.

Then it gleamed in the quieter light, as it once did in an iron chest washed up from the wrecked *Calypso* with its canny captain, onto the shores of Whiskey Beach.